The Butcher of Beverly Hills

a novel

THE BUTCHER OF BEVERLY HILLS. Copyright © 2005 by Tessera Productions, Inc. All rights reserved. No part of this book may be reproduced or transmitted in any form or by any means, electronic or mechanical, including photocopying, recording, or by any information storage and retrieval system, without written permission from the publisher. For information, address Broadway Books, a division of Random House, Inc.

This book contains an excerpt from the forthcoming book *The Mangler of Malibu Canyon* by Jennifer Colt. This excerpt has been set for this edition only and may not reflect the final content of the forthcoming edition.

Excerpt from *The Mangler of Malibu Canyon* by Jennifer Colt copyright © 2006 by Tessera Productions, Inc.

PRINTED IN THE UNITED STATES OF AMERICA

BROADWAY BOOKS and its logo, a letter B bisected on the diagonal, are trademarks of Random House, Inc.

Visit our website at www.broadwaybooks.com

First edition published 2005

Book design by Caroline Cunningham

Library of Congress Cataloging-in-Publication Data
Colt, Jennifer.
    The butcher of Beverly Hills : a novel / Jennifer Colt.—1st ed.
        p. cm.
    ISBN 0-7679-2011-2
1. Women private investigators—California—Beverly Hills—Fiction.
2. Beverly Hills (Calif.)—Fiction.   3. Sisters—Fiction.   4. Twins—Fiction.
I. Title.
    PS3603.O467B88   2005
    813'.6—dc22

                                                      2005042191

10 9 8 7 6 5 4 3 2 1

For Rajeev,

who always starts my day with a laugh

acknowledgments

I want to thank the friends and family members who have read my manuscripts-in-training for years, giving me notes, corrections, and encouragement. Amazingly, some of these people still answer the phone when I call:

Claudia Hoover	Pat Sinnott
Beth Bornhurst Preminger	Jeff Franzen
W. Keith Border	James "Meese" Louis
Ginger Smith	Janet Tanner
Mary Linda Thomas	Jane Gordon
Lisa Bandy	John Quinn
Daphne McAfee	Aaron Ockman
Patty Holstine	

And just in case you thought that hunky, funny cops were merely the stuff of fiction, I give you Detective Paul Holstine, who tries to keep me honest on matters concerning the police.

The
Butcher
of Beverly
Hills

prologue

Scientists say that character is encoded in your DNA.

If that's true, how do you explain me and Terry? Identical, down to our toe hairs. Exact same green eyes and reddish locks, exact same anatomy, even the same damn freckle constellations. If one sister left skin cells at a murder scene, the other could be convicted of the crime.

But she's left-handed, I'm right-handed. She played with trucks; I played with dolls. She frequently got expelled for smoking or worse; I made straight A's and was elected class president. She had a series of unrequited crushes on girls; I went steady with chess-champ Brent Graebner, while secretly lusting after quarterback Rick Davis.

On graduation day I gave the valedictory speech, urging my fellow students to go forth and do Burbank High

School proud, while Terry, her diploma lit with a Bic and flaming in her hand, yelled *Wahoo!* and tore up the school's front lawn doing doughnuts on her scooter.

I call her my evil twin. She calls me good for organ transplants. But the truth is we're like a single, double-headed, multilegged organism—conjoined emotionally like Chang and Eng were at the spleen—helpless to go our separate ways.

We had a happy, ultranormal suburban childhood. Summer barbecues, Girl Scout cookie drives, ponies at our birthday parties. Next to ours, the Brady home was a crack house. But the bottom fell out in adolescence.

Our stay-at-home mom, Jean, died from breast cancer when we were fifteen. Our dad, Joe, a gaffer for the movies, hung on for another four years, then the day after we turned nineteen he suffered a massive coronary, waiting for a bus.

Terry found him—swear to God—slumped over in front of an ad for a funeral home. She called the 1-800 number on the bench and had him taken away. There were over two hundred Teamsters at his funeral and not a dry eye in the church.

Except for Terry. She was all cried out.

She took out her grief in nose candy, then was busted for possession after they clocked her doing seventy on a residential street in Brentwood—a search of her person revealing an eight-ball cleverly concealed in her bra, her arrest cleverly timed to dovetail with new mandatory sentencing guidelines.

I dropped out of UCLA after two years to work off her legal fees at the offices of Elijah "Eli" Weintraub, criminal attorney extraordinaire. Big heart, scary clientele. That's where I learned the rudiments of investigation.

When Terry got out of prison, I set us up in business:

DOUBLE INDEMNITY INVESTIGATIONS

Kerry McAfee, *Private Investigator.*

Terry McAfee, *Operative.*

It's been life at the end of a bungee cord ever since.

one

"*Y*ou've got to come right away, girls. I'm trapped in this damn hotel, and I need you to do something for me *desperately*."

Lenore Richling managed the trick of sounding needy and haughty at the same time. I looked at Terry, who was listening in on the extension. She rolled her eyes at me and made a rude hand gesture.

"We're kind of busy right now, Lenore," I said.

Busy trying to think of a way out of this situation. Lenore was the bosom buddy of our rich Aunt Reba, the Canasta Queen of Beverly Hills, who had called minutes earlier to say that her dear friend was in a pickle, and she'd be ever so grateful if we could help her out.

It wasn't the "pickle" bit that had us concerned. Pickles, you might say, are our business. No, it was the word "help" that gave us pause. Like Aunt Reba—in fact, like most members of the moneyed class—Lenore was famously cheap. She would probably expect the help in the form of a favor, and we doubted she'd be all that grateful. Rich people are hardly ever grateful for anything, since they think they're *entitled* to everything.

Terry had made me promise to pawn Lenore off on someone else.

"I can give you the name of someone who can help you—" I started to say.

"Oh, but I need *you*," the older woman wheedled shamelessly.

I hesitated for a second, mindful of the consequences of blowing off Reba's best friend, then caved. "Could it possibly wait till tomorrow?"

Terry's boot connected painfully with my shin. Mouthing the word "wimp" at me, she waved the property tax bill in my face. Our business had slowed to nothing, and the tax bill had arrived along with a notice that our checks were going *boing* at the bank. There were no jobs on the horizon and unless we got some paying work quickly, we were going to lose our little love shack to the county. There was simply no time for running down Lenore's runaway new husband, which we assumed was the reason for the call.

"No! It can't possibly wait. I need you this *minute*," Lenore said, an emotional quaver working its way into her smoke-ravaged voice.

I sighed. Clearly there was no getting out of this.

"All right. Look for us in an hour," I said, rubbing my shinbone. "You're at the Dauphine on Layton Way, right?"

Terry stomped around the room, whipping her long red braid around like a cat-o'-nine-tails as she cursed me for a turncoat.

"Yes," Lenore answered. "If asked, say you're visiting 'Mrs. Templeton' in Room 308."

A false name, no less. Very cloak and dagger.

"*Beverly Hills 213* printed a blurb saying I'm visiting a contessa in Monaco," she explained, referring to a throwaway paper that featured gossip and social items of interest to its denizens—*213* being the former area code for the infamous 90210 region. "Only Reba knows I'm here. It's terribly important that you not mention my name to anyone."

Lenore was using this subterfuge because she'd just had her third face-lift in fifteen years, according to Reba. There are more cosmetic surgeries per capita in Beverly Hills than chopsticks in Shanghai, but few self-respecting BH residents will ever admit to having had tummies tucked, faces winched, or thigh fat sucked through a straw. This is why Lenore had leaked the contessa story before going under the knife, then checked into the hotel to be pampered by the "superb staff" while she recuperated away from prying eyes. Afterward she would appear in the driveway with her suitcases looking very "relaxed" after her fictitious trip. *Ah, there's nothing like the fresh air of Monaco to stretch your skin as tight as panty hose on a rhino.*

"Lenore, just out of curiosity—is this about your husband?"

She snorted into the speaker. "Did Reba tell you about that?"

"Uh, she mentioned something."

She had, in fact, told us the whole sordid story. After the death of Lenore's ancient first husband, Myron Richling, she had married a valet from the Beverly Hills Hotel named Mario Vallegos, twenty-eight years old to Lenore's seventy. She tried to reinvent Mario as an Argentinean polo player on the theory that no one noticed the help at five-star hotels, so no one would tumble to the lie.

Then barely two months later, Mario had run out, leaving Lenore Richling-Vallegos thoroughly humiliated. The face-lift was a way of perking herself up—a kind of surgical shopping spree.

"I called the INS on him," Lenore said. "But they haven't been able to catch the slimy little wetback."

Whoa, I thought. A woman scorched.

"Mario's an illegal alien?" I said.

She laughed, phlegm gurgling in her throat, and I heard her light up a cigarette. "He's an illegal everything. Look, come over here and I'll fill you in. I can't get into this on the phone."

Terry revved the Harley in the driveway as I locked up the house. She was pissed, I could tell by the thunderous volume of the throttle. I walked up to the front tire and made a helpless gesture.

"She's Reba's best friend, what could I do?"

"You could let *me* talk to her. I'd tell her what to do with her boy toy."

"It's twenty minutes away. What can it hurt to go see her? She might even pay us."

"Yeah," Terry snorted. "And monkeys might fly out of my butt."

These days, everyone's a detective. Just buy the software, and you can *Find Out Anything About Anyone!* online.

Fortunately for us, people don't steal from their employer's warehouses, fake insurance claims, or cheat on their spouses online, though occasionally some idiot going through a divorce will post pictures of himself in compromising positions with leather-clad swingles or bewildered farm animals on his very own website. (Even in a no-fault divorce state, illicit sexual activity or just plain spousal bizarreness can be taken into account when dictating monetary settlements or custody arrangements.)

It's not glamorous work—hunkering down with a telephoto lens behind a Dumpster at the Motel 6 or the Good Guys Electronics store, or trying to bust some worker's-comp faker waltzing behind a mower on his front lawn—but it allows us to postpone thinking about what to do when we grow up, and keeps the credit card company wolves from our door in the interim.

We'd even done our share of locating runaway mates, mostly dads of the deadbeat variety, but I found myself getting queasy as we made our way east on Santa Monica Boulevard toward Beverly Hills. I doubted that Lenore wanted us for anything so straightforward as finding out where that darn man of hers had gone. She'd sounded too bitter, too bent on revenge.

And I didn't much like the idea of sacrificing some poor Mexican national for the sake of Lenore's wounded pride.

Terry slowed in front of the Dauphine Hotel, an elegant façade that blended in with the pricey condos and apartment buildings on either side of it. She waved to the valet standing out front, signaling him that she had things under control, and zipped into the underground parking garage.

The valet did what a lot of people do when they see identical redheads on a shocking-pink Harley. He laughed.

With its eye-catching custom paint job, our bike looks like something from the *Barbie Goes Hog Wild!* collection. Plus, Terry wears a matching pink leather jacket with fringe and a pink helmet with a purple flower-power daisy on the side—not exactly stealth transport.

She'd bought the Softail Deuce after we cashed in Dad's insurance policy, and in the lean times following her arrest we'd never managed to trade in her drug- and grief-induced purchase for something more suitable to our line of work.

Terry found an empty parking space in the subterranean garage and we climbed off the bike, grinning at the surveillance cameras aimed at our faces, then hiked up the incline that said Not a Walkway to the street level and back past the valet, who asked the question we heard—on average—twice a day.

"Hey, are you two twins?"

"Identical strangers," Terry said, never very charitable toward the stupid of the species. We breezed up to the doorman, who reached out a white-gloved hand and swung open the brass door.

"Hello, ladies. Welcome to the Dauphine."

We gave him a quick smile that said we hung out in fancy hotels all the time and strolled into the lobby.

The space was done in pink marble, reflected on all sides by floor-to-ceiling mirrors. Massive Japanese flower arrangements protruded from gilded ceramic urns, their stems reaching almost to the ceiling and drawing attention to its Renaissance-style fresco of angels and puffy clouds on a light blue background. Impressionist reproductions, or possibly originals, hung on the mirrors in heavy gold frames, and everyone who was not anyone was attired in an anonymous black hotel uniform.

Everyone, that is, except the short, slick Armani-suited man who headed us off at the elevator.

" 'Allo. May I help you?" he said in a tone that conveyed: *I am French. I am better zan you.*

"No, thanks," Terry said, punching the call button.

"May I know to whose room you are go-*ing*? I am *ze* hotel managère."

"We're here to see, uh, Mrs. Templeton," I said, remembering to use Lenore's alias.

"Room number?"

I glanced over at Terry, who made a face at the back of the manager's pomaded head.

"Room 308," I said.

"Ahh." He ignored the edge in my voice and stepped onto the elevator with us. "I will accompany you. At *ze* moment she is in 302 with *ze ozzer* ladies."

He wore an overpowering cologne that sucked all the oxygen out of the small elevator, a cloying mixture of spring posies and animal musk that spoke of goats frolicking in the meadow. I held my breath and watched as he straightened his Givenchy tie in the reflection of the polished bronze doors.

"Madame is expecting you?"

"*Mais oui*," Terry said.

At the sound of French, he went all charming, almost bowing. He held out a puffy manicured hand. "I am Alphonse."

Alphonse. One name only—like Prince, Madonna, Butthead. Obviously a local celebrity in his own right.

"Thérèse," she said with a phony French accent, crooking her hand into a palsied little hook, which he took by the fingers and squeezed.

I rolled my eyes at her. "Kerry McAfee," I said, holding out my hand to him in the normal manner. "And that's my sister Terry."

I got a quick, jerky shake that left my hand reeking of all the perfumes of Araby. "You are relations of Madame?" he said.

"No, we're here on business," I said.

"*Beeziness*? What kind of *beeziness*?"

Terry lowered her voice. "Private business."

"Of course," he said unctuously.

The doors opened on the third floor. "Thanks, Alphonse. We can find it." I hoped he'd take the elevator back down and give my nostrils a rest.

Instead he bolted out the doors ahead of us. "I'm afraid I must accompany you. You understand, our guests expect *ze* utmost in discretion, *zhey* come here for privacy."

We stepped out into the subdued light of the hallway and

followed Alphonse down to 302, where he rapped delicately on the door. " 'Allo? Meezus Temple*tohn* . . . ?"

"Come in!" a voice warbled from within. Alphonse tried the door, but it was locked. I stepped up beside him and knocked again.

"Mrs. Templeton, it's the McAfees."

"Dash it, come in!" I heard a craggy voice grumble, then the door flew open.

I stepped back and my breath caught in my throat.

In front of me stood someone of elfin proportions, balanced on three-inch platform heels and swathed in animal prints. Her face was swollen and oozing at the edges, her beady brown eyes peering out over cheeks that looked like rumpled purple pillows. A large turban crowned her tiny head, giving her the appearance of a genie who had recently escaped from a miniature Aladdin's Lamp.

"Yes . . . ?"

"We're here to see Mrs. Richling, I mean Mrs. Templeton," I said, choking on the words. Just looking at her bruised face made my stomach lurch and my hamstrings ache.

She turned and yelled into the room, "Len, honey! It's for you . . . !"

Beyond the woman in leopard-skin bell-bottoms was a sur-realistic scene—a table surrounded by bandaged persons of smallish stature, their ages impossible to guess without the usual markers, their hair caught up in sleek blonde ponytails or bloodred French twists and rich brown bouffants. And under-neath the meticulous coifs were bandaged, mutilated masks.

This was obviously a way station for women who, like Lenore, were taking their third or fourth dip into the Fountain of Youth, the hotel standing in for a number of exotic ports-of-call that would never actually be stamped in their passports.

There appeared to be a high stakes game of canasta going on. The playing cards were grasped in hands with long, multicolored talons, the knotted knuckles and spotted skin revealing the years that facial surgery had sought to erase. A Louis Vuitton umbrella bag lay on the satin coverlet of the sprawling bed, stuffed with cash, bundles of one hundred dollar bills carelessly massed in its opening. Another large stack of greenbacks sat on the table in front of a woman with dark hair in a Flamenco dancer's bun, who had normal breasts that sagged perceptibly, something of a belly, and a pleasing roundness to her arms. I guessed that liposuction and breast augmentation were next on the menu.

A big, cellophane-wrapped gift basket caught my eye, sitting on the bureau near the table, stuffed with a profusion of goodies. Perfumed soaps and gourmet comestibles, probably compliments of the hotel.

Lenore looked up from her scorecard and waved to us. I assumed it was Lenore, but only knew for sure when she spoke. I recognized the husky nasal drawl. "Hello, girls. Be right with you."

She totaled up their scores and handed the paper to her neighbor, a woman with a Hermès scarf wound around her face.

"I don't know how," the woman said, "but you've been cheating, Lenore."

Lenore hiked a bony shoulder. "Sore loser."

"We're all sore, duckie!" another one quipped, then they all burst out laughing, their cackling following us as we left the room and all the way down the hall.

When we got to room 308, Lenore turned and dismissed Alphonse with a curt nod.

"Will Madame be needing anything?" he asked, ever the eager toady.

"Later," she snapped. He bowed and disappeared.

Lenore attempted to smile at us. "Thank you for coming, girls. I really need your help." She put her key card in the lock and pushed open the door. Something dashed out of the room, tan-colored and sleek, the size of a large rodent. It ran straight through Lenore's feet and spun around.

"Rat!" Terry yelled.

I jumped back, slamming into the wall, my heart pounding in my chest. I hate rats. Hate the *idea* of rats.

"Don't be stupid," Lenore said, bending at the waist to scoop it up. "It's Paquito. How's my precious?" she cooed at him.

It was a dog. A rat dog.

He'd had fur at one point in his life, judging by the brown and white mane encircling his neck. But his puny torso was now completely hairless, revealing a rib cage the size of a Cornish game hen's.

"Jesus," Terry said, peering at the diminutive pup. "What's wrong with him, mange?"

"Poppycock," Lenore said, bussing him on the head. "He's in the pink of health. Pomeranian pups always lose their coats at six months. It's called the *puppy uglies*."

The ugly puppy stared out from the crook of Lenore's arm—round eyes popping from the terror of being tiny and helpless—and quivered like a plus-size vibrator with a lifetime battery. He was barely larger than Lenore's hand, sporting a baby-blue rhinestone collar and matching muzzle. With the bald body, electrified mane, and face mask, he looked like some sort of Frankendog.

"You leave him in the room by himself?" I asked.

"I can't take him to the game, he makes the other girls nervous," Lenore said. "Angela Pillsbury says he reminds her of a miscarriage she had in fifty-eight."

Terry rolled her eyes at me, and I shrugged back. We followed Lenore into the room, where she sat on the bed, placing Paquito on her lap and snapping off his muzzle. Freed from the constraint, he barked several times in rapid succession—*Yapyapyap*—then hunkered down between Lenore's thighs and sniffed her crotch. Terry leaned against the wall, and I pulled up a gilded chair from the antique secretary, which I saw was topped with another of the fancy hotel baskets.

"I suppose I should tell you why I called," Lenore said, picking a stray piece of lint off the spread.

"That would be good," Terry said with barely concealed sarcasm.

Lenore glanced over at Terry, then averted her eyes. "I need you to find my soon-to-be-ex-husband."

"Why?" I said, trying for a more sympathetic tone. Terry's ham-handed approach was obviously making Lenore skittish.

"He has ten thousand dollars of mine," Lenore said with a self-righteous flick of her chin. "I'd like it back."

Ten thousand dollars? Surely that was chump change for someone in Lenore's economic bracket. She probably spent that much on Lancôme products and body waxes every month. But maybe there was a larger issue here.

"Did he take the money from a joint account?" I said.

Lenore stuck out a cinnamon-hued nail and scratched Paquito behind the ear. "I may be a romantic fool, but I'm not stupid," she said archly. "We *had* no joint accounts."

"Then how did he get it?" Terry said.

"It's the money he got for selling my jewels. He stole them, then hocked them. I had to pay to get them back from a cheap little storefront on Pico Boulevard."

So it wasn't the money. It was the humiliation Lenore had suffered when Mario abandoned her, his pockets full of baubles. Well, at least it didn't sound like she wanted him handed over to the INS.

"Any thoughts on where he might be?" I said.

"I have no idea, that's why I called you. You can find people, can't you?"

"If he hasn't skipped the country," Terry said. "Or even if he has, actually. It just takes longer and gets more expensive."

A wave of alarm spread over Lenore's features. "How . . .

expensive?" The facial pain was apparently nothing compared to the agony of parting with cash.

"We charge three hundred dollars a day, plus expenses," I told her. "We like to get one week in advance, pro ratable if we find what you're looking for in less time—"

"Three hundred dollars a day! What are you, lawyers?"

This from a woman who had just racked up ten thousand dollars in elective surgery followed by a five-thousand dollar hotel bill.

"It's a fairly standard fee," I said. "On the low side, really."

"Well, fine. But I can't give you an advance. Obviously I don't have cash here at the hotel."

Terry frowned. "There was a suitcase of bills in that other room."

"Not mine, I assure you. Those Mexican gals are something else. Come up here with a suitcase full of dollars to get their faces done. I guess Hattrick doesn't take foreign checks."

"Hattrick?"

"Daniel Hattrick. He does all of us. Oh, there are plenty of surgeons around—Beverly Hills is fairly bursting with them. But I wouldn't let those hacks near me. Hattrick is magic. I can spot his work a mile away. Anyone can, who's been around."

Now that was fascinating—the same people who could spot a Dior bag or a Valentino dress or Gucci shoes could spot a Hattrick tuck. I wondered if he signed his work, and looked on Lenore's neck for his initials, carved or perhaps branded into her flesh.

"Maybe you could pay us out of your canasta winnings," I said.

Lenore brushed aside the suggestion like a nettlesome insect, her hand flapping in the air. "Oh, I never actually take their money. How tacky would that be? It's a win on paper, only. Purely for sport."

"We can take a check," Terry persisted.

Lenore jumped up from the bed with a grunt of annoyance, causing Paquito to roll off her lap sideways. The poor little thing righted himself, claws digging into the satin coverlet as the mattress rocked beneath him.

"You're just going to have to trust me for it. I can't go to the bank and get the money, not like this. And when I recuperate it will be too late. You have to find him *now*. Before he slinks back to Mexico."

Terry gave me an *I told you so* look, then tried another tack. "Okay, how about this? We'll take a twenty percent recovery fee when we get the money. That way you're not on the hook for anything unless we're successful."

Lenore considered it, her mouth bunched into a little fig. "Ten percent," she countered.

"Twenty percent," Terry said. "Take it or leave it."

"Dash it all, you've got me over a barrel. Very well then, twenty percent. But I'm going to have a word with your great-aunt about this. I would have expected some consideration, as a friend of the family."

Terry's hand balled into a fist, and I knew she was giving Lenore's face some consideration as a punching bag.

"We're working stiffs, Mrs. Richling," I said quickly. "I'm afraid we can't afford that kind of consideration."

"Oh, all right." Lenore did a disgusted little toss of her head. "Just bring me the money."

"Good," I said, glad to be done with the negotiations. "Where do we start? Does he have family in the area? Friends? Anyone special—?"

Lenore moved to the floor-length gold mirror and stared fixedly at herself, as if she were gazing into a magic glass and could see straight through the swelling and the stitches to her glorious new designer face.

"He may have a girlfriend," she said.

Aha, so there *was* more to the story.

"But that's not the issue," she added defiantly. "I just want what's mine."

"Who is she?" I asked.

"She's a medical assistant in Hattrick's office. Her name is Tatiana, and I think Mario may have been infatuated with her. But I'd rather you didn't speak to her unless you have absolutely no other way of finding him. I'd hate for her to think I was . . . jealous."

We sat in awkward silence for a second.

"Does Tatiana have a last name?" Terry asked, obviously losing patience with the process of pulling teeth.

Lenore snorted. "Something Russian. What's the difference? They're all the worst sort of peasants."

Bigoted, coy, *and* a tightwad. All in all, Lenore was shaping up as my favorite candidate for Pain-in-the-Ass Client of the Year.

"Okay then, we'll start at the Beverly Hills Hotel," I said. "Isn't that where you met him?"

Lenore spun around in dismay, her eyes going wide. "How did you know that?"

Terry and I looked at each other—had we just finked on Reba?

"Mrs. Richling, if we're going to get your money, we have to dig around in places Mario might go," I said, reasserting our professionalism. "That would mean speaking to his alleged girlfriend and asking around at his previous place of employment, where somebody might have a line on him. We have no other avenues to pursue. He won't have an address on file with the DMV. He probably has a fake Social Security card, if he's illegal . . ."

Lenore deflated and leaned on the mahogany dresser, her pride going out of her with an audible rush of air.

"I'm sorry. This has all been so humiliating." She grimaced, pawing at the side of her face as if there were an itch she desperately wanted to scratch underneath the bandage. "I was silly, girls. I fell for a handsome face and he took complete advantage of me. I guess I should have known he didn't love me for myself, but I thought that my *social position* . . ." The words tumbled out of her in a pathetic gush. "You're too young to understand. It's . . . it's a hard thing for a woman to admit that she can no longer hold a man with her looks."

I felt sucker punched, a burst of sympathy overriding my previous assessment of Lenore as one of Satan's minions. Whatever her defects, the woman was aging, she'd been ripped off by a gold-digging Lothario, and possibly dumped for a babe in a white smock, and she was asking for our help now with heartbreaking humility.

"Help me out, won't you, girls? It's not the money," she said, pulling out a Dunhill and torching it with a silver lighter. "It's my pride."

$\mathcal{W}e$ $\mathit{decided}$ to go straight to the doctor's office in spite of Lenore's reservations. Tatiana Something-Russian was the only real contact we had for Mario, and we didn't know much else about him, aside from what he looked like, bare-chested and sweaty next to a kidney-shaped pool. Lenore had given us a snapshot of him that she carried in her otherwise empty billfold.

Back in the garage, Terry hooked her leg over the bike, frowning at me. "There's something funky about this. She's not telling us everything."

"I know," I whispered, pointing to the cameras overhead, peering at us from every possible angle.

"I doubt they have audio," she whispered back.

True, but the Pentagon itself couldn't have had better visual coverage. It seemed like overkill for a hotel in a relatively crime-free neighborhood. My eyes traveled around the spotless garage—no pools of oil under the carriages of Jaguars, Lamborghinis, and good old-fashioned Mercedes sedans. Then I glimpsed a man in a blue shirt and a black coat lurking just inside the glass-paneled office. The parking attendant.

I sauntered over to him and he lowered his large black eyes, as if he'd been caught spying or eavesdropping.

"We parked ourselves." I pulled a couple of crumpled bills out of the pocket of my light green capris. "This is for you."

He reached for the money, then the phone on his desk started beeping. He jerked around and grabbed the receiver.

"Hello?" His eyes darted sideways and he lowered his voice. "Not yet. . . . Yes, sir."

He hung up and waved the bills away with a guilty look. "That's okay, miss."

I tossed them down next to his lunch, a burrito wrapped in grease-stained paper with a half-eaten jalapeño lying next to it. Either they didn't send duck à l'orange down for the help or he simply preferred a lump of green chili and beans wrapped in a flour tortilla. Couldn't blame him.

"Keep it," I said, my mouth watering.

As soon as Terry started up the engine and made a circle to leave, I saw the man pick up the receiver again. Maybe it was paranoia, but I got the distinct impression he was calling to let someone know we had gone.

two

*H*attrick's office on Bedford Drive was about what you'd expect for a swanky plastic surgeon. Plush salmon-colored carpeting, subdued lighting, tasteful prints on the walls, and piped-in Muzak offering a soothing orchestral rendition of "Like a Virgin."

"Before" and "after" candidates were grouped on blue leather couches. An exotic-looking girl of fifteen with an aquiline profile and long dark hair sat next to her mother, who had bleached-out tresses and a scooped-out ski-slope of a nose. Like mother, soon-to-be like daughter. Further down, a middle-aged woman with blackened eyes and a nose bandage sat across from a man with hair plugs who might have been there to get a chin implant, since his neck started at his lower lip. A little boy with a large purple raspberry on the side of his face sat on his mother's lap sucking a lollipop.

We were just about to announce ourselves at the reception

window when *she* walked into the waiting room, taking our breath away.

She was five-foot ten, partly on account of the four-inch heels. She had flaxen hair that hung straight, brushing turbocharged breasts that were bound in an impossibly tight red sweater. A taut, tanned face with a tiny little nose wedged between two mountainous cheekbones. Lips that were one-inch thick, poking out from her face like those of a hungry perch. Eyes that sparkled an arctic blue. She held out a leathery hand with inch-long acrylic nails done in a French manicure.

"Hi, I'm Barbie! Dr. Hattrick's beauty consultant. Is this your first visit?" Terry and I internally debated taking the hand—then I offered mine.

"Yes, it is. Hi, Barbie. I'm Kerry McAfee."

We shook, then she held out her hand to Terry.

"Hi, I'm Barbie!"

"Hi, I'm Terry McAfee."

She was like a robotic blonde cyborg, stuck on the word "Hi." We were afraid if we didn't respond in kind she'd go into some sort of hyper-confusion and explode.

"Would you like to take a look at our samples?" She ushered us over to a couch that was situated apart from the rest of the waiting room, then plopped down on it, motioning for us to sit beside her. She opened up a large binder on her lap with dividers that read: *Nose, Eyes, Cheeks, Breasts, Liposuction,* and so on.

"Now, what are you here for? Let me guess." She glanced back and forth between us. "Well, we can surely fix that bump in your noses. That's easy as pie. And we could take care of those icky freckles—don't you just hate them? And if you don't mind an opinion, your chins could be stronger. And looky there, you've hardly got any breasts at all!"

Terry and I looked at each other, speechless.

Barbie flipped to the first section of the book. "Let's start with your noses—"

"Uh, Barbie?" Terry said.

"Mmm-hmm?"

"Was your name always Barbie, by the way? Or did you change it, you know, after you had some work?"

"I get that a lot," she chirped. " 'You look just like the doll, Barbie. Bet you changed your name.' But, no—born Barbie, always will be Barbie, till Barbie is no more." She paused, then went on, "You seem a little nervous, but I guarantee the pain is totally worth it, and we can have you looking just like me in four easy surgeries! Then, if you want to, you can change *your* names. But somebody's already got the name the Barbie Twins. Too bad. You'll have to think of something else."

I had to nip this conversation in the bud. If we listened to her much longer, we'd end by moving to Stepford, Connecticut, packing a case of Mop n' Glo.

"Actually, we're not here for surgery," I said. "We wanted to speak to Tatiana. Is she in?"

Barbie deflated like a punctured blow-up doll. "No surgery?" she said in a wounded tone.

"I'm afraid our insurance won't cover it."

She brightened. "We can put you on a payment plan. Just like buying a car!"

"It's okay," Terry said. "We enjoy being flat-chested and freckled with bumps in our noses. Could we speak to Tatiana?"

Barbie pouted, her swollen lips pressed together. "She doesn't work here anymore. I replaced her."

Oh, that's why she was so disappointed. She was new on the job and eager to prove herself. I wondered if she got a commission on the procedures she talked people into.

"Tatiana was the 'beauty consultant' before you?" I asked her.

"Yeah. She just took off, I guess. That's how I got this job, which was a really great break. Acting jobs are hard to come by these days, what with all the free sex sites on the Internet."

"Yeah, that must be tough," I said. "Would you know where we could reach her?"

"Barbie!" a sonorous female voice boomed from the inner office. Barbie looked up like a startled deer at an African American woman in a white coat who gestured from the reception window. She was big-boned and rich-colored, with naturally full lips, naturally full cheeks, and a short natural hairdo. Real out of place, with all that naturalness.

"Yes, Janice?" Barbie squeaked.

"I need you for a moment, please."

"S'cuse me." Barbie swung herself up from the couch and teetered for a minute on her heels—butt waving perilously in our faces as she tried to get her balance. Terry and I reached out and gave the tush a little push, and Barbie was back on her feet.

"Thanks!" she said, tottering to the window. The woman waved her through the door and Barbie was out of sight.

Terry leaned over to me. "Buns of steel," she whispered.

"Tell me about it. I think I sprained my ring finger on her left cheek."

We cooled our jets until Barbie returned a few moments later, looking considerably less happy than when we'd first met her.

"Tatiana's moved," she said, "and we don't have a forwarding address. Or a phone number. So . . . 'bye!"

She spun on her spiked heel, heading back to the office.

"Wait! Does anybody else know how to get in touch with her?" Terry said.

"Nope. 'Bye!" Barbie said, running to the door on tiptoe.

"Well, could we speak to the doctor?"

"Nope. 'Bye!" And Barbie disappeared for the last time.

"Well, that was a total bust," I said, as we went down in the elevator.

"Not really. At least we know that Tatiana is persona non

grata at Hattrick's office. The black babe obviously told Barbie to blow us off."

"But if she's skipped, where does that leave us?"

"Oh, we can get a line on her."

"How? We don't even know her last name."

"I think we can get something out of that Janice woman."

"You do?"

"Oh, yeah. She may look tough, but she's *mush*."

"I don't know." But even as I said it, I knew to trust Terry on these matters. She had an uncanny knack for reading people and almost never missed with her gut instincts. Except when they turned out to have been menstrual cramps.

"Let's stake her out," Terry said.

"Where?"

"Where does everybody in an office building go, sooner or later?"

I frowned. "The ladies' room?"

"Like I'm gonna hide in a stall, breathing bathroom fumes!"

I stared at her for a second. "Oh, the coffee shop."

"Duh," she said, rotating her eyes to the ceiling. "It's next to the front door. She'll have to pass it on her way out."

I ordered chamomile tea from the teenage girl behind the counter, thinking we'd better not have caffeine at five-thirty. Then I sat back down at the table and thought, *Nah.*

"Oh, miss?" I called to the girl. "Could you make that two lattes instead?"

"Sure thing," she said. "Would you like them no-fat?"

"No," Terry said.

"No fat?" the girl asked.

"No, yes to the fat. No to the nonfat. Okay?"

The girl frowned in confusion.

Terry sighed. "Please put fully fatty milk in our coffee."

"Well, you don't have to get snotty," the girl said.

"She's in withdrawal," I said, hoping it would deter the girl from spitting in our lattes. Teenaged coffee clerks can be vicious creatures when provoked. Once, after complaining about being forced to say *venti* when I wanted a large coffee—the server even pretending ignorance of the meaning of the word "large"—I found a venti-sized roach backstroking in my cappuccino.

"Great people-watching here," Terry said. "Lots of celebrities have shrinks on this street. You see 'em here all the time."

"Thought you were too jaded for celebrity spotting."

"I'm not gonna climb over their fences or tackle 'em for an autograph or anything, but if they walk past the window, sure I'll look. Hurts them deeply if you don't. There's a pharmacy across the hall, did you notice? I'll bet the place is crawling with them, going in for their Zoloft and Xanax and Viagra."

I sighed, bored with the whole subject. "Probably."

"Hey, look! It's John Malkovich!"

My head jerked around to the window.

"Made ya look."

"It *is* John Malkovich," I said, squinting. "And I think he's already picked up his prescription of Xanax. Looks like he's moving underwater."

"That's not him. It's someone *being* John Malkovich. He's a lesser actor who wants to be him, like Christian Slater trying to be Jack Nicholson."

"Oh. You could be right."

Terry pointed toward the entrance of the coffee shop. "Yo! Here comes Janice, now."

Janice strode past the window in a butter-colored leather coat, on the way home at the end of her workday.

"Let's book," Terry said.

We jumped up and I threw ten dollars on the table even though we hadn't been served, and we followed Janice out the front door and onto the street.

We followed her for two blocks. The sidewalk was already filling up with people leaving their workplaces, providing us with good cover in case she turned around. Eventually, she came to a bus stop and sat down. We hesitated behind the bench. Should we walk up to her, tap her on the shoulder, and start right in with *Where's the Russian, lady?* before her bus arrived?

But she knew we were there. She turned around and looked us in the eye. "Why are you following me? You with the plaintiff's attorneys?"

Terry could spot 'em, all right. This woman had spilled a very interesting tidbit before we'd even asked a single question.

"We're Terry and Kerry McAfee," Terry said.

"I heard that much in the office," Janice snapped, daring her to say more.

Terry refused to be intimidated. "We're private investigators. We work for someone whose husband has disappeared with a bunch of her money."

This got Janice's attention. "Who?"

"Lenore Richling, a patient of Dr. Hattrick's. Know her?"

"Yeah, I know her." Janice seemed more intrigued than annoyed now.

"Look, could we buy you a cup of coffee?" Terry said.

"No," she said, "but I wouldn't turn down a drink."

Hey. The *mush* theory suddenly had legs.

Janice took us to a sleek yuppie bar around the corner. It was long and narrow, a richly appointed upscale place with a second-story balcony.

"Let's sit up there," she said, pointing to the balcony. "That way if someone comes in from the office, they won't see me talking to two private dicks. Or is it *dickettes*?"

"Investigators," Terry said, "but I could go with *dickettes*."

"Nah," I said, "sounds like a chorus line of men doing high kicks in tap shoes."

Terry nodded. "True."

We placed an order at the bar for three sour-apple martinis, then made our way up the steep staircase. The balcony gave us an unimpeded view of the front door and a godlike perspective on the mosh pit of young singles below, trolling for dates after a hard day at the gallery or the clothing store or the shrink's office.

Janice had ditched her conservative office look for brown flared pants and a cream-colored sweater that clung to her curves like a second skin, gold hoop earrings, and shiny cinnamon gloss slathered on her generous lips. Her transformation from officious boss to Happy Hour sex goddess was a mindblower, like she'd gone into a phone booth as Nurse Ratched and bounded out again as Tina Turner. As she swayed up the stairs she extruded *come-hither* pheromones that turned all male noses in our direction.

"So the sweet young mister left with Mrs. Richling's money," she said as the martinis arrived. "That figures."

I thought we'd caught her just at the right moment. She gave the impression of being disgusted with something or someone, and anxious to unburden herself.

I lifted my glass. "*Cin cin.*"

"Cheers," Janice said, clinking. "So . . . how much did he get?"

"Not much," Terry told her. "Ten thousand dollars."

"Pay my bills for a while."

"Ours, too."

We all drank to that one.

"Did you ever meet Mario?" I asked Janice.

"Mmm-hmm. He came to the office a couple of times with Mrs. Richling. He's *fine*," she said, wagging her head appreciatively. "Way too young for that old—I mean, for your client."

"It's okay," I said. "We know she's a bitch on wheels. Did he ever come to the office on his own, without Mrs. Richling?"

She gave us a wise look. "Yeah."

"Do you know if he was involved with Tatiana?" Terry asked, getting right down to it.

Janice's head bobbed up and down, but her lips were firmly pressed together. Like she wanted to confirm, but wouldn't say it out loud.

"So she *was* involved with him?" I asked to be sure.

Janice leaned in, a wicked gleam in her eye. "He wasn't the only one she was involved with. She was doin' the doctor, too. Girl spent more time on her back than a June bug."

Hmm. I wondered how Tatiana's sexual proclivities might play into this scenario. Could she be some femme fatale who had set everything in motion, seducing Mario and getting him to steal from Lenore?

"She was a medical assistant, right?" I said, causing Janice to spray some high-priced vodka right past my ear.

"Ha! Girlfriend had no medical training. She didn't do nothing except spend a couple of hours in the office meeting with prospective patients. And got paid plenty for it, too."

"But what did she do, exactly?"

"She was a model. One of Hattrick's masterpieces. He'd drag her little ass in and tell people they were going to look just like her when he was done with them. Of course they didn't. Lately, people have been coming out looking like freaks. The doctor—" she expelled a breath, "started messing up bad. Was named in a bunch of malpractice and breach-of-contract actions. But when the lawyers started coming around for depositions, our little Russian hottie was nowhere to be found."

"I don't get it," I said, remembering the crowd of surgical

hopefuls in Hattrick's office. "He had an office full of pa-tients—"

"Not like he used to. A few insurance cases, people who don't know any better. But the money people, the society crowd, they been staying away in droves."

"But what about Lenore?" Terry said. "She said he was the best in the business or something."

Janice made a face. "She's a freebie."

"Free surgery?" Terry and I said together. "Why?"

Janice shrugged. "Dunno. But you'd think she was paying top dollar, the way she bosses him around."

A gratis face-lift. This was an entirely new wrinkle, so to speak. *File it away under W for weird*, I beamed to Terry, a de-gree of mental telepathy coming with the twins territory, then brought the conversation back around to the missing assistant/model.

"Where do you think Tatiana went?" I asked Janice.

"Don't know. She's probably still around somewhere, living off some dude. Maybe Mario, who knows?"

"Do you have an address for her? Or a phone number?"

Janice sobered up instantly, fear crossing her eyes. "Oh, uh, I don't think—"

"What's the matter?" I said, surprised at the abrupt change in her demeanor, from gleefully catty to completely cowed in just under two seconds.

She looked over Terry's shoulder as she answered. "Ta-tiana's not someone you want to mess with. She's cold, you know? Out for herself. I wouldn't want her mad at me."

I tried to reassure her. "She wouldn't have to know you gave us the address. In fact, all we need is a last name. We'll find her."

Janice studied me for a moment, then shrugged. "Oh what the hell. She probably took her act someplace else, anyway. I have an address in Hollywood." She pulled a day planner from her bag and flipped it open. I caught a glimpse of a dog-eared school picture on the inside of the front flap. A six-year-old with a sassy smile, missing two front teeth.

"Cute." I pointed to the picture. "Yours?"

She expanded with pride. "My baby," she said, showing the photograph to Terry, who smiled in appreciation.

Janice studied the picture for a moment, her eyes misting over. "He's a smart boy. So smart. And he was so proud of me when I got this job. I'd worked long and hard to get here. There's nobody better at running a medical office." She dabbed at the corners of her eyes with a cocktail napkin.

"Now all I do is field calls from dickhead lawyers and pissed-off patients. I was better off in Fox Hills, but you couldn't have told me that. No ma'am, I was going to the Hills of Bever-leee . . ." She snorted into her martini glass. "Swimming pools, movie stars."

This Janice was not only *mush*, she was a very cheap date. I hoped she wouldn't ask for another drink, even if it *did* mean we'd get more information out of her. I didn't want her to go home to her kid sloppy drunk.

"Look, we're sorry," Terry said. "We didn't mean to dig into all this other stuff. All we really need is a way to get in touch with Tatiana. She's our only contact for Mario."

Janice ran a finger over the plastic shield on the photograph. "Sure, sure," she said, then flipped to the address pages. "Here it is. She lives off Franklin on Argyle." She pointed to an entry for *Tatiana Pavlov*. Terry quickly wrote the name and address on a napkin.

"Thanks a lot," she said. "We owe you."

"Just don't tell her where you got it." Janice looked at her watch before swilling the last drop from the bottom of her glass. "Well, I got to get home to my boy. Thanks for the drink."

We stood and shook her hand.

"Thanks, Janice," I said. "Good luck."

"Uh-huh. I'll need it, I'll need it," she said, giving her head a little shake as she made her way carefully down the stairs, then disappeared through the front door.

Terry looked at me. "Wonder what's up with the doctor?"

"Who knows? Maybe he got too successful. Took on too many patients and got careless."

"Hmm. Still early. Want to pass by Tatiana's?"

"Suits me." I chugged the rest of my martini. "I bet Mario's using the ten thousand dollars for fun money with his floozy."

Terry slammed her glass on the table. "Let's go nail the little Russkie slut."

The sun was setting as we arrived at Tatiana's address on Argyle Avenue, a cluster of 1940s-style stucco bungalows around a courtyard planted with yucca and bright orange birds-of-paradise. Terry continued past the building, then pulled up to the curb in the next block, parking the Harley out of sight.

We went back to the complex and across the well-maintained grass, locating apartment 4 square in the middle of the horseshoe-shaped complex. We knocked, and as we waited, a head poked out of the door to our left.

"She's gone," a young man lisped past his tongue stud.

One look told me *he* was gone—his eyes glowing pink, surrounded by a cloud of wacky-tabacky smoke. He favored the current trend of circus geek chic: industrially dirty jeans slung from his pelvic bone, pigeon-chest and shaved head covered with spiky tattoos, metal pins and studs skewering the soft tissue of cheeks, lips, and eyebrows.

"Tatiana?" Terry said. "We're looking for Tatiana."

"She took off," he said, shrugging. "Like a few days ago."

"Any idea where she is? We're friends of hers."

"Don't know, man. She left with that dude she used to hang with. Had a couple of bags, and was all, like, amped."

"Hmm," I said, not wanting to sound like I was ignorant of Tatiana's friends, since I was supposed to be one of them. "Uh, young guy? Dark—?"

He nodded. "Thinks he's the shit?"

Probably. "Mario?" I asked, to be sure.

"Never heard his name."

"Okay, thanks," Terry said, attempting a last look through the curtained windows.

The bald, tattooed, half-naked man disappeared back inside, then Terry whispered to me, "I'm gonna see if there's a back door. Keep watch out here."

"Okay," I said, moving away from the door. I didn't think the neighbor would jump on the phone to the police if he saw us lurking around, but it didn't hurt to be cautious. I walked back to the front sidewalk and leaned on a palm tree, thinking Terry would join me in a few moments. Even if there were a back door, it would probably be locked, and we'd be no wiser to Tatiana's movements . . . *unless*.

Unless Terry had broken into the apartment.

Oh shit, say it ain't so! But I knew that she had, the same way I always knew when she crossed a line—a sinking feeling in the pit of my stomach.

Before I'd had time to formulate my next thought, I heard a noise behind me. I turned to see a short man in a plaid sport coat exiting a beat-up Toyota Tercel. He punched the lock on his door, slammed it shut, then scooted across the grass, headed directly for Tatiana's apartment.

I followed him across the lawn, keeping to the sprays of orange blossoms for cover. What if he had a key? What if Terry had actually managed to get inside? He knocked on the door and sure enough, Terry opened it—probably thinking it was me.

"Tatiana Pavlov?" the man said to her.

She didn't lie outright, so much as nod her head faintly. He shoved a brown envelope at her. She took it, wearing latex gloves.

"You've been served." He turned on his worn heels and hustled back down the walkway past me to his Tercel.

As soon as he pulled away, I came out from behind a bush and made a *What are you doing?* gesture to Terry, who was still in the doorway. She waved me in with the envelope, a finger across her lips, and I ducked into the apartment.

"Put on your rubbers, please," she said, handing me a pair of latex gloves. I nudged the door closed with the toe of my platform tennis shoe, then snapped the gloves on. I peeked out the front curtains, but Tattoo Man hadn't made another appearance.

"You can't accept a summons intended for someone else," I fumed at her. "That's against the law!"

She was busy perusing the document. "Honest misunderstanding," she mumbled.

"Yeah, and the credit card you used to get in the back door was an honest misunderstanding, too."

"Hey, you can believe it or not, but the door was unlocked."

I didn't believe her for a second. Terry was a world-class liar, dating back to childhood. She was always able to convince our mother that I was the one who'd dismembered all the dolls, pulverized the hutch window with a baseball bat, or spent my milk money on the malt liquor in the garage. It took Mom years to realize I'd been framed every single time by my silver-tongued sister.

"I'll look out here for the money," she said. "You take the bedroom."

I headed into the bedroom as instructed, though I was increasingly nervous about being here at all. I searched the closet, felt under the mattress, and rifled through the drawers of the dresser next to the bed. Tatiana had left behind some stray articles of clothing, probably because they weren't worth taking. A couple of T-shirts, worn cotton panties, a pair of Guess jeans.

Underneath the clothes I spotted a window flier advertising an evening of Russian folk music at Trotsky's Cafe. I knew the place—a downtown restaurant specializing in heavy food, balalaika music, and angry poetry readings. The walls and booths were red, and the outdoor sign bore a hammer and sickle insignia—twenty-first-century nostalgia for the Evil Empire. If Tatiana was a recent immigrant, it would make sense for her to frequent a place that catered to homesick Russians. It was probably worth a shot if we didn't turn up anything else.

Terry came into the room, waving the subpoena. "This is a summons to appear as a witness in *Pilch v. Hattrick*. A breach-of-contract action."

"When?"

"Next Thursday. She's got to be there or show cause."

I showed her the flier for Trotsky's. "Maybe we should deliver the summons to Tatiana ourselves."

"Good thinking." She gave me a thumbs-up. "Even if she's not there, I'll bet *someone* will know who she is. Find any money?"

"*Nyet.*"

"Well, I've been all through the rest of the place. No money anywhere. We'd better get out of here before the guy with the tattoos sobers up and gets nosy."

We started back toward the living room, but I suddenly felt Terry gripping my arm. She put her finger to her lips and nodded toward the back door. We paused, deadly silent, listening.

Footsteps on the porch.

A heavy tread. Maybe work boots.

We darted back into the bedroom, and I pulled Terry behind the door. We waited breathlessly for a knock, but none came. Instead the back door opened and a man called into the apartment.

"Tatiana . . . ?"

I peered through the crack, but all I could see was the back door itself, opening toward us.

"Tati . . . ?" The man pushed the door further inward. "It's me."

He came all the way inside the apartment, looking around, then closed the door behind him. He was average height with an extraordinary build. Smooth, predatory movements. Lots of dark hair, big bedroom eyes, and Gina Lollobrigida lips.

Mario.

One look, and you knew the guy was a total sexual athlete. Maybe that was what had tempted Lenore into marriage with someone so obviously wrong for her. Wrong side of the tracks on the wrong side of the border and probably the wrong side of the law.

He tossed a black leather shoulder bag on the dinette table and went into the small kitchen. He opened the refrigerator door and looked inside.

"Shit. No *pinche* cerveza."

He slammed the door. Glass bottles rattled inside, but they obviously weren't beer. He sat down at the table and looked at his watch, then reached into his bag and pulled out a pen and a candy bar wrapper. He scribbled a note, grabbed up the black bag, and started for the door.

Then he stopped.

He unzipped the bag and took out a large business envelope, grabbing a couple of dollar bills out of it and stuffing them in his pants pocket. Then he looked around the living room, his gaze settling on the couch.

He crossed the room in two strides, grabbed a cushion, flicked open a switchblade and deftly sliced the side of the cushion underneath the piping. He stuffed the envelope into the opening, then tossed the cushion back on the couch.

I swallowed hard. This guy was mighty handy with a blade. I didn't want to think about what he could do to our fair, yielding flesh if he was this good at slicing through tough poly fibers.

A minute later, he let himself out the back, taking the black bag and testing the knob before closing the door behind him. It was still unlocked.

I heard his footsteps receding into the distance, and I let out my breath.

"That was too easy," Terry scoffed. "Let's get out of here." I grabbed the back of her jacket.

"Hold on," I whispered. "Let him get down the alley, at least."

We waited another couple of seconds, then Terry lost patience. "Come on. He could be back anytime."

We rushed into the living room. She grabbed the cushion while I read the note on the tabletop. *Back in five. Went to get beer.*

"Hurry it up," I said, waving my hand. "He's coming right back." I looked out the back window for a car, but didn't see one. Had he come on foot?

Terry opened the envelope and thumbed through a stack of bills that were bound with a thick rubber band. "Hundreds and fifties, mostly."

"How much?"

"Gotta be close to ten thousand. Let's bail."

Beads of sweat were popping out on my upper lip. "I don't know. Can we take it . . . just like *that*?"

"It's Lenore's."

"She *says* it's hers."

"Ah come on. Whose word you gonna take? He stole her jewels and hocked 'em."

"I don't know. Breaking and entering, theft. This is real borderline stuff. What if we get caught?"

"Quit fucking around and we won't get caught! We're acting as recovery agents now, not PIs. How were you planning to get the money back, anyway?"

"I thought we'd confront him and, you know . . . guilt him out."

"Yeah, that'd work. You'd guilt him out and he'd stab you through the heart."

She was right. Mario looked a lot more dangerous than we'd been led to believe, and it was a good thing we hadn't had to talk the money out of him. I decided we'd better count our blessings and hit the pavement while we still had the chance. Terry stuffed the envelope in the back of her jeans, covering it with her shirt, and we started for the back door.

Then we heard the footsteps again. A shape appeared in the pebbled glass of the window. We froze.

Terry pointed to the front door on the opposite side of the room.

We scrambled toward it.

Then we heard someone turning the knob on that door as well.

We lurched toward the bathroom door, jamming ourselves through and getting stuck for a second, popping through to the other side like twin bowling pins. Terry closed and locked the door behind us.

"What do we *do?*" I whispered frantically.

But Terry was already working on the lock of the bathroom window, which by some good fortune was not painted shut. She shoved open the sash, took a quick look outside, and dove headfirst onto a hawthorne bush, bouncing off and rolling across the grass.

I wasn't about to dive headfirst.

I jumped up on the sink and stuck my feet through the window, grabbing the bottom of the sash for leverage as I tried to ease my way over the bush.

Then I heard—*SLAM!*

It was the front door in the living room.

SLAM!

The door at the back of the house.

Terry grabbed me by the ankles, yanking me outside. I had almost cleared the hawthorne when I heard a man scream.

"Mother*fucgggg* . . . !"

I released the window in panic and landed on a thousand sharp twigs with exposed skin, my skimpy vintage leather jacket having hiked all the way up my ribs. I cried out in pain at the same instant we heard the explosion.

It sounded like the roof had been blown off.

Terry dragged me up by the arm and we stumbled through the fir trees bordering the backyard and tore off down the alley, hearts thudding in our chests, eardrums throbbing like homebound fans after the Ozzfest.

three

$\mathscr{I}$ don't remember running to the bike. Barely remember jamming the helmet on my head and leaping on as Terry fired up the engine and burned rubber down the street. We were two miles west on Franklin when the shaking subsided, my vision cleared, and my brain flashed me a big neon sign that said: *Guilt!*

"Stop!" I yelled at Terry.

She shook her head.

"*Stop!*" I slugged her in the kidney.

The bike angled over to the right and she turned onto a residential street, pulling into an apartment driveway, where she cut the engine.

I ripped off my helmet. "We left the scene of a crime!"

She turned and gave me a pitying look. "Could you speak a little louder? I'm not sure they heard you in Rancho Cucamonga."

I tried to rein in my hysteria. "What *was* that?" I said, climbing off the bike.

"I'm guessing large-gauge semiautomatic."

I paced around the driveway. "We have to go back. Someone could have been killed. We're material witnesses."

"Okay," she said, "let's go back. It's your first offense, so they'll go easy on you. Two, three years max in Sybil Brand for breaking and entering and grand theft. It's my second strike, so I'm two-thirds of the way to a life sentence. But hey. When you're right, you're right. Let's go turn ourselves in."

"You . . . ! You were arguing the other way ten minutes ago! You said we were perfectly within our rights to take that money!"

"That was my perspective. I think Johnny Law might have a different perspective. He might see us as a couple of sneak thieves. There are two sides to every story, Ker."

My teeth were grinding themselves into chalk dust. I unhinged my jaw and took a deep breath. "Tattoo Man. He can identify us."

"Maybe." She casually took a tube of cherry-flavored lip gloss out of the pocket of her cargo pants and applied a coat. "Or maybe the ganja caused him to see double. Or maybe it was yesterday and he thought it was today. The guy's fried to a crispy crunch. He's useless as a witness." She snapped the cap back on the gloss and smacked her lips.

I bonked myself on the head with the helmet. "How did I let you get me into this?"

"How did I get *you* into this? Ms. I-Couldn't-Turn-Down-a-Friend-of-Reba's?"

I looked down, my cheeks flaming.

"Listen, what's done is done," she said. "We need to put some miles between us and that apartment. Now."

"But who got shot? Mario? Tatiana?" Then a more frightening thought occurred to me. "Or were they shooting at *us?*"

She shook her head, eyes narrowed as she tried to put it together. "I don't think so. We heard two doors open, one shot fired. Somebody screamed, a man—" She checked her watch. "If we hurry over to the hotel now, we can get home in time for the ten o'clock news. Maybe they'll have the story."

"But what do we tell Lenore?"

Terry's eyes went sideways. "We *could* tell her we didn't find him. Keep the money as hazard pay. After all, she neglected to mention switchblades and gunplay. We could cover the property taxes and have enough left over for a weekend in Vegas."

I glared at her.

"Or not."

"This could be blood money," I said. "I don't want any of it."

"Look, if we don't take our twenty percent, it will show consciousness of guilt."

Damn. This girl could rationalize anything.

"But what do we say about how we got it?"

"How many times do I have to tell you? A good lie is one that sticks close to the truth. We saw him leave the apartment, then we went in through an unlocked door and found the money in a cushion. Then we left. We have no idea what happened after that."

Sirens began screaming a half-mile away.

"There's the cops, they'll take care of it," she said, reaching for the key. "Let's go give Lenore her money and be done with this."

I was beyond resisting. I threw my leg up and it flopped over the seat like a big dead thing. Exhausted after the adrenaline rush, I had all the willpower and motor control of a Raggedy Ann doll.

Terry, however, was cool as a cuke. She made a skillful turn in the driveway, looked both ways, then buzzed into traffic on Franklin like it was just another day.

Twenty minutes later we were back in the lobby of the Dauphine, where Alphonse materialized out of thin air.

" 'Allo-o-o," he crooned. "Mrs. Templeton is expecting you?"

He had to ask, either out of habit or just to be annoying.

"No, she's not," Terry said. "Guess we'll be going now—"

I was not going to let her walk with Lenore's money. "Would you like to call her, Alphonse?" I said, grabbing Terry by the hem of her jacket. "Let her know we're coming up?"

Terry gave me a resigned look, as Alphonse snapped his fingers at a young woman behind the counter. "Call Mrs. Templeton," he said. "Try 302 and 308, and let her know *ze* young ladies are here."

The clerk made the call and nodded to Alphonse. "She's in her room. Number 308."

I punched the call button expecting Alphonse to accompany us for the ride, filling the elevator with his musky pungency. But I got a shock when the doors opened.

The elevator contained a woman with a face like a Braque canvas, gray and green alternating blotches on cheeks that looked like they were stuffed with wadding and overwhelmed by giant Jackie O. sunglasses. She was hunched with osteoporosis, leaning precariously on a gold-tipped cane.

"Mrs. Magnuson!" Alphonse two-stepped it to the elevator. "You should have told me you were ready to leave *ze* hotel! I would have brought *ze* wheelchair!"

"I don't need a wheelchair, you ponce," she croaked, thrusting the cane in front of her like a blind person and nicking Terry in the shin.

"Ouch!" Terry scuttled backward.

The woman lurched out of the elevator without a word of apology. Alphonse ran to her side, gripping her bony elbow as she staggered forward. Either Mrs. Magnuson had inner ear problems or she'd spent the entire afternoon on a minibar bender.

"A basket for Mrs. Magnuson!" Alphonse yelled.

The young female clerk dipped down below the counter and came back up with another of the ubiquitous gift baskets.

Terry gave me a puzzled look—*Okay, getting a basket when you check in makes sense, but getting one when you leave?*

The clerk hurried around the counter with the basket, cellophane crinkling. A bellhop came zipping out of another elevator pushing a brass cart loaded with designer suitcases. The clerk ran to him, stuffed the basket next to Mrs. Magnuson's brown lizard hatbox, then watched as the bellhop wheeled the cart out to a beige Rolls Royce that was parked at the curb. A uniformed chauffeur stepped out and installed the luggage and the basket in a trunk big enough to picnic in.

Alphonse helped the wobbling little figure into the backseat of her Rolls. She slapped his hand away and he responded with an ingratiating bow, clicking his heels together before closing the door.

The clerk returned to her post at the registration desk. She had straight blonde hair, a button nose, and an apple-cheeked pudgy face that seemed to be at odds with her tall slender body. Straight off the boat from Nebraska, I thought. Splits her time between working at the hotel and auditioning for Burger King commercials. Terry sauntered over to her. I let the elevator doors close and followed.

"That's a nice going-away gift," Terry said, leaning on the counter with a confidential air. Just a little girl-to-girl chat while the men were out of earshot. "What's in it?"

"Don't know, exactly," the girl said. "You think they ever give the employees one of those, even at Christmas?"

"They don't?" Terry looked appalled. "What's the big deal? It's just promotional items, I'll bet. Probably get 'em for free."

"Who knows? They treat them like gold. They put them to-gether in the back office under lock and key, like we're a bunch of thieves, gonna steal their little prizes. These rich peo-ple, they can't get enough free stuff."

"Pathetic," I said, shaking my head.

"And it's not just when they leave. They've got to have them all the time while they're here, delivered up to their rooms. Some of those women can go through a basket like that in two days. I don't know where they put it. Most of them weigh about eighty pounds, soaking wet."

When Alphonse returned from seeing Mrs. Magnuson off, he looked surprised and not at all pleased to see us still on the ground floor. The clerk caught his eye and suddenly got busy with some paperwork, ducking her head.

Since when was it a crime for front desk personnel to be friendly?

This five-star hotel had the locked-down feel of a prison camp, with Alphonse doing duty as a Froggy Colonel Klink. He gave us a little wave and a superior smirk as we turned to get on the elevator.

"Give my best to Mrs. *Reeechling*," he said, using her real name this time.

I wondered at the breach of security, then shrugged it off.

We knocked at the door to room 308. We heard scratch-ing on the door and whimpering, then Lenore calling out, "Coming . . . ! Out of the way, precious, Mommy has guests."

The door swung open and Lenore stood there, resplendent in a red silk kimono and black bell-bottomed slacks, fresh fire-engine red enamel on her nails, her watery blue irises peering out at us from ballooning eyelids.

She shoved Paquito into her armpit and clamped down on his body with a skinny, viselike arm to hold him in place as she let us in the door. Then she plopped down with him on the bed and rubbed the heel of her hand against her face, apparently still plagued by itchy stitches.

"So . . . any luck? I didn't expect you back this quickly."

Terry pulled the envelope out of her shirt and Lenore's mouth flapped open. "Is that all of it?"

"We haven't counted it, but it looks like ten thousand," Terry said.

Lenore snatched the envelope, squeezing its sides and dumping the contents on the bed. She riffled through the stack of bills, looking at the denominations.

"Count it, will you, dear?" she said, tossing the bundle to Terry. "My nails are still tacky."

Terry rolled her eyes and took the money over to the little desk next to the window. She snapped off the rubber band and began counting, stacking the bills according to size.

"Where did you find him?" Lenore said to me, her eyes glinting in triumph.

"At Tatiana's," I said, watching her carefully. But there was no hint of pain on learning that her husband was consorting with the Russian honey.

"Little tramp." Hatred deepened the color of her bruises. "How did you get him to give up the money?"

I looked over at Terry, whose head was bent in concentration. I was on my own. The Glib One was busy at her task.

"Uh, the money was there. *He* wasn't."

"You just said he was."

"I mean he left."

"And you went in and got the money."

"I'd rather not discuss our methods," I said. "Trade secrets."

"Fine. I don't really want to know," Lenore said. "Now I need you to follow him."

"What?" Terry shrieked from the other side of the room.

I shot her a look—*Chill.*

"Why?" I said to Lenore, dreading the answer.

"Well, he won't be happy about this. I want you to make sure he doesn't come after me."

"But you said the money was yours!" I said, as Terry went back to counting, shaking her head in disgust.

"Of course it's mine! But he might be . . . peeved that I took it back."

Yes, he might. And I could imagine him flicking open his switchblade and punching air holes into someone's skull if sufficiently peeved.

If he was still alive, that is.

But whether Mario was dead or alive or somewhere in between, I wasn't about to offer our services as human buffers. Lenore's story was getting murkier by the minute, and I wanted our business with her concluded as soon as possible.

"Mrs. Richling, you don't want us for that job," I said. "You need a bodyguard. We couldn't guarantee your safety."

"Whyever not?"

"Well, for one thing we don't carry weapons."

She gasped. "You went after Mario without weapons?"

Terry gave me a sideways smile. She was always after me to buy a gun, since her felon status prevented her from getting one. I couldn't tell her that my main reservation, besides taking a life, was that I didn't entirely trust Terry herself around firearms. You don't keep guns around someone with the impulse control of a three-year-old buzzed on Frosted Flakes.

"We're not licensed to carry them," I said. "Incidentally, if you thought there'd be a call for weapons, it would have been nice of you to warn us."

"I thought it went without saying Mario was dangerous!" Lenore said, her nostrils flaring like a stallion in a sweat.

To my mind, the things that go without saying are—*The sun rises in the east and sets in the west; Things that go up, must come down*; and *All things must end*. Everything else in life is up for grabs. What Lenore meant, of course, was that she hadn't *wanted* to say that she was sending us on an errand that could land us toes-up in the morgue.

"Sorry, Mrs. Richling. We're done here. We did what we agreed to do and got your money back. Pretty good work considering we did it in one night."

Terry finished counting the money. "Nine thousand, seven hundred and sixty-seven."

Lenore got a cagey look on her face then stood up and grabbed three hundred-dollar bills, thrusting them at me. "Now let's see . . . that's three hundred for today. And I'll give you two days' advance for tomorrow and the next day. That should be long enough."

"No deal!" Terry stood up so fast she overturned the small gilded chair. I flashed her another warning look.

"Long enough for what?" I said. What the hell angle was Lenore working now?

"I'll be satisfied if you keep a watch on him. If you see him go near my house, notify the police immediately and tell them there's a burglary in progress. If he comes near the hotel, alert Alphonse. He'll get his security people involved . . . Take another six hundred, there's a good girl."

Terry crossed her arms over her chest, hip slung in her best tough-slut posture. "Our contract was for a twenty percent recovery fee."

Lenore sniffed. "You don't mean to tell me you expect eighteen hundred dollars for one day's work? That's highway robbery!"

"That was our *deal*." Terry's voice was low, and to my ear, dangerous.

Lenore let out a Scarlett O'Hara sigh. "Oh, sweetheart. Don't be so difficult. If you only knew the *agony* I'm in with these stitches!"

She lurched to the mirror working her jaw up and down,

as if the movement would somehow scratch the itch, and brought her hands up to her face, the long red nails curved millimeters away from it, dying to dig in.

"Maybe you should call the doctor," I said, feeling her discomfort. "I don't know if that much itching is normal."

"I *have* been calling, all day! These doctors . . . glorified cosmeticians. Think they're gods, but where would they be without *us*?"

Sensing Lenore's distress, Paquito jumped off the bed and began humping her ankle. She kicked out sideways, sending him sprawling.

"Yah!" Terry and I yelled, echoing the dog's piteous cry of surprise and pain.

"Behave!" Lenore barked at him. "Mommy's in anguish! Oh, if only I could scratch my ear, just once . . ." She tugged at the edges of the bandage.

Terry and I looked at each other in alarm. Was she going to rip it right off her face?

"Lenore, no!" Terry said. "Your stitches!"

"Your manicure!" I said.

But it was too late. She'd got a purchase on the tape and she yanked on it, tearing it away from her face with a revolting ripping sound.

Then she let out a scream of terror.

Time was suspended as we gaped in horror at the white strip that hung to Lenore's shoulder. There, nestled in the gauze and stuck to the tape was a purplish-black lump. Blood was caked around the hole in the side of Lenore's head, where only a piece of flesh remained . . .

The rest of the necrotic ear now dangling at Lenore's neck.

"*Uh-h-h-h-h!*" she fainted dead away before we could even make a move.

I felt my stomach flip over and heard Terry gagging on the other side of the room. I ran to Lenore's side but Paquito beat me to her. He grabbed the bandage in his teeth and tugged on it, fighting to pull it free from her head like it was a great new chew toy.

"No, Paquito!" I lunged at him but he got the tape free, squirming away from me and running with it into the black marble bathroom.

"Call 911!" I screamed at Terry.

I ran into the bathroom after Paquito, casting about wildly for the crazed mutt with the sow's ear. I spotted his tail wagging behind the bidet and knew he wanted me to chase him. I reached out and grabbed at him, but he squiggled away and raced out of the bathroom, claws ticking jauntily on the marble.

I chased him back into the main room and saw his tail disappearing under the bed. I threw myself to the carpeting and yanked up the gold-trimmed dust ruffle.

Terry was yelling hysterically on the phone. "She ripped it off her *head!* She's bleeding from her *hole!* The dog's gonna eat her goddamned *ear!*"

Jesus, we'd be lucky if they didn't hang up on us.

I peered into the shadows under the bed. A panting yellow lump sat right in the middle of the space, beyond the reach of my arm, his tiny pink tongue jabbing the air. I saw the bandage with the ear stuck to it lying in front of his paws, and the look on his face said, *What a prize!*

Terry was behind me putting a pillow under Lenore's head, slapping her wrists to stimulate circulation, as Lenore moaned semiconsciously.

"You'll be okay," Terry said, her voice choked with revulsion. "You'll be just fineohmygodinheaventhatwasthegrossest-thingIhaveeverseen!"

"Good doggie," I cooed breathlessly. "Good Paquito. Bring me the ear! *Bring me the ear!*"

He responded with an *aarf* of pleasure. Poor little guy was play deprived, I thought, trying in vain to picture Lenore going a few rounds of fetch with him. This was a really good game, he seemed to think, and he was making the most of it.

Aarf, he said again. *Nothing doin', Two Legs! Come and get it!*

I heard Lenore behind me muttering in shock. "My ear, what did the prick do to my *ear?*" she said.

And then she blacked out again.

In the ensuing melee of sirens and blinking red lights and EMTs chasing down the dog with a bandage trailing from his jaws, I didn't notice Terry stuffing the envelope of cash into her jeans. It was only after Alphonse had left, glaring at us as if we were personally responsible for maiming one of his guests, and after Lenore had been whisked away to Cedars-Sinai Medical Center to have her ear reattached—if that was possible, given its unfortunate condition—only then, when we were alone in front of the hotel holding a shivering and hairless, homeless lapdog, did Terry admit to taking Lenore's money.

"We're just keeping tabs on it. It's not safe in the hotel," she said, zipping Paquito up in her jacket, his minuscule head poking out the top like that of a preemie papoose.

"She has to have a full-time maid, they all do," I said. "We'll leave the money with her first thing in the morning, along with the dog."

"No! That's a breach of our fiduciary duty! You don't give ten thousand dollars of somebody's money to someone you don't even know because that person happens to clean the toilets of the person whose money it is—is that *smart?* She could say she never got it!"

"We'll get a receipt."

"What if she doesn't speak English?"

"Then she can give us a receipt in Spanish or Chinese or Swahili."

"Racist pig!"

"Or Swedish! Oh, never mind," I said. "We'll give it directly to Lenore when she's better."

"*Less* our twenty percent."

"All right, all right!" I yelled. "You're a mono-fucking-maniac, has anyone ever told you that?"

She gave me a pout. "I could call you a few things, too."

Paquito loved the ride home—tongue flapping in the breeze, nostrils quivering as he sucked up an olfactory city smorgasbord at forty miles an hour. He didn't seem at all worried about being separated from his mistress. In fact, he seemed to be having the time of his life.

First a game of keep-away with a rotten ear, then a ride on a motorcycle snug between two human teats, his wet nose alfresco. It doesn't get better than *that* for a dog.

The phone was ringing as we entered the house. Terry answered and I knew immediately who it was. Evidently, our great-aunt was not pleased.

"We . . . she . . . it . . . *our* fault?" Terry stammered. "Well it serves her right. She kicked her dog!"

I grabbed the receiver from Terry and mouthed: *Turn on the news.*

"Right!" She ran to the TV.

I braced myself for the whirlwind. "Hi Reba. How are you?"

Her words came out fast and furious. "I don't know what you girls think you're doing. I ask you to come to the aid of a friend and this is how you help? What's this I hear about your attacking Lenore, ripping off her bandages and . . . and is it true her ear came off—?"

"We didn't *touch* her . . . Who told you all of this?"

"Alphonse gave me the short version. And my phone has

literally been ringing off the hook with people wanting to know what happened."

"Well, hold the phone. Lenore is in Cedars recovering from a little mishap with her surgical tape, and beyond that I don't think you should spread any more rumors."

"Rumors? So it's not true about the ear?"

"It *is* true but it's not for public consumption." Bad choice of words, I thought, almost gagging. "But I'm sure she'll be fine, and if it's any consolation, she's bound to receive a gigantic settlement from Dr. Hattrick's insurance company."

"*If* Hattrick still has insurance."

I paused. "What are you talking about?"

"Giselle Fairweather says the good doctor has lost his hospital privileges, and is minutes away from losing his license," Reba declared with a hint of malicious glee.

If Reba was in the know about the doctor's troubles, then it stood to reason that Lenore was, too. The next question was: Why in hell would Lenore let Hattrick operate on her if his license was in question?

"Psssst! Psssst!" Terry was waving me over to the TV.

"Listen, Reba. I'd like to talk to you more about this—"

"Well I certainly wish you would."

"Let's do it in person. How about we come over tomorrow?"

"Fine. Be here for brunch at eleven."

"Okay, see you then." I hung up and ran to the screen.

Terry was cuddling Paquito with one hand and biting the thumbnail on her other hand as she watched the ten o'clock newscast. An excited young woman with platinum hair and a microphone stood in front of Tatiana's Hollywood apartment building. Crime-scene tape was strung up in front of the bungalow, and police lights lent an eerie strobe effect to the scene, as though the disco ball of death were rotating swiftly overhead. The reporter stood next to a witness who shielded his eyes from the camera lights. We leaned in for a closer look at him. Bald and nude from the hips up, body generously decorated with spiky designs.

Uh-oh. Tattoo Man.

"I'm standing here with the next-door neighbor, a Mr.—"

"Potato," he said.

"Wha'?" The reporter was momentarily stunned. But she recovered immediately, the consummate professional. "You heard the gunshot?"

"Sounded more like a cannon shot to me."

"Did you see anyone leaving the scene?"

"No, man. I got under the bed . . . and stayed there." He leaned into the camera, driving the point home. "Didn't see a thing."

The reporter gave him a brisk nod.

"Thank you, sir," she said gravely, as if he'd just revealed the coordinates of Amelia Earhart's plane. He stumbled away into the darkness and she turned to face the camera again. "And there you have it. An unidentified young Latino, dead of a gunshot wound. But no suspects, no witnesses. Truly, a mystery. Back to you, Hal."

Terry flipped off the TV. "Shit."

"Got that right," I said.

"Whoever shot him must have taken his identification."

I paced the floor. "Think this is coming back to us?"

"No. There were no other witnesses. And Tattoo Man obviously doesn't want to get involved. Saw nothing, knows nothing. Name of Potato."

I snorted. "Great alias, huh? The bonehead's never heard of Smith?"

"Best he could do on short notice with no neurons."

"Think he mentioned us to the police?"

"No. He doesn't want to cozy up to the police, either. On account of his tendency to self-medicate."

We pondered the situation for a moment. Terry sat down with Paquito on the couch.

"You think Lenore had something to do with it?" I asked.

Terry sighed, shaking her head. "Obviously she didn't know Mario was going to be out of commission, or she wouldn't have tried to hire us to follow him."

"But she said 'two days should do it,' meaning she didn't think he'd be a problem after that. So what did she *think* was going to happen to him?"

"I don't know. But it's a safe bet that Mario and his blushing bride were into *something* extralegal."

"Yeah, but what? What were they into?"

She tugged on her braid, mulling it over. "Hey, what did Lenore's first husband die of, anyway?"

"Old age? He was in his nineties."

"Hmm. Makes ya wonder, doesn't it? She marries the young guy as soon as the old guy's in the ground, then the young guy gets shot."

I got a mental image of Lenore as a psychopathic black-widow murderess, cackling with delight as she bumped off a series of hapless husbands. It didn't seem like too much of a stretch, actually. "You think she's a killer?"

Terry responded with a neutral shrug.

Suddenly it was all too much for me. Dead husbands. Purloined money. Severed ears. "Look, we're going to have to give a statement to the cops—"

"Don't start with that again!"

"This is not playtime, Terry. This is real. We're involved with a murder."

"Peripherally," she said. "Let's talk to Lenore, first. See if she'll come clean."

"Oh all right. But if the police find out we were there—"

"They won't. We wore gloves. We're covered."

I gave her a skeptical look.

"Hey, rest easy," she said, looking at the dog curled up next to her leg. "Speaking of which, we'd better figure out some sleeping arrangements for Paquito."

We fed our new houseguest a meal of canned turkey chili, then made a little sweater nest for him on the couch, stoking the fake logs in the stone fireplace for warmth. Our house is a tiny, shingled two-story cabin, 850 feet square, apparently built for and by Keebler Elves in the 1940s. It's freezing in the winter because there's no insulation, and freezing in the summer because of a huge canopy of trees that completely blocks the sun during the day. I sleep upstairs in the loft, a six-by-eight-foot platform with a closet and a skylight, that has a half-wall and no door. Terry sleeps on a mattress on the floor of a little alcove downstairs, an add-on slightly lower than floor level, with a window seat she uses as a dresser.

We inherited the house from our mother's father, Pops. It sits off of Beverly Glen, a winding road that cuts through the mountains that separate the San Fernando Valley from Los Angeles proper. The structure isn't worth its weight in matchsticks, but property values around us have shot up insanely, and real estate agents are always dropping by to see if we're willing to sell. But we would never think of it. In an age of tract homes and mini-malls and smog, our little homestead is like a magic wooded getaway, tucked deep into the curves of the narrow canyon road. We have a family of possums that lives under the house, sparrows that nest on the outside deck, and a wild deer that visits our backyard. But no real pets, not since childhood.

"He's kind of cute for vermin," I said, stroking Paquito's bony spine.

"He's much more relaxed here with us," Terry observed. "He probably knows we'd never kick him or make him wear a Hannibal Lecter mask."

"Lenore doesn't deserve him," I said.

She perked up. "So we can keep him?" she said like a kid with ice cream on the brain.

"First you want to keep her money, then her pet!"

"She probably won't want him back. After all, he ran off with one of her body parts and left little carnivore holes in it."

Uck.

"We can't have a dog in our line of work," I said. "We never know when we'll be home."

"We could get a doggie door!"

"Are you kidding? We can't let him outside. He'd be a coyote snack so fast it'd make your head spin!"

She petted him, dejected. "I guess you're right."

"Anyway, she'll probably want him back. I would."

"Me, too," she said, a little quaver in her voice. "I think . . . I think I'm falling in love with him."

"Yeah." I kissed his fuzzy skull. "But he isn't ours to love."

four

We pulled up to Lenore's coral-colored Spanish mansion at ten o'clock the next morning, the dog and the money envelope in tow. We were going to say a sorrowful farewell to Paquito, drop him off with the maid, and then pop over to Reba's for a gab session before seeing Lenore at the hospital.

As we made our way up the walk under forty-foot palm trees, my eyes traveled to the upstairs balcony, where smoke drifted skyward. A young Latina fanned at the smoke, looking down at us as she stubbed out her cigarette, and then disappeared. We rang the chimes, just as she pulled open the heavy oak door.

She was sleek-skinned and pretty in a skanky kind of way. Low-riding jeans and a short T-shirt that showed off her trim midriff, a gold navel ring shining from its epicenter. Her hair was long and gleaming blue-black, her eyes heavily lined, her lips pouty pink. I put her age at around nineteen, her attitude at fifty-year-old, burned-out barfly.

"*Señora Richling-Vallegos no está*," she said.

"Yeah, we know," I told her. "Do you speak English?"

The girl's expression said that she was withholding that information until she knew what we'd be *saying* to her in English.

"We were hired by Mrs. Richling to find something," Terry said. "We went to see her at the hotel and she's, uh, had an accident."

"Accident?" the girl said, frowning.

"Yes, unfortunately," Terry said, unzipping her motorcycle jacket while letting her eyes travel from the girl's cleavage down to her exposed navel. "She's in Cedars-Sinai Hospital."

"*Qué pasó?*" she said casually, no alarm in her voice.

"She needs some restitching after her surgery, is all," I said, taking Paquito out of Terry's hands and holding him out to her. "We brought the dog so you could take care of him."

The girl leaned on the door and sighed, giving Paquito a look of disgust. "That's no dog. *Es una rata*."

"Yes, but he belongs to Mrs. Richling. You kind of *have* to take him."

She shrugged and reached for him. "Sure, give him to me. I'll put him down the garbage disposal. I put a whole chicken down there once, bones 'n' everything. I'll say he got squished by a truck."

Paquito seemed to comprehend the girl's diabolical threats. He started trembling and whimpering and a thin trickle of pee-pee ran down the front of my leather jacket. Terry saw it first and guffawed.

I thrust Paquito out to arm's length and another little stream shot out and hit Terry's arm, dousing her spiked leather watchband. Terry winced and shook her arm frantically.

I looked back at the girl, who was now the only one laughing. "Think you could spare a few paper towels?" I asked her.

She gave me a sly look that said, *Told you he was a pain in the ass*. Then she turned and walked toward the kitchen through the foyer, past a sweeping staircase with Moorish tiles on the steps and a wrought-iron balustrade. I noticed she was barefoot, with a chipped pedicure in blue glitter nail polish.

"Does she strike you as the typical Beverly Hills servant?" I whispered to Terry when the girl was out of earshot.

She shrugged.

"I mean, she's smoking on the balcony, has total attitude, and dresses like one of Britney's backup singers."

"Yeah," Terry jeered, "and *you* want to give her the money."

Before I could reply, the girl reappeared with a handful of paper towels. We thanked her and wiped off the piddle.

"What did you say your name was?" I asked her.

"Rini," she said.

"Pretty name."

"Short for Irina." She laughed. "Pussy name."

Indeed.

"Well, Rini, we've decided to hang on to Paquito until Mrs. Richling gets out of the hospital."

"Fine with me." She gave me an engaging smile. "But you know, I wasn't really going to put him in the disposal."

I wasn't even remotely convinced of that. If not the garbage disposal she'd find another way for him to meet a horrible end, like accidentally stepping on his itty-bitty spine in four-inch stilettos while she rushed down the stairs for a night out.

"I didn't think you were," I said, "but we've gotten kind of attached to him, so we'll just keep him for a day or two."

"By the way, what kind of food does he eat?" Terry asked.

"You won't believe it." Rini rolled her big black eyes dramatically. "She feeds him caviar and goose liver pâté."

Caviar and pâté? For a dog? That was the wretchedest excess I'd ever heard of, and doubly astonishing for someone of Lenore's thrifty habits. It had to be terrible for the pup's health, in any case.

"That's okay," Terry said. "We've got lots of that around. Does he drink champagne or just water?"

Rini snorted. "Bottled water."

"Well, we'll see to it that all his needs are taken care of." Terry turned and began striding purposefully back down the walkway toward the motorcycle, stuffing the tiny dog back inside her jacket as she went.

I handed the bunched-up paper towels to Rini, damp side in. She took them between the tips of thumb and forefinger like a soiled baby's diaper.

"Do you know Mrs. Richling's husband, Mario?"

"Of course. I'm the *maid*."

She gave the word extra emphasis, as if she were trying to convince me.

"Seen him lately?" I asked her.

Her eyes became mean little slits. "No."

"Did he say anything about where he was going? Or who he was going with?"

"Nuh-uh." She moved to close the door in my face.

"Just wondered." I thrust my hand in the doorway with our neon-pink business card. "Give me a call if you want to check up on the dog or anything."

She took the card and glanced at it, before looking back at me. "Double Indemnity?"

"Yep."

"What*ever*." She slammed the door.

Yeah, I thought as I turned to leave, whatever quacks like a duck is a duck, and Ms. Rini didn't begin to quack like a housekeeper for a Beverly Hills mansion.

She was a street-smart chiquita who'd probably never scrubbed a floor in her life. So who was she, really? My money was on some kind of connection to Mario. Sister, cousin, compatriot. But why would Lenore be giving her shelter if that were the case? And why the pretension of being a maid?

Maybe for the same reason Lenore had pretended that the tough guy she married was a famous polo player from South America.

Jerry was ecstatic about keeping Paquito. This could be a real problem, I realized. She had a talent for neurotic attachment, and I knew that if she bonded with him too closely she'd spend days in bed with psychosomatic chest pains and migraines when we had to give him up.

"Look, why don't we see if Aunt Reba and Cousin Robert will keep him?" I said to her.

"No way."

"He belongs in Beverly Hills. Not in the canyon with no heat and hungry predators. Come on, it'll be no trouble for them to take him."

"Grizzie'll stomp him to death. What if he pees on the furniture? She'll wind back and hurl him all the way to Culver City!"

Griselda was Reba's stout Irish housekeeper. An honest-to-god scullery maid with big, beefy red hands who worked like a fiend, sighed really loud about ten times an hour, and muttered to herself with occasional outbursts of "Aye, ye'll soon see" and "Aye, that'll fix yer boat," like a chunky female Popeye.

"He *won't* pee on the furniture," I said. "They can keep him in the kitchen. Or maybe Robert will like him and take him into his studio."

Cousin Robert was Reba's bouncing baby boy of fifty, a would-be artist who lived with Mama in the fifteen-room Tudor mansion on Palm Drive, dabbling in painting and swilling a never-ending stream of inspiration in the form of Armagnac, Tanqueray, and Cristal.

"Oh, great. What if he gets drunk and steps on him?" Terry whined. "He can't even see past his own stomach!"

I gave her a withering look. She was pulling out all the stops in order to keep Paquito, even stooping to defaming her own flesh and blood.

"What an awful thing to say," I scolded her. "You should be ashamed of yourself."

"Oh bite me," she replied.

We arrived at Reba's mansion and punched in the security code at the gate. It opened slowly and ponderously like the entrance to Buckingham Palace, and we pulled into the large circular drive.

We'd decided to get as much information as we could from Reba about Lenore's marital woes without mentioning Mario's death. We didn't want to alarm her unduly, and hearing that Lenore's husband had been gunned down in cold blood just might set off an alarm or two.

"What did you think of the maid?" Terry asked me.

"She's no maid."

"That's what I thought, too."

"She may be related to Mario," I speculated.

"Why? Just because they're both Latinos?"

"No, because they're both bad news."

I rang the bell and Cousin Robert answered the door, satin

robe open over his hairy, rounded gut, breath one hundred–proof before the day had even begun.

"*Entrez*, my lovelies!" He planted sloppy flammable kisses on each of us.

"How's it going, dude?" I said, stepping over the threshold. "Setting the art world on fire?"

"Well, I had a nibble from a gallery that represents emerging artists," he said. "They loved my work until they met me, then evidently decided I could stay submerged. I don't think they could picture trotting me out at their chichi little cocktail parties, could you?"

"Yes," Terry said. "Yes, I can picture you at a cocktail party, actually."

"Thank you, sweets. I can always count on a kind word from my cousins." He scuffed across the marble foyer in his pink satin mules. "Mumsy? The Nancies Drew are here."

"Come on in, girls," Reba called from the dining room.

Reba Price-Slatherton is our great-aunt on our mother's side. The second wife of Jeffrey Price, who was Cousin Robert's father. Reba married two more times after Jeffrey's death for a total of five husbands—each richer and more infirm than the last—and had more money than God as a result. (Not that I'd recommend He hit her up for a loan any time soon—she was just the tiniest bit tightfisted.)

As far as Reba knew, we still had funds from our father's life insurance. We never told her otherwise. We were too proud to let her know the extent of our poverty, and besides, we were afraid she'd try to rectify the situation by rustling up some nice, terminally ill millionaires for us to date. Not that it could be much worse than the series of dwarves, losers, and misfits I'd been out with lately—Los Angeles is a breeding ground for them. The truth is, I was jaded beyond my years when it came to men. But Terry managed to remain a hopeless romantic, with stars in her eyes for every pretty girl she met.

Reba was reading the paper in a quilted pink bed jacket and paisley silk pajamas, her face made up like a road map despite the early hour, her hair sprayed into a stiff hennaed helmet. She was avidly soaking up items from the crime blotter, riveted by the mayhem that existed just outside the borders of her rarefied world.

"How about this one?" she said. "A Long Beach factory worker took a blowtorch to his shift manager, then sued the company for stress leave. Mmm-mmm. What *is* the world coming to?" She nibbled on an English muffin with orange marmalade and a slice of mango. It was all we ever saw her eat. I guess it's how she kept her birdlike figure. Either that, or she was visited by liposucking vampires that came through the French windows at night.

Robert tipped a bottle of cognac into his coffee. "This, girls, is called a *carajillo*." He drew out the double *l*'s, grinding them in his throat. "I learned to drink them on the Costa Brava. They start the day with them over there."

Clearly we were to infer that if you were sophisticated enough to learn the name of a drink in Europe, you weren't a lush if you had a snootful with breakfast—you were continental.

"Isn't it kind of early?" I ventured.

"Oh, just a little hair of the dog." Robert poured a skosh more cognac into his cup. "Speaking of which, is that a dog under your jacket, Teresa, or is an alien about to spring forth from your stomach, gnashing its horrid little teeth at us?"

"Oh, we wanted to talk to you about that—" Terry started to say.

Reba gasped at the breach of etiquette. "You brought an animal to the table?"

"Don't worry. He's very clean," Terry said, unzipping her jacket.

Grizzie entered with a tray of English muffins just as Terry set Paquito on the floor. The poor woman took one look at him and threw the muffins up in the air, the silver tray clattering to the floor behind her.

"R-r-r-a-t!" she screamed, as muffins rained down around us.

I guessed right away there weren't too many mutant lapdogs roaming the emerald hills of her homeland.

Terry leaped up from her chair. "Jesus, Grizzie! It's not a rat! It's a dog!"

Paquito dived at a muffin on the floor, grabbing it in his teeth and running under the table. Terry and I got down on our hands and knees, reaching for him. "C'mere, Paquito, c'mere boy!"

But he wouldn't come. He dodged our hands and growled, thrashing the muffin back and forth like it was a gazelle and he was the fierce dingo that had felled it. *Paquito devour carcass on Serengeti! Grrrrrrrr!*

I finally managed to snatch him under the belly and clambered to my feet, extracting one muffin from the tiny jaws of death and peeling another one off of my elbow.

"Well, I'll be a kitten's knittin'." Grizzie squinted at him. " 'Tis a dog, is it?"

"Of course, Griselda," Reba said. "It's Lenore's little beast. I recognize it now. What on earth happened to its hair?"

"He shedded it," Terry said.

"Shedded it!" Grizzie shouted, as if it were some sort of excretory function. "He'll not shed on my floors, filthy little beggar!"

I cradled him in my arm. "He's not filthy. He's very sweet. We were going to see if you wouldn't mind keeping him for a few days. He's really no trouble."

"Not on yer life!" Grizzie exploded.

"Puh-*lease*," Robert groaned.

"Darlings, what a dreadfully stupid idea," Reba said.

"Told ya," Terry chimed in.

And that settled it. Paquito would stay with us.

When things had calmed down, and we'd been served fresh muffins and coffee, we finally got down to business. Paquito was snoozing in Terry's lap, and Robert was either asleep or passed out, his chest resting against the edge of the table, head dangling forward as he inhaled with loud, wet sucking sounds.

"So, have you had any word from Lenore?" Terry asked Reba.

She shook her head and sighed. "I haven't been able to speak to her. The staff told me she's not taking calls, but I mean, not even from me?"

"So," I said, lowering my voice, "we don't know the . . . disposition of the ear."

Reba shuddered, reaching up to twirl a two-carat diamond in her own lobe. "No. I can't believe it. I simply can't believe it. Daniel Hattrick was the most sought-after surgeon in Beverly Hills for the longest time—"

"We were told that Lenore got her surgery for free," Terry said.

"For free?" Reba sniffed. "Well, you certainly get what you pay for."

"That's very unusual, don't you think? Does she have a relationship with the doctor that would account for it?" I asked.

"Not that I know of. Although she *was* always tooting his horn. Even got me to go in for a consultation once, which come to think of it was a *free* consultation. I didn't use him, but perhaps others did on her recommendation, and he repaid her with a free face-lift. Of course, he's having so much difficulty now with the lawsuits and whatnot . . . maybe he had to do some pro bono work to get people back."

"Any chance he'd do something like this on purpose?" Terry asked.

"What, maim a patient? I hardly think so." Reba sliced into a dewy bit of mango. "I imagine he merely slipped with the knife. Stranger things have happened, you know. I could tell you stories about plastic surgery that would curl your hair," she added, waving the blade at us.

"No thanks," I said.

"Not that you need your hair curled. Straightened is more like it. I do wish you girls would let me treat you to an appointment with Jordan. He could give you a much more sophisticated look than this Pippi Longstocking do you're sporting, Terry."

Terry rolled her eyes at me, and I attempted to bring Reba back to the subject at hand.

"We have a feeling there's more to this situation with Lenore than meets the eye," I said. "It all seems pretty weird. Sending us after this guy for a lousy ten thousand dollars—"

"Well, he stole her jewels, didn't he? That justifies prosecuting him to the fullest extent of the law. You can't let people get away with things like that."

"But that's just the thing—she called us, not the police."

Reba thought about it, casting her mind back. "I remember now. She told me she *had* called the police but they refused to pursue the matter since she and Mario were married. Hmmph. She might have expected something like this when she got involved with such an *unsuitable* young man."

Terry looked at me and nodded. Reba was playing right into our hands. "What do you think she saw in him?" Terry asked her.

Reba's eyebrows did a tiny dip—the closest approximation of a frown the Botox would allow. "I never understood it, myself," she said. "I suppose anyone can be led down the garden path in later life, but I always thought there was more to it than mere animal magnetism. She married him only three months after Myron's death, you know . . . although at our age, a year's mourning does seem excessive."

"Do you think they could have been involved before Myron died?"

Reba drew herself up. "Well, I just have no way of knowing, do I? She never mentioned a lover."

"Okay," I said, "but you might have heard things. Were there any whisperings about it? Rumors about Myron's death?"

"Oh my yes, although I would hate to repeat them."

We stared her down. At length she continued.

"Poor Myron had suffered so in recent years. His death was a blessing, really. The more vicious wags in the neighborhood said it was an assisted suicide, but I for one am *positive* Lenore had nothing to do with pushing his wheelchair into the pool."

"What?" we yelled.

Reba nodded. "An accident. It could have happened to anyone. You're wheeling along the slick tile, not really paying attention, you push the little lever to the left, when you meant to go right, and the motorized chair takes you right over the edge of the pool and into the water, electrocuting you before you can even drown."

"Uh-huh," we said.

"Tragic," Reba said with a sigh. "She really ought to have sued the manufacturer, but I think she was too distraught to think of it at the time."

"Let me get this straight," Terry said. "A ninety-year-old man is tooting around the edge of the pool in his motorized wheelchair, doing what? Soaking up the sun? Trying to get more liver spots on his scalp?"

Reba shrugged. Not for her to second-guess her fellows and their strange habits.

"And then he accidentally spins the hundred-pound chair with no turning radius completely around, aiming it at the pool, and gasses it hard enough to send it over the raised concrete lip—"

"Brick, it was brick," Reba said helpfully.

"Over the brick edge of the pool and into the water and is electrocuted?"

"That's how it happened, apparently."

"Was he compos mentis?" I said. "I seem to remember your saying that Myron hadn't been able to play canasta since the nineties. As in the 1990s."

"That's right. But he was still completely charming and debonair, kind of like Bob Hope in his later years. He had that little twinkle in his eye that completely distracted you from the drool running out the side of his mouth."

"He was a vegetable," Terry said.

"No-o-o," Reba said, shaking her head. "You're much too harsh, dear. He was just more relaxed in his waning years. He preferred to sit back and enjoy the fun from a distance rather than actually participating in the games. And the eating. And the breathing."

"What?" I said. "He had an oxygen tank?"

"Mmm-hmm."

"He didn't eat?" Terry said.

"Oh, he did, now and then. But the oxygen mask made it awkward. Mostly he sat in the corner and . . . enjoyed."

Terry gave her a jaundiced look. "You mean she propped him in his chair and ignored him."

"Oh, have it your way." Reba sniffed. "But it's not like she locked him in the attic or anything. She did an admirable job with Myron, poor dear."

This qualified Lenore for sainthood, I guess. Not locking the old guy away in the attic when he got too feeble for canasta.

Reba pursed her lips. "You girls are too young to understand. It's difficult to see someone you love so changed."

"But if what you're saying is true, then he couldn't have managed the trip into the pool by himself," I said. "It sounds like he'd have trouble even finding the switch, let alone operating the chair."

"And maybe it *was* too difficult for Lenore to watch him suffer. Maybe she took matters into her own hands. You couldn't blame her," Terry said, using the sympathetic interrogator method to elicit a confession. Or an accusation, as it were.

"Well, I hardly see that it matters," Reba said, waving a bejeweled hand, brushing the scandal away like a bad smell. "There was an investigation and no foul play was alleged. Poor Myron's but a memory now, and those heartless individuals who want to think the worst of Lenore can just go ahead and do it. Most of them live south of Sunset, anyway." Sunset Boulevard was a sort of DMZ in Beverly Hills, separating the obscenely rich from the merely extremely loaded. "As far as the police are concerned, Myron Richling died an accidental death."

Okay, but . . .

If Lenore *had* helped Myron into the pool, she'd probably had an accomplice. I really couldn't picture her doing it on her own. And then maybe that accomplice had forced her to marry him in exchange for keeping quiet about the whole thing. But when she realized she couldn't control him anymore, she'd sought to shut him up permanently.

Terry looked at me, and I could see she was thinking the same thing.

"Snerrrk," Robert said, his head bouncing up once and back down in his sleep.

I turned to Reba. "How about finances? Did Myron leave her well off?"

"We don't talk about money, of course, but I haven't noticed any belt tightening. Although come to think of it, she did let something slip right after Myron's death, and I inferred from it that she wasn't entirely happy with her circumstances."

"What was it? What did she say?"

"Mmm, let's see if I can remember . . . It was on the order of, 'The old prick left me high and dry,' or words to that effect. But she was quite tipsy, you understand. It was at the funeral reception and she'd put away quite a few Tom Collinses."

Terry slammed her hand on the table. Robert's head hit the wood, jogged loose by the table's movement. He landed *splat!* on his right cheek, snoring the whole time.

Reba gave us an affronted look. "What?"

"Aunt Reba, I don't want to sound cynical," I said, "but did it ever occur to you that maybe Lenore *was* left high and dry? And that if she's been able to maintain her lifestyle since Myron's death, maybe it's because she's been up to something in the intervening months? Something not entirely legal—?"

"Well, I hadn't thought of it."

She thought of it now and it almost caused an expression of concern, which was prevented only by the cosmetic paralysis.

"Did you ever socialize with them? Ever hang out with Lenore and Mario?" Terry asked, leaning in.

Reba rolled her eyes. "NOCD," she said.

Terry looked at me, baffled. "Not our crowd, dearie," I translated.

"Not only was he not *your crowd*," Terry said, "I'm pretty sure he'd be right at home with the Crips."

"Oh? I wasn't aware that he was *handicapped*."

"The Crips are a gang, Reba," Terry told her. "Not cripples."

"Oh-h-h-h, of course." Reba nodded thoughtfully. "It never occurred to me that Mario might actually be a gang member. Although he did pull a gun on me once and threatened to kill me."

Terry slumped forward, shaking her head. I looked over and saw Paquito jump down from her lap. He began sniffing intently in a small circle on the Oriental rug. Terry saw this and scooped him up, then took him out to the backyard to do his business.

Aunt Reba just had time to tell me the rest of her long-winded story about Lenore and Mario before her masseur arrived. I'd have to recount the whole thing to Terry from memory later.

We retreated to a coffee shop on Robertson to talk things over before we went to the hospital. Housed in the base of a professional building, it served tuna sandwiches and a thinnish brew from a Bunn automatic drip machine to the working people from upstairs. We had to order something, but our caffeine meter was already in the red zone, so we asked for toast.

A waitress brought the order and spotted Paquito seated next to Terry in the booth. She looked a little conflicted.

"Do you allow dogs?" Terry asked her.

She shrugged. "No, but I don't think he counts. We got rats bigger 'n that in the kitchen. Cuter 'n that, too."

The waitress walked away and Terry made an indignant face at her back. "Don't you listen to her," she said, nuzzling Paquito. "She's just jealous because she wouldn't look half as fetching in a rhinestone dog collar." Then she got him situated under the table with a saucer of water.

I pulled out a steno pad and started to make notes. I scribbled *Who, What, Where, Why,* and *How* across the top of the page, then drew a circle in the middle with lines radiating out to the sides.

"Oh no," Terry said, jamming her finger down her throat. "Not the diagram."

She hated my diagramming technique. It smacked too much of *school* for her, a place she was only too happy to see in her scooter's rearview mirror.

I ignored her, running a hand through my unruly hair, and then wrote the names of the characters in our little soap opera on the lines. *Mario, Lenore, Tatiana, Rini,* and *Hattrick.* I put an arc between Mario and Lenore and wrote underneath it—

Murder?

Terry yanked the pen from my hand. "Hey! I'm sitting here. Let's talk and we'll *diagram* it later."

"This is how I get it straight in my mind!"

"Quit messing around and tell me what I don't know, and then we'll take it from there."

I dropped the pencil and began to fill her in on the rest of Reba's story. "Reba was going to Hattrick's office, at the insistence of Lenore—"

"*Where's* his office?" Terry said.

"You know where it is."

"*When* was this?"

"Couple of months ago."

"*Why* was she going there?"

"For a pre-op consultation."

"*What's* that?"

"You're trying to annoy me."

"Just covering the bases on your little steno pad," she said, pointing to the four *W*'s. "One *H* to go."

Sigh. "He put a three-dimensional image of Reba's face on the screen, revising the image with his fancy-schmancy software to show her what she'd look like after he performed surgery on her."

"And *how* was that?"

"Just like Cindy Crawford."

"Just like my *ass*."

"You *wish* your ass looked like Cindy's. Anyway, Reba said she ran into Mario and Lenore in the underground parking garage."

"Coming or going?"

"Going. And they seemed to be in a real hurry."

"Hmmm."

"And Reba was chatting them up when she noticed that Lenore was carrying a black Judith Leiber bag that Reba had loaned her ages ago, and it struck Reba that the bag would be perfect for the do she was going to attend that night."

"What sort of do?"

"Charity."

"*We* could be a charity, if she wants a charity."

"No margin in it with us. No rubbing elbows with Angie Dickinson and Connie Stevens."

"Silly of me."

"So Reba spots the bag and says, 'Oh dear, you know I've simply *got* to have my bag back, it'll go perfectly with the Donna Karan. Could we possibly switch bags right now?' She didn't think Lenore would refuse, seeing as how it was Reba's own bag, and she was offering her a Prada to use in the interim."

"That as good as a Judith Leiber?"

"It's probably a wash. Anyway, Reba had the moral high ground, the bag was *hers*, and she needed it for that night, but Lenore fought her off."

"How so?"

"She squeezed the bag to her side so hard it would take The Rock to pry it loose."

"Reba's analogy or yours?"

"Hers, believe it or not."

"Reba watches the WWE?"

I shrugged. "Evidently."

"Must be the hole in the ozone layer."

"Anyway, Lenore ran to her car, saying, 'I'll get it to you tomorrow, shall I dear?' "

"But Reba wasn't taking no for an answer?"

"Nope. The bag had set her back three thousand dollars. It was perfect for her outfit and she wasn't about to buy another exactly like it, although she could go out and get a new Tom Ford, but didn't want to, as a matter of principle."

"Okay. So then what happened?"

"Then Reba ran to Lenore and grabbed the bag—the straps were digging into Lenore's shoulder—and Reba was yelling, 'Give me the bag, it's mine!' and Lenore was shouting, 'Not now! I'll bring it to you tomorrow!' and in the middle of all of this, the gun went off."

"The *gun*?"

"Reba looked over and saw Lenore's bridegroom with a handgun pointed at the roof of the garage, and a big hole in the concrete."

"And?"

"And Mario said, 'Leave it alone, bitch. Or the next one goes in your bony ass.' "

Terry gasped. "Aunt Reba said 'ass'?"

"Direct quote. She said 'prick' earlier, if you'll recall."

"It's the end of life as we know it. So then what happened?"

"Lenore and Mario got into her BMW and sped out of the garage. Then the security guards got there and Reba said, 'They went thatta way,' then she hopped in her Mercedes and fled the scene." I gave Terry a sardonic look. "Guess it runs in the family."

"What?"

"Fleeing the scene."

She smiled. "It's the only way."

"So the question is—what was in that bag?"

"Who knows?" Terry sipped her water. "Maybe nothing. Maybe it was truly about the fashion statement."

"Could it have been the ten thousand dollars?"

"Why would she be hauling it around? Not to pay the doc, since she got free surgery." Terry sat back in the booth, rubbing her forehead. "Anyway, all this speculation is hurting my brain. I say we go over to the hospital and get it right from the horse's mouth. Lenore needs to do some talking. You ready to give her the old one-two punch?"

"Ready as I'll ever be."

"I think Paquito needs a rest stop, first."

As soon as we got outside Paquito ran to a scrawny tree poking out of the sidewalk, sniffed its trunk, then squatted in the twelve-inch-square opening around its base. A Beverly Hills patrolwoman appeared out of nowhere and walked up to us, swinging her nightstick, her other hand on her holster. She had sandy blonde hair in a ponytail and a curvaceous figure, but the mirrored shades gave her a somewhat fearsome appearance.

"Be right back with the scooper," I said with an apologetic grin. I tore back into the coffee shop and snagged a dozen paper napkins from the dispenser, then ran back outside to the scene of the crime, where I was surprised to find that Terry had not fled.

Instead, she was engaged in a passionate discussion of the relative merits of k. d. lang and Melissa Etheridge with the lady cop.

Who was no lady, needless to say.

The cop hitched up her belt and inched her jacket away from the holster on her ample hip, accidentally on purpose revealing her 9mm Glock.

Terry tossed her hair and "oohed" and "ahhhed" and asked her what it was like to be armed, did it give her a sense of power? And the officer assured her that yes, it certainly did, and Terry said her wimp sister wouldn't let her have a gun, and the cop gave me a sour look.

Then the wimp sister picked up the poop and deposited it in the trash bin that exhorted her to Keep Beverly Hills Clean! and the cop nodded her approval. Terry handed her our business card, then the patrolwoman went on her crimefighting way.

Hmmm. Looked like Terry's attitude toward law enforcement was evolving.

She picked up the dog, weighing him in her hand. "Amazing. He's at least two ounces lighter. You know, he might slide by in a rat-infested coffee shop, but I doubt we can get him into a hospital."

"Unless we're fiendishly clever," I said.

We swung by the drugstore and grabbed a Hello Kitty backpack and half a dozen knockoff Beanie Babies for sneaking Paquito into the hospital. Terry shoved the beanie knockoffs into the bottom of the pack for a booster seat, and we picked up a bag of low-fat, high-protein kibble, a few cans of tuna-flavored cat food we were hoping to pass off as caviar, and a Lilliputian blue leash to match his collar.

A woman with permed yellow hair and thick glasses on a chain totaled up our purchases. Her name tag said *Marge— Since 1989,* although I was pretty sure she'd been Marge since Cadillacs had fins.

"You were flirting with that cop," I whispered to Terry.

"Was not."

"Were so. You went all woogly-woggly when she showed you her gun."

"Oh give me a break."

"And you were discussing lesbian singers. Is that some kind of code, like fishes in the sand or something?"

"Oh, so they're *lesbian singers*. Not first-class lyricists, not kick-ass rockers. You have to categorize them according to their sexual preference, Reverend Falwell?"

"I'm only saying—"

"I *hate* the word 'lesbian,' " Terry fumed, swiping her ATM card in the machine.

"I hate the word 'vagina,' " Marge said, shrugging, "but what're ya gonna do?"

five

We pulled off of Beverly Boulevard into the parking garage of Cedars-Sinai Medical Center, scoring a motorcycle parking space on the first level. I stuck Paquito into the bottom of the backpack and attempted to camouflage him with the beanbag toys.

"It's just for a minute, honey," I assured him as I closed the flap.

Terry swung him up on her back, and then we headed for the double glass doors at the rear entrance.

A black guard sat behind the inside counter. "Hello, ladies. Can I help you?"

"We're here to visit Lenore Richling," I said.

He consulted his computer, found Lenore's name, and confirmed that she was allowed visitors. "Room 509. You can take the elevator there."

We thanked him and started toward the elevator, but he

grabbed Terry's arm. "I'll need to check your bag," he said, pointing to the backpack.

"Oh, uh, sure," she said, looking at me sideways. Then she flipped it open nonchalantly. "It's just Beanie Babies, that's all. Got a Princess Di one, even. It's worth a lot of money. Got a little crown on its head and everything . . ." She started to close the flap again.

"Just a second," the guard said. He grabbed the pack and peered in. "Uh-huh," he said, thrusting his enormous mitt right down in the middle of the beanies and fishing around. Then he grabbed something and pulled it out butt-first. Something tan-colored and squirming.

"Is this it? This don't look like Di, to me. More like the Taco Bell dog on a bad hair day. I wasn't aware they were making Taco Bell dog beanies. This is one of a kind. I'll have to add him to my collection."

Busted. Time for the sympathy angle.

"We've gotta take him to see Aunt Lenore," Terry said, a tear pooling in the corner of her eye. "She's dying and this may be her last chance to say *good-bye* to the little guy."

Paquito licked the guard's hand and whimpered, right on cue.

"It would mean the world to her," I said. "Please?"

The guard gave us a wise look, then gently placed Paquito back on top of the Beanies. "You get caught, don't tell anyone what door you came in."

"Our lips are sealed!" I said, and we hurried over to the elevators before he could change his mind.

We were greeted at the fifth-floor duty station by a plump nurse with red hair who smiled warmly at us. Natural redheads are members of an unofficial club—like-minded souls who were tortured for our differences as kids, developing great personalities or serial killer tendencies as a result.

"Hey, great hair," Terry said.

"Back at ya," the nurse said.

"We're here to see Mrs. Richling in 509. Is she awake?"

"Yeah, I think so. The police just left."

We kept smiling.

"The police? Surely she's not in trouble with the fashion police again, is she?" I turned to Terry. "I told her not to wear heels with shorts, didn't I?"

"Ha ha," Terry said.

"Seriously, um, why were the police here?" I asked oh-so-casually.

"No idea." The nurse shrugged and went back to her work.

We wandered down the hallway, dread slowing our steps. "They must have identified Mario's body," I said in what was supposed to be a whisper but may have come out as more of a shriek.

An old man passed by in a wheelchair, pushed by a young orderly with spiky hair whose jaw was working a wad of gum like a lump of pink pizza dough. The old man's watery eyes lingered on my face as if trying to place it from an episode of *America's Most Wanted*. Then he looked at Terry and said, "Hmmm."

"We're not on the lam or anything, honest," she said sweetly.

"Hmmm," he said again. The orderly winked at us and popped a bubble as they continued down the hallway.

"I think he heard us," I whispered when they had past.

"They can't hear you if you don't *say* anything."

"This is making me nervous. I talk when I get nervous."

"Well, shut your hole," she said, "or I'll stuff Princess Di in it."

We slipped into Lenore's room and found her alone. The police had gone and no staff were present. She had a large lump of gauze taped to the side of her face and bands of adhesive circling her head. If she had looked bad before the accident, now she was positively gruesome.

"Girlsssth," Lenore slurred, doped out of her mind. "C'mere."

She crooked a finger and we went to her bedside. This was not an occasion for one-two punches, I thought, feeling very sorry for her in spite of myself.

"Were they able to save your ear?" I asked gently.

Lenore's head wobbled back and forth, and she poked her tongue out of her lips, trying to wet them without success. I grabbed the plastic cup of water by the side of the bed and put the straw to her mouth. She craned her neck forward and sipped, a little water dribbling onto her hospital gown, then she leaned back and closed her eyes with a sigh.

"What are you going to do?" I said.

"Thsssue."

"Can they do anything for you at all?"

"Prosssthetic ear."

"That thsssucks," I said. "I mean, that's too bad."

Terry rolled her eyes at me. "Lenore, why were the police here? Was it about Mario?"

Lenore cracked open her eyelids. "What about Mario?"

"We didn't tell you last night because you were preoccupied with the ear thing," I said, "but there was some trouble at Tatiana's yesterday—"

"What kind of trouble?" Fear had crept into Lenore's voice.

"Mario was shot," Terry said.

"What?"

"Killed."

"Eee-eh-h-h." Lenore covered her face and made a high-pitched keening noise like a fruit bat on the wing. It was hard to tell whether she was weeping or emitting sonar distress signals.

"Lenore, you haven't told us everything about this situation, have you?" I said. She shook her head and sniffed up tears.

"Well, you'd better come clean with us," Terry said. "We're getting in deeper than we bargained for."

Lenore looked up at us, pleading. "Girlssth. I need you to do thssomething for me. It'ssth vitally important." She gripped the safety bar on the side of the bed, her knuckles going white.

"Sure. Anything," I said, suckered by her distressed condition.

Terry kicked me in the calf. Apparently she was not similarly moved by Lenore's plight.

"Find Tatiana," Lenore said, gasping as if each breath might be her last. "Find her and . . . tell her . . . I don't have it."

Terry squinted at her. "Have *what*?"

"I . . . I can't tell you that." Lenore cast her tearful eyes to the curtained window.

"Okay," Terry said. "Who *does* have it? Just in case she wants to know."

"No one hassth it. It'ssth gone. Completely gone. Tell her that. Tell her to tell *him*."

"Who?" Terry shouted. "Look, if you don't tell us what this is about, we're through with you, Lenore. Do you understand?"

Lenore rolled her head back and forth on the pillow. "Oh, the horror . . . the *horror*," she moaned, covering her face with her hands again.

Great. Now she was totally freaked out.

Even knowing that Lenore was about as trustworthy as a snake, I wanted to reassure her, to tell her we would help. But in order to do that, we needed more information. I had to drag her out of her despair and get her talking again.

I know what she needs! I thought. Something cheery. Something life-affirming . . . a visit from Mr. Good Feelings.

I took Paquito out of the backpack and brought him over to the bed. He smiled down at Lenore, panting. "Look who's *he-e-e-re*," I sang.

Lenore opened her eyes and screamed.

Okay. Maybe she wasn't completely over the ear incident.

I rethought the situation immediately and stuffed Paquito back in the bag just as the red-haired nurse appeared in the door. Terry and I spun around to meet her startled gaze.

"What happened?" she said, rushing over to check Lenore's pulse. Lenore's head lolled to one side, her tongue protruding from the parched lips.

"I don't know," I said innocently. "We were just here talking, and suddenly she screamed and passed out."

The nurse narrowed her eyes at me, and I sensed we'd used up all our red-haired capital with her. "You'd better leave," she said. "And I don't think you should come back."

Terry and I started for the door as Lenore muttered something in her semiconscious state.

"Pah . . . lahv," she moaned. "Pah . . . lahv."

What was she trying to say?

Paquito . . . love?

Was she trying to tell him she still loved him? That in her drugged state she had mistaken him for a hostile life-form from another planet?

Or was it *Pavlov*?

What exactly was going on between Lenore and the enigmatic Russian woman?

When we got to the parking lot, I tried to suss things out.

"Okay, the police were there for some reason, and it wasn't to tell her about Mario's death, so what could it have been?"

"I don't know and I don't care," Terry said, firing up the engine. "I vote we shitcan this case."

"But we agreed to talk to Tatiana."

"You agreed, I didn't. Listen, I don't like this. Lenore's up to no good. Obviously she took something that belongs to somebody else—"

"Yeah, and she thinks they might kill her for it."

Her eyebrows went up. *"So?"*

"So it would be pretty bad for business if one of our clients, who's also Reba's best friend, got snuffed on our watch."

"Our watch? We're not her keepers!"

"No, but we may be the only thing standing between her and some kind of danger."

She sighed. "Dammit Ker, we're PIs. Not avenging angels."

"Look, we still have her money. It obligates us to her. Let's take a quick run by Tatiana's and see if she's there. Then we can deliver the message and be done with the whole thing."

"But—"

"But nothing! I say we're going and that's that."

Terry answered by revving the bike at full throttle, rattling the concrete pillars of the garage.

She hated it when I pulled rank, but I *was* her boss. Also, I'd been born a minute and thirty seconds earlier, and age has its privileges.

She pulled out of the garage and back onto the street, and then we headed out past the Beverly Center shopping mall in the direction of Hollywood.

We rolled past Tatiana's apartment like rubberneckers who'd heard about the murder on TV. The apartment was still sealed up with crime-scene tape. Tatiana had not returned.

Terry pulled up next to the curb a few houses down.

"She's not there," I said.

"Would you be? You know, she may even be the killer, and Lenore's sending us right into her clutches."

"But she said she wanted Tatiana to tell *him*. So *he's* the dangerous one."

She threw up her hands. "Okay, so how do we find her?"

"I think our best bet is to go by Trotsky's. See if anybody there can put us in touch with her."

"Now?"

"Later tonight. It doesn't get hopping until dinnertime."

"What do we do until then?"

I pondered this a second. "Lenore said she didn't have 'it' anymore. That means she had it at one time."

"Yeah?"

"So let's go talk to Rini. Maybe we can get her to tell us what this mystery object is."

"Your wish is my frigging command," Terry said, laying down tracks to Lenore's mansion.

As soon as we pulled around the corner onto Rexford we heard it—"La Cucaracha" blaring on a car horn loud enough to start a rock slide on Pacific Coast Highway ten miles away. We parked directly behind a lime-green gas guzzler with hydraulic shocks that might have been a GTO when it came off the assembly line in the 1970s, but had been transformed into one badass eyesore of a lowrider. The *cholo* version of *Pimp My Ride*.

It was covered chockablock with well-endowed girls showing lots of titty, surrounded by sparkles and squiggles and other swirly hallucinogenic designs. Dice hung from the rearview mirror, a hula girl shook her booty in the back window, and the Virgin Mary sat in holy contemplation on the dashboard. Long brass horns affixed to the sides of the car blasted another impatient stanza of "La Cucaracha." The driver, a Latino in his twenties with a lightning bolt of black hair on the back of his bald head, bopped in time to a salsa beat coming from the nuclear-powered stereo.

Terry switched off the engine and turned to me. "Rini's boyfriend?"

I shrugged and we started up the walk just as Rini came out

the front door. She had an orange duffel bag slung over her shoulder, and she was pushing a perambulator down the sloping walk. She spotted us and stopped cold, releasing the baby buggy in her surprise.

The pram barreled down the walk, making a rapid squeaking noise as it went. Terry catapulted herself toward it and caught it before it crashed into the side of the car. The driver jumped out of his door and screamed at Rini over the hood.

"*Coño!* You want to kill your own nephew?"

"Sorry . . . *sorry!*" Rini ran to the infant, who gurgled happily and reached for her with plump little hands, blissfully unaware that he'd come *that close* to baby whiplash. "*Estás okay, mi'jo?*"

"Hey, Rini," I said. "Where are you going? Looks like you're skipping out on Lenore."

She looked up at me with a pitiful face. "Look, I'm sorry, okay? I can't take it no more."

"What can't you take anymore?" I said.

Lightning Bolt advanced on us and Rini glanced in his direction with unmistakable fear. We wouldn't get any information out of her now.

"Can't talk. Gotta go." She hustled the perambulator over to the man, who was short but wide, almost a doublewide, with the pleasant demeanor of a pit bull on steroids.

"You're not coming back?" Terry called.

Rini shook her head. "She can clean up that shit herself!"

"What shit?"

"*Whaddayou want?*" the man roared at us.

Terry held up the backpack with Paquito, who was bleary from a road nap. He blinked his big brown eyes against the sunlight and yawned, displaying fangs that looked like they belonged on a catfish. "We're dog-sitting for Mrs. Richling. The little guy's sick. We need to take him to the vet and we don't know who that is. Does she have some phone numbers on the refrigerator or anything?"

Rini hastily dug into the pocket of her stretch jeans and pulled out a gold key chain. She tossed it to Terry.

"She's got some files in the office and numbers next to the kitchen phone. You'll give her back the keys? I was gonna mail them to her."

"Sure," Terry said. "Thanks."

The man grabbed the baby, which looked like a bundled-up summer squash in his massive arms, then buckled it into a child seat in the back. I saw that the interior of the car was covered from ceiling to floor in purple fake fur.

"Irina! *Vámanos!*"

Rini hurried to the car, stuffing the duffel onto the floor before jumping in the passenger side.

"Hey, is the burglar alarm activated?" Terry asked.

"No!"

Rini slammed the door and the lowrider took off, screaming down Rexford Drive with a lethal slipstream of hydrocarbons.

Terry shrugged and turned to me. "*Vámanos.*"

We unlocked the door to Lenore's manse and pushed it open. The house felt abandoned.

No, it was *trashed*.

The raw silk cushions of the rose-colored couches were slashed. Chairs upended, their sapphire-blue upholstery shredded. Drawers and their contents strewn everywhere. Oriental rugs were ripped from the floor and tossed against the walls. And everywhere you looked, on every surface— black fingerprint dust.

Terry gaped at the mess. "What the hell? Did Rini do this?"

"I don't think so. She wouldn't have stopped to talk to us." I pointed to the dust. "Besides, the police have been here."

"So that's why the cops were at the hospital? To report a burglary to Lenore?"

"Guess so." I shook my head, looking around. "Could this woman's life get any worse? What's next, an IRS audit?"

"Let's figure out what happened here," Terry said, pacing the floor as she did the nervous lip-gloss thing, stroking her bottom lip over and over with it. "Rini was gone when the house was robbed, and she called the police when she got back?"

"I think it's more likely someone else saw it in progress, like a neighbor, and called the police. Then Rini came back to a house crawling with cops and wigged out."

"Lenore was afraid Mario was going to break in, remember? She said so at the hotel."

"Yeah, but we're pretty sure he was in no position to. So who *else* might have done it?"

Her eyes popped. "Maybe someone who was after whatever-*it*-is? The thing Lenore claims she doesn't have?"

"Could be. Let's have a look around."

We took Paquito out of the pack and set him on the floor, expecting him to take off like a shot on his home turf. But he stood on the tile floor and looked up at us in confusion.

What, he didn't feel at home here anymore?

I picked up a cushion from the floor and laid it on the bare couch frame, setting him down in the middle of it for a nap while we explored.

Lenore had been pretty well off before she was left "high and dry," that much was clear. Even in its vandalized state the house was like a spread from *Architectural Digest*. The massive fireplace was decorated with hand-painted tiles and topped with a gnarled wooden mantelpiece that looked like it had held up a wall in a Spanish mission. There were oak beams across the vaulted ceiling, arched doorways, indigo slate tiles on the floor, original oil paintings on the walls . . .

Wait a minute.

Was that a Francis Bacon in the corner? I waded through the flotsam to take a closer look.

If it was a fake you could have fooled me. I'd only taken one art history course in my years at UCLA but the style was unmistakable. It was a simple portrait, a man slumped in a chair facing the lower left corner of the frame. His face was a double image—like an X-ray superimposed over flesh and blood. His black eyes stared vacantly, his teeth seemingly floating in space. A naked lightbulb cast a pale light in the darkened room, illuminating the man's oversized wristwatch.

The effect was unsettling. Like someone marking time until his death, unaware that he'd already passed on.

"Hey, up here!" Terry called from the second floor. I ran up the stairs and found her standing in the doorway to Lenore's bedroom.

There was an enormous four-poster bed of antique wood with a white lace coverlet, big enough to ice skate on. The drawers from the dresser were lying empty on the floor, lingerie flung pell-mell around the room.

Terry pointed to a wisp of black lace that hung obscenely from a lampshade. "Crotchless."

"God, I don't *even* want to know," I said with a shudder.

We moved down the hallway and found that the other upstairs bedrooms were in the same condition. Furniture toppled, bric-a-brac smashed, throw rugs tossed.

We wandered back downstairs and found Lenore's office, a small wood-paneled room off the kitchen. We sifted through the books and papers that were strewn all over the floor, looking for a clue—anything that might provide an explanation of who had been here and why. After a few minutes Terry jumped up waving a small piece of yellow paper.

"Oh my God, look at this! It's a receipt from a pawnshop!"

"What, for redemption?"

"No, it's the original pawn transaction. Check it out: a twenty-two carat gold and diamond Koala bear, diamond pavé bracelet and earrings, an emerald ring with matching pendant and earrings, a ruby hatpin—"

"Sounds like it's worth a fortune."

"Less than you'd think, but still a pretty penny." She shoved the paper under my nose. "Ten thousand dollars."

"What? Does it have Mario's signature?" I looked at the bottom of the page. The contract was signed by Lenore Richling in an elegant, feminine hand.

"Lenore hocked her own jewelry," Terry fumed. "That lying skank!"

"Whoa, wait a minute, wait a minute," I said, trying to wrap my mind around this. "What does it all mean?"

"The story of jewel theft was total BS," Terry declared triumphantly. "She said it to make herself look like a victim."

"Well, okay. But maybe she hocked the jewels and then Mario took the money from her. And she was too embarrassed to tell us the truth." I figured Lenore's secret shame about her husband's unsavory habits had to run pretty deep.

"Either way, she lied through her capped teeth."

I sat on the carpet, surrounded by the contents of Lenore's desk, surveying the opulent surroundings. "But why did she need to sell off her jewels?"

"She was desperate for the money we got from Mario," Terry said, narrowing her eyes. "You could practically taste the desperation. She probably needed it to pay her bill at the hotel."

"But why not sell the house or some of the stuff in it? There's a valuable painting in her living room, probably worth millions."

We sat there for a moment, stumped.

I got up and leaned on the desk, running my finger along the decorative scrolled carving on its edge. "Okay, Lenore pretended that getting the money back from Mario was a matter of principle, not necessity, right?"

"Right."

"But she actually *needs* the money. Needed it enough to hock her own jewels."

"Right. But Mario stole the proceeds and took a powder. Why?"

"Because it was getting dangerous," I said. "They took something—Lenore's *it*—from someone who wanted it back bad enough to kill Mario. Then that someone came *here* and ransacked the place looking for it. It was just dumb luck Lenore wasn't home or she'd be dead, too."

Terry sighed. "Well, all I know is I can't do any more of this advanced theoretical thinking on an empty stomach. Think she's got anything to eat?"

"Let's go see."

I followed her into the kitchen, figuring a little glucose might be just the thing for my muddled thought processes. Terry pulled open the stainless steel refrigerator door. It was crammed with goodies. A bottle of Dom Perignon, a tin of French Paté de Campagne—for the dog, no doubt—and other assorted gourmet foods, from pickled Vidalia onions to something called a Torteau Fromage Soufflé sponge cake, to a can of wild burgundy snails from La Maison de l'Escargot.

I knew we couldn't defy the law of thermodynamics forever, and the day would come when a binge like the one I was contemplating would result in thighs of thunder. But we were still in our twenties and that day seemed a long way off.

"What's that?" I said eagerly, pointing to a Tupperware container toward the front. I could see a swirly brown substance through the lid that just had to be chocolate.

Terry reached in and grabbed it. "Mousse, I'll bet, from some fancy restaurant like The Ivy. Those women always order dessert and squirrel it away for later. They like to eat it in bed 'cause it's totally sexual for them," she said, snapping the lid off the container and taking a deep whiff.

"Oh my God!" she screamed. "It's dog poop!"

I jumped back. *"What?"*

"You heard me!" She held it out to me, gasping for breath.

I heard the happy click-clicking of Paquito's toenails on the kitchen tile. We'd said the magic words, apparently, and he'd come running.

"Sniff it yourself," she said.

"No way!" I shouted, motioning for her to put the lid back on. "You think it's Paquito's?"

She leaned down to him with the Tupperware. "This yours, buddy?" He wagged his tail and lunged as if to dig right in, but she jerked it away from him in the nick of time.

"You don't think . . . ?" she said with a look of utter horror.

"That she feeds him his own leavings? Come on, Ter, Lenore may murder her husbands in crotchless panties, but she's no *monster*."

"Well, what's it doing in the fridge?"

"Maybe he really has been sick and she needed a stool sample for the vet. They do that with dogs, you know. See any worms in there?"

She peered into its depths. "What do they look like?"

"You're asking me what *worms* look like?" I looked, but there didn't appear to be any critters in the doody.

"Besides," Terry said, "why wouldn't she have dropped it off at the vet's before she went in for surgery?"

"Excellent question."

I remembered Rini's original instructions and found a list of numbers next to the phone. There under NM Tea Room and The Spa was a listing for *Vet—Dr. English*. I picked up the phone and punched in the number.

A young woman answered cheerily. "Good afternoon, Beverly Animal Clinic."

"Hello, I'm dog-sitting for Lenore Richling and—"

"What's the name again?" The clacking of computer keys.

"Lenore Richling."

"Is that the dog's name?"

"No, his name is Paquito."

"We file under the pet's name. Oh here it is, Paquito Richling."

Okay. "Uh, were we supposed to bring in a stool sample for him? Mrs. Richling mentioned something, but I can't remember exactly what it was. Were you expecting anything?"

More clacking. "Let me pull his file." She was gone for a few moments then came back on the line. "The only thing I have scheduled is his shots in April, and of course his weekly grooming and nail clipping. Oh, I see he hasn't been in for a while. Want to make an appointment?"

What's to groom? I thought, but I didn't want to look like a bad parent. "I guess we could do that."

"How's Tuesday at four o'clock?"

"Okay, sure." She gave me the address and I committed it to memory, then gave her our home number for the reminder call.

"Fine, I'll put you down. Have a nice day," she said, clicking off.

I hung up the phone and looked at Terry. "It wasn't for them. But Paquito has to go in for a grooming."

"Go *in* for a grooming? We could groom him with a drop of Ivory liquid and a toothbrush."

I shrugged. "Maybe we'd better get it done by professionals. Maybe he needs to be fumigated for fleas or something."

"Okay," she said, shaking her head, and she snapped the top back on the Tupperware. She opened the refrigerator door and put the container inside.

"You're putting it back?" I said.

She gave me a look. "And you'd like me to do what with it?"

"Flush it. *Something.*"

"Uh-uh. It's a crime scene. Better not tamper with the Tupperware."

"I won't be able to eat, knowing there's a container full of dog poop in the fridge!"

"It's not our refrigerator."

"*Anyone's* refrigerator!"

"Buck up, sis," she said, stuffing Paquito into the Hello Kitty backpack. "This is a tough business."

We passed a small park a few blocks from Lenore's house, a beautifully landscaped enclave planted with red, white, and purple petunias, and shaded by lavender-flowering jacaranda trees. There was a gleaming jungle gym and a brightly colored swing set in the middle of the spotless playground.

In other parts of LA, the drug dealers and derelicts would have made short work of this little oasis. There'd be filthy encampments spread over the grass, walls covered with graffiti, and slavering creeps waiting in the bathroom for any kids naïve enough to think that parks were actually for playing in. But here it was only a weak echo of the surrounding neighborhood, where everyone had gardens that put Versailles to shame, and where kids were raised with Olympic-sized swimming pools, in-home theaters that rivaled the local multiplex, and video game players as technologically advanced as the average missile guidance system. Beverly Hills youngsters wouldn't even know what to do with a regular swing set, I thought cynically.

Something caught my eye as we rode by: a group of dark-haired young women clustered on the benches, each with a perambulator containing a little blond baby with milky fat cheeks. The women were laughing and pushing the strollers, gabbing away, having a grand old time.

"Hold on!" I shouted to Terry.

She slammed on the brakes, pulling up to the curb.

"What?"

"Did you see those girls back there?"

"What girls?"

"Nannies. A half-dozen of them."

"So?"

"So Rini had a baby with her when we saw her."

"And?"

"Why would she have a baby with her? Obviously, it wasn't hers."

"Her nephew, the guy said."

"Did she strike you as the devoted auntie type?"

"No, but—"

"Let's head back to the park," I said. "Maybe one of those girls will admit to knowing her."

Terry nodded and made a U-turn and parked next to the greenway, a hundred yards from the nannies. They watched the Harley's approach cautiously; we were unwelcome invaders of their private little paradise. I got off the bike and strolled up to them casually, trying to look like a weary traveler out to stretch her legs.

"Hi," I called out.

A sweet-looking girl in a yellow cotton blouse gave me a smile, and I zeroed in on her. "How's it going?"

"Fine."

The other women avoided looking at us. They got busy wiping pabulum off their babies' faces or bouncing them in their carriages.

"I'm looking for Rini," I said. "Do you know her?"

"Rini Vallegos?"

Bingo. I didn't dare look at Terry, who'd come up beside me.

"Yeah," I said. "Seen her around lately?"

"She was here before with the baby, but she left. She's

quitting her job, going back to Boyle Heights." Boyle Heights was an east-side neighborhood of quaint, 1930s-style houses that had been primarily Jewish ages ago, but now was home to a big, lively Latino population.

I nodded at the girl sympathetically. "Working here can't be easy."

The women all looked up now, rolling their eyes in agreement.

"You don't even know," the sweet-looking one said.

I handed her my card. "If you see Rini, will you tell her we're looking for her?"

"Sure." The girl looked at my card. "What's this mean? Double Indemnity?"

"It means we're private investigators," Terry said.

Four of the women sprang up and made off with their prams like contestants jumping the gun at a supermarket sweepstakes, scattering in all directions.

"Hey, we're not cops or anything," I shouted after them.

The sweet one got up, dropped my card on the grass, and rolled the wheel of her buggy right over it, then raced down the sidewalk, her raven hair streaming in the breeze.

I looked at Terry. "Boy, you sure know how to break up a party."

She shrugged. "Illegals, easy to spook. But hey, at least you got Rini's last name—and it's the same as Mario's!"

"So . . . Rini is related to Mario—a sister, maybe. And she comes here with a baby, pretending to be a nanny like the rest of them. Why?"

"For the company?"

"Yeah, but she's not like them. She's much more 'street.' I doubt she'd be that anxious for their company, unless they could do something for her."

"What could they do for her?"

I let my eyes wander. On both sides of the palm-lined streets were rambling mansions filled with dozens of rooms.

I did a quick calculation of the help that would be needed in each house to keep it running. Four to five servants minimum, I estimated, to maintain the house, chlorinate the pool, cook the meals, trim the lawn, cart the kids to soccer practice . . . Someone in every corner of the household, tending to all the details of daily life, seeing all, hearing all . . .

Then it came to me.

"What do you think these girls talk about while they're here?" I asked, smiling.

Terry followed my gaze around the neighborhood, probably the richest this side of Brunei. "What does anybody talk about? Their work."

"More specifically, their rich employers. Who knows more about what goes on in a house than the hired help? They hear every conversation, every phone call, they know who comes and who goes. They're literally in charge of the dirty laundry—"

"Right!" she said, as understanding dawned.

"And maybe while they're taking the air with the babies, Rini talks to the girls from the other households and finds out that *la señora* is doing the pool man, that *el señor* is hiding money from his partners, that the valuables they reported stolen to the insurance company are hidden in the attic—"

"Information like that could be worth a lot."

"Yes, it could."

Terry blew out a breath. "So Lenore's been blackmailing her own neighbors? The crafty little bitch! *That's* how she's maintained her lifestyle!"

"It might explain her little gang of three. Rini gets the scoop, Lenore does the dealing, and Mario the enforcing."

"And maybe the break-in was one of her victims trying to retrieve something she had on them. That's why she wants them to know she doesn't have it, because they're coming after it now."

We were just about to slap each other five when Terry

frowned, thinking of a complication. "But if she's blackmailing people, why doesn't she have any money? Why would she be so desperate for the ten thousand?"

"Maybe she's on the verge of a big payout, holding on by her fingernails till it comes."

"*A big payout*, huh? You know, that makes total sense!"

"It's just a theory."

"But it's brilliant, baby!"

"Elementary, my dear."

six

That evening when it was time to go downtown, we made the difficult decision to leave Paquito at home. We didn't want the attention he was bound to draw at Trotsky's, so we filled a bowl with kibble and left a pile of newspapers in the kitchen for bathroom breaks. But when we tried to leave, he lunged on his little toothpick legs trying to get outside, whimpering so much it almost shattered our hearts.

"Stay," I begged him. "Honey baby, stay!"

Whimper, whimper. Which translated to *Take Paquito on moving machine! Paquito stick nose in air, have fun with new mommies!* Or words to that effect. And you can believe me when I say we were very affected.

How on earth were we going to part with this little three-pound love muscle? We managed to close the front door, obliterating the sight of his quivering nose.

Terry blew out a sigh. "That wasn't fun."

"It was torture," I agreed.

The bouncer at Trotsky's looked like he'd just gotten off the boat from Siberia. Six-foot-five, face a foot-and-a-half wide, mean little eyes that said he preferred work as a Mongol horseman but this was the only gig he could get in LA. He fixed us with a freezing stare, until Terry batted her eyelashes and popped out with, *"Zdratsvuitye. Kak vui pahjhivaetye?"*

He grinned and answered her in Russian, then hotfooted it to open the door for us.

"I hope you didn't just offer him a blow job," I whispered.

She gave me an affronted look. "I said, 'Hi, how are you?' "

"Pardon me. I wasn't aware you knew any non-obscene foreign words. Where'd you learn Russian?"

"You don't want to know," she said, as the hostess approached us with menus.

"Two, please," I said to her. "Away from the band if possible."

A four-piece ensemble was playing folk songs that sounded like dirges, but nobody seemed at all depressed. It was a big crowd, happy and red-faced, a mix of Russian nationals drunk on vodka and college students intoxicated by Dostoyevsky. I was looking forward to a Stoli martini myself.

We were seated in a booth in the back directly below a large mirror tilted at a fifteen-degree angle. Terry faced the crowd and I faced the mirror.

"Are we gonna ask around?" I said.

"We should order something first. It's harder to throw out real patrons for being nosy."

The waitress appeared, a woman in her forties wearing a

red skirt, black T-shirt, and lace-up boots, her hair covered by a flowered babushka. Terry ordered borscht and straight vodka for both of us.

"I wanted a martini," I complained, as the waitress left.

"You can't drink a martini here, Ker. That's for capitalist running dogs."

We spent the next couple of minutes scanning the room, looking for friendly faces we could approach with our query. I made eye contact with a guy with a Lenin beard and a peaked worker's cap, and was just about to go over and speak to him, when the waitress reappeared.

She deposited bowls of beet soup with dollops of sour cream in front of us, followed by two large shot glasses of cold, clear vodka. *Yum.* I could already feel it biting my tongue, searing my throat, and obliterating the microbes in my stomach lining. Sort of a health tonic, really.

"Excuse me," I said to the waitress. "I have a question—"

Terry cut me off with a raised hand, shaking her head.

"Yes?" the waitress said.

Terry lifted her glass. "Could you send two of these to that table over there?" she said.

The waitress looked around. "Which one?"

"The one with the two women—one black and one white."

"Sure," the waitress said, walking away.

I looked in the mirror over Terry's head and who did I see two booths away? Janice, deep in conversation with a young woman with lush brown hair in a French twist. The woman wore an embroidered peasant blouse with a scoop neck and large silver earrings.

"It's Janice!" I said. "Is that Tatiana with her?"

"We'll know soon enough."

The waitress put two vodkas down in front of Janice and the mystery woman, then pointed in our direction. Janice's mouth dropped open, and her friend spun all the way around in her booth to see what was going on.

The woman had to be Tatiana. And no wonder she'd been used as a sales tool. She could stun a man senseless at fifty paces. Any woman would gladly pay a million bucks to look like her.

That Hattrick was a genius. Or *had* been.

Terry got up and walked over to their booth. She spoke to them and shook their hands, and even at a distance I could see a sort of worshipful look on Terry's face as she gazed into Tatiana's eyes.

She pointed over at me. Janice gave me an ambivalent little wave, then the two of them picked up their drinks and followed Terry to our table. They sat on the opposite side of the booth, and Terry slipped in next to me.

"Hi, Terry," Janice said.

"Kerry," I corrected her. "Hi, Janice."

"I am Tatiana," the other woman said with a thick Russian accent.

Her flawlessness was so intimidating that I actually found it hard to look her in the eye. She had a broad face with perfectly honed cheekbones, almond-shaped dark brown eyes, a little rosebud mouth, and eyebrows that arched theatrically but gracefully over her wide-set eyes. I'd never thought of foreheads as being beautiful, but hers was so elegantly proportioned, such a perfect complement to the pointed chin, that it might actually have been the best feature among many. It wasn't exactly a kind face, but she didn't strike me as a cold-blooded killer either. I wondered if she was aware of what had befallen Mario in her own apartment.

"I told Janice and Tatiana about Lenore's accident," Terry said.

Clever, I thought, using the gossip about Lenore's mishap

as an opening. Everyone secretly enjoys talking about the misfortune of others, whether they admit it or not.

"You hadn't heard?" I said, and they shook their heads.

"I can't believe it. Did the dog really eat her *ear?*" Tatiana said, sounding so much like Natasha Badenov I almost laughed. *Deed the dog eet herrr eerrr?*

"No, not really," Terry said. "But they weren't able to save it."

"Terrible," Tatiana said.

"They didn't notify Dr. Hattrick?" I asked Janice.

Janice looked over at Tatiana. "The doctor's on an extended leave," she said.

I was going to ask if the leave involved a suspension of his license, but Terry jumped in first. "So is that a normal . . . I don't know . . . hazard of a face-lift?" she said. "An ear coming off?"

"Let me put it this way," Janice said. "I never heard of it happening. But I'm not a medical doctor or a nurse. I guess anything's possible."

"Have you ever actually watched a face-lift operation?" Terry asked.

Janice nodded. "Put me off plastic surgery for life, I can tell you that. They won't get *me* under a knife." She leaned in, taking on a ghoulish tone. "You see the person's face, and they're unconscious, almost lifeless. Which is damn creepy, their mouth hanging open and their personality just . . . *gone.* It's like looking at dead lumps of flesh."

I quickly slurped a spoonful of soup before I heard the rest of what she was going to say, afraid that afterward I would lose my appetite forever. First dog-poop leftovers, now lumps of flesh on the operating table.

"First they draw lines all over the face, then they start cutting—" Terry and I crossed our legs simultaneously, "slicing off big hunks of skin around the forehead and the side of the face. Then they dig underneath the skin—" she made thrusting motions with a knife, "separating skin from muscle. Then they grab hold of the face and yank it up like it was droopy drawers, and the whole saggy thing goes tight, but it's still dead.

"Then the doctor pulls out this huge needle and just starts whipping it around the bloody edges with strokes as big as you please. I'm trained as a seamstress, and I thought maybe they'd take their time with it, making careful little stitches like I did when embroidering handkerchiefs, but no siree. You ever see a fisherman repairing his net?"

We nodded and gulped.

"That's just what it looks like. Jabbing that needle, pulling it through the dead flesh, yanking it tight, over and over again. With those big, sweeping strokes. Then they go for the eye area . . ."

I wasn't sure if it was the vodka or the face-lift talk, but the room was swimming in front of me. I put a hand on the table to steady myself.

"Wait a sec," Terry said. "What about the cutting part on the side of the face? Couldn't the knife slip at that point, slicing under the ear?"

"Yeah, I guess so," Janice said.

"But there'd be blood, wouldn't there? Wouldn't somebody notice the ear had been . . . severed?"

"Baby, there's blood all over, anyway. They just mop it up every now and then and keep right on slicing."

"What Terry's trying to get at," I said, "and I realize this may be touchy because he's your boss, but do you think that Hattrick was capable of doing something like that on purpose?"

"No," Janice said. "The man's simply incompetent."

"He should not be practice medicine," Tatiana added.

"Well, he certainly did a good job on you," I said, feeling more than a touch of envy.

Janice let out an explosive laugh, putting a hand over her mouth to stifle the giggles.

Strange, I thought.

"Are you going to testify in his lawsuits, Tatiana?" Terry said, obviously thinking of the summons we'd intercepted.

Tatiana took her time answering. "I cannot testify," she said finally.

"Why not?" Terry asked. "If he's that incompetent, you'd be doing the world a favor."

"She's afraid of being convicted," Janice told her.

"Of what? You didn't do the operations."

Janice rolled her eyes. "Of *fraud*."

Terry and I looked at each other, then back at the two women across the booth. Something wasn't making it past our skull bones to lodge in the gray matter.

Janice made a noise of disgust at our naïveté. "Oh, you don't think you get looks like that from surgery, do you? Get real, honey!"

It took us a full five seconds to comprehend what she was saying, maybe because we couldn't have imagined any-one being born as beautiful as Tatiana. But of course she had been. Her perfect face had not been manufactured on the op-erating table.

"Ohhhhh," I said to Tatiana. "So Dr. Hattrick *didn't* do any surgery on you, after all."

Tatiana leaned her dainty chin on her palm and exhaled. "I was working in video store in his neighborhood. He comes to me and says he will pay me to meet with—" she looked at Janice, "what is word?"

"Prospective?" Janice said.

"Yes, prospective patients," she continued, shamefaced. "He says they will look like me. He will give them my cheek-bones, my eyes, my nose, my complexion . . . I am not proud, but that is what he did."

"And they bought it wholesale?" Terry said, astonished. "They didn't even ask to see a before picture or something?"

Janice smirked. "He had a before picture. On his computer. He distorted her face, then told them he fixed her with surgery."

Well, this was definitely fraud. No getting around it. But I found it hard to believe that Tatiana would bear the brunt of a prosecution. She was just an immigrant getting the best work she could. I said as much to her, but she wasn't convinced.

"I am not citizen. I have only green card. If I do not have job, I can be deported." She looked down at her hands, and I noticed she was wearing a gold signet ring with a scrolled *P* on the third finger of her left hand. A man's ring.

"I wanted to be actress. Big star," she said, pronouncing it *Beeg starrr*. "But they say I have too much accent."

Oh dear. Another Hollywood casualty. Sometimes I wished that on the signs leading into the city, they'd post the odds of actually making it in the movies.

Welcome to Los Angeles! Population: 6,000,000. Your chances of succeeding as an actress: 10,000,000,000,000 to 1! Registration for dental hygiene school begins in August!

Still, dreams are dreams. And she'd been right to think she had something to offer, physically at least.

"Did you ever think of working as a model?" I said to her.

She nodded. "But I needed green card. Dr. Hattrick got it for me. INS will not like that I got job to defraud."

"He told the INS that Tatiana was a highly qualified medial technician," Janice said.

Ah, more lies, and to the government. That wasn't good. That tended to land your butt—no matter how attractive— on an outbound boat to Greenland.

"Have you had any contact with Hattrick since you left the job?" Terry asked Tatiana.

"No, I hate that bastard!" Tatiana covered her eyes and Janice put a comforting hand on her shoulder. "He's ruin my life!"

I gave her a minute to get a hold of herself, then turned to Janice. "How about you?" I said. "Are you going to testify?"

She sighed. "My lawyer tells me that if I don't I can be named as a codefendant in these cases, since I had knowledge of . . . malfeasance."

"You were in on the meetings with Tatiana?"

"No, but I knew what was going on. That's not why they want me, though."

"Why do they want you? That is, if you can tell us."

"Oh, why not? I'm screwed either way. I'll either be in prison or on the line for millions in damages I could never pay off if I lived to be a thousand."

We waited for her to continue.

"I stood in for his nurse during surgeries," Janice said.

I squinted at her. "But you just said you weren't a nurse—"

She nodded, eyes open wide. *"Uh-huh."*

"You're not a nurse and you assisted in operations?" Terry said. "Oh. That could be a problem, huh?"

Or it could be a violation of ethical conduct on a par with amputating the wrong foot.

Janice nodded in glum agreement with Terry's statement.

"But what . . . what happened to the real nurse?" I said. "Surely a doctor in his position could have hired the best."

"She was disgusted with him and one day she just didn't show," Janice said. "Should have had more than one attending nurse in the first place, but I don't think he could afford it."

"Amazing," Terry said.

"Let's have another drink," I said. "Waitress!"

I ordered another round of vodkas, wondering how to

subtly work Lenore's message into the conversation. The hell with it, I decided—just come out with it.

"When we saw Mrs. Richling in the hospital she asked us to get in touch with you, Tatiana."

She pinched her perfect brows together. "Why would she want me? I hardly know this poor woman."

But you knew her husband intimately, I thought. "She said to tell you she doesn't have *it*," I said.

Terry and I watched Tatiana closely, looking for a flicker of recognition. But her face was blank as copier paper.

"Doesn't have *what*?"

Terry shrugged. "We don't know. She wouldn't tell us."

Janice laughed. "Well, that's fucked up."

"Yeah, I guess it is. But we promised to pass on the message," I said. "She wanted you to tell *him* that she doesn't have it."

"Who?" Tatiana said.

"We don't know."

Tatiana began a slow burn. "I cannot tell *who* I don't know she does not have *what* I don't know!"

I held her eyes in a stare-off, neither of us so much as blinking for a full fifteen seconds. "Well, someone evidently thought she had something they wanted," I said finally. "Because Mrs. Richling's house was broken into today."

Tatiana and Janice both sat back in the booth, giving each other a nervous glance.

Terry turned a strand of hair around her finger and pressed into dangerous territory with her next remark. "Lenore thought you might have been involved with her husband, Tatiana. She was even a little jealous of you."

Janice looked away, focusing her attention on the band.

"Ridiculous!" Tatiana snapped.

"So you're not seeing Mario?"

"Of courrrrse not. He is nothing to me. Oh, he came

to office and gave me big doggie eyes, but I was not interested."

I knew her indignation was false—after all, we'd heard Mario calling her name upon entering her apartment. We were indeed in the presence of a major acting talent, I decided—Meryl Streep of the Caucasus.

"So if he was nothing to you," Terry said lightly, "I guess you wouldn't have blown him away. I guess it was sheer coincidence that he was shot in your apartment."

Tatiana's eyes turned to glass and she leaned into Terry. "I did not do it."

Janice frowned and put a restraining hand on Tatiana's arm. Tatiana shrugged it off angrily.

"Who did?" Terry said, refusing to let up. "Was it the guy you're supposed to give Lenore's message to?"

Janice rose quickly from the booth, dragging Tatiana by the hand. "Thanks for the drinks," Janice said. "And for the message. I'm sure Tatiana appreciates it."

Tatiana slid out of the booth after Janice, her rosy mouth turned down. "Yes, thank you so verrry much," she said.

Terry shoved me out of the booth, then jumped out herself. She got directly in Tatiana's face.

"You *know* who killed Mario," she said. "And you know why."

Tatiana gave her a tight smile. "You are private investigator? You figure it out."

She and Janice turned to leave the restaurant. "The police will want to talk to you, Tatiana," Terry called out, trailing after her.

I caught sight of someone in my peripheral vision—the guy with the Lenin beard, striding across the room in Terry's direction, ready to restrain her or beat the shit out of her, I didn't know which.

I threw two twenties down on the table and rushed over to

the exit. The bouncer was blocking the door, looking at my sister with murderous intent, no longer taken in by her charms.

Janice and Tatiana were gone.

Comrade Lenin came up behind me. I could feel his breath on my neck, but I didn't dare turn around.

We were trapped between him and the bouncer. I let my eyes travel around the room. The lively chatter had stopped. All the patrons were watching the unfolding situation wordlessly—a conspiracy of silence. I knew that none of them would come to our aid if things got rough.

"Terry," I said, quietly. "I think it's time to go."

She looked back at me and shrugged casually. "Sure," she said. "I was going to suggest that myself."

I felt Lenin back away from me, then the bouncer turned sideways to permit us access to the door, keeping a wary eye on us the whole time.

Terry breezed out the door, with me fast on her heels. To my surprise, we got to the bike unimpeded.

"Well, we tried," I said to Terry, breathing a sigh of relief.

"At least we delivered Lenore's message," she said. "That's all we had to do."

Right. We'd delivered the cryptic message to the Russian woman as promised, and we could now wash our hands of Lenore Richling's dirty dealings with the lava soap of righteousness.

Or so we thought.

The phone was ringing when we walked in the door at home.

"Probably Aunt Reba," I said, picking up the receiver. "Hello?"

It was Reba, and she was more than usually agitated. "Terry? Kerry? You'll never *believe*—"

Terry picked up the extension. "It's both of us. What's going on?"

Reba sucked in air. "Lenore is *dead*."

"Dead?"

Terry and I fell back onto the couch at the same time.

"When did she die?" Terry finally asked.

"This afternoon. Can you fathom that—right in the best hospital in the world!"

"What was the cause of death?"

"They think it was an aneurysm but they won't know for sure until after the autopsy."

"An aneurysm?" I swallowed hard. "Is that something that can be caused by a shock? Like a dog in the face when you're not expecting it?"

"What?" Reba said.

"Rhetorical question," Terry said, waving at me to shut up. "How did you find out?"

"The hospital called me. Evidently she'd put me on her forms as a local contact. You know, girls, there's something very *wrong* about all this."

She had *that* right.

"There's other news to report, too," Terry said. "We went to Lenore's house earlier today, and it had been tossed."

"Tossed?"

"Broken into. Everything was wrecked. Someone was looking for something and tore up the house in the process."

"Oh my, my, my," Reba said. "Was anything stolen?"

"Hard to say. But in any case, we think they were after something other than her valuables."

"*Oh* my, *oh* my," Reba said again. One of these days we'd have to teach her some new expressions of shock and dismay—like *Getthefuggouttahere!*

"You didn't happen to notice if there was a black Judith Leiber bag in the house when you were there, did you, dears?" she inquired.

Terry rolled her eyes at me. Here her best friend was dead, and all Reba could think about was her damn handbag.

"No, but I wouldn't necessarily know it if I saw it," I said. "I'm a Kate Spade girl, myself. Guess you'll have to wrangle with her estate to get it back."

"Oh don't be stupid," Reba spat out. "I don't care about the bag, it's last season anyway. But I can't help thinking there was more to that situation in Hattrick's garage than a mere catfight over a purse. I know I got a little out of control and so did she, but that's what bothers me. We're such . . . we *were* such dear friends. Much too close to let an *accessory* get in the way of our friendship."

I nodded at Terry. "So you think she had something in the bag that she didn't want you to see?"

"That's exactly what I'm thinking."

"We had wondered about that ourselves," Terry said.

We all three contemplated this development in silence. Lenore had gone to the Great Beyond with her mystery intact. Had she been a blackmailer involved in a criminal conspiracy with Mario and possibly Rini? Had her actions resulted in Mario's death as well as her own?

"Girls, here's what I'd like to do," Reba declared suddenly.

"What?" I asked.

"I'd like to get involved with this case."

"What case?" Terry said with her typical tact. "Our client is dead. There is no case anymore."

I flinched. Terry could be a little more sensitive to Reba's feelings, but she was right. Besides, if Lenore's death was somehow a wrongful one, that made it a police matter.

"The only thing left for us to do," I said, "is to get in touch with the executor of Lenore's estate. We have to find out who to turn the dog over to and who we should give the eight thous—"

The phone was knocked out of my hand. It sailed across the room before clattering to the floor. Reba's voice barked through the speaker. "Hello? Hello . . . !"

"Sorry," Terry said. "Kerry dropped the phone, she's such a klutz."

She shook her head at my woeful lack of coordination, as if completely convinced of her own lie. She knew I'd been seconds away from telling Reba about Lenore's money and she'd made sure I couldn't.

"Now what were we saying?" she said to Reba, inspecting her nails casually.

I got up from the couch to retrieve the phone. Terry frowned and waved me off. I shot her the finger. I shot her both fingers, then I put the pieces of the receiver back together, lifting it to my ear.

"I'll give you whatever Lenore was paying you," Reba was saying.

Reba wanted to finance us?

"Well, she was supposed to pay us four hundred dollars a day," Terry said, "but obviously she didn't get the chance."

I couldn't believe it. Terry wanted to keep the money *and* hit Reba up for inflated fees. What a crook!

Of course, we did have those pesky bills.

"I'm back," I said into the phone, keeping it cool. "Want to fill me in, somebody?"

Reba's voice was full of conviction. "I want to know what's been going on. I want to know why somebody's tossing around my friend's house and possibly knocking her over."

Oh boy, she was really getting into this. Throwing out what she imagined to be detective slang. Crimespeak. "Reba, have you been watching cable TV by any chance?"

"Just a little HBO," she said defensively. "And MTV."

Terry made a face of astonishment. "Well, you don't knock over a *someone*," she corrected her, trying not to laugh. "You knock over a some*thing*. Like a jewelry store."

"I'll learn, I'll learn," Reba said eagerly.

What did she mean by that?

"Look, Reba, I don't know if this is such a good idea," I said.

Terry's arms started flailing at me again.

"I won't hear any arguments," Reba said. "For one thing, I know Lenore's family lawyer. It's Hugh Binion, of Hartford, Huntington, and Binion, on Rodeo Drive. I'll call him first thing in the morning to find out who's executor of the estate. I'm onto it, girls!"

And with that she hung up.

Oh boy. Reba was *onto* it. I'd sleep much better knowing that.

seven

$\mathcal{T}$he next morning Reba called while we were still in our pajamas to say she had spoken to the hospital administrator. He told her that Lenore's postmortem would be conducted that afternoon. If there was anything unusual about her death we'd find out about it then.

"I spoke to Hugh Binion regarding Lenore's will, and what do you know? He's executor of her estate, and *I'm* her beneficiary," she reported, bristling with excitement.

"What about Mario?" I said. "He was still her husband. Doesn't he get something under community property?"

"Well, Hugh says not."

Terry made a face. "What do you mean, *Hugh says not?* Mario's not entitled to anything?"

"Not her *husband*. You won't believe this, girls, but it turns out they weren't married at all! The whole wedding business was apparently a charade. There were no nuptials in Las Vegas or anywhere else!"

Terry and I shook our heads at each other. Our woman of mystery just kept getting more mysterious.

"Lenore told you they'd eloped to Vegas?" Terry said.

"Yes and it turns out that was a blatant lie."

"What's *that* about?" I said. "Lenore didn't want people to think she was living in sin with a man a third her age?"

Terry laughed. "Well, there's no sinning going on at all anymore."

"Look," Reba said, annoyed, "just get your tushies over here and we'll talk about it over breakfast. Then I want you to go to Binion's office with me. I've got an appointment with him to discuss the will."

We had to say yes. After all, she *was* our new boss.

"He's on Rodeo Drive, dears, so do wear something decent. I got a whole new outfit for the occasion."

The occasion? Reba didn't already have an outfit suitable for going to a lawyer's office? She had enough clothes to stock a dozen department stores and enough shoes to make Imelda Marcos look like a slacker. Then again, you get a new outfit anytime you want when you're that loaded.

By "decent" I hoped she didn't mean a darling little suit off the showroom floor at Neiman Marcus marked down to $1,500. These days, our definition of decent was boot-cut jeans without holes in the crotch or the knees. We dug around and found a clean pair each, threw on leather jackets over our baby tees, and figured we were well enough attired for government work.

We arrived at Reba's at eleven o'clock. The large black door swung open before we'd even touched the brass lion that served as a knocker.

Grizzie stood in the open doorway looking panicked. "Ya got to *do* somethin', girls. She's lost 'er mind. She's like some kind of Catwoman creature. Ya got to stop her or I won't be able to show m' face at Bristol Farms, ever again!" Bristol Farms being the market where the elite went to buy their gourmet eats.

"I'll be right there, dears," Reba called from the living room. "Wait till you see my new look!"

Grizzie stomped past us into the kitchen with a full-body shudder, shaking her head and muttering Popeye-isms. We waited in the foyer next to the sweeping staircase, and in another few moments Reba scurried in—looking like a seventy-year-old chemically peeled Emma Peel.

She was wearing skintight black stretch pants that were tucked into knee-high, black patent leather stiletto-heeled boots, and topped by a form-fitting black turtleneck sweater, with a thick black belt that cinched her insectile waist. Her hair was suddenly platinum, a chin-length blunt cut with bangs, and her lips and fingernails glistened in blue-black hues.

Oh dear God in heaven.

I hazarded a sideways look at Terry and saw her shoulders shaking, her hand over her mouth.

Hold it in, I beamed to her telepathically. *Keep it together* . . .

"How do I look?" Reba said, spinning around. "Ready to catch some evildoers?"

Oh sweet Jesus.

"It's just a little something I put together to start work as a detective," she said, looking at herself in the Rococo mirror in the foyer. "Do you like the wig?"

Oh good, it was a wig. It could be removed and burned. But how to tell Reba tactfully that she looked ridiculous? Terry mumbled something about having to use the bathroom, and then scurried off to the powder room before her laughter gave away her true opinion.

I had just made up my mind to hint that maybe Reba could

find something a *wee* bit more age-appropriate for catching evildoers, when I heard Robert's voice croaking on the stairs.

"Hello-o-o! Do I hear the dulcet tones of the Bobbsey Twins . . . ?" he said. Then he saw Reba and his eyes bugged out.

"Mother!" he cried, startled. "What in the name of—?" But before he could finish, he lost his footing and slipped off the top step, landing on his rear end, and—to our horror—sliding down the remaining twenty stairs at an alarming pace, his body picking up speed like an olympic luge contestant, screaming his brains out. He arrived on the floor's marble surface without slowing down and zoomed across the entire foyer, slamming into a free-standing pedestal holding, you guessed it, a priceless Ming vase.

I got to the vase before it crashed on the marble. But I neglected to catch the pedestal before it toppled over and crashed onto Robert's head, knocking him unconscious. He lay there motionless, mouth agape, bare belly hanging over his pajama bottoms.

"Well!" Reba exclaimed. "That reaction was a bit extreme, don't you think?"

I reached down and felt Robert's pulse. Thin, but steady.

I hollered for Terry and called 911, while Reba huffed off to change her outfit, ripping the wig from her head as she mounted the stairs. Underneath it, her hennaed hair was slicked to her head and surrounded with a thick elastic band. The resemblance to Gloria Swanson in *Sunset Boulevard* was more than just a passing one, I thought, and it was definitely a better look for her.

"No sense ripping around town *detecting* at my age," Reba said. "Besides, I have a child to think of."

Terry came out of the bathroom, wiping tears from her eyes and blowing her nose.

"What's up with Robert?" she said. "Is he dead?"

Robert was not dead, just slightly concussed. He refused to go to the hospital, probably because his room wouldn't have a wet bar. The EMTs were relatively sure that he was okay to stay at home, although he failed an examination in which they asked him to name the current U.S. president and to list the states that border California.

He told them that anyone could be expected to repress the name of our current president, given who it was, and that the "provinces" bordering California held no particular attraction for him—hence his decision not to clutter his mind with their names. The paramedics left convinced that his brain was functioning well enough, within obvious limits.

Reba put him to bed with a toddy, and we were seated at her dining room table for coffee and muffins. She'd canceled the meeting with Binion during the hubbub, telling his secretary she'd call to reschedule later.

She was now attired in a more subdued version of her previous outfit. A leather bolo jacket over a silk blouse, and jodhpurs tucked into knee-high riding boots. It was an elegant ensemble, if a complete sham. Reba had never ridden a horse in her life.

"So Lenore and Mario weren't married at all," Terry said to Reba.

"Apparently not," she said, dabbing marmalade on her muffin. "I suppose she had her reasons for associating with him, but undying love was not among them."

Surprise, surprise.

"As I said, Hugh Binion is the executor of Lenore's will," Reba continued. "I was pleased to hear that she left the contents of her house to me, then I remembered you said the house had been robbed. I wonder if everything of value has been ruined."

"There are some crotchless panties that are still in working order," Terry said.

Reba made a little moue of distaste.

"She had a very valuable painting on the wall," I offered.

Her penciled eyebrows twitched greedily. "Oh?"

"A Francis Bacon."

"No, you must be mistaken, dear. Lenore had no paintings by masters of any era."

"I'd bet you money," I said.

She allowed herself a little excitement. "What did it look like? What did it depict?"

"It's a portrait of a man with a kind of ghostly grimace, sitting in a chair. There's a bare lightbulb hanging from the ceiling and the man has a large wristwatch on his arm."

"Hmmm. I wonder if it was part of a series. My friend Suzie Magnuson also has a Bacon—a real Bacon—which is also a portrait of a man in rather the same surroundings."

Was this the same Mrs. Magnuson we'd encountered at the hotel?

I looked at Terry and saw that she also remembered the little old lady who'd nicked her in the shin getting off the elevator. The one with the bruised face who got a parting gift basket from Alphonse.

"She didn't by any chance just have facial surgery?" Terry said. "I ask because we saw a lady leaving the Dauphine by the name of Magnuson."

"Why, I believe she *was* due for a touch-up, now that you mention it. Give me a sec, I'll get her on the phone. She can help us settle the issue of Lenore's Bacon."

"Or settle Lenore's hash," Terry whispered.

I rolled my eyes and we waited for Reba to complete the call, but no one answered.

"Tell you what," Reba said. "Suzie's just three blocks away. Why don't we see if the maid's home, then we can have a look at her Bacon. And when I get the keys to Lenore's house we can compare them."

"We have the keys to Lenore's," I said. "The maid gave them to us."

"Fabulous! Then there's no need to wait for Hugh Binion. We can let ourselves in, take an informal inventory, and check out that painting." Reba pushed up from her seat. "Let's rock it, girls!"

We were at Lenore's in less than ten minutes. I started to put the key in the lock, but Reba put a restraining hand over mine, shaking her head.

"What?" I said.

"Well, we can't just *barge in.*"

Terry shrugged. "Sure we can. You're her beneficiary, and we were employed by her as investigators."

"I don't mean that," Reba said, her eyes tearing up.

"Oh, I'm sorry," I said gently. "I should have realized this would be emotional for you."

Reba nodded, then lowered her head and sniffed, dabbing at her nose with a linen handkerchief.

Terry looked at me and raised her shoulders, palms out— *What do we do?* I shrugged, but then Terry got an inspiration. She cleared her throat, stood up straight, and began to speak in a reverential voice, like a preacher delivering a eulogy.

"We stand here today on the front porch of Lenore Richling, who was taken from us all too soon . . ."

Oh no. I was afraid Reba would find this offensive, but she kept her head lowered and made a sign of the cross over her chest.

Okay, nobody here is Catholic, I thought. But I went along with it, crossing my chest. Terry crossed hers, too, without missing a beat.

"She was a good woman. A kind woman. A faithful friend . . ." Terry intoned. "A woman who, when you were in need, would give you the shirt off her back . . ."

Reba nodded again, sniffling.

"Or the handbag right off her arm. Be it a Prada, a Gucci, or even the humble Coach. These earthly labels had no meaning for a woman of Lenore's spiritual qualities . . ."

Reba frowned and I made a *cut it* gesture to Terry across my throat, followed by a *wrap it up* gesture, waving in a circular motion. She nodded, but then stopped—at a loss as to how to continue.

"We bless this woman's memory," I jumped in, "and commend her to . . . her Higher Power . . ."

Reba cast a dubious look at me. I don't think she was familiar with twelve-step speak.

"Who is, of course, our Father in heaven. I wouldn't be implying that she would have any gods before thee, O great and good . . . God in heaven . . ."

Oh shit, now I was stumbling over a definition of God. Terry cut in again.

"And so, in conclusion, we say to thee, Amen." A little abrupt, but what the hell. This wasn't the Crystal Cathedral and we weren't Robert Schuller.

Reba took a deep breath and squared her shoulders bravely. "Thank you, girls, that was just what I needed."

I unlocked the door and we stepped over the threshold.

The house was in the same condition we'd left it, looking like the aftermath of a typhoon. Furniture askew, cushions flung everywhere—her friend's house ruined, and Reba's whole inheritance dashed to splinters.

She gasped, shocked by the extent of the damage. She took it all in for a few moments, goggle-eyed, then finally she found her voice.

"Well, thanks for nothing, Len," she snorted.

Terry rolled her eyes.

"So where's that painting?" Reba said.

I pointed, then blinked.

"It was right over there!" I yelped, running to the opposite side of the living room, dodging fallen chairs and strewn cushions.

"Right here!" I slapped the wall. "I swear to God, it was right on this wall!"

But the painting was gone.

We went through the house, taking stock of the wreckage. Reba noted that the Oriental rugs were unharmed, estimating their worth in the tens of thousands.

"Well, that's something," she said. "I wonder about her jewelry. She kept it in a wall safe in the office."

"Oh, uh, we're pretty sure she hocked her jewelry," Terry said.

"Hocked her . . . oh dear." Reba fingered a diamond pendant hanging from her own neck.

"She might have more," I said, trying to be optimistic.

We went into the office and found the wall safe behind a picture. Reba didn't know the combination, so we couldn't take a look inside, but the outside seemed to be intact. No one had dynamited it or anything.

I glanced at the floor and saw something we'd missed the other day—an insurance file lying on the piles of paper. I picked it up and skimmed the homeowner's policy and the attached inventory. Surely it would list something as valuable as a Francis Bacon painting, I thought. But two careful readings of the inventory produced nothing.

"The Bacon's not listed on her homeowner's policy," I said.

"Maybe she'd acquired it recently, and hadn't had time to add it to the policy," Reba said.

"Nobody's *that* busy. Besides, she's got everything else listed, down to a gold-plated dog bowl."

Terry laughed. "A gold-plated dog bowl? Well, Reba, unless you want to melt it down and make a brooch out of it or something, I guess that little item will go to Lenore's relatives, along with the dog."

"Lenore doesn't have any relatives," Reba said. "Not any that she had anything to do with, at least. Obviously there was no one she was closer to than me, if she's left me everything in the house."

Terry clapped her hands. "That means we get to keep Paquito!"

We were so overjoyed at hearing this news—already imagining the fluffy bed we would buy for him, the miniature pink motorcycle jacket to match Terry's—that we didn't even think of the next logical question. But Reba did.

"Come to think of it, who'd she leave the house to?"

The doorbell rang and we all froze.

"Hell-o-o-o-o! Anybody ho-o-o-me? It's Sally Firth!"

Ding-dong, ding-dong, ding-dong. She must have been holding her finger down on the doorbell. Sally Firth was either at the wrong address or the world's most aggressive Avon Lady.

"It's Sally Firth, with Century 21!"

Century 21, the realtors?

I hurried to the front door, Reba and Terry in tow. I swung it open and was met with a dazzling smile spread across the face of a tall skinny woman who stood on the porch, dressed head to toe in sunflower yellow, looking like a giant, anorectic bumblebee. Her brown hair was cut helmet-style, the bangs obscuring her eyes and leaving only the wide smile and long nose poking out from underneath.

She thrust her hand out to Reba, whom she'd pegged as the lady of the house. "Sally Firth, Century 21. We spoke on the phone? And these are the Benisons." She pointed to a well-dressed couple behind her.

"Oh, uh—" Reba began.

"Nice to meet *you,* Mrs. Richling," Sally said to Reba, shoving her out of the way and barging into the foyer. "May we?"

She gestured for the Benisons to follow her in. When they saw the state of the house they did a series of comic double takes—eyes popping out to the whites, heads swiveling 360 degrees. Sally paused for a millisecond, then flashed them a blinding grin.

"As we discussed," she said to the Benisons, "the house is for sale *as is.*" She turned to Reba. "We'll just have a look around, shall we? You go right ahead with your packing. I know you're anxious to get to France."

France?

She led the Benisons through the living room, dodging the debris as she went, behaving rather convincingly as if it weren't there. She pointed out features like the fireplace, the ceiling beams, the doors leading to the pool in the backyard.

Reba and Terry looked at me, as if I should know what to do. I stood open-mouthed, watching the trio continue upstairs.

"And upstairs is the master bedroom," Sally said, consulting her clipboard. "It has its own fireplace and its own balcony . . ."

Oh no. Lenore's lingerie.

Somehow it seemed like the ultimate indignity for a roomful of strangers to see the dead woman's boudoir looking like ground zero in a sorority house panty raid.

"I'll just see if there's anything amiss in the bedroom," I said as I bounded up the stairs past the house hunters. I dashed into the room and ripped the crotchless panties off the bedside lamp, then whipped up all the undies off the floor just as Sally and the Benisons appeared in the doorway.

I looked up at them and smiled over the armload of lingerie.

"Really," Sally sniffed. She pulled the Benisons out into the hallway, her heels clunking on the hardwood.

"Some people are such slobs . . ." she said in a stage whisper.

I found myself getting pissed off. What was I doing? I threw the panties in a pile on the bed. There was no sense in letting this continue.

"And this is the guest bedroom," Sally said, as I reached out and tugged on her yellow jacket sleeve.

"Uh, Sally," I said. "There's something you should know."

"Yes, yes, what is it?"

I glanced at the Benisons, who were frowning at the state of the guest bedroom, shaking their heads.

"Could you come with me for a second?"

She sighed and followed me down the hallway, arms crossed under her breasts.

"Mrs. Richling *wasn't* a slob—" I started to say.

"Since when? This is the worst state I've ever shown a house in, I don't mind telling you. If it weren't for the address—"

"Sally, Mrs. Richling is dead."

She gasped. "What—heart attack? Did you call 911?" She ran for the stairs. "We haven't signed a contract yet! Is she still breathing . . . ?"

I grabbed the hem of her jacket and yanked her back from the balustrade.

"That's not Mrs. Richling downstairs," I said. "That's her friend, Mrs. Price-Slatherton. What I'm trying to tell you is that Mrs. Richling was robbed. They ransacked the house and she died on the same day. Yesterday."

"She was murdered in the house?" Her eyes widened under the bangs. "Well, I have to *disclose* that, I have an absolute professional obligation—"

"No, no. She died in the hospital. Someone robbed the house while she was there."

"Oh." Sally sucked in her cheeks thoughtfully. "Well what about the place in the south of France? Mrs. Richling obviously won't be occupying it. Who's got the contract on that?"

"*What* place in the south of France?"

"She said she was in a hurry to sell, on account of she wanted to live in her new villa. She was in a rush, said we'd take care of the contract when I came by."

"And she told you to come today?"

Sally nodded her bangs.

"When did you speak to her?"

The Benisons peered out into the hallway. "Maybe we'd better come back another time," Mr. Benison said.

"Be with you in a jiff!" Sally sang. "You've simply *got* to see the kitchen. It's got a Sub-Zero refrigerator!"

"DON'T look in the fridge," I said.

The Benisons ducked back into the guest bedroom.

"What is going on here?" Sally demanded.

"Please, just tell me when you spoke to Lenore Richling."

She shrugged. "I don't know, two or three days ago. She said she was recovering from an operation and would be home today. She said not to scream if she answered the front door wearing a mask. And she was moving to France later this week."

With what, the proceeds from the sale? But it sounded like she planned to skip the country before the house had even made it into escrow. Then I remembered . . .

The Big Payout.

I convinced Sally that she wasn't going to be able to make a sale today because we didn't know the disposition of the house in the will. I gave her my card and took hers, telling her we'd be in touch after we'd spoken to the executor of the estate.

She was fiercely disappointed, but I didn't think the Benisons were. They couldn't wait to get out of the house, having correctly sensed that something wasn't right with this picture.

The three of them hustled out the front door, Sally apologizing all over herself for the mix-up, offering to show them a darling Cape Cod four blocks away.

When they'd left, I turned to Reba and Terry. "The Realtor said that Lenore was moving to the south of France."

"With what?" Reba said.

Terry raised her eyebrows at me.

"Should we tell her?" I said.

Terry nodded, plastering a mock-serious look on her face. "Oh, definitely. She's part of the team, now."

I shot her a look—*What team? The A-Team?*

"Yes, do!" Reba said. "*Do* tell me!"

"This may come as a shock," I said, taking her arm. "Let's sit for a minute."

"Don't be ridiculous," she said, letting me drag her along. "Nothing you say can surprise me now."

I led the way into the breakfast room and we seated ourselves at a glass-topped table with a view of the pool. "We're not sure," I said, "but we think Lenore was involved in blackmail."

Reba's mouth flew open. "Blackmail?"

"Like I said, it's just a theory that we're working on that seems to make sense in light of . . . recent events."

"What recent events?"

"Lenore was desperate for money right before she died," Terry said. "She sent us after Mario to get it, claiming he stole her jewels and hocked them—"

"Why, that's what she told *me*."

"But we found proof that she hocked them herself. She

seems to have been hard up ever since her husband died. But she might have been expecting a big payday and needed the money to tide her over. We think she was working with Mario and the maid on the blackmail part."

"What maid?" Reba said. "Maggie or Martha or whatever her name was?"

"A girl named Rini," I said. "Possibly related to Mario."

"Well whatever happened to Maggie or Martha? She'd been with Lenore for twenty years! Dowdy thing, devoted as a dog. Missing a couple of incisors, so she never smiled. And you say she was replaced with this Rini?"

I nodded. "By the looks of it, Lenore was scraping bottom. Maybe she had to fire Maggie or Martha because she couldn't pay her. Anyway, we don't think Rini was a real maid. She performed other duties."

Reba blinked. "What other duties?"

"She took a baby to the park and pretended to be a nanny," Terry said, "hanging out with the other nannies in the neighborhood, trying to get dirt on their employers."

"That's the theory, anyway," I said. "And then Lenore and Mario put the screws to the people in question, threatening to air their dirty laundry if they didn't pay."

Reba's eyes got wide and she began to nod. "Yes, yes . . . You know, Lenore always *was* asking a lot of questions about people. Nosy questions. She seemed morbidly interested in the misfortunes of others—"

"We saw her at the hospital before she died," I told Reba, "and she pleaded with us to tell an assistant in Hattrick's office that she wasn't in possession of some item, although she wouldn't say what it was."

"But someone came here looking for this thing," Terry said. "And tore the place up."

"Do you think Lenore was blackmailing the doctor?" Reba asked excitedly.

Terry and I exchanged a look. We hadn't thought of this—it didn't fit with our squeeze-the-neighbors theory.

"I guess it's possible," Terry said. "The message was delivered to his former assistant."

"I don't know," I said. "He's on the ropes, professionally. About to lose his license. And it seems that everyone knows it. What could she hold over him?"

Reba's mental wheels began to grind. "Hmm . . . what's worse than losing your livelihood?" she asked with a sly, Jessica Fletcher expression.

I shrugged. "Prison?"

"And why do people go to prison?" Reba was really getting into it, her eyes shining with intrigue.

"Murder, extortion, fraud—" I glanced at Terry, "drugs."

"That's an interesting thought," Terry said. "Doctors have access to lots of drugs."

Okay, I figured we could take this speculative detour for a minute. All we had was conjecture anyway. "Reba, you went to Hattrick for a consultation. What was your impression of him?"

"Well, I knew immediately I didn't want the man to operate on me. I'd only gone as a favor to Lenore. This was before everyone knew about his troubles, of course."

"Was there anything in particular about him that you didn't like?"

"No, more of a general impression. Something I didn't trust. Maybe it was the dark glasses."

I frowned at her. "He wore dark glasses during your consultation?"

"He said he'd been to the optometrist and his pupils were still dilated. But I could see his eyes behind the lenses, and something about them frightened me."

"What?" Terry asked. "Was it the dilated pupils?"

"Hmm . . . I don't think so." Reba closed her eyes to focus

on her memory of Hattrick. "Oh, I know! His eyes didn't blink. Not once in the whole time I was in the room!"

She smiled, pleased with herself. "Isn't that remarkable? I'd never been able to put my finger on it before, but that's exactly what it was. He didn't blink his eyes. I'm more observant than I knew."

Well, it was strange, but not necessarily indicative of anything illegal.

"Did it seem like he was high?" Terry asked.

"No, only five-foot-eight or so," Reba said, "although he was sitting on a stool."

"What Terry means," I said patiently, "did it seem like he was on drugs? His pupils could have been dilated for reasons that had nothing to do with optometry."

"Oh. Well, how would I know?"

"Slurred speech, uncoordinated movements? Did he nod off, anything like that?"

"No-o-o-o," she said, thinking back. "But now that you mention it, he did wrap a rubber band around his arm and pumped his fist to get a vein, then injected himself with a hypodermic needle. He said it was Vitamin B, but I suppose it *could* have been drugs . . ."

Terry threw herself down on the table, burying her head in her arms.

Reba gave her a look. *"What did I say?"*

"Reba," I said, "the doctor is a junkie, an addict. One that's so far gone he'll even shoot himself up in front of a patient."

"Jesus," Terry muttered, sitting back up. "I guess that's blackmail material, all right."

"Lenore wanted us to give her message to Hattrick's assistant," I said. "Did you meet her when you were there? A gorgeous Russian he used as a model, named Tatiana?"

"Model? No. He used his computer to show me the results. Of course, I've always *thought* I bore a resemblance to Cindy Crawford."

"It's the beauty mark," Terry said.

"Mmm-hmm."

"This is all very interesting," I said, "but let's not forget why we're here in the first place. What about the painting? There's no record of it on her insurance. She was hurting for money, but she didn't sell it. And now it's missing."

"Well, perhaps it wasn't hers to sell," Reba said. "Maybe it was on loan from Suzie Magnuson and she took it back."

Terry was incredulous. "You think Suzie walked into the burglarized home of her friend and took it off the wall?"

"There's only one way to find out," Reba said. "We'll go to Suzie's now and see if she's got her painting. She's only a couple of blocks away."

"You're the one with the wheels," Terry said, and we locked up the house, hopped into Reba's Mercedes, and sped over to Suzie's in two minutes flat.

Suzie Magnuson lived in a redbrick Colonial mansion with a white colonnade running the length of the façade. The house sat between a granite French house topped by a mansard roof, and a stark, Frank Lloyd Wright–inspired split-level.

Jefferson goes to Paris, then retires to Arizona.

The neighborhood resembled Lenore's block: open, without the massive security walls that existed on Reba's older, more exclusive street. *Nouveau riche*, maybe, but still *filthé riche*.

We pulled up in the circular drive and parked behind the beige Rolls Royce we'd seen at the hotel.

"That's strange," Reba said.

"What?"

"She wasn't home when I called, so what's the car doing here?"

"Maybe she just got back," Terry said.

Reba shrugged, her shoulder bones knifing through the silk fabric of her blouse. She rang the bell.

No answer.

"Hmmm," Reba said, ringing again. "The maid's *always* here. Wonder what's taking her so long."

We heard a noise. The now-familiar sound of claws on the tile floor, scrambling to the front door to greet whatever human happened to appear. Dinner guest, UPS guy, Ed McMahon with a big friggin' check. They were all equally exciting to a certain class of creature.

"Does she have a dog?" I said.

Reba shuddered. "If you want to call it that. Little monster."

Do you see a pattern emerging here? I asked Terry telepathically.

"What? A rat dog, like Paquito?" Terry asked.

"A wiener dog?" I said. Whatever it was, it sounded small.

"An abomination. One of those with the smashed-in faces and bulging eyes. You know, like a Chinese statue."

"Oh, a pug."

"Well, I guess we'll have to come back later," Reba said, "although it seems strange that the maid wouldn't be here."

I looked around the side of the house. "Should we go around to the back and look for the chauffeur?"

Terry elbowed us aside in a huff. "Does anybody ever think of the obvious?" She reached out and tried the door handle— it was unlocked—and the door swung open.

The smell hit us with the force of an A-bomb.

It was unmistakable: the sickening-sweet rot of human flesh.

Someone was very dead in there.

Terry slammed the door. Reba gagged, tears springing into her eyes. She brought her handkerchief to her face, and I suddenly became afraid for her. Would this be too much of a shock, coming right on the heels of Lenore's death?

"I . . . I . . . can't," she choked.

We took her arms and guided her back to the Mercedes. Terry lowered her into the front seat, turning on the engine to blow air-conditioning into Reba's bloodless face.

"We've got to go back," I said to Terry.

"I know! We left the dog in there!"

"Yeah, but we need to go in and see who's . . . who's—"

"Smelling."

But how could we go back in? How could we plunge head-long into that hateful odor?

I looked at Reba, who was fanning herself in the front seat. "Do you have any perfume on you?" I asked her.

She nodded and pulled a small bottle of Chanel No. 5 out of her bag. She didn't have a clean handkerchief, so she handed us each a kid glove. We doused the gloves and held them against our noses as we made our way back up the drive.

Terry pushed open the front door again and we saw the tiny creature, wagging its curly pig tail. He was about a foot long. A solid, barrel-chested stump of a thing, with a black velvety mug that looked like it had collided with an anvil. His lips curled up in a smile and he panted heavily, a thick pink tongue lolling out of his mouth. He seemed very happy to see some live humans, diving forward to snuffle at our feet.

I held the glove against my nose and mouth and bent down to scoop the little guy up. He squealed, wriggling around in my arms like a greased hog. But I held on to him, couldn't let him run out into the street and be squashed by an oncoming Jaguar. It seemed awful to take him back into that house, but he'd apparently adjusted to the gaseous vileness of the corpse, and had already mourned his mistress, who'd perished days ago.

He would have to come with us.

We stepped over the threshold into the front entry hall, and immediately began to sweat bullets. Someone had turned the thermostat up full blast. It had to be eighty degrees inside.

Although I'd never been there before, the interior of Suzie Magnuson's home looked like a dead ringer for the White House. It was elegant and stuffy and classic in the extreme, with nothing that spoke of the century just past—no deco items from the Jazz era, no atomic designs from the fifties, no psychedelic vinyl from the sixties, to say nothing of the forty years since then. It was pure nineteenth century, all the way. Hand-painted china was displayed in a mahogany hutch, chairs and couch were nondescript early American, paintings on the walls depicted English hunting scenes or poetic American vistas. There was leather and chintz and spotless eggshell plush-pile carpeting, but no paintings by modern artists. Nothing even remotely avant-garde.

We followed our instincts, since our noses were otherwise engaged, and went up the stairs to the second floor. We found Suzie Magnuson in the bedroom, splayed on the bed. We took one look and stepped back, repulsed by the bloated monstrosity.

Suzie's head was still wrapped in bandages. Her face was purple, spotted with black bruises. She wore white silk culottes and a maroon dressing gown that was tied loosely with a sash. One hand was draped over her breast, the manicure done in a deep eggplant color that was almost a perfect match for her skin.

Suzie's other hand clutched a brown medical vial with several pills spilling out of the top. On her cherrywood bedside table was another assortment of pill bottles and a half-drunk glass of water.

And there on the floor beside the bed was the gift basket from the Dauphine. The cellophane had been ripped open, the little goodies and gold netting tossed aside. But something remained in the bottom of the basket, nestled in the shreds of brightly colored paper.

Terry stuck her hand into the perfumed glove and, pinching her nostrils with the other hand, reached down into the basket. She retrieved another brown vial, flipping the lid to look inside. Then she rattled it under my nose.

It was full of green and black capsules.

eight

$\mathcal{I}$ t was two hours, a lot of blinking lights, officers with questions, various crime-scene techs, and a coroner's van later. Terry and I had been shunted aside as soon as we gave our statements, but continued to loiter on the front lawn. Terry was hopping up and down, trying to get the attention of anyone who exited the house in order to wrest more information out of them.

A uniformed officer walked out the front door on the way to his patrol car, still wearing a face mask.

"What happens to the dog?" Terry asked him, holding the pug up for maximum heartbreak effect.

The policeman pulled off his mask and gave the dog a sympathetic scratch. "Oh, he'll go to the pound, I guess."

"Can we keep her?" I asked, because by then we'd determined that it *was* a she. Her anatomy was our first clue, but her dog tag confirmed it. Her name was Muffy. "We're friends of the . . . deceased."

"Sure," the officer said. "You'll have to sign a receipt."

Aunt Reba was long gone. She'd given a statement to one of the first officers on the scene, then Terry drove her home in the Mercedes and brought our motorcycle back to Suzie's. Reba'd given the police as much information as she could manage in her anguished state: Marital status of the victim, widowed. Known relatives, none. A maid named Phoebe and a chauffeur named John. As for their descriptions, she'd never taken stock of their personal features, and could only offer that they were both white, average height, middle-aged.

That narrowed it down.

She thought they were a married couple, but couldn't swear to it. She thought it was possible that the two of them were "shacking up" in the garage apartment that served as their home.

The deputy coroner came out the front door, followed by two attendants pushing a gurney that bore Suzie's tiny, body bag–encased form. He supervised the loading of the gurney onto the coroner's van.

Terry approached him, looking distraught. "We're friends of the family," she said again.

"I'm sorry," he said as the doors were slammed on the van. "You're the ones who found the body?"

She nodded gravely. "Did she die of an overdose? There were all kinds of pills lying around—"

He shook his head. "Sorry, miss. Can't discuss the case," he said, before making his way across the lawn to his car.

"Shit, got nothing from him," Terry said, watching him get into the driver's seat.

Suddenly we both noticed a man in a beautifully tailored suit exiting a black BMW at the curb. He was in his fifties or sixties, distinguished-looking, with an exquisite head of silver hair. He hailed the coroner, who rolled down his window to talk to him. I figured he might be someone closely connected to Suzie, or just someone with enough authority to get the death doctor's attention.

They conferred for a few moments, and then the distinguished man walked straight up to the front door of the house where he was admitted by a uniformed officer.

"Huh, who was that?" Terry wondered.

I shrugged, watching as the van pulled out of the drive and made its way down the street, passing another group of officers. Then someone in the group caught my eye. I smiled and punched Terry in the shoulder.

"Maybe we could get more information from your friend over there," I suggested, pointing to the female cop from the coffee shop. She stood with her hands on her round hips, deep in conversation with another officer on the other side of the street. They were part of the group assigned to keep away gawkers, yelling occasionally to a curious motorist, *Everything's fine. Nothing to see here!* before waving them on.

"Huh!" Terry said. "What a coincidence."

"Did you get her name?"

She looked sideways, searching her memory. "Uh, yeah. It's Officer Lott, like Trent."

"How about her first name?"

"Dinah. Like Shore. That's how we got on our discussion of female singers. And golf."

It took me a second, then I shrieked, "Oh my God! Her parents named her *Dinah Lott?* And she didn't *change it?*"

Terry gave me a contemptuous look. "I can't believe this reaction from someone who's put up with *Are you two twins?* her whole life. I think it shows character that she didn't change her name."

I looked over Terry's shoulder and saw the cop facing our way. I waved to her and she started walking toward us.

"Did she see us?" Terry said.

"Yep. Here she comes. Friendly Officer Eats-a-Bunch."

"Kerry, shut up or I swear to God—"

She shoved the dog at me, then turned around and flashed a smile at the cop. Dinah pulled off her mirrored sunglasses as she approached, and I could now see that she had lovely brown eyes and rather delicate, feminine features. But she walked with a strange cowboy swagger—hands tensed at her sides, as if she was ready to whip out a pair of six-shooters at any second.

"Hey girls," Dinah said. "What are you doing here?"

"Just walking the dog," Terry said, pointing to Muffy.

"Another one?" Dinah attempted to pet Muffy on the head, but got a handful of dog slobber instead. "What you got against real dogs?"

"*Real* dogs?" Terry said, an edge to her voice.

Dinah was unaware that she'd offended. "I got a German shepherd named Helga. Maybe we could get them together for a playdate some time. Of course, I can't guarantee that my Helga wouldn't eat your little pooches' lunches," she chuckled, topping it off with a convulsive "Huh-*yuk*."

I could see Terry's eyes bugging with the onset of an outburst. Before she could give the armed woman with a badge a lecture on breed sensitivity, I jumped in to save the situation.

"We'll take a rain check on that, thanks," I said to Dinah. "So, um, we're friends of Mrs. Magnuson's. Can you tell us what happened here? No one else will."

Dinah shrugged and hitched up her belt. "Haven't heard yet. All I know, it's a ten fifty-five—coroner's case. No idea if she died of natural causes, or what."

"Well, we're pretty sure it wasn't natural causes," Terry said. "Unless you call overdosing *natural*."

Dinah's eyes widened. "Huh. This is turning out to be an interesting call. Sounds like you already know quite a bit."

"We found her," I said. "We came over to visit with our Aunt Reba, walked in and encountered . . . the smell."

"And the body," Terry said.

"Was she expecting you?" Dinah studied me intently, causing a rush of adrenaline to flood my bloodstream, as if I were suddenly the prime suspect in a murder.

"Uh, no," I said casually. "We were just passing by, thought we'd drop in."

Dinah nodded, one eye narrowed. "Hmmm."

Terry and I started backing up. "Well, we'd probably better let you do your job," I said. "Do you mind if we call you later? Get the update?"

"Sure, but I can't promise I'll be able to tell you anything about an ongoing investigation."

"Oh," Terry said. She did her best to look crestfallen and fluttered her eyelashes at Dinah just a tad.

"Tell you what," Dinah said, apparently moved by this feminine display of disappointment. "I can't talk about it on my watch, but if you want to meet for a beer later, maybe I could give you some info, strictly on the QT."

"Great!" I said. "Where and when?"

"How about Barney's Beanery? Nine o'clock."

Barney's Beanery was a joint on Santa Monica Boulevard that served chili burgers and beers and boasted a couple of ratty pool tables. And cottage fries, I remembered. They served cottage fries. The thought set my mouth to watering.

Terry gave Dinah a confused look, and I suddenly realized why. Barney's was in West Hollywood, a notoriously gay city that was incorporated back in the eighties. There'd been a problem a couple of years back, accusations that Barney's discriminated against gay patrons, so most of them—including Terry—avoided it like the plague.

Oh well, I decided. That was probably ancient history.

"We'll be there," I said, smiling. "And the beer's on us."

"Later." Dinah winked at us and headed back toward her cohorts in the street, still with that strange, rolling gait. If she'd been bowlegged, I could have understood. But there was no light breaking between those thighs. *Whatever*, I thought. We all have our little pretensions. If she wanted to walk like she was the Law West of the Pecos, it was nothing to me.

"You could have been a little nicer to her," I said to Terry when Dinah was out of earshot.

Terry rolled her eyes at me. "Get *out*."

"Come on, play your cards right and she could be an excellent source for us, not to mention a hot date for you."

"I'm not playing anything with that woman! She's a cop, and she walks like a cowpoke. And did you hear that laugh?" she said, mimicking Dinah: *"Huh-yuk!"*

Methought she was protesting too much. "Want to borrow some makeup?"

"Pimp!"

"Skag!"

"Snluggg!" Muffy chimed in.

Terry looked at the dog, who was happily snorting all over the sleeve of my jacket. "So, what do you think? Have we acquired another dog?"

"She'd be good company for Paquito," I said, nodding. "And this way, you can have one, too."

Her eyes nearly popped out of her head. "Oh, so you're claiming Paquito? Who died and left you in charge of him?"

"Lenore."

"You know what I meant!"

"Well, I don't see why we can't share him," I said. "We're grown-ups, aren't we?"

"Yeah . . ." Terry said skeptically.

"She's kind of cute, too, isn't she?" I scratched beneath Muffy's chin.

"Adorable."

"Good," I said, shoving the pug at Terry. "You take her and I'll take Paquito."

She grabbed the orphaned dog around her solid little middle and huffed off toward the bike. "You get any more grown-up, we're gonna have to potty-train you soon," she said, trying to zip Muffy up in her jacket. But the jacket was too small or Muffy was too big. When I got to the bike, Terry thrust her back at me.

"She was your idea. You hold her."

I was about to hop on the bike, when a vintage blue Renault pulled up to the curb in front of us. The driver beeped lightly on his horn, waving his arm out the window, then clambered out of the car and came toward us with quick little steps.

He was around thirty. Pleasant-looking, if forgettable. Thinning brown hair, average height, dressed in neatly pressed khakis, golf shirt, and white running shoes. Mr. Normal.

"Hey, is that Mrs. Magnuson's dog?" he said.

"Yes," I said. "Who are you?"

He pulled a business card out of his wallet. "Sidney Lefler. Nice to meet you."

I handed him the dog and took off my helmet, reading his card. He was an investigator with Whitechapel Mutual.

"I'm Kerry McAfee." I handed him one of our cards. "My sister, Terry. You know Mrs. Magnuson?"

"We're her insurers. I came as soon as I heard."

"That was fast," Terry said. "I don't think they've even notified her next of kin, and the insurance company got a call?"

He stammered, embarrassed. "I'm, uh, kind of a police radio junkie. I was in the neighborhood checking on another account and I heard the call, recognized the address."

"Oh," I said. "So you know."

"Yeah, how'd it happen?" he said, handing Muffy back to me.

"Looks like a drug overdose."

"That's terrible." He tried to look deeply affected, but his head kept jerking toward the house, like he was dying to get a look at the corpse.

"They've taken away the body," I said, dashing any voyeuristic hopes he may have had.

"Wow, first the break-in, and now this," he said, blowing out a little whistle.

"What break-in?" Terry said.

"Mrs. Magnuson had a burglary a few weeks ago. Closer to a month, actually."

"Really?" I looked at Terry. "Was anything stolen?"

"Oh, not much. Just some silver and whatnot. Jeez. I wonder if the two incidents could be related."

Now we wondered, too.

"You're investigators also?" he said, looking at our card.

"Private," I said.

"Are you here in a . . . professional capacity?"

"No, our aunt is a friend of Mrs. Magnuson's," Terry told him. "We just dropped by for a social visit."

"Mmm. Well, keep my card. Maybe we could go out to lunch one day and swap war stories."

"We'd like that," I said.

"Call me." He scurried up the walkway toward the cop on the front porch.

When we got home, Paquito was yapping at the door. We cracked it open and he poked his nose outside, nostrils working furiously. Terry carefully pushed the door in further and he ran outside and dodged at our feet, spinning in circles like a tiny whirling dervish.

"Mommy's home!" each of us said, then glared at the other.

Paquito started leaping into the air, yelping at Muffy, who was in my arms and straining to get down. She was a strong little thing and so determined I almost lost my hold on her.

But something distracted Paquito from his new friend. He lunged at my feet, sniffing the hem of my jeans. Then he jumped from my pants leg to Terry's, performing the same doggie reconnaissance.

"The body," she said. "He smells the body."

"You think?"

"They can smell a single molecule of meat from a mile away."

We had plied our nostrils with the expensive perfume, but the fumes were evaporating and I was beginning to detect a little eau-de-decomposition under the Chanel No. 5. It smelled like the proverbial French cathouse, housing a big dead cat.

"I'm gonna burn these clothes and sandblast my skin," I said.

Terry grabbed Muffy from me.

"Here's a little girlfriend for you, precious," she said to Paquito. "Her name's Muffy." She placed the girl dog nose-to-nose with the boy dog.

It was love at first sight.

They quivered. They lunged. They ducked and feinted. They did their version of the minuet, noses daintily inserted into backsides, as violins played *How Much Is That Doggie in the Window* in the flickering candlelight of their imaginations.

Then Muffy rushed Paquito from behind, threw her front paws on his back and began humping him.

"Muffy, no!" I yelled. She looked up at me with bewildered black eyes. "You're the girl, Muffy. You don't do the humping!"

Terry got in my face. "Why don't you let them do what comes naturally, instead of trying to force them into a puritanical ideal of proper sex?"

"Well, okay," I said, chastened. "Hump away, Muff."

And she did, for a full thirty seconds. By then we became afraid for Paquito's backbone. She was a sturdy little thing, weighing in at about ten pounds to Paquito's three. Feminist principles aside, we were afraid she might snap his spine. Terry pulled her off Paquito's back and took her into the kitchen, promising a nice treat to make up for the humpus interruptus.

Paquito shivered and fell to the ground, panting. If his male ego had suffered from being pinned by a female aggressor, he gave no sign of it. His eyes were big, his tongue darting in and out, and he seemed to be saying to me, *She's a firebrand. What's her name, again?*

After taking extra-long hot showers, we watched Muffy and Paquito snapping up kibble companionably side-by-side. It was clear that this tiny match had truly been made in heaven.

Domestic tranquillity established, we went to meet Dinah.

Barney's Beanery was already hopping when we showed up at 8:45. The jukebox was rocking with bar hits by the likes of Bruce Springsteen, ZZ Top, and George Thoroughgood. Patrons with meaty arms in sleeveless denim vests plied their pool cues under fake Tiffany lamps. A ponytailed waitress in a midriff and bell-bottomed jeans balanced orders of huge burgers and fries on a tray as she wended her way through the crowd, wagging the butterfly tattoo above her tailbone.

There was no sign of Dinah, so Terry and I ordered beers. The bartender set down two frosty mugs of Beck's, weighing in at about five pounds each.

"To Lenore," Terry said, hoisting her beer.

"Lenore." I tried to clink the hefty mug, but it came out as more of a *clunk*. "Sounds like greed was her undoing."

"Yeah, but who 'undid' Suzie?"

"The demon drug," I said.

She squinted into her beer. "You know, I've got an idea about Suzie and that basket from the hotel."

"Yeah, how sad. Hiding her drugs in her little goodie basket."

"But did *she* hide them? Remember what the clerk said? These women 'have to have' the baskets delivered to their rooms all the time. What do you call someone who 'has to have' something all the time?"

I slapped the bar. "An addict!"

"Bingo, babe." She knew what she was talking about. "Now follow me for second . . . we think the doc was a druggie, and all those post-op girls at the hotel were patients of his—"

"Right, right."

"And at least one of them, Lenore, was getting her surgery for free. And she was *pushing* the doctor on Reba."

"Yeah . . . ?"

"So maybe the operative word here is *pushing*, with Alphonse and Hattrick doing the honors. Maybe the surgery is free 'cause they get all the girls hooked on painkillers, then they go home and push them on their friends! 'Menopause got you down, dear? Try one of these. Another frightful tension headache? I've got just the thing.' "

I nodded, encouraging her to continue.

"Then before you know it," Terry went on, "you've got the Mary Kays from hell—a pyramid marketing scheme, with an army of Beverly Hills broads spreading the drugs around town like candy!" She slapped the bar for emphasis and the bartender appeared immediately at her side.

" 'Nother one?" He smiled at her flirtatiously, taking her in from the purple low-rise jeans to her slinky black camisole, not even sparing me a glance.

"No thanks," she said, tossing her hair behind her bare shoulder.

"Let me know when you do," he said, then moved to the other end of the bar, where a yuppie with an empty mug had been desperately trying to get his attention.

Okay, this was something I was used to, but it still pissed

me off on occasion. I slap the bar—nothing happens. Terry slaps the bar—the guy comes running, practically panting. Why, when confronted with two identical women, were men always attracted to the one who had no use for them? Terry had this *energy* that reached out and snared them, reeling them in like brainless big-mouthed bass.

"A ring of painkiller pushers operating out of a five-star hotel," Terry continued, oblivious to the bartender's ardor. "It's insidiously brilliant, isn't it?"

"It would certainly give Lenore some raw material as a blackmailer," I agreed.

"So how do we confirm this?"

"I guess we'd better go back to the hotel. See if we can get something out of that blond registration clerk. Better yet, somebody on the housekeeping staff. They're bound to have noticed pill canisters lying around the rooms, or guests facedown in their own vomit—"

Just then, I looked over Terry's shoulder to see Dinah walking in the front door. My smile froze on my face. She was outfitted in urban cowboy finery that would put Clint Black to shame, hitching up her jeans as she moseyed on over to us.

"Here she comes," I said, stifling a chuckle.

Terry read my expression correctly, without turning around. "She's dressed weird, isn't she?"

"Yup."

"Hi, girls," Dinah said as she arrived, tipping the brim of her Stetson.

Terry spun on her bar stool to greet the policewoman. "Howdy, Sheriff," she said, and got a Huh-*yuk* in response.

$\mathcal{W}e$ *sat in* a booth and munched cottage fries and burgers. Once Terry and I got over the initial shock of Dinah's getup we found she was good company, if a tinge red on the neck. Turns out she came by it honestly, though—born and raised in Norman, Oklahoma.

"Why'd you leave?" I asked her, after she'd rhapsodized about the southwest for some time.

"Oh, it's fundamentalist country." She looked at Terry. "Not too tolerant, you know what I mean?"

Terry nodded sympathetically.

Dinah said she'd attended Oral Roberts University in Tulsa for two years before deciding to come west. "My original plan was to be a stunt rider, but they don't make too many westerns these days, and even the ones they do make don't have many women riders. Historical accuracy, and all. So I got interested in law enforcement and, well, here I am."

"Glad it worked out for you," I said.

" 'Course, patrol work isn't my ideal. I hope to work my way up to homicide."

Perfect. She was providing the very segue we needed.

"There aren't too many of those in Beverly Hills, are there?" I asked, playing the wide-eyed innocent. "Might be kind of boring."

"You'd be surprised. Take your friend Mrs. Magnuson," she said, leaning into us and lowering her voice. "It looked like an overdose at first, but it turns out she was stabbed in the heart with an ice pick–like instrument."

Terry and I leaned back in our seats.

Dinah took a swig of beer. "It's lucky the dog didn't eat her," she said. "That sometimes happens . . . the owner dies, and the poor little pet has no choice between that and starving."

The tail of a cottage fry dropped from my lips, hit the table, and bounced to the floor.

"That didn't happen with your little guy, though," Dinah said cheerfully.

"Little girl," Terry said. "The dog's a she."

"You've got her," Dinah said, "don't you?"

"Yeah, we took her home. I guess we'll adopt her."

"So poor Suzie Magnuson was murdered," I said, shaking my head. "Any leads?"

Dinah gave us a long, appraising look. "I can trust you not to repeat any of this?" We nodded, with all the sincerity and trustworthiness we could muster. "We got fingerprints off those pill bottles. No matches yet, but it's something."

"What kind of drugs, were they?" I said.

"Percocet, Darvon, Dilaudid."

"Jesus, all of them?"

Dinah nodded. "In quantities that would kill a darn hippo."

"But she didn't overdose?" Terry said.

"She was heavily drugged, but no, it didn't kill her. Just incapacitated her to the point where she probably didn't even hear her attacker come in the house."

"Wait," Terry said. "If she was stabbed in the chest, why didn't we see it?"

"Her blood pressure was really low," Dinah explained. "That's why there wasn't more blood at the scene. She might have died anyway from the drugs, but somebody saw to it that she would never wake up."

Terry and I took a moment to let this sink in. The wrongful death of another of Reba's dear friends was unsettling, to say the least.

"No chance she stabbed herself?" I asked.

"None. There was no weapon. And besides, people don't usually stab themselves in the heart. Don't know why, but they'd rather cut themselves almost anywhere else. They'll bleed themselves till they stop it pumping, but don't go straight to the source. Makes you wonder if people who kill themselves by cutting really do want to die at all.

"Now, I've told you what I know," Dinah said, "how about a little coming back?"

The moment of truth. Time for a girls' room strategy session. "Uh . . ." I hesitated. "Will you excuse us for a minute, Dinah? We have to pee."

Dinah nodded, frowning as Terry and I slid out of the booth. Once inside the bathroom, I looked under the stalls to make sure we were alone.

"*We* need to pee?" Terry said. "That's pretty lame, Kerry."

"We're twins. What does she know about it? Maybe our bladders are in complete sync."

"Yeah, right."

Satisfied that we were alone, I leaned up against a stall. "So, what do we tell her?"

"About what?"

"About everything."

"*Nothing.*"

"We can't get away with that! She knows we know something, and we need her on our side."

Terry laughed. "Why?"

"She's a cop!"

"First of all, we don't know anything. We've guessed a few things, but we don't *know jack*."

"But she's smart. And she has aspirations to homicide. Maybe we should tell her about our . . . our theories, and see if she can help us from the inside."

Terry skewered me with her evilest eye. "You want to tell her about Mario?"

Dang. Forgot about Mario.

"I guess not."

"Then I guess we tell her nothing. 'Cause I'm pretty sure it all ties in."

"But if someone else dies—?"

"Look, if things get out of hand, yeah. But let's find out more before we jump into anything half-cocked. Hell, we might be able to put it all together ourselves and get paid by

Reba in the process. Maybe we'll even get a citizen's medal of honor or some shit from the cops."

"Yeah, *that's* gonna happen." I rolled my eyes. "They hand out lots of medals to citizens who break the law and withhold information while impeding investigations."

She put her hands on my shoulders. "If things change in the next day or two, we can revisit it, okay? I promise. Now let's go soak Dinah for everything she's worth."

Cold. My sister could be cold.

We slinked back into the booth. "I take it you've decided not to tell me what you know," Dinah said, searching our faces. "That's not exactly fair, is it?"

Terry waved at the waitress. "Could we have the bill, please?"

The girl hurried over to place it on the table, but Dinah wouldn't let Terry off the hook. She kept her gaze fixed on my sister's darting eyes.

"Look, we're sorry," Terry said. "But we have to keep confidentiality. You understand—"

Dinah gave her a crooked smile. "Yeah. But I know you've got something that pertains to this case, and sooner or later it's gonna come out. I just hope it doesn't bite you both in the behind."

I cast guilty eyes down to my plate.

"Well," Dinah said, standing. "I'd probably do the same in your shoes. But I want you to know that if you *do* need help, I'm here."

She reached for the bill, but Terry grabbed it first.

"It's on us," she said to Dinah, who gave us a little nod, then rolled on out of the restaurant.

As we made our way out to the bike, I did some thinking about our policewoman friend. She was wily, a smart cookie in spite of her redneck duds. She hadn't set up this meeting as a favor to us, she'd suspected we had information on the case all along and had come here to pump us for it. She was likely headed straight to the homicide squad, I concluded, probably in less time than it took most rookies to get their shoes shined.

Maybe with a fashion makeover and diction lessons, there'd be hope for her and Terry, after all.

It was past midnight when we got home, and we were pleased to see that the pups had behaved like housebroken little ladies and gentlemen in our absence. After we took them outside, we returned Reba's frantic calls, each of us on an extension.

"Where have you *been?*" she demanded.

"Sorry, we had legwork to do," I told her.

"I apologize for losing my composure this afternoon. But the death of one's peers does tend to—" She paused, sighing. "Poor dear Suzie . . . did you find the Bacon in her house?"

"No, but things were a little out of control," Terry said. "We could have missed it."

"But there's been another development," I said to Reba. "And this is strictly between us. We got it from a confidential source on the police force."

"What?"

"Suzie was murdered. Stabbed through the heart."

"Dear God," Reba breathed. She was silent for a long moment. "That does it!" she said. "I'm going to hire a bodyguard."

"Not a terrible idea," Terry said. "Where were you thinking of getting one?"

"Well, I was rather hoping you two would know some big, handsome brute who'd take a bullet for me."

I ran down the list of big, handsome, suicidal brutes of my acquaintance and came up empty. "Not right off hand," I said. "But we'll look into it."

"First Lenore, and now Suzie . . . *murdered*," Reba said with a shudder in her voice. "Right in her own home!"

"But it's not like there's been a *rash* of murders," I reminded her. "Lenore was pronounced dead of an aneurysm. If she was murdered, it would have to have been some clever method that escaped the scrutiny of the medical staff."

"Oh, scrutiny my patootie," Reba blurted out. "You could stampede a herd of elephants through that hospital and they'd never notice. They're completely understaffed, and the ones who are left are always bellyaching about how overworked and underpaid they are. What's the world coming to, anyway?"

Reba was having a crisis of confidence where her cherished institutions were concerned. Only yesterday she'd pronounced Cedars-Sinai the best hospital in the world. The deaths of her friends seemed to be upending her entire worldview.

"Try not to worry, Aunt Reba," Terry said. "Just make sure you've got the house alarm on, even during the day. And tell Grizzie to keep her eyes peeled for any strange vehicles or persons on foot around the neighborhood."

"I will. So, see you in the morning? We're due at Binion's office at noon."

At the mention of Binion, a lightbulb went on over my head. "What does he look like, anyway?"

"Who?" Reba asked.

"Hugh Binion."

"Oh, he's handsome. Matinee idol looks, although I doubt you girls would find him 'hot.' He's much too old for your tender libidos."

Reba had not quite processed the fact that Terry's libido ran in a different direction altogether.

"Tall, about six-foot-one?" I said. "Graying hair? Well-dressed? Tan, but not excessively, just a hint of outdoor color?"

"*Ye-e-s,*" Reba said. "That sounds like him. Why?"

"Because he was at Suzie's this afternoon. He spoke to the coroner as they . . . took her away."

Terry smiled at me, impressed. I even got the coveted thumbs-up from across the room.

"Maybe he was passing by," Reba said. "I'm sure he lives in the neighborhood."

"Uh, I don't think so. The coroner wouldn't give us the time of day, but he had a nice long chat with the well-dressed man. And then they let him into the house without any trouble."

Reba paused, thinking it over. "Well, wouldn't that be an interesting coincidence? Hugh representing both Suzie and Lenore?"

"Sounds like he represents a good portion of the wealthy widows of Beverly Hills," I said.

"The dead ones, anyway," Terry quipped.

Reba's phone clanged to the floor.

"Reba? Reba!" I shouted.

Terry and I were just about to hang up and call 911, when we heard Reba pick up the receiver again, breathing heavily.

"Beverly Hills used to be the safest place on earth," she said.

nine

*W*e got to Reba's house next morning at the stroke of eleven. When the door opened, we were greeted by a mountain of a man in a black suit and Raybans with a squared-off jaw, who sported a blond military brush cut.

"Morning, ladies." His voice was low and Eastwood-raspy. "I'm Lance. Mrs. Price-Slatherton's security consultant."

Well, that was fast work, I thought. Reba'd acquired a bodyguard in one morning.

"Hello, Lance," I said, starting across the threshold.

He body-blocked me, sending me flying into Terry, whose wind went out of her with a startled *Ugh!*

"Sorry, ladies. No one gets in without a once-over. House rules."

Was he seriously going to frisk us?

He slapped the outside of my arms before I could protest, then yanked them out to the side and ran hands that were like huge, inflated airbeds down the sides of my appliquéed pink tee and low-riding khakis.

"Lance!" Reba said, rushing into the foyer, her fingers fluttering. "That won't be necessary!"

He gave her a flinty look. "I'm afraid it is, ma'am. I can't guarantee your safety if I don't follow established procedures. You never know who's gonna jump out at you with a gun or a knife. Don't know who might be carrying."

"But they're my nieces!"

"Everyone's someone's relative, ma'am. Mark David Chapman had parents. Ted Kasczynski had a brother. Charlie Manson had one *hell* of a big family."

"Oh, all right. You don't mind, do you girls?" she said, then whispered, "Just until he gets to know you."

Terry and I sighed and held out our arms. We were patted down the hips, the legs, then briskly about the ankles. Lance grabbed my bag and rummaged around inside, extracting a metal nail file before handing the bag back to me.

"Sorry, miss. This stays with me," he said, secreting the file inside his jacket. "You may retrieve it when you exit."

He turned to Reba. "They're clean, ma'am."

"Thank you, Lance."

"My pleasure." He gave her a salute. "Your security is my foremost concern at all times."

"Come on girls," Reba said. "Coffee's ready."

Terry and I straightened our clothes and followed Reba to the dining room.

"Well, he certainly seems to know his stuff," I mumbled to Terry. "Still, he could afford to tone it down a *tad*."

We sat down at the dining room table and Reba poured us coffee from the silver service. "Muffins and mangoes all right with you girls?"

"No, we'd like French toast and eggs with Tabasco sauce," Terry said.

Reba was momentarily speechless.

Terry flashed a devious smile. "Just kidding."

Reba placed a hand on her heart. "Grizzie will be right in."

As we waited for the food to arrive, I could see Lance's sleeve in my peripheral vision. He was stationed just outside the living room door, still as a statue.

"May we speak freely?" I whispered to Reba, motioning toward Lance's massive presence.

Reba cut her eyes in Lance's direction. "He's absolutely guaranteed to be trustworthy," she said in a hushed voice.

"Where did you get him so quickly?"

"An agency."

"A security agency?" Terry said.

"No," Reba said, "a casting agency."

"*What?*"

"My friend Stella Longstreet has a son who's in casting. He's gay, of course, but a charming boy. Lance is between movies right now, and Stella's son thought he'd be perfect for the job."

"You hired an actor to protect you?" I said. "Wouldn't you rather have a professional?"

"Oh, he *is* a professional. You should see his résumé. He's played a robot policeman, a special ops soldier twice, and an army colonel in the last Gene Hackman movie. He even had a speaking part in that one."

"But what does he know about bodyguarding?"

"Well, he's done a lot of research for a new role. But there's nothing like on-the-job experience, so Stella's son suggested he could guard me until I get the real thing. He certainly looks the part, don't you think? A criminal would definitely think twice about coming at me with Lance around."

"Well, that's probably true," Terry said, looking pretty dubious all the same.

"He's very forceful. Watch this." Reba called out, "Oh, Lance?"

He stepped inside the room, maintaining his military bearing. "Yes, ma'am?"

"Do it for the girls."

"Ma'am?"

"Come on, don't be shy. You said it for me, say it for them. One little line reading."

He blushed. "Oh, no. I feel stupid."

"Just once!" She turned to me and Terry. "This is from the Gene Hackman movie. Go ahead, Lance."

He acquiesced, planting his feet, then rolled his head on his neck and shrugged his shoulders to get loosened up. He frowned, jutting out his lower jaw, and jabbed his forefinger in the air.

"Incoming!" he shouted at a phantom missile.

He held the pose for a few seconds, then grinned and gave us a little bow.

Reba applauded in delight. "Isn't that something?"

Terry and I clapped our hands. "Thanks, Lance," Terry said. "We'll look forward to seeing it in Cinemascope."

Lance slipped out of the room and took up his post again.

I cleared my throat. "Well, that was impressive."

"Now, about the Bacon painting—" Reba started to say, but she was interrupted by a sudden outbreak of pandemonium.

"Get your-r-r foul giant's mitts off me muffins!" Grizzie screamed, followed by the sound of crashing metal. Lance howled in terror.

Terry and I jumped up from the table and ran into the foyer. Grizzie was bashing Lance mercilessly on the head with her serving tray. Muffins were strewn all over the floor.

"Grizzie, stop!" I yelled.

Lance was backed against the wall, making a sound that sounded a lot like whimpering.

"Get her off me!" he wailed.

Terry grabbed Grizzie by the apron strings and pulled her off, ducking to avoid the still-swinging serving tray that sailed over her head. Grizzie and Lance backed away from each other, breathing heavily and shaking with emotion.

"What the hell were you doing?" Terry shouted at Grizzie.

"He was grabbin' and eatin' all the missus' muffins!" she yelled, red in the face.

"Lance, why didn't you just ask for a muffin?" I said in a conciliatory tone. "I'm sure Grizzie would be happy to toast one for you."

"I . . . I was checking for poison," Lance sniffed.

"Poison, indeed! As if I'd be poisoning me own mistress! Why you big bugger!" Grizzie darted forward and slashed at him again with the tray, screeching like some sort of Ninja housekeeper.

He fought her off the best he could, his huge hands *pinging* off the tray, then ducked past her and ran for the front door. He threw it open and tore across the porch without looking back, racing across the wide front lawn, sending up tufts of freshly mown grass as he went.

"Well," Terry said philosophically, watching as Lance plowed through the front gate, "I guess we call that 'outgoing.' "

"*That didn't go* so well," Reba observed, as we sat back down at the table. "Maybe I'll just skip the bodyguard and get a gun."

"*No!*" Terry and I shouted.

"Why not? I'm entitled, as an American citizen."

"Reba, do you know the number of fatalities that occur

just from accidents with guns?" I said, my mind reeling at the thought of my great-aunt packing a piece.

Her lips turned down in a pout. "Well, I thought it might make me a more effective member of the team, but . . ." She waved a hand in the air. "Oh, never mind. I can always gouge out their eyes with nail scissors."

Terry started to blink rapidly. I wondered if she was having a seizure.

"Now, about that Bacon," Reba said. "I remembered something about it—"

"What?" I said, keeping an eye on Terry. The blinking had stilled to a simple twitch, thank God.

"Well, we were playing canasta a couple of weeks ago," Reba said, "and I noticed it was missing from Suzie's living room. I asked her about it and she said she'd moved it upstairs, said it didn't go with the decor and it gave her a migraine. She told me she might consider selling it and buying another landscape. It was one of her husband's purchases sometime in the sixties, and she'd never really liked it."

"So instead of moving upstairs, it looks like the painting made its way into Lenore's hands," Terry said.

Reba nodded. "Yes, it does."

"We forgot to tell you last night," I said to her. "We ran into a man from Suzie's insurance company yesterday. He said she'd reported a burglary a few weeks ago."

Reba looked at me in surprise. "He did?"

"Yeah, he said some odds and ends were stolen, silver and things, but he didn't say anything about the painting."

"How odd. I heard nothing about it." Reba got an impish look on her face. "In any case, I've been thinking about it, and I believe I know where the painting is now. It must have been taken from Lenore's house by Hugh Binion!"

"Huh?" Terry said. "You're saying Binion has the Bacon?"

"Yes! Consider this—he already *knew* that Lenore was

dead when I called. Let's say he got the call about her death the same time I did, which would have given him a few hours to take advantage of the situation, dashing over to her house to take anything of value before I could see what there was to be had—"

"Hmm," we said.

"And he knew that Suzie was in no position to claim the painting," she added, "because she was dead!"

"But the painting disappeared *before* Suzie died," I said.

"Before we found her, but *not* before she died," Reba said. "She'd been dead for a couple of days before you discovered the painting was missing from Lenore's."

"Hey, she's getting pretty good at this," Terry said to me.

"But how would Binion *know* Suzie was dead?" I said. "We found the body before he even got there . . ."

Terry suddenly made the connection, turning startled eyes to Reba. "Wait a minute. Are you accusing Binion of . . . involvement with Suzie's death?"

"It's the simplest explanation possible," Reba said, matter-of-factly.

"Unbelievable," I said, shaking my head. "Is there anyone in this town that isn't dirty?"

Reba gave me an indignant look. "Well, I'm not," she said.

A half hour later, we were on our way to the law office. Terry and I had decided to play the part of supportive family members, sitting in on the meeting to see if Binion said anything to implicate himself. We figured he'd see us as simply a Beverly Hills matron and her two young nieces, no reason to be especially cautious.

We grilled Reba on what she should know, and more importantly what she *shouldn't* know for the purposes of this meeting. She could know about the deaths of Lenore and Suzie, of course, but she couldn't appear to know anything about the break-in at Lenore's house. That would tip Binion off that we'd been there and seen the painting before it disappeared.

I was sure Binion would have ascertained that we had discovered Suzie's body, but Reba shouldn't know about the stabbing. I instructed her to feign ignorance of the exact manner of Suzie's death, even evincing a healthy curiosity about it. *Was it a heart attack? An overdose?*

"Needless to say," I felt the need to say, "no mention of the Bacon."

"Got it," Reba said. "No break-in, no Bacon, no stabbing." She winked at us. "Don't worry about me, girls. I'm the body and soul of discretion."

We entered the reception area of Hartford, Huntington, and Binion, full of the requisite brass fixtures, gleaming wood paneling, and leather furnishings of all high-end law firms. *Forbes* and *Harper's* were stacked neatly on the table in front of a brown Chesterfield couch. Polished office plants thrived in hand-beaten copper planters. A pretty brunette in a gray Ann Taylor suit greeted us, then announced us on the phone with a smooth FM-radio voice.

Within seconds, Binion was hurrying down the corridor to meet us, the rustling of his trousers the only noise in the tomblike silence of the hallway. The thick carpeting sucked up all sound, giving the offices the appropriate hush associated with professionals toiling away for six hundred dollars an hour.

I recognized Binion immediately as the distinguished man from Suzie's house. Terry gave me an almost imperceptible nod of her head. She recognized him, too.

He took Reba's bony hand in his, leaning in for two air kisses. "Reba," he said in a satin baritone.

"Hugh, so nice to see you," Reba said, then pointed to us. "I've brought my great-nieces with me. Terry and Kerry McAfee."

He gave us an oily smile. "Oh, but surely they're your sisters?"

Reba actually tittered. "No, they're the daughters of my dear deceased niece, Jean."

Binion's face went solemn. "You have my condolences, Reba. It must have come as a terrible shock, losing both Lenore and Suzie so close together."

Reba's lower lip quivered. "Thank you, Hugh. Most kind. Can you tell me how poor Suzie died?"

"It was an overdose, an apparent suicide."

Reba gasped. "Well, you think you *know* someone—"

"Yes," Binion said, "but so many of us have dark secrets."

Terry threw me a look.

He ushered us down the soundless cavern of a hallway past miles of leather-bound law volumes and into his corner office. We sat on another stately couch and crossed our ankles, resting our feet on a plush Persian rug. A different gray-attired young woman took our drink orders—water all around.

I scanned the walls behind Binion's massive wooden partner's desk. Framed certificates and diplomas, and a couple of prints of Englishmen on horseback out to cadge a few foxtails. No modern oils. No abstract modes of expression. Nothing to upset the aura of historical continuity and mind-numbing stodginess.

Binion picked up a file from his desk. "I have good news for you, and bad too, I'm afraid."

"Oh?" Reba said. She was doing a fair impersonation of someone who was completely innocent of what she was about to hear.

"As you know, your dear friend Lenore thought of you

when she drafted her will, and it was clearly her intention to leave you whatever she had of value in her house."

Reba gave a wan smile. "I'd have done the same for her. Who did she leave her house to, if I may ask?"

"The bank, to be perfectly blunt about it. She was in arrears on her third mortgage and they were just about to foreclose."

Reba *tsked* at this disheartening news. "I'd have been glad to help in any way I could."

"I'm sure," Binion said, his voice low and confidential. "But the situation had gone beyond . . . help."

"Alas," Reba said. "You were saying, the contents of the house?"

"Well, unfortunately there was a mishap."

"A mishap? Whatever sort of mishap?" Reba cocked her head like a curious little bird, her voice high and querulous. Okay, maybe she wasn't such a great actress.

"A break-in, while Lenore was in the hospital."

Reba clapped a hand to her cheek. "No!"

Oh God. Binion's going to see straight through our little act, I thought in panic, but he kept his professional mask in place with nary a flicker of skepticism.

"I'm afraid so," he said, clucking his tongue. *"The times we live in . . ."*

"Was anything taken?" Reba asked.

"I sent one of my associates over to the house yesterday with an adjuster from the insurance company. They had brought along an inventory, and there was nothing missing as far as they could tell. But many of the household items have been destroyed. The furniture is almost a complete loss."

"What a pity." Reba looked over at Terry and me. "Well, what about her jewels? Were they in the safe?"

"I'm afraid not. Apparently she'd been forced to sell them."

"Oh-h-h-h," Reba said. "Too bad. I was very fond of her koala pin."

"It was a lovely koala," Binion said, nodding. "She wore it to our meetings on several occasions."

"Well, what about her rugs?" Reba said. "As I recall, she had some valuable rugs."

"The rugs were ruined. My associate took them to a repair shop but they declared them beyond salvaging."

This was a complete lie. The rugs had been tossed aside, but they were in fine condition. They weren't slashed. Hadn't been doused with acid. Now we knew for sure that Binion was a bald-faced liar, and probably a thief as well.

"Oh, really?" Reba said, sounding a little cagey. "Still, I'd like to have them for sentimental value. Perhaps I can salvage a square foot or two and make a patchwork rug to remind me of Lenore."

Ha! A patchwork Persian. Let him try to wriggle out of that one. If Reba was willing to take rugs that were trashed, it'd be no business of Binion's to withhold them.

"They've already been disposed of," he said, puckering his lips as if tasting something rancid. "They were utterly destroyed, I doubt you would have found any use for them."

"You're quite sure?" she said to Binion, her words clipped.

He gave her a regretful nod. "I'm so sorry."

Reba was getting hot under her linen collar, I could tell. Those rugs were worth tens of thousands of dollars, and she was choking on an upsurge of anger. The righteous anger of the ripped-off.

"Well, I don't want to sound greedy or anything," Reba said with a tight little smile, "but was there anything worth having in the *whole stinking mess*?"

Binion's eyes widened a hair, but he maintained his lawyerly aplomb. "I'm afraid not. That was the bad news I had to impart."

"Oh really? Well, what about her Francis Bacon painting?" Reba blurted out.

Three jaws dropped simultaneously. Binion's, Terry's, and mine.

"*What* painting?" Binion said, sounding genuinely perplexed.

Reba jumped up and pointed a brick-colored fingernail directly at his nose. "I'm on to you, Mr. Slick! Don't you tell me those rugs were ruined! I know what you've been doing!"

I grabbed Reba by the arm and started dragging her from the office. "I'm sorry, Mr. Binion. She's been under a lot of stress—"

"You stabbed Suzie Magnuson, didn't you?" Reba shouted as Terry seized her other arm. Reba wrestled against our grip, trying desperately to break free and rip Binion's face off. Her own face was purple, the muscles of her neck straining through her mottled skin.

"She doesn't know what she's saying," Terry assured Binion. "She's on medication . . . for Alzheimer's!"

A crowd was gathering in the hallway outside Binion's office, a wall of gray silk and striped ties and curious faces. Binion's pert secretary had just arrived with a tray full of water glasses, frowning in confusion.

"Killer of defenseless women!" Reba screamed, spittle spraying from her mouth. "Rug stealer! Art thief!"

I grabbed one of the glasses of water from the secretary's tray and jerked it in Reba's direction, sloshing its entire contents in her face.

She sputtered and spat, blinking her eyes and wiping the water from the front of her blouse in stunned silence. Then she looked up at Terry and me with a shit-eating grin.

"Oh my," she said.

"Oh yeah," I said, reaching over to grab her purse from the chair.

"I guess we'll be going now," Terry said. "Thanks, 'bye!"

We hustled our way through the throng of stunned on-lookers, who parted like the Red Sea to let the psychotic woman pass unimpeded. I looked back over my shoulder at Binion, who had stood to watch us go. His hands were clenched at his side and he was shaking with rage.

And the look in his eyes made me want to run and hide.

ten

  erry drove, while Reba repaired her makeup in the backseat of the Mercedes. As soon as we were out of the garage, I called Eli Weintraub on our cell phone. Eli was my mentor in the PI business and surrogate daddy. He was also a lawyer of great renown, at least among the criminal classes.

I was put through immediately.

"Eli, it's Kerry. You busy?"

"Never too busy for you, doll."

"Listen, I need a little help with something. Could we come by? We're in the neighborhood."

"Who's we?"

"Me, Terry, and Aunt Reba."

"I'm finally gonna meet the famous Aunt Reba?"

"Yeah," I said, "she's really looking forward to it."

The truth is, I had avoided putting the two of them

together for years. I was sure that Reba would think Eli a to-tal slob, with his decades-old polyester suits, scuffed wingtips and perpetual five-o'clock shadow, and I didn't want to risk hurting his feelings when she looked down her delicate nose at him. But the times had changed. Reba had just made slan-derous accusations against a Beverly Hills bigwig, and she was hardly in a position to be choosy about who rode in to her rescue.

"I'm with a scumbag," Eli said matter-of-factly, "be free in ten minutes." He hung up.

A "scumbag" meant a client who was a criminal defen-dant. Similarly, Eli referred to his divorce clients as "idiots." The names were apt, since the scumbags usually *were* guilty of whatever they'd been charged with, and the idiots usually *had* been totally blind to the faults of their spouses. But it never ceased to amaze me that Eli got away with essentially insulting his clients to their faces. The truth was that his was such a naturally foul mouth, and the names and impreca-tions sounded so much like his normal speech, that no one ever appeared to notice.

We pulled up to Eli's office building and I could tell right away that Reba was unimpressed. It was a utilitarian sixties high-rise, the planters beside the entrance full of dead stalks, with no doorman, not even a parking valet. This wasn't the skeeviest of Los Angeles neighborhoods—they certainly came more rundown and past-their-prime than this—but the "Mid-Wilshire" district was one of the more nondescript. There was absolutely nothing Hollywoody or beachy or rus-tic or postmodern about it, nothing to distinguish it like other areas of LA.

We opened the door on the tenth floor office and Priscilla jumped up from her desk to greet us. "Honey, how are you?" she said, grabbing Terry in a bear hug. "It's been too long."

"Hey, Priss. Over here," I said.

"Oh, sorry," she said, blushing. "I can never tell you two apart."

Priscilla was one of those extremely capable people who juggle work duties like dinner plates, never letting one crash to the floor. Now in her mid-thirties, she served as receptionist, legal secretary, office manager, and cook—the backbone of Eli's one-man firm. I had worked with her for three years, and she'd become a good friend and confidante during the rough years after our dad died, when Terry hit the skids. I didn't see Priss that much since I'd gone out on my own, but whenever we did get together it felt just like old times.

She hugged me, then shook Reba's hand.

"So nice to meet you," Priscilla said to Reba, her plastic Mardi Gras bracelets clattering.

"And you, dear." Reba's lips pursed as she took in Priscilla's white vinyl hip-hugging miniskirt, hot pink pumps, and long platinum hair extensions with purple stripes. The nose ring didn't seem to be doing much for Reba, either.

"Eli's on the phone right now," Priscilla said, kneeling on an ergonomic chair that looked like a torture device for joints. "But you can go on in."

I led the way to Eli's office. He jumped up, phone to his ear, and leaned over the cluttered desk to plant a kiss on my cheek, simultaneously waving at Terry. Then he turned his attention to Reba.

"Reba, at last," he said, taking her hand to kiss it.

She looked pleased, if a little conflicted, at his gallantry.

"Have a seat, ladies. I'll be right with you."

Reba peered into the threadbare seat of a chair as if checking it for dirt or lice, then gave it a little brush and sat down, straightening her skirt.

I looked at Eli as he spoke on the phone, trying to see him as Reba must be seeing him—objectively, without the smoky lens of my affection. He was like a sixty-five-year-old human tuber, a big round middle tapering up to sloped shoulders and a pointed head with thinning black hair. His big nose was cratered with pockmarks, his green and red suspenders clashed with his pink Oxford shirt and navy suit, and he reeked of expensive stogies and cheap cologne.

All in all, Eli Weintraub was one of the least glamorous guys you could ever meet. But without a doubt one of the best and the smartest.

He finished up his conversation. "Yeah, yeah. I know," he said into the phone. "These things happen . . . Now take care of that cold, and *don't* kill anybody else, okay? Later."

He hung up and smiled at us, hands open wide. "Now, what can I do for you lovely ladies?"

Where to begin?

I gave him the short version.

We were working for Lenore Richling. We'd seen a valuable painting in her house before she died. We suspected her executor, Hugh Binion, of taking the painting. We went to Binion's office and Reba had accused him outright of stealing it.

I toned down Reba's outburst to leave her a little dignity, not mentioning the water in the face, for example, or the banshee screeching. I did say that she'd raised her voice while making pointed accusations and that there was quite an assemblage of witnesses outside the office by the time we left.

Eli slapped his thigh and congratulated Reba. "Good for you! I only wish I coulda seen the motherfucker's face when you lit into him!"

Reba smiled and blushed, apparently reveling in her new role: muckraker of motherfuckers. She even seemed to be enjoying Eli's colorful use of language. *As seen on TV!*

"Binion seemed furious when we left," I said. "Mad enough to kill."

"Nah," Eli said. "He's highly unethical, but he doesn't kill people. He couldn't bleed 'em dry with his fees if he did."

"He represented two of Reba's friends," Terry chimed in, "and both women ended up dead."

"Who's the other woman?"

"Suzie Magnuson," I said. "Another—sorry Reba—rich Beverly Hills widow. We have it from a source on the BHPD that she was murdered."

"Listen, don't get me wrong," Eli said, leaning back in his chair. "I detest Binion, and I have no trouble believing he stole your painting. But you're gonna have to look some-place else for your widow killer. It's just not his style."

Reba made a disappointed face.

"I'm assuming this painting is worth a lot," Eli said, "if he bothered to steal it."

"Millions," I confirmed.

"The guy who painted it is dead?" I nodded. "Say no more. Now, let me get the chronology straight here. You girls were initially hired by the lady who had the painting in her house, right?"

Terry nodded. "Lenore Richling. She originally wanted us to retrieve some money her new husband had run away with."

"Which you did?"

"Right," I said.

"And what happened to the husband?"

"Oh, uh. He's . . . *gone*."

Eli scrunched up his brow. "Who sent him packing?"

"We don't know," I said, glancing at Reba—signaling to Eli that she didn't know about Mario's death.

Eli looked at Reba and cleared his throat. "Well, what about Richling? Did she . . . stamp his ticket?"

Reba was openly staring at me now.

"Uh, no," I said. "Not personally. She couldn't have. She

was recuperating from a face-lift with her Pomeranian in a hotel room at the time."

"What the fuck's a Pomeranian?" Eli said.

"It's like a Chihuahua," Terry told him. "Only hairier."

Eli's eyes popped, then he exploded with laughter. "*Ah-haaaaaa-haa-ha!* Recuperating from a face-lift in a hotel room with a hairy Chihuahua? Forty years in the business, and that's the absolute best alibi I ever heard!"

Just then Priscilla buzzed him on the phone. " 'Scuse me, I gotta take this," he said to us, still guffawing. He punched a button. "Hey, Jerry!" he said into the receiver. "By any chance, were you recuperating from a face-lift with a hairy Chihuahua in a hotel room when your wife's head got bashed in? Ha ha. Didn't think so. Just kidding. Call you back in ten."

He slammed down the phone and honked into a handkerchief, wiped his eyes, and then attempted to pull a straight face.

"Forgive me," he said. "Please continue."

"Just a moment," Reba snapped. "I'm not completely thick. Obviously, Mario's dead. Why the devil didn't you girls tell me?"

"Sorry," Terry said. "You've been on a need-to-know basis on some of this."

"Well, thanks for the vote of confidence!"

This from the woman who'd virtually blown our whole investigation in the past hour with her flapping gums.

"You weren't on the team when Mario got killed," I explained.

"Oh." She looked somewhat appeased. "But if he's dead, who killed him?"

I sighed. "We have no idea."

"So how'd you find out about it?" Eli said.

"Someone was shot as we were leaving the apartment he

was in. We saw on the news that a young unidentified Latino had been shot and killed there."

Eli gave us a wise look. "So you don't even really know that it *was* Mario. I mean, if he was unidentified."

I frowned. "Not . . . a hundred percent, I guess."

"Has anybody contacted you about it," Eli asked. "The police?"

"Not yet. I thought we should go to them and make a report—" I gave Terry an accusatory look, "but we didn't."

"Why not?"

Terry glared back at me. "Because we broke into the apartment and took Lenore's ten thousand dollars, which could be construed as theft," she said. "And we could also be pegged as suspects in his murder."

"Excellent thinking! I guess I taught you something." Eli beamed at me. I saw Terry smirking in my peripheral vision.

Reba blinked in our direction. "Did you say you have ten thousand dollars of Lenore's money?"

Busted.

I shrank down in my seat. "Well, technically, we only have around eight thousand of hers. She owed us the other two as a recovery fee."

"Yeah," Terry said, "we were only keeping the rest for her while she was in the hospital, but I guess the proper thing would be to turn it over to the estate, to that nice Mr. Binion—"

"You'll do no such thing!" Reba said.

"Or we could give it to Lenore's favorite charity . . ." I put in.

Reba made a disdainful face. "Lenore was Lenore's favorite charity. You girls keep that money and buy yourselves some decent clothes. I won't have you going around in rags."

Whew. We were safe from the county comptroller, and with an almost clear conscience, too.

I then told Eli about seeing Lenore in the hospital, and her desperate plea that we pass a message to Hattrick's former assistant, who was a Russian immigrant. I explained that when we gave her the message, the Russian woman claimed to have no idea what we were talking about.

"We think we've stumbled onto a massive conspiracy, involving blackmail and prescription drugs and these dead widows," Terry said.

Eli frowned and sat forward, planting his forearms on the desk.

"Lenore may have been blackmailing Dr. Hattrick, the plastic surgeon," she continued. "And we think the plastic surgeon might be involved in a drug ring that operates out of the Dauphine Hotel."

"Wait, hold on," Eli said. "A drug ring in a hotel?"

Terry nodded. "It's a kind of halfway house for Beverly Hills broads who've had plastic surgery. We saw Suzie Magnuson leaving the hotel with a gift basket, and then later when we found her body, she was surrounded by painkillers. They were spilling out of these plastic vials—"

"Hold it hold it hold it! What does all of this have to do with Binion?"

Binion. He said it with such venom. I wondered if there was more to Eli's dislike of the man than simple resentment of his pricey law practice, his fancy clients, his European suits.

"Well, nothing yet," I said. "But he may be tied in."

Reba spoke up. "As we said, he represented both Suzie Magnuson *and* Lenore Richling. We think the painting in question may have actually belonged to Suzie. I'd seen it on several occasions at her house, and made the connection to the one the girls saw at Lenore's."

Eli gave Reba an approving nod. "Excellent."

She smiled and brushed the hair back from her forehead coquettishly.

"So maybe Lenore was also blackmailing Suzie, and took the Bacon as payment," I said. "And Binion was in on it all somehow, and—"

"Whoa whoa whoa!" Eli said, waving a pudgy hand in the air. He shook his head, jowls flapping violently. "What *proof* do you have of any of this?"

Proof?

I swallowed hard. "Um. None, really."

"You girls are all over the place. You got Binion drug dealing and blackmailing and stealing paintings from dead women, and you've got your auntie believing all this and making accusations, without even a shred of evidence?"

He stared directly at me. I looked down at my khakis, brushing off some imaginary dust.

"Well, it kinda makes sense . . ." I started to say.

"Okay, but you don't go accusing politically connected Beverly Hills lawyers of theft, and you don't go finding monsters under the beds of hotshot plastic surgeons until you got the goods! Jeez. What did I teach you?"

We sat in silence for a while, lambasted and completely humiliated in front of our employer, who also happened to be our great-aunt. I felt like a boob and a loser. A loser boob.

I decided to take the focus off me.

"Why do you hate Binion so much?" I asked Eli. "What did he ever do to you?"

He swiveled in his chair, hoisting up his legs and plopping the worn heels of his wingtips on the desk. His pants hiked up to his calves and we were treated to a glimpse of what looked like rolled dough sprouting bristly black hairs.

"Well, I hate him on principle 'cause he makes much more money than I do. But also, he stole a client from me a few months ago, which is a big ethical no-no. I thought it was funny—Binion's business is strictly white-collar scumbags, know what I mean? What did he want with my creep from the streets? But he goes in and makes a pitch to the guy that he won't have to do time if Binion takes his case, right when I was in the middle of negotiating a plea bargain."

"Does Binion still represent him?"

"Well, that's the beauty part. He takes the scumbag on as a client, and I'm left with egg on my face with the DA. Then as soon as he's in Binion's tender care, the guy disappears, never to be heard from again."

"He was out on bond and skipped?" Terry asked.

"Exactamundo."

"Huh," I said. "What was the guy charged with?"

"International drug trafficking."

"Heroin?"

"No." Eli blinked once or twice. He scratched his nose. Something was gnawing at his consciousness.

"What, then?"

"Uh, prescription drugs," he said. "Hijacked painkillers from Canada."

"Hmm," Terry said. "That's an interesting coincidence. But I wouldn't want to jump to any conclusions or anything."

"Yeah—no," Eli stammered. "That kind of thing goes on all the time."

"Right," I said. "So what was the scumbag's name, just out of curiosity?"

"His name? Oh, it's a—" he cleared his throat, "it was a Russian name, come to think of it. Who was the guy that tortured dogs with bells and shit?"

"Pavlov?" Terry and I said in tandem.

Eli stabbed the air with his finger. "That's it," he said, grinning.

Okay, in all fairness to Eli, we hadn't mentioned Tatiana Pavlov's name. If we had, it might have precipitated a cascade of connections in his mind. We learned that *his* Pavlov was named Sergei. Thirty-two years old and part of a big wave of Russian immigrants during the eighties. A known felon who'd bounced in and out of the penal system starting at the age of fifteen.

Eli described him as slender and wiry, on the short side, with blue, soulless eyes. He'd never mentioned a sister or a wife, or any female relative, so we couldn't establish a definitive link between Sergei Pavlov the international drug trafficker and Tatiana Pavlov, the "medical assistant" in Hattrick's office. But the common last name seemed more than coincidental.

The good news was that we now had a partner and ally in Eli. He was intrigued by the idea that Binion might be involved in some indictable criminal activity, and he was more than happy to help us bring home the Bacon.

"I'll leave things in your capable hands," Reba said to Eli as we stepped into the hallway, seeming buoyed by his interest in the case. "I'm off to plan Lenore's memorial. There's so much to do."

It was the first I'd heard of it. "You're planning her funeral?"

"Yes. The hospital confirmed that she died of a thrombosis, a not uncommon occurrence, sadly, after cosmetic surgery. So I'm having her body transferred to the crematorium."

I must have made a face, because Reba put a hand on my arm. "There's really no one else," she said. "Lenore deserves better than to go into that good night without a remembrance. No matter what she'd got into recently, she was a dear friend at one time."

"Hey, that's aces," Eli said. "Really decent of you."

Reba blushed again. "Ta," she said, heading down the hallway.

"Toodle-oo," Eli said, wagging his fingers at her.

" 'Bye, Reba," we said.

And with that she slipped into the elevator, waving at Eli once again.

Eli gave us access to his stealth weapon, Greg Adams, a law clerk and investigator who worked out of Eli's office, and who had a genius for dealing with people. When I had been employed by Eli, Greg usually worked the phones and I did the legwork.

At first glance, Greg defined the word "nerd." He was in his late twenties, tall and scrawny, with a too-big shirt collar around a pencil neck, and traces of teenage acne still scattered across his cheeks. But he had the patience of a Zen master and the soul of a Yakuza assassin.

He had amassed an incredible Rolodex over the last seven years, which he kept on a state-of-the-art PDA, and he could put his hand on the most amazing, arcane sources of information you could ever want due to his uncanny knack for cultivating personal contacts.

He billed Eli yearly for thousands of dollars in gifts, flowers, and liquor for weddings, christenings, Christmas, Ha–nukkah, bar mitzvahs, anniversaries, and probably Flag Day celebrations. He had the important dates meticulously recorded for all of his contacts in various bureaucracies, agencies, private business, and on the streets, and he never, ever, missed a life event, no matter how small. He always made people feel valued, thus there was always someone willing to give him valuable information for the asking.

He was also relentless in his efforts to get me to sleep with him.

Within two hours of catching our case, Greg had landed some interesting scoop on the doctor. Hattrick had been investigated by the Medical Board of California, and the results had been sealed. But not well enough to keep Greg out. He ushered us into his office excitedly.

"What'd you get?" I asked him.

He gave me a crooked smile, waggling his eyebrows. "What's it worth to you?"

"Greg, we've been through this before," I said. "We're colleagues. I don't mix business with pleasure."

"Oh, right," he said, turning his attention to Terry. "How 'bout it, Ter? Still batting for the other team?"

She gave him a warning look.

"*Kidding!* Just wanted to see if you were paying attention," he said, straightening some files on his desk. "Okay, here's what we've got on your doctor . . ."

He opened the top file and began to fill us in. It appeared that Hattrick had been reported to the board by a former nurse named Tish Werner who lived in an apartment on Doheny Drive. Ms. Werner's allegations had been nothing short of bizarre.

She contended that Hattrick had decided his eyes needed a lift, and he had performed the operation on his own lids while looking in a mirror.

"He botched it," Greg said. "I mean, how could you know how much flesh to take from the very eyes you were looking out of? He took too much, and as a result, he has perpetually open eyes."

"My God," Terry said. "That's exactly what Reba told us! He wore dark glasses and he never blinked his eyes!"

"He's operating on people with eyes that never shut?" I said.

Greg shrugged. "He should have been defrocked, but he had some high-priced legal talent, a guy named Hugh Binion—"

Terry slapped the arms of her chair. "That's beautiful!"

"What?"

"Binion represents everyone in this scenario. Our conspiracy is really shaping up. Sergei gets the drugs, the doc distributes them, and the shyster Binion keeps them all out of prison."

"Well, Binion definitely got the doc off the hook. Hattrick passed peer review, probably on the grounds that he hadn't hurt an actual patient, and there was nobody to sue but himself."

"Unbelievable," I said.

"But here's the best part," Greg said. "This is hot off the medical grapevine. Hattrick became a hopeless drug addict. Because of his eye thing he was using drops containing narcotics—"

"Which breed tolerance," Terry said.

"Yeah, and soon he moved up to pills, as many as twenty a day—eighty-milligram tablets. Finally, he started shooting up morphine."

"Jesus," Terry said. "Everyone knew this and he was still practicing medicine?"

"You know doctors," Greg said. "They'd rather turn in their own mothers than rat on a colleague."

"But there'd be a limit to what he could prescribe to himself without raising suspicions," I said.

Terry nodded. "So he tapped into a prescription drug ring, fronted by Sergei Pavlov. And that's how he came to hire Tatiana."

Which brought us back to the Russian beauty.

"So who is Tatiana to Sergei?" Terry said. "A sister? His wife?"

"I'll look into it," Greg said. "See if there's a marriage record. And if I come up with some invaluable piece of information . . . ?" he asked, hope springing eternal.

"We'll see you in your dreams," Terry said, giving him a wink.

eleven

$\mathcal{I}$n the course of his sleuthing, Greg turned up an interesting tidbit on Sergei Pavlov's personal life. He had indeed married one Tatiana Dmitriyevna, but she had instituted divorce proceedings immediately after his arrest. A fair-weather wife, it seemed. Greg also discovered that she'd moved out of the apartment on Argyle Avenue a week before Mario was killed, but he couldn't find a current address of record.

By four o'clock, we were brain-numb from grubbing after blackmailers and drug dealers. We gave Eli a briefing, and Greg went back to working on another case for the rest of the day. Terry and I were left sitting alone in the small conference room beside Eli's office, drinking coffee from Styrofoam cups, pondering the situation.

"Sounds like Tatiana's out of it," I said. "She bailed on her husband *and* on the doctor. Hit the road."

"She still could have murdered Mario." Terry had kicked

back in one of the gray pleather chairs, her long legs and chunky black biker boots resting on the table.

"Maybe. But she didn't strike me as the murdering type. Women like that are usually content to slay people with their looks."

"I wonder why Janice was meeting with her? Especially after all the not-nice things she had to say about her."

I shrugged. "Maybe they were dishing the doc. They could have been discussing strategies for dealing with the lawsuits—"

Terry suddenly sat up, excited. "Listen, why don't we call Janice and see if we can get her to admit to the drug thing."

"You think she's involved?"

"She's the office manager. She has to know what's going on. She's in charge of the drug supply, knows every package that comes in or goes out."

"Yeah, but why would she tell us? Why would she give up her boss?"

"Because she likes us. And she doesn't like *him*."

"You've got a high opinion of us," I said, raising an eyebrow.

"Besides, the police are bound to connect Suzie's death with the funny stuff going on at the hotel, which will lead them directly to Hattrick. We should tell Janice what we think we know, then let her decide if she wants to go to the cops herself. Turn state's evidence or something. Especially if they get the doc for murder."

It was the first time either of us had said it out loud. Had the doctor murdered Suzie Magnuson? And possibly, in some invisible way, Lenore Richling?

"You think a prominent plastic surgeon would go around murdering his patients?" I asked.

"It's not a big leap from maiming your patients to killing them, is it?"

She had a point.

"Okay," I said, "I'll get Janice on the phone."

I called Hattrick's office, announcing myself as Ms. McAfee and using a fake, high-society voice, hoping the receptionist wouldn't remember me or see through my attempted disguise. She told me Janice couldn't come to the phone, so I gave her our cell phone number and hung up.

Terry looked out the window. "I feel like we're leaving loose ends somewhere. Something's bothering me."

"Well, perhaps it's time for the diagram," I said, pulling it out.

"Yippee, the diagram!" She pushed back from the table with her foot, spinning herself in the swivel chair. "We're having some fun now!"

"Do shut up."

I'd been tinkering with my "case graph" for the past couple of days, and it was a mess of crisscrossed lines and arcs. It looked like someone had done his geometry homework on acid.

"Okay, we got Hattrick, Sergei, Tatiana, and Binion, all connected to each other, and all associated with Lenore, Suzie, and Mario," I said.

"And Alphonse. Don't forget Alphonse," she said, getting interested in spite of herself.

"He's a second banana."

She tapped the pad with her finger. "Humor me."

I drew an arc between Alphonse and Hattrick, sketching a picture of a banana underneath.

"And you need to indicate who's dead now."

I drew a skull and crossbones next to Mario, Lenore, and Suzie. As I did, Suzie's name popped out at me.

"Suzie's the wild card," I announced.

"Why do you say that?"

"She may have been both victim and perpetrator, know what I mean?"

"No. 'Splain me."

"A perpetrator in the sense that she was working with Lenore and Mario on blackmail or whatever dirty doings they had their hands in. But what if they turned on her for some reason and killed her, making her a victim?"

"Why?"

"I don't know, a case of dishonor among scumbags?"

Terry sighed and leaned on the table. "Look, we think it was her painting that was at Lenore's house. We know she was murdered. And we know she reported a break-in prior to her murder—"

"Right!"

"What?"

I dug through my pockets and found the card I'd gotten from Sidney Lefler of Whitechapel Mutual. "Let's call this Sidney guy and see if we can nail him down on the painting. He might be able to give us a gigantic piece of the puzzle."

Priss drove us home to pick up our bike, and within an hour we were back on the road going east.

We took the 10 Freeway to the Pasadena Freeway, curving past the Staples center, and hooked a right on Sixth Street, then a left onto South Grand on the western edge of downtown LA. There are a lot of "downtowns" in the area, since most of what people think of as LA is actually a bunch of small towns connected by the freeway system: Century City, Culver City, Pasadena, Burbank, Santa Monica, and so on.

But downtown LA is the mother of all area downtowns, the one with high-rise buildings, public artworks and fountains, the Mark Taper Forum and the Disney Concert Hall, a garment district, a financial district, and ethnic neighborhoods like Little Tokyo, Chinatown, and El Pueblo. There's lots of hustle and bustle during the workday, but at night it's as lively as Tombstone, Arizona. The professional types head back to the West Side or the Valley, the wind whistles through the high-rises and trash blows down the deserted streets, and gun- and knife-slingers come out to infest the night with mayhem. At the moment, though, it was full of people in suits and sensible shoes toting leather briefcases, blabbing on cell phones, rushing to their meetings, as buttoned-down and slick as the denizens of midtown Manhattan. You'd never know they coexisted with the fruits, flakes, and nuts of California legend.

We hung a left on Fifth Street and pulled into the underground garage of a granite skyscraper, then took the elevator up to the lobby. There we caught the express, whizzing up twenty-one floors to the offices of Whitechapel Mutual.

Sidney met us in the lobby. "Hey, good to see you again," he said, extending a hand. "Didn't expect the pleasure this soon. Come into my office."

He turned and headed down the hall with short, quick strides. Terry and I fell in behind, following him until we reached a cubbyhole of an office that was crammed with map books, camera equipment, and volumes on every conceivable subject from anatomy to biology, metallurgy to stamp collecting. It would have been suffocating, but for his window on the world—a floor-to-ceiling pane of tinted glass that gave us a view all the way to the snow-tipped San Gabriel Mountains.

He plunked himself down behind his desk, the vinyl executive chair *whooshing* as he sat due to a hole in the cushion. He pulled up an Igloo cooler and opened it on his desk, displaying a range of soft drinks and a couple of sandwiches.

"Drink?"

"We don't want to drink your lunch," Terry said.

"It's not my lunch, it's my stash. I take it with me when I do surveillance."

"You do a lot of that?" I asked, as we each took a bottle of spring water.

"It's what I do most of the time. Investigating injury claims, theft claims, that kind of thing."

"We've done our share of surveillance, too," I said, glad we could establish a rapport along these lines.

"So what can I do for you today?" he asked, looking magnanimous.

Terry sandbagged him. "You can tell us the truth about Suzie Magnuson's claim."

So much for rapport.

Sidney blanched and leaned against his desk. "Th-the truth? What do you mean, the truth?"

"She reported something stolen other than the silver, didn't she?"

He frowned and hunched his shoulders. "Who do you represent, again?"

"We represent our aunt, who was a friend of Suzie's," Terry said. "Two of her women friends have met with an ugly end in the past few days, and we're trying to find out why."

"I see." His nose twitched and his eyes darted, giving him the furtive look of a ferret in human drag.

"How did you get to the scene of Suzie's death so quickly?" I said.

He leaned back in his chair and made a temple out of his hands. "Can I expect reciprocity?"

Terry looked at me. "Yes," I said. "You tell us what you know, we'll tell you what we know."

Some of it, anyway.

"I had her under surveillance," Sidney told us.

Terry's mouth fell open. "Who, Suzie Magnuson?"

"Yeah. She had submitted a theft claim on a valuable painting—"

"A Francis Bacon," I said, and immediately heard his foot thumping under the desk. At least I hoped it was his foot. I was relieved to note that both hands were present and accounted for above the desk, nervously worrying a pencil.

"Yes. How did you—?"

"In a minute," Terry said. "Please, go on."

He tapped his lip with the pencil eraser. "There were questionable aspects to the case. She put in a claim of three million, but the company was stalling on payment in the hopes the painting would be recovered."

"What were the questionable aspects?" I said.

"The whole thing was hinky. She made a police report of a break-in, but there was no sign of forced entry. The maid and the chauffeur both had the evening off, said they went to a movie and dinner. But when they were asked what movie they had seen, they had a sudden attack of amnesia. Couldn't remember the story, who was in it, nothing. They said that they were tired and overworked, and may have slept through most of it."

"Uh-huh," Terry said, smiling. "Pretty hinky, all right."

"But the police found a letter of resignation from them, dated Tuesday. That's the day they estimate Mrs. Magnuson . . . died. I actually saw them hustling away with their suitcases earlier in the day."

"Do the police consider them suspects in her murder?"

He hitched up his eyebrows curiously.

"We know she was killed," I told him.

"How'd you find out?"

"Confidential source," Terry said.

"Well, the servants haven't been ruled out completely, and they're certainly suspects in the attempt to defraud Whitechapel. But as of yet, they haven't been located."

"Where was Mrs. Magnuson when the alleged burglary occurred?" I said.

"She claimed she was playing canasta with some other ladies, and it checked out."

Terry gave me a quick sideways glance. "So how long had you had her under surveillance?"

"For a few weeks, ever since she reported the burglary. The day her body was discovered, I'd been pulled away. I had to run over to another house to do an inspection, and I guess that's when you found her."

"Do the police know about your surveillance?" I said.

"Hell, yeah. They've got my tape from the night of the murder. I got an image of someone going into her house."

"You did?" we both said at once.

He nodded, pleased. Then his smile turned down. "Unfortunately, whoever it was is dressed in dark clothes and a hat, and his face isn't visible. They have their experts working on it right now, or I'd show it to you."

"Amazing," I said.

"Okay, your turn. How did you know about the Bacon?" he said, squinting at us.

"We saw it at the home of another friend of our aunt's, Lenore Richling."

"Are you fucking kidding me?" He clamped a hand over his mouth, suddenly conscious of appropriate office conduct. "Sorry."

He jumped up from his desk to close the door, then rushed back to his seat and *whooshed* into it, oblivious of the comic effect. "I was *at* Lenore Richling's when the call came through about Mrs. Magnuson!"

"You insured Mrs. Richling, too?" Terry asked him.

"Yeah, it was all set up through her lawyer."

I looked over at Terry. "Hugh Binion?" I said.

"Yeah," Sidney said, laughing. "*Puke Pinhead*, I call him."

We laughed along with him, and it eased the tension in the small room.

"So, this is great," Sidney said. "Is the painting still there?" I heard his foot thumping again, and realized he was practically jumping up and down at the prospect of running over to Lenore's to recover the painting. He probably got a bonus in cases like this, and though I hated to disappoint him, I hoped our news would stop the thumping. It was making me feel like he was slightly unhinged.

"No," I told him. "It's gone."

"Oh." The thumping ceased and his facial muscles went flaccid with disappointment.

"Our aunt was Lenore Richling's beneficiary," I explained to him. "She was supposed to inherit the contents of the house. We took her over there the morning after Lenore died, but the painting had apparently been stolen."

"Shit, not again!" He pounded the desk. "Can you describe it to me?" he asked to be sure. "The painting you saw at Mrs. Richling's?"

"Yeah, it was a man seated on a wooden chair, with a kind of floating smile. He was facing down into the left-hand corner of the canvas."

"You an art major?"

"No, but I did take an art history class at UCLA, and I recognized the style and some of Bacon's trademark items, like the watch, the cigarette butts, and the naked lightbulb."

Sidney wasn't convinced. He reached over into his filing cabinet and riffled through some hanging files, pulling out a color slide. He handed it to me, and I held it up to the light of the window.

"That's definitely the painting I saw," I said, feeling my shoulders loosen. I would have felt like the world's biggest dingbat if I'd been wrong about the whole thing.

"So what's going to happen to the claim for three million?" Terry said.

Sidney shrugged. "If we can't recover the painting, it'll become part of Mrs. Magnuson's estate. It's being administrated by Binion, and he's after us big time for the money. Threatening to sue and everything."

"Just out of curiosity, did Mrs. Magnuson have any heirs?" I asked.

Sidney smiled and shook his head. He knew where I was going with this.

"So," I continued, "Binion's in charge of the estates of two recently deceased women whose deaths were untimely, to say the least. And the missing painting will add three million to the kitty."

"Looks that way," Sidney said with a fatalistic sneer.

"This just keeps getting hinkier, doesn't it?" Terry said.

There wasn't much more to say. We got up to leave, promising to let him know if we got any good scoop. He said he'd do the same, especially when it came to the identification of a suspect in Suzie Magnuson's murder.

But when we got to the door, I had a sudden inspiration.

"Hey, do you mind if we have a look at that police report?" I asked Sidney. "The original one for the break-in at Suzie Magnuson's house, when she reported the Bacon stolen?"

"Sure." He rustled through some more files and produced the report.

I scanned it quickly, noting the time and date of the report, the claim of theft, the chauffeur and maid's statements, etc. Then I saw something that almost made me jump.

I handed the report to Terry and pointed to the names of the responding officers. One of them was Dinah Lott.

"What?" Sidney said, seeing my obvious interest.

"Nothing." I handed the report back to him. "Just a little déjà vu. Thanks a lot, Sidney."

Terry and I left the office in thoughtful silence and remained that way during the twenty-one-floor trip down to the garage.

"Pretty interesting, Dinah being the responding officer at Suzie's fake burglary," I said when we got to the bike.

"What of it?"

"I don't know. It just seems funny that she took the burglary report and was also there directing traffic after Suzie was killed."

"Yeah, but she's a cop, it's her beat. Beverly Hills is only a couple of miles square."

"But when she was pretending to be so open with us at Barney's, she was actually withholding an important piece of information—the burglary at Suzie's house."

"Hey, she gave us more than we gave *her*," Terry said, swinging her leg over the bike.

I shrugged. "So Suzie was defrauding the insurance company, with the help of her buddy Lenore."

"Three million would buy a lot of umbrella drinks on the Riviera."

"Was that the Big Payout?" I wondered. "They were waiting for the insurance company to come through on the claim?"

"Don't know," Terry said, revving the engine. "Sounds like there was a lot of red tape and a possible legal hassle. Maybe when they realized it wouldn't be so quick in coming, they went for another big kill."

"And got themselves killed for it."

twelve

Terry said she'd felt the cell phone vibrating in her pocket while we were on the freeway, but decided to answer the call from home.

We opened the front door and were greeted by our new little pets, who wiggled their little behinds in excitement, licking our hands and prancing around at our feet. When we got through petting them, Terry checked the display window on the cell phone and found a return number that neither of us recognized.

"Hmmm," Terry said. "Want to take a flyer on who the mystery caller is?"

I held up my hands. "I can't begin to guess."

"Maybe it's Janice, ready to spill the beans on the whole drug-dispensing operation."

"As if," I said, rolling my eyes. "Probably a phone solicitor."

I picked up the extension to listen in as Terry dialed the number from the land line. To my surprise, Janice did indeed answer (chalk up another one for Terry's intuition), but she was clearly not in the doctor's office.

"I'm at a pay phone in the coffee shop," Janice said, sounding bone-weary. "I didn't want anyone to know I was talking to you—"

Terry decided to deploy her sandbags straightaway. "We know about the doctor's drug trade, Janice." There was no response, but I thought I heard sniffling on the line. "And there's something else you should know. One of the doctor's customers was found dead—murdered—with a bunch of your goodies in the room."

"Who?" Janice said, sounding like a frightened little girl.

"Suzie Magnuson."

"When?"

"Yesterday."

"My . . . *God*," Janice whispered. "I can't believe this is happening."

"The walls are closing in on you, girl," Terry said, pressing her cruel advantage. "You've got to tell somebody what you know."

"But my *son* . . ." Janice moaned.

I felt a knife go into my gut. "It will be even worse for him if you don't do something," I told her.

She sighed, then seemed to make up her mind. Her voice came out stronger, more resolute. "Can you meet me at the office? I'll show you some things. Evidence. Then maybe you can advise me what to do."

I waved my hands at Terry, frowning.

"Yeah," Terry said into the phone, ignoring me. "We can do that. What time?"

"Come by at eight o'clock. Everyone will be gone."

"What about the doctor?"

Janice made a disgusted sound. "The doctor's in Rio, for all I know. I don't think he's coming back. Don't know why I bother hauling my ass in anymore."

"All right. We'll be there at eight," Terry said. "Keep your chin up. It's going to be okay."

Janice laughed bitterly. "Right."

Afterward, I had a rapid sinking feeling, like something really bad was about to happen. I tried to read Terry's face, to see if she had the feeling, too.

"Was that a little too easy?" I asked her.

She gave me her best *Now what?* glare.

"I didn't expect Janice to roll over that quickly. People don't usually just jump up and implicate themselves in criminal conspiracies."

"That's why you slam them right away," Terry said, as if it were the most obvious thing in the world. "You knock 'em off balance. That way they don't have time to BS you."

I went upstairs to change into some sleuthing clothes, with Terry following along behind me. "But why is she going to confess everything to two women she's met only twice?" I said, as I zipped up my miss sixties jeans, slipping on some raspberry-colored Pumas. I topped it with a hooded pullover.

"Know what I think?" Terry said. "She's been wrestling with her conscience for a long time. She didn't mean to get involved with illegal drug dealing. She's a hardworking single mom who got swept up in things and now she's stuck. She's probably grateful we're forcing her hand, especially if people are getting killed."

"I don't know—"

"Hey, who's the one with the golden gut?"

"You are," I admitted grudgingly. *"Usually."*

"And I'm telling you, Janice is a good egg. Don't worry. She'll make a deal and be outta there with minimum time served. Maybe no time at all, thanks to our early warning."

$\mathcal{S}ince$ *we had* an hour to kill before we met Janice, we decided to go by the Dauphine. We were going to try to talk to the desk clerk and persuade her to open one of the gift baskets for a little peek inside. *Toblerone and OxyContin, anyone?*

We parked a block away so the garage attendant couldn't alert anyone that we were on the way. But we'd have to go in the front door, and there was little doubt that Alphonse would pop up in our faces soon after we got there. If he did present himself, we planned to fake him out. Ask him direct questions about Suzie Magnuson's "overdose" to see if he blanched or stammered or pulled out an ice pick and stabbed us.

This time around, the doorman didn't smile. He picked up a phone next to the outdoor bellhop station and I assumed we'd been fingered, but we walked on into the lobby anyway. The blonde Burger King girl was indeed behind the counter. She looked up without any apparent recognition.

"Hello? May I help you?" Pert and professional.

I was tempted to ask her to supersize our order.

"Hi," Terry said. "We were here a few days ago, visiting the lady who called herself Mrs. Templeton, remember?"

The girl pointed a pen at Terry, wagging it. "Oh, yeah."

"We're fine," I said, even though we hadn't been asked.

"We were here when she had her, you know, ear problem," Terry said.

"Uh-huh." The girl was getting cooler by the second. I read her name tag. *Sandy Gratz.* Might want to rethink that one if she had show business aspirations.

"Well, Sandy," Terry said, "Mrs. 'Templeton' is dead."

"Oh!" Sandy gasped. "Oh, how terrible!"

"And so is Mrs. Suzie Magnuson," I said. "She was here at the same time. Remember her?"

"Mrs. Magnuson OD'd on prescription drugs," Terry added, omitting any mention of the stabbing.

Sandy blinked a few times, her blue eyes wide, cheeks going spotty red.

I felt a tingling at the back of my neck and sensed that

Alphonse was about to appear in a puff of smoke, so I slipped our card onto the counter. Sandy glanced at it, but made no move to pick it up.

"Well, it's *you* again," Alphonse sang as he exited the executive offices behind the registration desk, the place where Sandy had said the baskets were assembled. Out of the corner of my eye, I saw her palm the business card, slipping it into her jacket pocket.

"Hello, Alphonse," Terry said.

"Monsieur Alphonse," he corrected her, and I gathered we were no longer on a first-name basis. "What are you do-*ing* here?"

"We're making a few inquiries," I said.

Alphonse cut his eyes to Sandy. She gave her head a little shake, as if to assure him that she'd said nothing to me.

"I have *nozzing* to say to your inquiries," he said, glaring. "And you are not a guest of *ze* hotel."

"I know," Terry said. "We were thinking we'd go to your lovely piano bar for a little drinky-poo. Care to join us?"

Alphonse gave a curt nod to the doorman. He swung the door wide open, looking like he'd throw us out bodily if we didn't leave by the count of three.

"No, I don't sink *zat's* a good idea. I *sink* you should go somewhere more appropriate for you. *Ze* Airport Holiday Inn, perhaps?"

Terry leaned on the counter and stuck out her chin.

"Sure. Happy to. But we were just wondering—what with Easter coming up and everything—could we buy a few of those gift baskets from you? You know, like the one you sent home with Mrs. Magnuson just before she croaked?"

Alphonse's nostrils flared outward. "*What* are you implying?"

"I'm implying that those gift baskets would make terrific Easter presents," Terry said, all smiling innocence.

"Get out!" Alphonse fairly screamed.

Terry let out an exaggerated sigh. "Oh well, Ker. I guess we'll just have to keep shopping for all those rich old ladies on our list."

She pushed herself away from the counter, eyes fixed on Alphonse's. Then she sauntered toward the front door, pointing to the elaborate flower arrangements that reminded me of science fiction monsters, with their gnarled Japanese twigs, beaked orange flowers, and elephant-ears with the penile protuberances.

"Killer flowers," Terry said, giving Alphonse a little finger wave good-bye. "Ciao!"

When we got back to the bike, Terry was wearing a huge grin. "We hit a nerve, baby. A big hairy nerve."

"Yeah, but what does it get us?" I wondered. "Alphonse won't let us near the place again. We won't be able to talk to the housekeeping staff—"

Terry shrugged. "The girl's got our card. And now she's got the word on a couple of suspicious deaths. She might come back to us with some information."

"Yeah, maybe."

"Also, backing Alphonse in a corner might force him into making a move."

I gulped. "A move on us?"

She punched me in the arm. "Now don't go all wimpy on me. Can you picture Alphonse getting violent? Please. He wouldn't want to muss his suit."

I gave her a game little smile and hopped on the bike, sincerely hoping she was right. It was a very nice suit, but whoever said homicidal maniacs couldn't be snappy dressers, as well?

•   •   •

$\mathcal{W}e$ $\mathit{arrived}$ at Hattrick's office at 7:59. The coffee shop next door was closed. The hallway was dark on the other side of the glass door, which strangely enough, was unlocked.

"Not locked?" I said, as Terry pulled open the door. "At this hour?"

"Janice probably left it open for us." Terry led the way and we walked down to the elevator bank.

"Come on, let's take the stairs," Terry said. "We don't want to risk running into anyone in the elevator."

"Isn't it kind of . . . dark?" I said.

"Scaredy-cat." She entered the stairwell and bounded up the stairs two at a time to show off. I followed, shaking my head, listening to her boots slap the concrete.

She stopped suddenly.

"Uh, Kerry?" she called down to me.

I tensed at the sound of her voice. "Yeah, what is it?"

"Um, blood," she said.

I raced up the stairs and found her on the third-floor landing, Hattrick's floor. She was looking down at a splatter of dark viscous fluid, smeared where someone had stepped in it.

"Holy shit! Did you step in it?"

She turned over her foot to look at the sole of her black leather boot. "Uh-huh."

"Are you sure it's blood?"

"Only one way to find out." She started to pull the boot off her foot.

"Don't you dare touch it!" I said.

She sniffed the sole. "Smells like boot."

"Great."

She got down on her knees and sniffed the liquid on the concrete. Finally, she looked up at me and smiled. "Taco sauce."

"Are you sure?"

"I don't think you want me to tongue it to find out, do you?"

"What's taco sauce doing in the stairwell?"

She got to her feet, shrugging. "We'll see if Janice has a flashlight in the office, then we'll come back for another look, okay?"

She pushed open the door to the third-floor hallway and walked into the pitch blackness.

This didn't feel right.

"Ter?"

"Yeah?"

"Maybe we'd better go back downstairs and get someone to turn on the lights."

"Forget it. Janice is waiting."

"It doesn't look like anybody's here," I said, my voice taking on a shaky timbre. All I wanted to do was run back down the stairs and find a warm, well-lighted place and stay there.

"If she said she'd be here, she'll be here," Terry said, hustling down the hallway toward the office.

The door to the stairwell closed behind me and the ambient light disappeared. I forced air through my constricted throat and followed the sound of Terry's footfall on the carpeting, a muffled sound that spoke of creeping hatchet murderers.

"Here we go," she said, turning the knob on the office door. I ran toward the sound of the squeaking hinges. It, too, was unlocked, the office as dark as an underground cave.

I followed Terry inside and she felt around for the light switch. I heard the rasping of her hands on wallpaper, then all at once she exclaimed, "Got it!"

The lights went on and I covered my eyes. I told myself I was protecting them against the sudden brightness of the lights, but actually I was terrified of what I was going to see.

"Hey chicken drawers," Terry said. "I think you were right. Janice blew us off."

I peeped out between my hands and saw nothing out of the

ordinary. The office was clean and professional-looking. No hate language scrawled on the walls in blood, no body parts lying around. I felt like the world's biggest idiot. This reminded me of a childhood incident when Terry and I had let our imaginations run away with us. "Hey, this is like the time when we were kids, and we convinced ourselves that aliens had landed in the hallway in the middle of the night 'cause we heard their spaceship creaking, remember? And it turned out to be the hamster running in his wheel?"

Terry rolled her eyes dramatically. "I seem to remember that the alien theory was yours. I thought it was the rusty garden gate making the noise."

She was full of it, of course. We had *both* been convinced we were about to be sucked up in an electromagnetic beam and used as twin guinea pigs in unspeakable alien experiments. But she'd never admit it.

"Janice?" Terry called through the glass of the reception window. "Janice, it's us!"

Obviously, Janice had had a change of heart. She'd sounded confession-minded when we spoke to her, but she'd thought better of taking us into her confidence.

Still, it didn't seem likely that she'd leave the front door of the office unlocked. Terry pushed on the door to the inner office. "Come on," she said.

"That's not locked, either?" I said, wary. "That's strange. I mean, what about all the drugs? It seems odd that someone would leave the door to the office . . . Hey, wait for me!"

I followed her into more darkness. The odor of antiseptic permeated the white linoleum floors and walls, the sterility of the inner office contrasting sharply with the lush waiting room outside. And the shadows in the hallway made me think of any number of horror films I'd seen that were set in hospitals and mental institutions. Funny thing about those places, no one ever worked there at night. Just like this.

In real hospitals, of course, there's more noise and activity than in an airline terminal. And someone's always barging in every two hours all cheerful and apologetic about waking you up out of a sound sleep, poking you in the butt with a needle the size of an electric drill bit. Who needed Chuckie or Jason or Leatherface when you had nurses and doctors licensed to stab, maim, and kill?

Terry found a light switch and flipped it on. A buzzing accompanied the blinking fluorescents, which formed a pool of unnatural green light next to the reception desk. But the rest of the clinic remained dark. Further down the hallway, we could make out an examining room, its door open a crack.

"Janice?" Terry called again, walking toward the open door.

I heard a rustling at the end of the hallway. I grabbed the back of Terry's jacket. "Did you hear that?" I whispered.

"Nuh-uh," she said, straining to listen.

"There's someone there, and they're not answering. That's not good."

She looked at me, gauging the extent of my fear. "Stay here," she said, turning. I grabbed her again.

"What if someone's in there, waiting for us with a scalpel? Or a needle? Or a chainsaw?"

She reached down to the reception desk and picked up a stapler, hoisting it like a cudgel.

"Oh, great. That's great," I said, looking around for a weapon of my own. I chose a round Lucite paperweight that bore the legend, "Zancutrol. When Nature *Isn't* Enough."

Armed for battle, we tiptoed down the hallway. It seemed to stretch longer into the shadows beyond, the walls curving into the floor in a trick of perspective that turned it into a fun-house terror tunnel.

Terry scanned the wall for more light switches. I saw one glowing like a night-light at the end of the hallway, next to the cracked door. I pointed to it and she nodded, creeping toward it on silent cat's paws.

She pantomimed to me that I should flick on the lights. She lifted her foot, and I understood that she was going to kick the door open, surprising whoever might be inside.

She held up her fist, then popped up her fingers, counting silently.

One! Two! Three!

We simultaneously flipped on the lights and kicked in the door, then Terry jumped into the breach. The door hit something inside and bounced back, slamming into her forehead.

Bam! She was knocked on her ass.

I ran to her, kneeling at her side. "Are you okay?"

She sat on the floor rubbing her head. I glanced inside the examination room and saw that it appeared empty. Thank God for that.

Then I heard the sound of rubber soles squeaking on the linoleum. Someone was running toward us. I spun around to see who it was.

A large shadowy figure kicked me in the jaw. The back of my head hit the wall, I saw fireworks, then everything went black.

I didn't know how much time had elapsed. Maybe a minute, maybe three hours. I sat up and felt the back of my aching head. There was a lump the size of a grade AA cage-free egg, and my jaw felt like someone had kicked it into Sunday with a metal-toed boot.

But it wasn't a boot. It was a rubber shoe on a large dark person. A man? Had to have been.

Although, Janice was an awfully big girl, now that I thought of it.

I heard a rustling and turned my stiff neck to see an old

Vietnamese man brandishing a mop. His waved it in the air, his eyes bugged.

"Porreece coming! *Now!*"

"What?" Terry's voice sounded like it was echoing at the bottom of a drum barrel. "Oh shit," she said, looking down at her arm. There was a needle mark in the pale, fleshy part of her forearm, with a trickle of dried blood. "Someone drugged us!" she yelled.

It was impossible to focus. My head was swimming, my vision shot. I forced my eyes to look down at my own arm and saw the telltale prick of a needle, along with a spot of red. And to make matters worse, I was holding an empty syringe in my other hand.

"Ugh!" I tossed it away, but it didn't fly down the hallway as intended. Just flopped onto my leg, stabbing me in the thigh before bouncing to the floor.

In spite of my mashed-potato brain, I was able to put it together. We had been ambushed and drugged. The Vietnamese man was the night janitor, who had found us lying there unconscious and called the police.

Terry dragged herself to her feet, using the wall for support. The janitor wielded the mop like a lance, swishing the dirty top as if to ward off fanged animals.

"Porrreece, coming now!" he shrieked, his voice eunuch-like from terror.

"Don't worry, we're not dangerous," I tried to say, but the words came out jumbled and thick. *Na flurry, wee da dangus.*

His reaction struck me as over the top, but I guess we did look like a couple of desperate junkies who had broken into the office and thrown ourselves a party. I tried to stand, too, but I put my foot on top of a plastic drug vial and slipped, falling back on my butt, landing hard on my coccyx bone.

"Owww!"

The janitor swung his mop in my face, granular dirt and lint flying into my eyes. I was blinded by dust bunnies.

"Stop it!" I yelled.

"Oh my God!" Terry shrieked. "Kerry, over here!"

I got to my knees and started to crawl in her direction. But the mop slammed down on my back and I sprawled on top of hundreds of drug capsules that were scattered all over the floor.

"Cut it out!" I yelled at the janitor, who took advantage of my prone position to jump in the middle of my back, springing over me to get to the exit.

"Don't *do* that!" I coughed into the linoleum, but he was long gone. Probably halfway back to Saigon by now.

I pulled myself up into a crouch, wiping capsules from the palms of my hands, where they'd stuck like pebbles after a schoolyard tumble on the asphalt. Where had all these pills come from?

I looked up to see Terry in the door to the examination room, her hand covering her mouth. She stood perfectly still, barely breathing. I got unsteadily to my feet and shuffled down to see what she was looking at.

"What is it?" I asked, then I stuck my head in the door and gasped.

I felt my stomach churning and fought hard not to vomit.

Inside the formerly empty examination room a body lay sprawled across the vinyl-covered table.

Dead, by the looks of him.

Hattrick, if I wasn't mistaken.

He was in his forties, with a thick head of black hair. Dressed in khakis and running shoes, a cotton shirt, a maroon V-neck sweater. The V-neck was drenched a darker maroon and his cotton collar was bright red with arterial blood. Sticky, but not yet dry.

His throat had been cut. Jagged white cartilage shone in the gaping maw of a wound.

But the killer hadn't stopped there.

After the fatal wound had been delivered, and as Daniel

Hattrick lay there bleeding to death, the murderer had plunged two hypodermic needles into Hattrick's staring eyes. Red-tinged ocular fluid ran from the needles down the sides of his temples, giving him the appearance of a crying saint.

"Jesus," I said.

"Joseph and Mary," Terry said.

"Police!" a voice said from the doorway. "Don't fucking move!"

thirteen

he cops had permitted Terry a cigarette even though it was against the law. She was milking the situation for all it was worth, blowing smoke through her nostrils, her chin thrust out for a *Fuck-you-I'm-so-tough* look.

"What happened to good cop, bad cop," she said.

Detective John Boatwright turned on a smoke-eating fan.

"We're all bad in LA, didn't you know that?" He smiled with what I had to admit was an adorable creasing of the lines down the side of his face, and his blue eyes actually twinkled in the overhead light of the interrogation room.

He was in his mid-to-late thirties, and horrifically sexy. I wished I'd had time to freshen my lip gloss before they cuffed me. *When did they start making cops so cute?* I wondered. How's a girl supposed to keep her mind on preserving her constitutional rights with such a hottie putting the questions to her?

We had been taken all the way down to Parker Center. The grisly murder was probably too big for Beverly Hills, requiring hard-core downtown talent. But this cop wasn't hard core. He was nice. He was polite. And as we sat there, I even began to realize he was kind of funny.

I felt an undeniable tingle of attraction, but caught myself. *Don't get hot for the cop.* I told myself. *He'll send your fanny straight to the slammer!*

"I'll take out the thumbscrews, if you ask real nicely," Boatwright said, giving me what I could have sworn was a flirtatious look, the word "nicely" getting a little extra thrust.

I was trying to think of a clever reply when I was interrupted by the arrival of Detective Hank Stedman, an older, more comfortably soft-around-the-middle guy who looked the way LA cops were supposed to look. He had oily skin and a bulbous nose with spidery red veins on the corners, and his gray irises didn't twinkle so much as float in the rheumy yellows of his eyes.

He dumped an armload of takeout food on the table, fishing around in a paper bag. "Great timing," he said. "Got there just before they closed. Now, who had the avocado and jack on whole wheat?"

I waved, limp-wristed. He handed me the sandwich with a stack of napkins and a small plastic container.

"I got the herb mayonnaise on the side," he explained. "Didn't know if you were counting calories."

"Thanks."

"And I guess you're the broiled chicken breast with roasted pepper," he said to Terry. She gave him a curt little nod. "Hope French roll is okay. Here's a little honey-mustard dressing. It's real good, try it."

I reached over and grabbed a plastic knife for my mayonnaise.

"Where the fuck's Eli?" Terry said. The more solicitous the cops were, the bitchier she got. That's Terry all over, I thought.

"Well, according to his secretary, Priscilla," Stedman said, "he's incommunicado. She says he had a hot date."

"Yeah, a hot date with his foot soaker and a fifth of scotch," Terry said. "Try him again."

Stedman shrugged. "That's what she said. But she left him a message, and she promised to get through eventually."

Well, it was better than nothing, I thought, but we'd already been stonewalling the detectives for hours, and it seemed too much to hope that we could keep it up until Eli got back from the sports bar or wherever he really was. He might have been bailing one of his clients out of jail, or giving him a ride home from the scene of a double homicide.

"So why don't you girls give us a *hint* what you were doing at the doctor's office tonight?" Boatwright cajoled. "We're not interrogating you. We don't think you murdered anyone. And we can't get you for possession again, Terry, since you weren't *in* possession of the drugs. They were just scattered around your feet."

So they'd run us through the system and come up with Terry's prison record. Maybe these cops weren't as harmless as they appeared.

"But wait," Stedman said. "They *did* have drugs in their systems—"

"We didn't take those drugs voluntarily!" I said, before a piece of red lettuce slapped wetly onto my cheek.

I looked over at Terry, who was aiming her sandwich at my head. I clamped my mouth down on a bite of avocado.

"What was that?" Boatwright said to me. "Want to say that again, into the camera?" He pointed to a tripod holding a top-of-the-line Super-8 video camera. The red light winked at us cheerily.

"Got any salt?" I said.

Stedman rummaged through the bag again, then tossed me a tiny bag of salt. "Here ya go."

"Thanks." I tore it open, and sprinkled it over the sandwich.

Terry hadn't even taken a bite. She was still fake-inhaling the cigarette and scowling. "We're not saying *nothing* till our lawyer gets here."

"And we wouldn't want you to," Boatwright said. "We wouldn't want you to say anything you don't want to say, or anything that isn't true. We just want to know why you were passed out in the office of a plastic surgeon who was brutally murdered tonight. I'm sure there's a good explanation," he added reasonably.

He was right, dammit. There was nothing improper about our being there. We'd been invited by the office manager herself, and had walked in through an unlocked door. We had stumbled onto a gruesome murder, it's true, and someone had apparently made a crude attempt to frame us for it, but these were intelligent men. They'd see through all that.

"I showed you my credentials," I said, dodging the toe of Terry's boot. She kicked the leg of the wooden table, instead. "I'm a licensed private investigator. Doesn't it seem reasonable to you that we were there in a professional capacity, investigating a case?"

"Your credentials don't say you're *licensed to shoot up*," Stedman said, his mouth full of turkey. He and Boatwright got a good chuckle out of this.

Aha. The bad cops were beginning to surface.

"You won't find our fingerprints on those syringes," I said, and instantly regretted it. I had been in such a haze when I woke up, I completely forgot about tossing the syringe away.

"We won't?" Boatwright said. "Well, that's a relief. We had thought we might. But hey, if you tell us those syringes full of morphine just jumped up and stuck themselves in your arms, we'll have to accept that, won't we?"

He looked at Stedman, who gave him an exaggerated nod of agreement.

"Obviously I'm not telling you they stuck themselves in our arms," I said, sarcasm dripping from my mouth. Oops, that was herb mayonnaise dripping from my mouth. Very unflattering. I wiped it off with a napkin.

"*Will* you shut *up?*" Terry hissed at me.

"I'm just saying—"

"And I'm just telling you to shut your hole until Eli gets here!" she snapped, her eyes bugging out of her head.

"Temper, temper," Stedman said.

I sucked in a breath, clenching my teeth. Thanks to Terry, we were looking like hot-tempered redheads who had something to hide.

I smiled, and said in my calmest, most relaxed voice, "I'm so sorry, gentlemen. I know you have a job to do, and I have the utmost respect for your work, bringing criminals to justice. But you see, we happen *not* to be criminals—"

"Then talk to us!" Boatwright said.

"And we're not unaware of our right to representation. If Eli Weintraub doesn't present himself in the next ten minutes, I suggest you provide us with another attorney free of charge, as is our constitutional right."

Boatwright exhaled and glanced over at Stedman. "Well, they're too smart for us."

Stedman shrugged and the two of them sat back in their chairs.

"So, how 'bout those Lakers?" Boatwright said, smiling at me, before taking a bite of his tuna salad sandwich.

They gave up after a few more minutes of good cop/good cop, then left us to our own devices in the interrogation room, having turned off the video camera.

Terry got up and looked at herself in the two-way mirror, running her hands through her hair and checking her teeth for lettuce. She found a piece stuck to her front tooth. She picked it out and flicked it onto the mirror.

"Eat *that*," she said.

"Terry—"

"Don't say a word, or I swear to God . . ."

I realized we were both extremely tense and, in spite of Terry's cocky stance, more than a little afraid to have found ourselves in this situation.

She punched the mirror with her fist. "Where the hell is Eli?"

"Calm down, he'll be here."

"It's been two and a half hours! Where *is* he? Ringside at a mud wrestling match?"

"He'll be here, he'll be here," I said out loud. In my head I chanted, *Please God, please God*.

And right on cue, a lady sergeant opened the door and ushered him in. He was wearing a coat and pants that actually matched, a tie that didn't clash with the ensemble, and a minimum of stains on his shirtfront. Had someone else dressed him tonight?

I jumped up and threw my arms around his neck. "Eli! You're here!"

I picked up the scent of a woman's perfume, a familiar aroma that I couldn't quite place, mixed as it was with garlic, scotch, and cigar smoke.

"Hey, girls. Sorry I was incommunicado. I had work to do tonight."

Work? Okay, but there was that dreamy cast to his eyes and the little matter of the perfume, the name of which was right on the tip of my tongue.

Terry was in no mood for apologies. "We've been sitting here being grilled by those bozos for three hours. It's about fucking time!"

"Whoa, baby, whoa!" Eli said, holding up a hand. "Now the

first thing we're gonna do is we're gonna chill right out, okay? We don't want to be looking like a couple of rage-aholics under the circumstances, know what I'm saying?"

"Listen, we've got dogs now," I said to him. "We have to get out of here."

"Really? What kind of doggies?" he asked, smiling.

Terry slammed the table with her palm. "The kind that has to eat and go to the bathroom! And we haven't been home for hours!"

"Well, this *is* serious," Eli sat, tossing his battered briefcase on the table.

"Can it, Terry," I said, shooting her a warning look.

"Yes, I didn't realize that there were innocent victims in this scenario," Eli continued. "That some poor little pups were going to go motherless, when they lock your asses up for breaking and entering, felonious drug theft, and murder one!"

Terry melted into the chair across the table from Eli. Tears swam in her eyes and she gripped his hand. "I can't go back in, Eli. I can't!"

She had always made light of her prison stint to me. *It wasn't that bad, Ker. It was actually kinda fun. Even made some new friends—junkies, whores, and killers, but really nice girls, underneath it all.*

But here was the naked truth. She was terrified of going back.

"You're not going in, sweetheart," he said, patting her hand. "Thing is, they know there's a story and they're gonna be real hard-ons about this unless we give them something."

"Give them something?" I said.

"First," Eli said, "tell me what happened tonight."

We explained that we'd accused Janice of complicity in the doctor's prescription drug trade. It was only a bluff, but we thought it had worked because she invited us to the office to show us some evidence.

"Looks like she called your bluff," Eli said.

I searched his eyes. "You think she set us up?"

He shrugged. "We'll let the cops figure that out. For now, I don't want you going into your blackmail and drug theories. Let's not muddy the waters. Our only concern is getting you out of here."

We nodded, agreeing wholeheartedly with that strategy.

"So, here's our line—you were concerned about your former client, Lenore Richling. She may have been the victim of malpractice, and you were investigating on that basis."

"But we got there and found the doctor murdered," I said.

"Right. That works."

"But why didn't he—whoever he is—kill *us* too?" I asked Eli.

"Or *she*," Terry said.

"Yeah, or she," I echoed. I wondered if it had been more than a setup, if Janice had done the deed herself. But I couldn't believe she was capable of the butchery we'd seen tonight, even if Terry *had* overestimated her good qualities.

"You weren't on his to-do list," Eli said. "Yet."

"But why not? It would have been easy enough," I said. "Why leave us there as witnesses?"

"Well, what did you witness, really?"

I thought about it. "Yeah, I guess you're right. I only saw a big dark shape."

Eli pointed a finger at me. "It was a warning, or a setup, or both. If you guys got nailed for the murder, terrific. If not, you'd probably be smart enough to leave it alone after this. If he'd killed all three of you, they'd be out looking for him right now, and the more time and obstacles he puts between the cops and himself, the better off he is."

"Or she," Terry said.

"Or fuckin' *she*, all right?" Eli shook his head. "Now, I'm gonna invite them back in, and I want you to look cooperative. But stick to our line—you went there to get information on the doc. All you know about him is that he operated on your client before she died, okay?"

"Gotcha," we said.

"And any question I don't want answered, I'll give you the signal—" he gave us a tiny shake of the head, eyebrows joined over his nose, "and you'll clam right up, okay?"

We nodded.

"Good," he said, standing up from the table. "I'll be right back with the dicks."

Boatwright and Stedman were all business when they came back in, no more game playing. They conducted themselves like complete professionals, for which I gave Eli all the credit. He had convinced them that we would answer their questions truthfully, and they were only too eager to get on with their investigation and find the real murderer, which they didn't seem to think was us after all.

The first part was establishing names, dates of birth, phone numbers, professional information, and so forth. They announced to the camera that we had been apprised of our rights, to which Terry and I readily agreed. Then Stedman put the questions to us.

"What were you doing tonight at 244 Bedford Drive, office number 303?"

Terry answered, "We had a meeting with the office manager."

"Name?"

"Janice."

"Last name?"

We both shrugged.

"What was the purpose of the meeting?"

"We were trying to get more information on her boss, Daniel Hattrick."

"Why?"

"We think . . . thought he might have played a part in the death of our client."

"Your client's name?"

I looked at Eli. He nodded.

"Lenore Richling," I said.

"So you were conducting a *private* murder investigation?" Boatwright said, giving me a sad-eyed look of disapproval. "You must know it's illegal for private eyes to investigate a homicide."

"No, no," I said. "We didn't think it involved *murder*, but the circumstances of her death were somewhat unusual. Lenore was a friend of our aunt's, and we'd been working for her when she died. Our aunt asked us to look into her death, that's all."

"You thought the doctor was involved in foul play of some kind?"

Eli gave me a little jerk of the head.

"*No-o-o.* But he's been investigated for malpractice before."

Stedman didn't seem too interested in this revelation. He took up the questioning again. "And where was this Janice?"

"We don't know," Terry said. "You'll have to ask her that."

"We will, we will," Stedman said, giving Boatwright a look from the corner of his eye. Boatwright jotted something down in a spiral notebook. "What were you investigating on behalf of Ms. Richling?"

Eli jumped in. "A confidential matter, gentlemen. Of a domestic nature."

Stedman turned to me. "How did you know the doctor had been investigated for malpractice?"

"We picked that up in the course of our investigation."

"From who?"

"It's a matter of public record."

"Okay. How do you know Janice?"

"We met her a couple of days ago," I said, "when we went to the doctor's office. We took her out for a drink and she told us Hattrick was losing it, emotionally and financially. He had several very angry patients."

"Uh-huh. Did she mention anybody mad enough to kill?" Boatwright said, knitting his thick eyebrows together.

I was finding this man distressingly attractive, especially in the face of a hard line of questioning. *Remember*, I thought, *he's a wolf in hunk's clothing*.

"No," I said, "she didn't mention anyone."

But even as I said it, Tatiana's voice came back to me—*He's ruin my life!* Had she hated the doctor enough to kill him? Or had our trip to the hotel caused Alphonse to strike out, as I'd feared?

But this was all speculative, I realized, and Eli had warned us against dragging in extraneous information.

"So you went to the office and Janice wasn't there," Boatwright prompted me.

"No one was there," Terry said. "Or so we thought. The lights were out. But the door was open and we went in, and then we thought we heard someone."

"At which point you left the office, like the smart girls you are, and called the police?" Stedman said, the sarcasm creeping back in. "No, wait. You didn't do that, 'cause the call we got was from a Mr. Nguyen, the night janitor. So I guess that means you went right into a darkened office, ignoring the sound of someone inside, and walked straight into an ambush."

"We weren't sure about the noise," I said, a little too anxious to exonerate us on the stupidity charge. "Sometimes we freak ourselves out and hear, or think we hear, bogeymen who aren't there."

Terry rolled her eyes all the way back into her skull.

"Bogeymen? Okay . . ." Stedman had a little chuckle at this, and Boatwright joined in. Even Eli permitted himself a short laugh.

"So," I continued, "we picked up a stapler and a paper-weight and went to see what the noise was—"

"Back up," Boatwright said. "What was this about a paperweight?"

"You know, for weapons. A stapler and a paperweight."

"Are you licensed to carry a paperweight?" Stedman said, and this time he and Eli and Boatwright all had a good, full-on laugh at our expense. I felt my cheeks broiling.

"Like I said, we didn't really think anybody was there."

"Okay, okay," Boatwright said, smiling at me. "Go ahead,"

"And Terry kicked in the door to the examination room, and it swung back and hit her in the head and knocked her on her ass—"

"Wooo-*haaaa-aaaa!*" all three men erupted at once. Terry shook her head at me with a deadly look in her eye.

Eli said to tell the truth—I telegraphed to her. In for a penny, in for a pound. Anyway, bumbling bimbos seemed like a better way to go than psycho hypo-killers at this point in the proceedings.

"And then what happened?" Stedman hiccuped. "Oh, excuse me. I should never laugh on a full stomach."

The three men hooted, while Terry scowled at them fiercely.

"I ran to see if Terry was all right. Then I heard rubber squeaking on the linoleum, and I turned around to look and somebody kicked me in the jaw," I said. "My head bounced off the wall and I passed out."

"Uh-*haw-haw-haw!*" the men responded.

Terry gave them the dirtiest look in her repertoire. The one usually reserved for guys with pick-up lines like, *Hey, what d'ya say? Can I double my pleasure, double my fun tonight?*

"Squeaking on the linoleum?" Stedman yukked. "Is this the Case of the Killer Nurse Shoe?"

Terry and I waited through another bout of hilarity, grinding our teeth, then I jumped in again, hoping to put an end to this torture session.

"And when we woke up, the Vietnamese janitor was there, and he hit me with the mop, knocked me to the ground, then jumped on my back to get out the door."

"Uh-*huhuhuhuhuh!*"

Stedman fell right off his chair. Boatwright plopped forward on the table, convulsing with laughter. Even Eli was wiping tears from his eyes with his dress tie.

"And then the cops came in and the rest is history," Terry finished.

"I gotta, I gotta, I gotta . . . go to the can," Stedman said, between hiccups. "I'm gonna lose my dinner!"

The interrogation went on for another fifteen minutes, having technically become a witness interview. We were released without further incident, none the worse off, except for the black smudges on our finger pads and a burning indignation at being ridiculed.

"*Aw, don't be* mad," Eli said, as he drove us back to our motorcycle. "I got you out of it, didn't I?"

"I think we did that ourselves," I said. "We convinced them we were too incompetent to murder Hattrick."

"Yeah, you were great." Eli laughed, his jowls jiggling like Hanukkah Harry's. "Really hilarious."

"I'm glad we could amuse you."

"Look at it this way—you're off the hook. And you did your civic duty, reporting a murder in your own, inimitable fashion. Did the janitor really jump on your back?" He cracked up again.

I slapped him on the belly. "Hey, whose side are you on?"

"Okay, okay," he said. "But you know, it could have gone

a lot worse in there. You should be happy you're going home to your doggies."

That was true. I'd never been so anxious to go home and snuggle with another creature in my life. Especially one with whom I had no hope of sexual intimacy.

The snuggling concept jogged something else in my memory. A certain *eau de toilette* on Eli's person when he walked in tonight. "By the way," I said to him, "who were you out with tonight?"

Eli got very sober suddenly, clearing his throat. "Oh, just some babe. Nobody you know."

Wait a minute, I had it now! Chanel No. 5!

Not the kind of perfume worn by the usual divorcées on the prowl. But it *was* worn by our great-aunt, whom he had been desperately trying to impress earlier . . .

He changed the subject quickly. "So who killed the doc, Sherlocks?"

"Well," I said, "we had been thinking the doc himself was the bad guy."

"Guess you need to keep thinking, huh?"

"I already have," Terry said. "I vote for the supplier—your former client, Sergei Pavlov."

"Oh? How come?"

"I figure it like this," she said. "The doc got too free and loose with the merchandise. It was interfering with his performance, and he was being sued to hell and back. If the guy's got no patients, then there's no one to get hooked on drugs."

"Besides, a junkie's a liability all around," I said. "There's always the risk he'll be picked up and spill the beans on the whole operation."

"Yeah, *if* Sergei was involved with this *alleged* drug ring at the hotel and *if* the doc was pushing the drugs to his patients," Eli said. "Still needs that little thing called *proof*."

"Well, *duh*, we're gonna prove it," Terry said.

I didn't see how, but hey. We could get lucky.

If we didn't get dead.

When we got back to Bedford Drive, there was a parking ticket on the motorcycle. Could have been worse. We could have been spending a heck of a lot more on a bail bond, while sharing a communal toilet with a lot of *really nice girls*.

fourteen

I didn't share with Terry my thoughts about Eli and Reba's budding romance. After all, It was only a suspicion. And with all the paranoia swirling around my brain, I hardly knew when to trust my instincts and when not to.

Despite the fact that we'd arrived home at close to three in the morning, Reba had called shortly after nine. She'd heard from Eli about Hattrick's murder and our arrest, and had insisted that we come over to talk about it, *immediately.*

I dragged myself down to the kitchen and found Terry seated at the breakfast table, hunched over a glass of orange juice. She was barefoot, her hair going in all directions, dressed in flowered yellow leggings under a black Harley-Davidson T-shirt. Muffy and Paquito were perched on top of the table, lapping at a saucer of half-and-half.

"No coffee?" I said.

She yawned, shaking her head. "Then I'll be tired *and* wired."

"That was Reba on the phone."

"I figured," Terry said. "She heard about Hattrick?"

I nodded.

"She got her panties in a bunch?"

I nodded again.

Terry took a sip of OJ and leaned back in her chair. "Maybe we should let her get a gun, after all. Beverly Hills is starting to look more like gang territory every day."

I had to laugh, in spite of my exhaustion. "She'd look very chic with an assault rifle strapped to her chest, don't you think?"

"Yeah, but it'll only happen when Louis Vuitton starts making cartridge belts."

To our surprise, we were greeted at the door to Reba's house by Cousin Robert.

"Well, if it's not the twin lovelies of the desert. How are my little cactus flowers this morning?" He gave us each a kiss, which amazingly didn't smell like alcohol. Not even yesterday's.

"We're fine," I said, then I noticed his outfit. He was covered head-to-toe in fuchsia velour. A zippered jumpsuit, with what appeared to be big white Bugs Bunny feet protruding from the bottom. Were those running shoes?

"What's up with the outfit, Robert?" Terry asked, trying not to sound appalled.

"Oh, these are my workout clothes." He smoothed back a wisp of frizzy red hair that had strayed into his face, tucking it inside a terry-cloth sweatband. "I'm on a new health kick," he announced, "but don't think this is a temporary fad. No way. There's nothing like staring death in the face to put you right with your maker. Henceforth, I'm treating my body like the temple it is."

A crumbling Jakartan ruin filled with rabid monkeys? I wondered.

Terry and I exchanged a look while Robert began jogging in place. He huffed and puffed, losing breath rapidly.

"See there? See there? That's with only one day's training." His stomach sloshed up and down like a water-filled garbage bag. He swung his arms into the air, stretching up on his toes, then bent over quickly and reached all the way down to his shins.

"Flexibility. It's all about flexibility. That's what keeps you young!" He ran toward the dining room, waving us forward. "Come, bambini. *Mangia!*"

We followed him into the dining room, where Reba sat motionless at the table. She didn't speak and her eyes never left the porcelain teapot in front of her. It had an engraving of a Shinto temple on its side, steam rising from its spout, and it sat in the exact spot where the coffee service should have been. She stared at it as if she were contemplating wiring it with explosives.

"Come on, Mother. Drink your ginseng. There's a good girl." Robert jogged to his seat across the table and plopped down with a satisfied *Ugh!* as if he'd just run down the side of Mt. Baldy. He pounded his chest with his fists. "Ah, it's incredible girls. I feel like a new man. Not a drop has passed these lips in twenty-four hours!"

Well, at least he'd stopped drinking. Maybe this would be for the best, even if it was a little annoying at first.

Grizzie entered with a silver tray holding four ceramic bowls, a milk pitcher, and a box of Kashi cereal. She gave Robert a look laced with daggers and slammed the tray down in the middle of the table, sending Kashi and milk flying into the air.

"She's a little resistant to change," Robert said, watching Grizzie stomp out of the room. "But she'll adjust in no time. Kashi, Mumsy? Clear those bowels right out. They'll be sparkling like diamonds in two weeks."

Reba lifted her eyes from the spilled cereal to Robert's face and then looked back at the cereal, not uttering a word.

"I'll have some," I said to defuse the tension.

"Good girl!" Robert pushed the tray toward me. "You can't *get* this much fiber without gnawing on the bark of a tree or munching whole stalks of wheat." He sucked in a lungful of air. "There's no disease but congestion, no cure but circulation!"

"Uh-huh." I put a spoonful of cereal into my mouth. "Mmm, even better than tree bark."

"So your little tumble kind of altered your outlook on life?" Terry said to Robert.

"Indeedy do. I realized I'd been letting myself go to an alarming degree. Eating poorly, getting very little exercise, drinking much too much."

Nah. Drinking too much?

Terry and I didn't dare meet each other's eyes.

"And I got up from my sick bed, and I looked around and I said, 'Robert, life is a gift. It's a treasure. And what are you doing with it? Squandering it, that's what. Soaking yourself in alcohol and digging yourself an early grave. Well, that's no way to be!' And then next thing you know, I'm off to the Big 5 Sporting Goods Store to buy some work-out clothes, and I got a personal trainer, and within twenty-four hours I'm feeling ten years younger. No, fifteen!"

Reba stared straight ahead, her expression unchanging, as if she planned to sit there in stony silence until this night-mare had passed right out of existence.

The doorbell rang.

"That'll be Sven, now." Robert jumped up from his seat. "See you later, lovelies. Got to get the lard out!"

I think he meant *lead*.

I leaned back in my chair and saw Grizzie open the front door. Outside was a man of thirty-five with the best physique I had ever seen on a live human being. He wore an orange tank top stretched over granite pecs, and shorts made of the same jersey material that hiked up on the sides of his bulging thighs, forming a shiny V anchored by his substantial package. He jogged in place, and so did it.

"Good morning," he said with a Scandinavian accent. "Is Mr. Robert—?"

The door slammed in his face.

"Grizzie!" Robert said, running for the door. "What's gotten into you?"

"What's gotten into *you*, ya great sack of jigglin' potatoes? Shut up and drink yer whiskey!"

"Why Grizzie, that's so insensitive," Robert said. "You know I'm clean and sober now." Robert opened the door to his trainer as Grizzie stormed off into the kitchen. "Ye'll be jogging out t' other side of yer mouth, soon enough!" she muttered.

Robert and Sven shook hands, then Sven whipped Robert around, pinning his arm behind his back. "Well, I can see we are going to have to work on your upper-body strength today, Mr. Robert."

"Come on," Robert squealed. "Race you to the backyard!"

The two of them jogged past the table, throwing their big white feet up behind them, pumping their fists with little hammer movements. They went through the French doors, and across the brick-paved patio out onto the grass, where Sven led Robert in a round of jumping jacks.

Reba picked up a little bell and rang it. Grizzie reappeared, sopped up the spilled milk, and took the cereal tray away without even being asked, and was back within seconds with the coffee service, muffins, and mangoes.

"Coffee, girls?" Reba didn't say a word about Robert's conversion to health nut, making no move to acknowledge his new life journey. A relapse was all but inevitable, she seemed to think, and the sooner, and the less said about it, the better.

We doctored our coffee and let her start the conversation.

"I've decided to drop the case," she said.

Terry sputtered her coffee onto the place mat in front of her. "What?"

"It's become far too dangerous. I couldn't live with myself if something happened to you two. You're my entire legacy, now that Robert has irretrievably lost his mind, and I won't be responsible for getting you killed."

I glanced out in the backyard and saw Robert trying to do push-ups. He was on his hands and knees, head hanging forward, his arms bent and shaking ferociously under his weight. They collapsed suddenly and Robert fell flat on his face on the grass.

I accidentally laughed.

Reba's eyes traveled from my face to the backyard where Sven was helping Robert up from the ground. Then, without warning, Sven hauled off and slugged Robert in the gut.

Robert stumbled backward, his arms pinwheeling in the air. Then he regained his footing and put up his hands for the boxing portion of the workout. Bouncing on the toes of his feet, fists punching the air, Sven ducking and weaving. Upper-body strength, here we come.

Reba sighed and rolled her eyes at me. "I'm thinking of having him committed."

"To a rehab program?"

"A psychiatric ward."

"Reba, you can't do that!" I exclaimed. "He's just trying to clean himself up."

"I'm changing my will. I'm afraid if I leave him everything, he'll donate it to a Swiss spa in exchange for a room with a Buddhist shrine, three bowls of hot gruel, and a cot."

"Give it a few days," Terry said. "This happens all the time. People swear they're going to turn over a new leaf, then within a week they're back to pounding Cheetos and guzzling beer and watching E! Entertainment biographies on the cast of *Gilligan's Island*. Just wait, he'll be better in no time."

"Nevertheless. I'm going to set up a trust fund."

"He's a fifty-year-old man," Terry protested. "He's too old to be a trust-fund baby!"

"He's unfit."

I shook my head, exasperated. "He's *trying* to get fit."

"Let's drop the subject," Reba said, putting a hand to her forehead. "It's too depressing."

Sven popped back in the door. "Excuse me, ladies?"

"Yes?" I said.

"Would you mind to call 911? I believe Mr. Robert has had a heart seizure." Then he jogged back into the yard and began pounding double-fisted on Robert's chest, as he lay motionless on his back in the grass.

Reba sighed again and turned around to pick up the phone, punching in 911. "Hello? Reba Price-Slatherton, here. Be a dear and send a cardiac unit to my address. Yes, that's correct. Well, I believe my son has had a massive heart attack. Thank you so very much."

As Terry and I sat there open-mouthed, she whipped out an alligator checkbook and readied a Mont Blanc pen.

"Now, how much do I owe you?"

●   ●   ●

We left Reba's with a two-thousand dollar check for services rendered, having promised to attend Lenore's memorial that afternoon, dressed appropriately. It would be held at Beverly Eternal Rest in the warm, still-beating heart of Beverly Hills.

"Curtain's promptly at three, dears."

"The curtain?" Terry said.

"Figure of speech."

Robert's prognosis was decent. In fact, the EMTs hadn't been certain he'd suffered a heart attack at all. When I told them he'd been slugged in the gut, they thought it might be something else entirely, like internal hemorrhaging. At which point Sven had jogged out the front door, suddenly remembering he had another client to train.

Robert would be admitted to Cedars-Sinai, and of course we'd try to visit him as soon as possible.

When we got close to Wilshire Boulevard, Terry pulled over and parked, signaling me to get off the bike. Time for a chat. We took off our helmets and sat on the curb.

"Well, are we gonna drop the case?" she asked.

"Yeah, the police are on it now. They're in a better position to investigate. But hey, we had a good run. And on the plus side, we're alive with money in our pockets and we're not in jail."

She made a face. "Doesn't feel right, just letting it drop."

"Yes it does."

"Wimp!"

"Suicidal idiot!"

"I'm not giving up."

Oh God. I could see that her mind was made up, and I was going to have a hell of a time talking her out of it.

"Think of it this way," she argued. "We still have Lenore's money. She's crying out to us from the grave to use it in a constructive way, to solve her murder."

"She *wasn't* murdered. And she wouldn't want us to keep investigating because we're only gonna turn up something slimy on *her*."

"Then consider it her karma. She was doing something bad and the universe conspired to give us her money so we could keep investigating and stop the madness. You know, there's no reason to think this is going to end with Hattrick's murder. There'll be other victims, you can be sure."

"Well, we can't use Eli's office anymore. He'll be on Reba's side about this."

"So we work out of the house, as usual."

"And no more Greg to help us out," I warned.

"What are we, chopped liver? This is our chance to prove ourselves, to make our bones as law enforcement agents."

"We're *not* law enforcement agents!"

"I meant . . . oh, you know what I meant."

"Yeah, you meant superheroines. You meant *Charlie's Angels*. You think this is some kind of TV adventure with good guys and bad guys and a happy ending where the only people who get killed are the ones with guest spots on the show."

"No, I'll tell you what my motivation is. You want to know?"

I nodded, fighting not to roll my eyes.

"I'm pissed!"

Why didn't that surprise me?

"I'm pissed at all the people who looked us in the eye and lied. I'm pissed at Lenore for getting us involved without telling us what the fuck it was all about. I'm pissed at Janice for pretending to be mother-of-the-year while she was setting us up to get killed!

"But mostly, I'm pissed at *us* for being taken in by everyone who had a bullshit story to sell us. And for walking straight into a murder trap and being assaulted with needles, then letting ourselves be laughed at!"

There was justification for being pissed, I had to admit.

I pulled up the sleeve of my scoopnecked tee and looked at the needle mark. My virgin arm had been violated. I'd never even dreamed of shooting up drugs, and now that I thought about it, it really got me incensed. And what about Terry? She'd had a major cocaine problem at one time. What if this malicious act had sent her into another spiral of self-destruction? Wouldn't that have been a kind of murder in itself?

She was right. We couldn't stop until someone had been brought to justice for all of this. If for no one else, we should do it for ourselves.

"Okay," I said. "I'm down."

She slapped me five and we jumped on the bike, off to right the wrongs of the world. Or at least the wrongs of Beverly Hills.

A truck rumbled past the corner and a guy with a greasy pompadour leaned out the window. "Hey, double your pussy, double your fun!" he yelled at us.

She looked back at me. But she didn't have to tell me, I knew.

She was pissed.

We parked in a public structure on the west side of Bedford, walking the half block up to Hattrick's building. We hoped to find Janice in the vicinity so we could grill her about why she had stood us up the previous night.

And who should be standing at the street door, waving away onlookers again?

Officer Dinah Lott.

She shook her head as we got closer, but it was more out of amazement than reproach. "You did it again!" she said. "How do you manage to be on the spot whenever a murder goes down in BH?"

Terry shrugged. "How do *you* manage it?"

"Just lucky, I guess."

I pointed to the building. "So what's happening in there? They still gathering evidence?"

Dinah twisted her mouth. "Yep, still gathering evidence. So, why *were* you there last night?"

"We were invited by the office manager, Janice. She isn't here by any chance?"

"Uh, yeah," Dinah said, nodding toward the front door. "Here she comes now."

A coroner's assistant pushed a gurney over the threshold with a full body bag. I lost my balance and fell against Terry, who caught me by the arm. I felt light and tingly and momentarily confused, like I'd been hit in the head with a fast-moving object I never saw coming.

"How . . . ?" I said, my voice cracking. "What happened?"

"They found her a couple hours ago. She bled to death in a locked storeroom on the fourth floor last night."

Terry frowned, confused. "Fourth floor? What was she doing on the fourth floor?"

"She was pursued there, apparently. They found blood in the stairwell. They think she'd been stabbed and was trying to outrun her attacker."

"Oh my God." Terry looked down at the boot that had stepped in Janice's blood, and scraped her sole against the sidewalk. "So she didn't mean to set us up after all. I feel terrible."

"She has a little boy," I said to Dinah. "Is someone taking care of her little boy?" My mouth was dry and I wanted to cry for that orphaned six-year-old with the brilliant toothless smile.

"I don't know. Better talk to the detective on the case. I think you know him," Dinah said, pointing into the coffee shop.

We looked in and saw Stedman seated at a table with the teenage counter girl, who was blowing her nose into a paper napkin. Her eyes traveled to the window and she said something to him, pointing at us accusingly.

Stedman turned to see us and smiled, crooking a finger in our direction.

"Oh shit," Terry said. "Here we go again."

In the hallway leading into the coffee shop I grabbed her arm. "What did we say about bringing in the cops if things got hairier?"

"We said we'd do it."

"They can't get much worse. We've got to tell him what we know, and let the chips fall where they may."

"You're right. But nothing about Mario and the ten thousand. Anything but that."

I gave her a look. "I'm not stupid, you know."

"Stupid is as stupid does, sis."

I shoved past her into the coffee shop, giving my hair an indignant flip.

$Stedman\ offered\ to$ buy us coffee, but we declined and asked for herbal tea instead. We sat at the same window table where we'd made the faux John Malkovich sighting, and he brought the cups to the table.

"So where's your partner?" I asked him, stirring in a spoonful of sugar.

"He's meeting the coroner at the morgue. But he's not actually my partner. He's BHPD. I'm with Robbery Homicide, Central Division."

We waited for him to elaborate.

"We're working together on an interim basis, a cooperative effort between departments."

"Huh," Terry said, sitting back and frowning.

"So," he said, "I guess we know why Janice didn't meet you last night. You want to talk to me now, or you want your lawyer?"

We shook our heads. "Go ahead, ask us anything," I said. "This is awful."

"You gotta catch this bastard." Terry poked a spoon at him for emphasis.

"But first," I said, "there's something you should know about." Stedman nodded for me to continue. "Well, if they're making imprints of the blood outside the third floor landing . . ."

Terry lifted her foot and pointed to the sole of her boot.

Stedman frowned at her. "You stepped in it? You didn't say anything about blood on the landing when we interviewed you."

Her voice went tiny. "I thought it was taco sauce."

"What? Did you say . . . *taco sauce?*" Stedman's shoulders started to shake and he pursed his lips, trying to stifle a laugh.

I glared at him in full-on hormonal mode. "If you start laughing again you can forget about any more cooperation!"

He sputtered a little, then took a deep breath and stirred his coffee, determined to keep a straight face. "Okay, it's passed. Anyway, we have you to thank for finding the victim's body."

We looked at him curiously.

"Yeah, after you told us that Janice didn't show, we went through the building more thoroughly. We had thought the blood on the landing came from the perp or the doc, but you pointed out another possibility."

"Glad we could help," I said, a lump swelling my throat.

"Now you can help by telling me the whole story. The real reason you were there last night."

I looked at Terry and she nodded. "We think the doctor was involved in prescription drug dealing," I said.

He gave me a poker face. "You do?" It was hard to tell if there was any sarcasm behind the remark.

"Yeah," Terry said. "And we told Janice what we suspected, and she offered to show us some evidence."

"And what were you going to do with this evidence?"

"Give it to the cops, of course. To you," I said. "If it was for real."

"Mmm-hmm."

"And we don't have proof of this yet," Terry said, "but we think the doc was supplying these drugs to the manager of the Dauphine Hotel, who in turn supplied them to guests in residence, patients of the doc's. The manager's name is Alphonse, a tight-ass Frenchy with a big cologne problem."

"Cologne problem?"

"He wears enough to shut down every nose from here to Bakersfield."

"Well, I don't think he's gonna have that problem anymore," Stedman said. "He wears too much cologne where he's going, he'll end up the snuggle bunny of some big hairy convict."

Terry and I frowned at each other, confused.

Stedman leaned in and lowered his voice. "We got Alphonse in custody right now. And guess what? We think he's been dealing drugs, too."

He pulled a card out of his pocket and slapped it down on the table. Our business card. We stared at it for a second, then looked back up at his grinning mug. "The blonde at the registration desk? Ours. Been on the inside for months. A great undercover gal."

I let my mouth fall open, then shut it again.

"She told us you were getting close, making veiled accusations and whatnot, so we decided to bring Alphonse in before he got the idea to zero you out."

Terry looked up at the ceiling, her tongue planted in her cheek.

"Is this what your cooperative effort is about?" I said.

He gave me his sternest look. "It goes no further than this table."

"What about Sergei Pavlov? Is he part of your investigation?"

"No, he *is* the investigation. The Organized Crime division has been looking for that rat bastard for months. He's a pretty big deal in the West Coast Russian syndicate. But he keeps giving 'em the slip, and now it looks like he's resorted to homicide to cover his tracks. That's how come I got involved." He paused. "How do you know about him?"

"In a minute," Terry said impatiently. "So he's your number-one suspect for these murders, Hattrick and Janice?"

Stedman nodded.

"There may be another murder attributable to him," I said. "There was an unidentified man killed in Hollywood a few days ago . . ."

Terry rolled her eyes at me, then fell forward on the table, head on her arms.

Stedman's furry eyebrows leaped to his hairline. "Yeah? What about it?"

"We believe it was Mario Vallegos, Lenore Richling's husband. I mean, the guy she was passing off as her husband," I said, with a mysterious compulsion toward the truth. There'd be hell to pay with Terry later, but I was pretty sure they wouldn't bring charges against us at this point—they had bigger fish to fry.

"Thanks for the tip, but we got that already. His sister reported him missing and we got her to ID the body."

Terry looked up. "What's her name?"

"The sister? Irina."

Terry looked over at me. "So Rini *was* Mario's sister."

Suspicion crossed Stedman's face. "How'd you know it was Mario who got offed?"

Terry kicked a new dent in my shin. "We saw the murder on the news," she said. "It was just a lucky guess."

Stedman gave her a sly smile. "Uh-huh."

"So you must also know that Mario was in Tatiana Pavlov's apartment when he was shot," I said. "Sergei's ex-wife, ex-employee of Dr. Hattrick, ex–Russian citizen. Is she a suspect as well?"

"Nah, she checked out. Solid alibi. She'd moved in with a new boyfriend, a big *macher* in the entertainment business. They had fifteen people at his house for a party. Movie executives, agents. That bunch."

So the dude Tattoo Man saw Tatiana leave with wasn't Mario, after all. It was some movie-industry person who "thought he was the shit." Well, didn't they all?

"Is the case still open?" I said.

"Yeah."

"Put Sergei Pavlov at the top of your list of suspects for that one, too."

"Why do you like Sergei for Mario's murder?" he asked.

"Jealousy. Tatiana may have been having an affair with Mario. She denies it, but it's been alleged."

He nodded. "I'll look into it."

"Janice also thought she was having an affair with the doctor," Terry said. "Maybe you can get Barbie to corroborate that."

"Barbie? Barbie who?"

I shrugged. "Didn't say. She's a first-name-only kind of gal. Calls herself a beauty consultant. She took Tatiana's job."

"What's she look like?"

"Barbie," Terry and I said at the same time.

He made a face, like we were yanking his chain.

"No, seriously," Terry said. "She has long blonde hair, tata's like heat-seeking missiles, great legs, and butt cheeks like boulders."

Stedman loosened his collar. "She was definitely not there this morning. I'd have remembered." He sat back in his chair. "Are you sure she worked for the doc?"

"Yeah," I said, "although she may have been new."

He made a quick note, circling her name. "I ask, because after we found Janice, we went through the employee records, just to make sure we weren't missing any more bodies. No mention of a Barbie."

Terry shrugged at me. "The first time we went to the doctor's office, she was there, all right. Tried to sell us on a bunch of procedures to correct all our glaring physical deformities."

Stedman gave her a head shake to indicate he thought she was just fine as is.

"I know," she said, "but that's how they make their money. Convincing perfectly normal people that they're repulsive monsters."

Stedman laughed. "Don't let it get to you, you're fine. Hell, if I was thirty years younger . . ." He leered at her and I could feel the heat radiating from his oversized pores.

Here we go again. Invisible sister.

"Detective, we're very concerned about something," I said, bringing him back to the present, in which he was a too-old cop lusting after a lesbian witness. "Janice had a son, a little six-year-old. Someone needs to find him and take care of him."

"You know his name?"

"No, but she had a photo of him in her day planner. Maybe the picture has his name on it."

"Got that right here." He reached into his briefcase and removed a plastic bag marked as evidence. He pulled on latex gloves and opened up the date book.

"There he is." I pointed to the tattered school picture behind the glassine window.

Stedman pulled out the photograph. There was a name scrawled in babyish letters on the back. He popped his reading glasses onto his nose and peered through the lenses.

"Thought you said it was a boy," he said, turning the back of the picture toward us.

Janice Gray. Age Six.

"What?" Terry said. "It's a picture of *her?*"

Stedman glanced at it again. "Looks that way."

"But why did she tell us it was her little boy?"

He hoisted chubby shoulders, shaking his head.

"So she could represent herself as something she's not," I said. "A hardworking single mom who's been caught up in circumstances beyond her control. To gain our sympathy so she could manipulate us."

"Jeez," Terry said, slumping back in her chair. "Everyone we talk to is always lying their asses off."

Stedman winked. "Welcome to my world."

We talked to him for another hour, outlining our theory of how the blackmail ring overlapped with the drug ring. We told him about the missing Bacon, too, and our belief that Suzie Magnuson had been involved with insurance fraud along with Lenore. His eyes lit up when we mentioned Hugh Binion, but he kept his own counsel on the big attorney. Maybe he suspected Binion of involvement in Sergei's disappearance and was playing that one close to the vest.

Overall, he seemed impressed, ready to credit our ideas. I glanced at my watch and realized we'd have to hurry home to get dressed for the funeral.

"Sorry, Detective. We have to go. Today is Lenore Richling's funeral."

"Richling's funeral, huh? Maybe I'll come, see if there's anyone of interest in attendance. Where's it at?"

"Beverly Eternal Rest on Beverly Drive, three o'clock."

He gave a short laugh. "Why the fuck is everything named Beverly around here? Who was this Beverly, anyway?"

Terry looked at me. "Any ideas?"

"No," I said. "But we're not detectives for nothing. We'll track her down."

"*Hope you feel* better, getting Mario off your chest," Terry sniped as we walked back to the parking garage. "I knew you'd have to say something."

"I couldn't help it. It just came up and out of my mouth involuntarily, like a burp."

"Ever thought of covering your mouth when you're about to belch up incriminating information?"

"At least we know they're looking for Sergei. That's a relief. They'll pick him up and nail him for the murders and everything'll be hunky-dory."

"Doesn't mean we have to stop investigating."

"Yeah," I said, "I still want to know what happened to the Bacon."

"Fuck the Bacon," she said. "I want to nail Sergei."

"Well, we better watch our step or we could be the ones nailed."

"Sure. I'm always watching."

"No, I mean it, Ter. The next time he could plug us with lead instead of morphine."

"I *said* I'd watch it," she said, as she hopped on the bike.

As we pulled out of the parking garage onto Bedford, I noticed a gray sedan behind us. The driver wore dark glasses and had short hair, and he was so focused on what was in front of him, namely us, that I immediately became suspicious.

Normal drivers never focus on what's in front of them. Normal drivers switch radio stations, talk on the phone, pick their teeth or check their makeup when they're stopped. Also while they're moving. His hands were gripping the wheel at ten and two o'clock, and his eyes were staring straight ahead.

The car was also suspect. A boxy gray thing in a neighborhood of sleek foreign cars and luxury SUVs. Nobody drove plain old cars around here. If they did, they risked being pulled over, a victim of vehicular profiling. Well, that was a bit of an exaggeration, but one thing was sure. This guy was so unremarkable, such a good driver in such a normal car, that he just had to be bad news.

When we were stopped at a red light on Santa Monica Boulevard, I tapped Terry's helmet. "Don't turn around. Someone's following us."

She peered into the rearview mirror. "Gray sedan?"

"Yep."

"How long?"

"Since the garage."

"Okay, don't worry."

The light changed and she burned rubber through the intersection. I turned around and saw the gray sedan lurch forward after us.

Terry darted into the middle lane and gassed the bike, zooming past a monster truck of a Lexus SUV, then ducking between the Lexus and a white Cadillac. The Lexus had to brake to avoid hitting our back tire and he laid on his horn, causing the Cadillac driver to hit his brakes in panic. Terry ducked out from between them and rode along the lane divider next to a Jeep Cherokee, whose driver could be seen behind his window shooting us the finger and yelling, *Fuggenidiotwhatdoyouthinkyerdoing?*

But I had no time to return the gesture because Terry braked, and the Jeep sped past us. She zipped into its wake, causing an older woman in a Lincoln in the next lane to slam on *her* brakes, sending her toy poodle sailing right into the windshield and then back down in the front seat, yapping his little head off.

Terry tore past the Lincoln and across two lanes of honking, screeching traffic to the green light at the corner, making the turn at an acute angle, my nose almost scraping the asphalt.

Then she gunned it down a residential street whose name I didn't catch because my eyes were running like leaky spigots, and she was halfway down the next block before she saw the crosswalk full of first-graders.

Our brakes squealed and the wheels locked and we spun ninety degrees to the left, sliding sideways toward the mob of wide-eyed kids, who were frozen like fawns in the headlights, and finally skidding to a stop six inches from the Nikes of a kid in a Dodgers cap, the stench of burning rubber in our nostrils.

We sat in silence for a moment, catching our breath and letting the adrenaline subside. I was so glad to be alive. I looked up at the sky, noticing for the first time today that it was clear blue and almost cloudless. Yes, Robert was right—it was important to take stock, to appreciate how fleeting life is, to breathe in every moment while we live.

Lost in these thoughts, I didn't see the crosswalk monitor stomping over to the bike until the last minute. She was forty, rotund, and quite indignant, swinging her stop sign around like a pair of nunchucks.

"What kind of monsters are you?" she screeched. "Endangering the children!"

Then Terry said something she shouldn't have. "Oh, bite me. We didn't kill anyone."

The stop sign came crashing down on her head.

It came down on her head again and again, the wooden spike making a terrible crunching sound, which I knew was even worse for Terry, but I guess that's why they make you wear helmets in California. I finally managed to wrest the stop sign from the woman's grip and hurled it to the grass at the side of the road, giving Terry enough time to reorient herself and rev up the bike so we could make our escape.

As we pulled to a stop at the corner, I looked to our left and saw the gray sedan idling by the side of the road. Terry evidently didn't see it, and I didn't say a word. She had almost killed us once, trying to evade a possible killer, and I wasn't going to give her another chance. She took a right, eventually getting us back to Santa Monica Boulevard, and we were on our way home to Beverly Glen.

The gray sedan behind us all the way.

It wasn't until we were inside the house pouring kibble into bowls for Muffy and Paquito that I told Terry we'd been followed.

"Goddammit, why didn't you tell me?"

"And risk my life in another high-speed chase?"

"Oh, you liked it," she said. "That's the most fun you've had all week."

"Well, let me think about that one," I said, my throat tightening and my voice rising a fifth. "No, I'd have to say that discovering a mutilated corpse—no wait, *two* mutilated corpses—was the most fun I've had all week. No, wait. I think I liked being arrested and hauled down to Parker Center like a common criminal even better!" My voice had crept up another third, making it a full octave higher. I sounded like Michael Jackson on helium.

"All in all, it's been a real fun week. But I think I would have had even *more* fun if we'd actually mown down that little first-grader. What do you think his name was? Timmy? Bobby? Think it would have been fun going to his funeral and laying a rose on his tiny coffin before we were hauled off to spend the next ten years in the slammer for vehicular manslaughter, which we wouldn't even serve 'cause we'd be shiv'd by a gang of angry crack mothers for cutting down an innocent child in the sixth year of his life. Don't you think that would have been even *more* fun? Think you could arrange it next time?"

Terry petted Muffy and Paquito, who were munching away happily. "You're such a worrier."

"So who do you think he is?" I said, sighing.

"Who?"

"The guy in the gray sedan!"

She made a face. "You see what you do? You go off on a rant and I forget the important things!"

She ran to the front room and pulled aside the curtain, peering out onto the street. I crowded in next to her.

The gray car was nowhere to be seen.

"I think it was paranoia on your part," she said. "It looked like a perfectly normal guy in a normal car."

"You think Russian assassins have big signs on the sides of their cars?" I demanded. "1-800-MURDERERS? Wekillem4u.com? Wouldn't you try to be inconspicuous if you were going around knocking people off?"

She gave me a weary look. "Kerry, you're coming unglued. I've been noticing it for a while, now—you're putting yourself under too much pressure."

I pretended to give it some thought.

"Well then how much pressure should I be putting myself under *when people are being killed left and right*? How many pounds per square inch? What exactly should my gauge be reading *right now*?"

"Right now I'd say you're hovering around nuclear meltdown. Know what you need? You need to get laid."

"I do not!"

"Yes, you do."

"I've had lots of . . . *laid* in my life!"

She gave me a patronizing smile. "You don't store it up like nuts for the winter. You need it on kind of a regular basis, you know, to function properly. You're wound way too tight, sis."

I nodded my head furiously. "Yeah. Yeah! Good thing I'm living with the world's foremost expert on these matters! Good thing I'm sisters with Dr. Brothers!"

"I think you mean Dr. Ruth. She's Dr. Brothers' sex-crazed Mini-Me."

"Whatever!"

"When was your last time?"

My teeth were grinding so hard I was seconds away from permanent lockjaw.

"That cop is kind of cute," she said. "What was his name, Boatman?"

"His name was Boatwright. And he wasn't cute, he was a schmuck."

"I'd do him," she said casually, looking at her cuticles.

"Don't you go near him!"

She grinned, poking me in the sternum. "Gotcha!"

God I hated her!

"You like him," she said. "Why don't you call him up and ask for a date?"

"Why don't we get dressed for the funeral?" I said.

I couldn't even yell at her anymore. My energy was spent. I imagined it going down the drain of my overwrought psyche, disappearing in a languid, liquid spiral.

"We'll pay our respects first," I said. *"Then* I'll think about getting laid."

"Good girl!" she said, poking me again for good measure.

fifteen

$\mathcal{I}$ kept an eye out for the gray sedan as we headed out to Lenore's funeral, but thankfully it didn't materialize. Either the driver was a murderer on a bathroom break or I'd been completely deluded about the whole thing. Gee, what were the chances?

When we pulled into the parking lot at Beverly Eternal Rest, it looked like an ecumenical foreign car dealership. Jaguars, Mercedes, Rolls Royces, Bentleys, and the occasional Duesenberg all sitting side by side. This was not your typical SUV crowd. Most of Lenore's friends and associates were upward of sixty, and clambering in and out of utility vehicles would have been too taxing on their elderly hearts, not to mention a potential hip-breaker for those suffering from osteoporosis.

We stepped into the soothing blue interior of the building, and a somber-faced young woman handed us programs. The auditorium was full of folding chairs adorned with blue satin sashes, and hundreds of calla lilies rising from art deco vases. Sarah Bernhardt herself would have been pleased with the profusion of high-priced blooms. We looked out over a sea of heads—gray, blue, black, bottle blonde, melon orange. They wore pillbox hats with black netting, big sweeping forties-style hats with foot-wide brims, and jaunty black berets. There was even a miniature black cowboy hat perched on the head of a woman in her seventies.

The organ played "Where Thou Art, I Shall One Day Be, Sitting at Thy Right Hand, or Failing That, at Least Somewhere Nearby," an old southern hymn. Actually I had no idea what it was playing. Our parents had never been too big on church attendance, and most religious songs sounded alike to me, especially when played at one-half time.

A grim man with squinty eyes approached us. "Are you fahm-i-lee?" he intoned lugubriously. The funeral home could have done a better job with their homework, I thought cynically. Lenore *had* no family to speak of.

But it was obvious Reba had gone to a lot of trouble for this memorial and I knew she had cared deeply for Lenore at one time. It would be too depressing for those reserved rows in the front to go unused, so I nodded my head and he led us up to the first row.

Well, maybe the first row was overdoing it. I pointed to the second row, hoping he would think we were second cousins or something, not actual offspring. He nodded, pulling aside a blue velvet rope to let us enter. We shuffled down a couple of spaces and sat down. He put the rope back in place, and I actually had the thought, *Hey, what if there's a fire? You're blocking my egress!*

Terry was right. I *was* wound way too tight. My fear was getting the better of my rational processes, and I had to get it under control. I might even consider going on a date, even though I'd only promised to call Boatwright because she'd bullied me into it. I had no actual designs on the man—

No sooner had that thought crossed my mind than he appeared at the side of the row.

Oh my God.

He was clean-shaven, his hair combed back with just a touch of gel to give it a slightly tousled look. With his hair off his forehead, I could better appreciate his thick eyebrows with their perfect proportions. His nose looked stronger and more prominent, curving down just a bit at the end as if pointing to the full lips below. The hollows under his cheekbones made him look kind of dangerous.

Until he smiled.

The grin sent his whole face into motion, giving him a charmingly goofy look. All that stoniness crumbling into laugh lines radiating from his eyes and surrounding his mouth.

And the *eyes*. Usually I wasn't big on blue, but these weren't the milky kind, or the scary ice-blue kind that you see in huskies and some human beings. They were clear with a navy circle around the edges, patches of lighter blues mixed up inside.

Take me, I thought. Right here between the rows. To the strains of "Amazing Grace" . . .

What?

I'd made a complete ass out of myself in front of this man the night before and *he'd* helped me do it. What was wrong with me? He probably thought I was a complete idiot, and I wasn't sure I liked him at all!

But my hand disassociated itself from the rest of my body, lifting up on its own power as if under hypnosis. I watched in detached amazement as it reached over and lifted the blue rope to invite him to sit with us, the *fahm-i-lee*.

Who could be using my hand? This was pure science fiction! It was Stephen King! *The Hand that Reached Out and*

Grabbed the Hunky Cop and Forced Me into Unspeakably Lascivious Acts of Perversion Against My Will, coming soon to a peep show near you!

Dontsitnexttome, dontsitnexttome, dontsitnexttome, I chanted mentally. *Keep on going, sit on the other side of Terry.* I was already starting to sweat.

So what did he do?

He sat next to me. His leg touching my leg, his shoulder brushing mine.

I choked, turning it into a dainty little cough, and used this clever ruse to move an inch to the left.

Ah, no more touching. I let my breath out in a silent, controlled stream.

Donttalktome, donttalktome, donttalktome, I beamed to him. But the moron wasn't picking up my signals.

"How you doing?" he said.

"Fine," I croaked, and felt Terry dissolve into giggles next to me. *She* was picking up my signals and loving my discomfort. Perverse bitch. Evil twin. Betrayer of your own flesh and blood.

She leaned over, digging her elbow into my ribs. "How are *you*, Detective Boatwright?"

He held his palms up in a so-so gesture, then smiled adorably.

Oh quit with the smiling already!

I turned and locked my attention on the dais, noticing for the first time that it was covered in something white and fluffy. Cotton, by the looks of it. Lots and lots of cotton on the top of the stage and bunched around the sides. Then I noticed the absence of a lectern.

Strange.

The organ music stopped, and with it the hushed whispering of the crowd—the silence commanding the mourners' attention. Throats were cleared and butts were adjusted in seats, as everyone faced front in anticipation of the preacher's appearance.

But no one came. The silence became oppressive. I had a momentary panic, thinking Reba had forgotten to book a clergyman, or he was lost, or he couldn't find a parking space in the jammed lot—

Come to think of it, where was Reba?

The lights dimmed. The lights dimmed? Were we in a theater?

Then a beautiful, clear voice rang out from the back of the auditorium. A full-bodied alto-soprano without accompaniment, but with great feeling:

"Did you ever know that you're my hero . . . ?"

Oh dear God in heaven—what was this?

I heard the other mourners turn in their seats to look at the singer, but I couldn't. I was afraid of what I would see. I heard her take a deep breath, then she belted out the next line:

"You're everything I wish-sh-sh-sh I could be . . ."

She really hung on the word "wish."

Her voice was getting closer. I stared forward, now completely overwhelmed by the fear of losing it in the middle of a funeral. Terry was on one side of me and I could feel her trembling with incipient laughter. Boatwright was on the other side, making me cringe with sexual discomfort. I'd be prime for exploding, if only to get release from the combined tension.

This was not fair, not fair at all! I was under altogether too much pressure. Would I crack? Would I spontaneously combust, singeing the blue satin sash on my chair and rising like a smoke ring above the crowd?

I guess it depended on what came next. The song was vaguely familiar, but I couldn't yet place it.

"I could fly higher than an eagle . . ."

And then the organ kicked in, blaring on all its pipes, with a rockin' drumbeat to underscore the signature line.

"For you are the wind beneath my wings!"

Oh no—I recognized it now! The theme song from *Beaches*, a Bette Midler movie about two women who were best friends, and the schmaltz anthem for middle-aged women and gay men the world over. A real tearjerker.

Well, I was about to burst into tears, all right.

Girls in white gowns emerged from the sides of the room, golden halos gracing their heads, white cotton wings fluttering from their backs. A candle-bearing choir, they moved quickly but gracefully to their places on the stage, while the lead singer made her way down the aisle at a clip.

I had to look at her as she passed.

She was a well-preserved sixty, with a huge bosom and a massive double chin, and I thought that if I were a little more cultured I would probably recognize her as an international opera star. She wore a headset microphone, her voice slamming against the walls and bouncing back to our eardrums with a decibel level just this side of Metallica.

Then the wind kicked up. Actual wind, coming from loud, whirring machines. And thousands of blue satin ribbons fluttered into existence out of nowhere, all over the room.

I *was* going to lose it, I thought. Right here, right now.

Terry took pity on me and got up from her chair, moving further down the row to avoid adding her psychic vibrations to my already dangerously high level of horrified amusement.

The opera star bellowed the next stanza from the stage, then she waved into the audience and shouted, "Everybody!"

And sure enough, all the mourners chimed in on cue, some of them sniffling and tone deaf, but all willing to give it a try. They hooked their arms and swayed with the music, which had truly reached an historic level of loudness and badness. More than a few hearing aids had been left at home as unfashionable accessories, that much was obvious.

They warbled about beautiful faces hiding the pain, swore

that they would be nothing without *you*, achingly sang about love hidden away in their hearts . . .

I still didn't know who was using my hand, but it reached out and grabbed Boatwright's. I laced my fingers into his, clenching in agony as a woman in labor does the hand of the guilty man. Or father, as they're sometimes known.

Then there was a cranking noise, audible even beneath the singing, and a bit of gold appeared beneath the blue velvet curtain hanging above the stage. Down came a gold-framed portrait, slowly and with great dignity. It was an oil painting done in the 1950s, to judge by the hairdo of a very young, smiling Lenore Richling.

She looked like Jackie Kennedy. Dark hair in a smart bob, bright red lips, and grease-pencil eyebrows. She leaned on a Corinthian pedestal strewn with grape leaves, surrounded by yards of emerald-green satin—the folds of her off-the-shoulder evening gown—and she wore a sparkling emerald necklace with matching earrings. The painting was enormous, at least eight feet tall, a pathetic monument to Lenore's past glory, her lost youth, her hocked jewels, and the dissolution of her physical body.

The giggles left me and I felt a sudden surge of compassion for the woman who'd been so desperate to maintain her standard of living that she'd stooped to selling off her own treasures and possibly to blackmailing others for theirs. The woman who'd fallen so far and met an ignominious end, one-eared and utterly alone.

The painting stopped its descent and hung suspended halfway to the floor.

Then through a trick of mechanics that I would have thought beyond Reba's imagination, and certainly beyond her ability to orchestrate, two large feathered wings popped out from behind the painting and began to flap up and down in synchronization with the song's refrain.

"Thank you, thank you,
Thank God for you, the wind . . .
Beneath . . .
M-Y-Y-Y-Y . . .
W-I-I-I-I-I-I-I-N-N-N-N-N-N-G-G-G-G-S!"

The audience jumped to their feet and applauded as if it were the climax of an Andrew Lloyd Webber musical, which it very nearly was. I found myself wondering if Reba actually knew Lord Andrew Lloyd or Lord Webber or whoever—I wouldn't put it past her to have such a big name pal in the wings—and I swear to God the moment the word "wings" had formed in my head, those on the back of the portrait sprang out of their moorings. The choir and the opera singer screamed and ran in circles, dodging the enormous bird appendages that plummeted to the stage.

Then the painting shifted, to the sound of wires creaking, and before you could say *crash landing*, the cable on the right side of the portrait snapped and it hitched to the left, *swooshing* down and clunking the opera singer on the head.

She teetered for a moment, then put her hand to her breast and collapsed to the ground with a long, melodic *"Uhooo-ohhh,"* and lay in a heap on the stage.

Very Wagnerian.

An appropriate ending, really.

The audience obviously agreed, because they started shouting *Bravo!* and *Encore!* and *Diva!* and the applause went on for what seemed like hours.

Eventually I realized that I wasn't applauding, and neither was Boatwright. He couldn't because his hand was between my teeth. At some point during the whole *Nightmare on Broadway* funeral production I had put the heel of his hand in my mouth and bitten down hard on it to avoid screaming.

I looked at him and smiled around his hand.

"Can I have it back now?" he asked.

I pried open my teeth, and he extracted his hand, wiping it on the side of his coat.

"Thanks," he said. And smiled in a way that made my heart go thump, even over the roar of the crowd.

You see, Lenore and Reba truly had been best friends at one time. I don't know who was the wind and who was the wings, but I thought it best not to be too literal about the whole thing. Either way, it was the sentiment that counted.

I thought about the possibility of having a lifelong friendship with a woman who wasn't my twin, and realized it would never happen. I'd had good friends, of course, I had some of them still. But that *Girlfriends4Ever* kind of giggly, nail-painting, talking about boys and trying on each other's bras kind of friendship that blossoms into mature woman-of-the-world friendship, *that* would elude me in this lifetime. Terry had never been into giggling and boys, and once when I'd made the mistake of borrowing her training bra at the age of twelve, she'd wrapped it around my neck and swung me around the room like a lassoed calf until I cried.

Terry simply took up too much space in my life. There was no room for a best girlfriend. And I guess I'd have to accept that there'd be no one for whom I'd be throwing an extravaganza of a funeral, like Reba just had. Terry and I would probably go within seconds of each other anyway, bickering our astral heads off even as they lowered us into the ground.

I covertly scanned the reception room looking for Boatwright. I'd lost him in the confusion following the opera singer's accident—the crowd surging toward the stage, the arrival of the ambulance and paramedics. They thought the singer had only suffered a mild concussion, but she'd been carted off to the hospital anyway as a precaution. Happily, nothing stopped the Grim Reaper from his appointed rounds, so the funeral reception had gone on as scheduled after the famous woman had been spirited away. Her name still escapes me, but I learned she had recently sung the role of Romeo in the LA Opera's production of *Romeo and Juliet*. Gender, age, and breast-size being irrelevant, apparently, in that fine art of yesteryear.

I was contemplating pouring myself a cup of punch when Boatwright walked up with two glasses of white wine.

"Ah, I had been thinking of punch," I said, taking the wine.

"Nah, after a performance like that, we have to toast."

I smiled and held up my glass. "To Lenore. May she have passed to the other side before she saw her send-off." We clinked.

This was a good idea, I thought, drinking half the wine in one gulp. It would hit my bloodstream unimpeded by food, giving me a false sense of relaxation, and might even keep me from swallowing my tongue while attempting to make witty conversation with Boatwright.

"Stedman told me about the statements you made today," he said. "I want to thank you for your cooperation. You and your sister gave us some good leads."

"You're welcome."

"I'm sorry we were a little rough on you yesterday. It's the job, you know?"

"I didn't really think you were that hard on us. Except for the laughing part . . . I felt a little ridiculous."

"Hey," he said, "laughter is a healing balm."

"So is sex," someone said, and I looked around to see who it was. But no one was there, and Boatwright was looking straight at me. Oops. I guess I said it.

Great, I winced. Now he's going to think I'm some horny nympho-beast.

"Yeah, I guess it is," he said, blinking. "I seem to remember that it was, anyway."

Okay, okay. That was good. He was trying to tell me he was available. So maybe he liked horny nympho-beasts. Was that a good thing or a bad thing? Maybe I'd better clear up my statement.

"I didn't mean to imply that sex with *you* would be, you know, you know, implicit, somehow, in all of this."

So much for the wine loosening my tongue. Yep, I was really lighting the rhetorical world on fire.

Then he did something so endearing, I shall never forget it. He actually spat his wine back into his glass. Apparently he'd had a mouthful when I made that last statement, and had been trying hard to swallow it without laughing.

"Oh God," I wailed, "everything I do around you is stupid! I'm *not* stupid, I was valedictorian!"

He laughed again and put his arm around my shoulders. "Congratulations. Would you like to go out some time?"

I stared up at him—the laugh lines, the blue irises, the nice teeth, the luscious lips—and my knees instantly turned to jelly. "You . . . you would go out with *me*?" I said, stumbling backward.

"Sure," he said. "How about tonight?"

My head began to nod furiously, as if it had a mind of its own. Who was using my neck muscles?

"Okay, then it's a date?" he asked to be certain.

I wasn't about to open my mouth. I wasn't going to blow it by saying something. *Anything.* But my damn head just kept bobbing up and down.

"Uh, okay then. I guess . . . I guess I'll get your phone number from your booking sheet?"

Nodnodnodnodnod.

Stop with the head bobbing! I yelled at myself inwardly. You look like a brain-damaged cockatiel!

"You're one of a kind, McAfee," Boatwright said, just as my identical twin arrived with a drink in her hand.

One of a kind!

That did it. I was in love. He saw me as an individual, as separate from Terry. And best of all, he seemed to like me better! I thought I could risk a little more conversation on the strength of this revelation.

" 'Bye!" I said.

Which I guess was a little abrupt.

He gave me a hesitant smile and set his drink on the table. "I should probably get back to the station," he said.

I gulped the rest of the wine and handed my empty glass to Terry.

"So, did you get any scoop?" she said. "You were talking to him a long time. Wring any good info out of him?"

"Uh, no."

She looked confused. "Well, what were you talking about?"

"Nothing." I wadded up a cocktail napkin and tossed it into a trash can.

"You were, too. You were nodding like a maniac! What did he say?"

"You want to know what we were talking about?"

"Yeah!"

"For such a long time?"

"Yeah, *what?*"

"Sex!" I shouted, as a hush fell over the crowd. Everyone in the place turned to stare at us, heads swiveling our way in super-slow motion.

Legend has it that when the whole room falls silent at once, an angel has passed overhead. So I guess the one who yells suffers from angel insensitivity.

Sorry, Lenore.

"I'm glad you weren't talking about fire," Terry said. "We would have been stampeded by senior citizens."

I closed my eyes and let out a breath. Then I opened them again to find Reba standing in front of us.

"Where *were* you?" I said, taking out my embarrassment on her.

"Backstage, darling." She was flushed and fluttery, stoked on success, like a playwright expecting rave reviews in the late edition. "The director can't just sit in the audience like the rest of the public. I had to make sure everything ran smoothly."

Smoothly? She'd almost killed one of the world's leading divas!

"Obviously, that last bit wasn't planned," she said hurriedly, anticipating this objection, "but I think it added something, don't you? A statement of the precariousness of existence, the whimsicality of fate—"

"The importance of ducking when giant wings fly at your head," Terry said.

"Yes, well." Reba gave her an irritated look.

"Where'd you get that magnificent portrait of Lenore?" I asked to get Terry off the hook.

"Wasn't it the perfect touch?" Reba was smiling again. "I found it in her garage. I had been contacted by a nice young man at the insurance company, and we went through the house together. You know, to put together a claim . . . and oh—" she suddenly remembered, "he said he knew you."

"The insurance company? You mean Sidney Lefler?" I looked at Terry, who gave me a shrug in return.

"Yes. We were poking around, and I found the painting right there in the garage, leaning against the wall. I knew immediately that I wanted to use it today. But the strangest thing, dears—"

"Yes?" Terry said.

"I found the Judith Leiber bag in the trash bin in the garage, and what do you know? It had been chewed! No wonder Lenore didn't return it to me."

Terry frowned at her. "Chewed? By what?"

"Well, I assume by her dog. The one you have."

"We haven't seen him chew on anything, have we?" I asked Terry.

"He's not really a chewer," she confirmed.

"Well, the corner of the bag was gnawed clear through. It's very peculiar, but there you go. Sidney said I could put in an insurance claim."

"Interesting," I said absently, while trying to put something together in my memory—something about Sidney.

"Lenore must have left it on the floor and the dog had his way with it," Reba said. "You'd think she'd have more respect for a genuine Leiber, but . . . oh, well. Can't take it with you, as today has amply illustrated."

She grabbed our hands, dragging us across the room. "Come, dears. I want to show you off to the girls."

Reba introduced us to a few of her friends and acquaintances, then wandered off, leaving us to our own devices. We made light conversation with two little old ladies, telling them that we'd known Lenore for a number of years and had wanted to pay our respects because we remembered her so fondly. That pleased them immensely, and a ninety-year-old dear named Harriet reached into her black silk purse and extracted a personal card with her name and number in raised gold ink.

"Send me your address and I'll put you on my invitation list," she said. "It's so nice to have young people at one's funeral, don't you think, Agatha?"

Her tiny wheelchair-bound friend agreed heartily, giving us a card of her own. I expected a phone number and address, but it was a poem, of sorts:

Here lies Agatha May.
Daughter of Zelda,
Mother of Bertha,
Beloved of Henry McBride.
She outlived them all,
By having a ball,
And keeping a man on the side.

I laughed and handed the card to Terry. "Is this your epitaph?" I asked her.

"You betcha. I carry it in my wallet. I want to make sure there are no typos when the time comes. I'd love it if you'd come to my funeral, too."

"We wouldn't miss it," I said.

"And be sure to talk about sex, real loud!"

Terry smirked at me. "We speak of almost nothing else."

The ladies tittered giddily, while my attention was drawn to the other side of the room. A group of women was huddled in the corner, deep in conversation. They wore large hats with black netting that covered their faces, which they hadn't removed for the sake of the indoor reception. I figured they were the post-op girls we had met in the hotel, and became even more certain of that fact when I saw one of them lift her veil to take a sip of punch, revealing bandages on the side of her face.

"Excuse me," I said to Agatha and Harriet. "We'll be right back."

I motioned for Terry to follow me and we made our way over to the sequestered group. Most of the women were older, but there was a youngish blonde with a killer body in a black panama hat.

"Hello, ladies," I said. "Remember us? We met you at the Dauphine Hotel."

One by one they nodded their heads. "How are you feeling?" Terry asked them.

They all muttered variations on *Fine, thank you.*

"So terrible about Mrs. Richling, wasn't it?" I said.

The women nodded in unison.

"Still, not as terrible as what someone did to Hattrick," Terry said, waiting for one of them to take the bait.

The Mexican woman finally did. "Hattrick was a putz." She made it sound like *poots.*

"Good riddance," another one of the veiled women said. Then they all lifted their glasses and clinked.

"Did you hear about Alphonse?" I asked breezily.

The drinks stopped in midair.

"What about him?" one of them asked.

I lowered my voice to a whisper, leaning in. "I heard he was picked up by the police for dispensing drugs to his guests in the hotel, using them like common pushers to keep the drugs circulating in Beverly Hills."

The Mexican woman was first to peel off. "Excuse me, *muchachas.* I must get to the airport. Please come to visit me in San Miguel. *Hasta luego!*"

They air-kissed through voile, then another one looked at her watch. "Oh, I'm going to be late for my acrylic fills. Darla gets so cranky when I keep her waiting." More kisses, then she scurried away.

And so it went, all of them making excuses and ducking out, as if Terry and I had let a bunch of mice loose on the floor that were about to skitter up their skirts.

Only the blonde remained. "Didn't mean to chase everyone off," I said to her, apologetically.

She giggled. "You guys don't recognize me, do you?"

I shook my head, then it came to me. I couldn't see her face clearly, but I knew that voice. "Barbie, is that you?"

She pulled up her veil. "Peekaboo!" The net dropped back in place.

"How are you?" I said.

She shrugged. "Back on the streets, looking for another job."

"Yeah, I guess so," Terry said. "Sorry about that."

"The police want to speak to you," I told Barbie.

"*Moi?* How come?" She sounded genuinely surprised, even a little alarmed.

"They want to talk to anyone who worked in Hattrick's office. It's standard procedure."

"I was only there for a little while, a couple of days at the most. I don't know anything."

"Even so," Terry said. "Sometimes little details can be helpful in an investigation, especially since you were there in the days leading up to Hattrick's murder. You should contact Hank Stedman of LAPD, or John Boatwright of BHPD. Want me to write those names down for you?"

"Don't bother. I'll remember. Stedman, Boatwright. See there? No moss growing on me." She tapped her hat with a long nail, then reached into her purse for a powder compact. "I heard you girls found the doctor all chopped up and everything. How icky."

"Yes," I said. "It was horrible. No one deserves to go that way."

"Well," she said, buffing her chin, "maybe he should have been more careful about who he took on as patients." She snapped the compact shut and tucked it back in her purse.

"Are you talking about anyone in particular?" I said.

"Well, no. But it's obvious he was killed by a patient, - isn't it?"

Terry gave her a piercing look. "I don't know. Were *you* one of his patients?"

"Uh, nooo . . ." Barbie flipped her hair behind her shoulder. "I don't want to speak ill of the dead, you know, but *quack quack!*"

"Yeah," I said. "That seems to be the consensus."

"Well, I just wanted to pay my respects," Barbie said. "And now I'm off to a hot date. See ya!"

She tottered away on her four-inch stilettos, her calf muscles bulging from the strain of balancing on her toes.

Reba came rushing up to us. "What did you say to the girls? They all left in such a hurry!"

"We just gave them a little heads up," Terry said. "They're going home to flush their goodie baskets."

Reba frowned, but decided to leave it alone. "Well, I've got to go strike the set. We'll get together tomorrow for brunch, shall we? We can discuss our next case. Ta!" She blew us kisses, and then she, too, scurried off.

Terry turned to me. "*Our* next case?"

"Don't look at me. You're the one who pronounced her a member of the team."

"I thought she'd get bored."

"She *was* bored and she didn't even know it. I guess getting her legs waxed and her brows tweezed and her feet sanded all day isn't doing it for her anymore. Now she wants to spend her golden years blinding evildoers with her manicure set."

"Well, we'll worry about it tomorrow," Terry said. "Let's go get something to eat. I can't deal with that finger food. I need something substantial. A *manwich*."

"It's been a long time since we went to Canter's."

"What a scathingly brilliant idea."

I hiked up my skirt and got on the bike behind Terry, and then we headed for Canter's Deli, which had been in the heart of the Fairfax district for God only knew how many years. Mr. Canter himself was featured on the front of the building, looking like a grinning Sephardic band leader limned in neon, welcoming one and all to sample his matzo balls.

The twenty-four-hour restaurant appealed to people of all ages, proclivities, and ethnic backgrounds. There were the elderly Jewish people who came for the wholesome chicken soup; the spiky-haired, tattooed types who went there to re-plenish their drug-depleted systems; the foreign tourists, be-cause the deli was a perennial stop on guided tours; and everything in between.

Terry and I were led to a booth right in the center of all the bustling activity and ordered pastramis on rye. Coleslaw and dill pickles were de rigueur, and didn't even need to be men-tioned.

The sandwiches arrived and we each took a bite of pickle, lodging it under our tongues, then took a bite of sandwich to be combined with the pickle, then we forked in coleslaw and chewed. We washed it all down with iced tea.

"You ever wonder why we don't just put everything on the sandwich if we want to mix it up?" I asked Terry.

She shook her head. As I've already indicated, Terry is not much given to introspection.

Nor, apparently, was she given to talking at the moment. That was good, because I needed time to concentrate on Sid-ney. There was something about him I felt I was missing, but I just couldn't put my finger on it.

I chewed and stewed, masticated and ruminated, gnawed and mulled, digested and reflected—

"What are you thinking about?" Terry finally asked.

"Nothing." Best not to tell her I was spending valuable case time on word games. But sometimes you had to come at things sideways. Terry never understood that. She was too straightforward, too dead-on, too head-in, too clear-cut, too on-the-nose—

"Are you playing word games in your head?"

"No."

"Are you doing synonyms or rhymes?"

"Synonyms," I confessed. "I was doing rhymes before."

"Well, cut it out!" she yelled at me. "I'm picking up your thoughts and it's making me crazy!"

The waitress turned to look at us, then rolled her eyes and kept going. She was used to chemically altered patrons here at Canter's, though not usually this early in the evening.

Before long, the greasy sandwiches had been converted into lead stomach weights and no epiphanies were forthcoming.

Then without warning, one arrived.

"I know!" I said.

"What?"

"Sidney Lefler went with Reba to check out Lenore's house, right? That's when she got the Jackie Kennedy portrait."

"Right."

"Well, when we went to see Binion, he said that a man from the insurance company had been to the house and reported that the rugs were trashed."

"Uh-huh."

"So the man had to be our friend Sid! Sidney told us he'd been at another inspection when the call came in about Suzie's death, and then it turned out the other house was Lenore's."

She bit on another pickle. "Yeah . . ."

"So if Sidney went through the house after the break-in, he would have seen that the rugs were in good condition. And he'd be duty bound to turn them over to Reba after the will was probated."

"You're right."

"He acts like he can't stand Binion, and maybe he can't. But that doesn't mean he can't be in league with him."

"So what are you saying, that Sidney has the Bacon?"

I opened my mouth to say *By George, we've got it!* but on second thought, it clamped shut. "No, I guess not. The timing's not right."

"Why not?"

"Because he was still looking for the painting when we were at his office. And he was real anxious to get it."

"He could have been faking it, pretending not to know where the Bacon was when he really did."

"I don't think so. He got too excited when he thought we could tell him where it was. You can't fake that level of anxiety."

"Hmm. But he *might* have the rugs."

"He might, indeed."

The waitress dropped off the bill. I was about to stand up to go to the cashier, when my eyes lit upon a heart-stopping sight: Eli strolling in the front door, holding the elbow of our dear Aunt Reba. They were looking very intimate.

"Duck!" I said to Terry.

She obeyed, quickly sliding under her side of the table. I peered around the corner of the booth, my head low.

"Who is it?" she demanded in a whisper, but I shushed her with a finger to the lips.

The hostess approached Eli and Reba, then led them toward the other dining room. Terry started to sit up.

"Don't let them see you!"

"Who?" She ducked again.

"Just *go*."

I grabbed the check and we made our way to the cash register, bent over in a running crouch. Terry flew out the door and I hid beneath the counter, throwing the cashier our bill and a twenty. She took them without question and started to make change.

"Give it to the waitress," I said.

"No problem."

"Thank you!" I scurried outside.

When I got a few yards away from the front windows, I straightened up and ran down the block to Terry.

"*What?*" she bellowed at me.

"Okay, okay," I said, catching my breath. "I haven't mentioned this before, but I think Eli is dating Reba. No, I *know* Eli is dating Reba, because I just saw them go into the restaurant together."

She gave me a look that would melt lead. "He's representing her!"

"Yeah, but when he came to the police station after our arrest, he was reeking of Chanel No. 5!"

"Oh, so what? For that we had to leave the restaurant like we were dodging bullets?"

She was right. What *had* I been thinking? Suddenly I felt ridiculously foolish. "I didn't want to embarrass them." It was weak, but it was the only explanation I could think of for overreacting the way I had.

"You're seeing conspiracies *everywhere*," Terry said.

"Nuh-uh."

"Yuh-huh." She broke out laughing. "Do you actually think Reba would go out with Eli socially?"

I started laughing, too. "It did cross my mind."

"Get outta here! I mean, I love the guy, but he's a terrible dresser, he has a total potty mouth, and he's way too poor for her!"

"You're right," I said, shaking my head. "Of course you're right."

"We didn't need to run out of the restaurant, you moron!"

I wiped a tear from my eye. "I don't know where my head is!" I admitted.

"You could probably locate it up your *ass*. Now let's go back in there and say hello. Maybe Eli's got some interesting scoop on Binion or something."

"Okay."

We went back in the front door. The cashier gave me a funny look. "Shouldn't you be crouching?"

"Turns out that was unnecessary," I told her.

"Well, good. That must be hell on your knees."

I followed Terry toward the back of the room, until she finally stopped next to the servers' station. She stood there, staring. I leaned over her shoulder to see what she was looking at, and what I saw took my breath away.

Eli and Reba were sitting on the same side of the short booth, their backs to us, and the two of them were making out.

Not billing and cooing, not smooching, not even kissing, but lip-smashing, teeth-splintering, tongues-down-throats making out.

I turned and ran, with Terry right behind me.

I raced past the cashier and flung myself out the door.

"Hurry on back, now!" she said.

We stopped running when we got to the bike, both of us sucking in air.

"I don't want to say what's the world coming to," I said, "but what the *fuck* is the world coming to?"

"They were doing the tonsil tango!" Terry gasped.

"Snogging each other in public!"

"He had his hand on her *boob!*"

I winced. "It was like seeing your parents doing it!"

"I'll never get that image out of my brain!"

"Well, it wouldn't be *in* your brain if you hadn't made us go back in again!"

"Oh, so this is *my* fault?" she fired back.

"I don't know how it could be seen any other way!"

"Oh, you don't?"

"No, I don't!"

We took a breath simultaneously.

"I think we need to go talk to Priscilla," I said.

We traveled south on Fairfax, took a left on Wilshire, and got to Eli's office at six-thirty. Priss was coming out the lobby door just as we arrived.

"Hey, girls! How ya doin'? Eli's not here."

"Yes. We. Know."

She frowned. "How'd you know?"

"We just saw him at Canter's, in a liplock with our great-aunt!" I cried.

"Oh."

"You *knew*," Terry said, shaking her head. "When did this start?"

"She's been calling a lot the last two days—"

"Yeah, and . . . ?"

"Well, at first she was making up excuses, like 'Tell him it's Mrs. Price-Slatherton, and I just had a wee question about blah blah.' But then I'd go, 'Oh, I can probably help you with that' and she'd go, 'Thank you, dear, but I really need to speak to Mr. Weintraub personally' and then—"

"And then?" I prompted her.

"And then she dropped the pretense. 'Let me speak to that big hunk of man,' she'd say, or 'Put the old sex hound on the phone'—"

"That's enough!" we yelled.

"How long has this been going on?" Terry demanded.

"Oh, since you brought her in. She called that afternoon, and they must have spent two hours on the phone. I couldn't get Eli's attention for anything. They talk about ten times a day."

Terry and I gawked at each other. What were we looking at here? A new step-great-uncle?

"Sorry, guys," Priss said. "I didn't think it was my place to blab."

"No, it's not your fault," I said with a sigh. "We're just . . . having a little trouble adjusting to the idea, I guess."

"Well, I don't see anything wrong with it. They're consenting adults. If they want to fuck like bunnies, it's nobody's—"

"Ewwwww!" Terry and I both wailed. That image put us right over the edge.

"Sorry."

"Look, Priss," I said, "we really shouldn't have even asked. It's none of our business. Do me a favor, don't tell Eli we know, okay?"

"Sure, I'd be happy not to mention it."

"Thanks." I promised to call her for lunch, then Terry and I hopped on the bike to head for home, our world rocked by a vision of senior-citizen horniness.

I thought I saw a yellow Volkswagen Bug following us for a good portion of the way, but I shrugged it off. Terry had told me I was seeing conspiracies everywhere, and in this case she was right.

The Bug turned off somewhere around Overland Avenue.

sixteen

It was twilight when we got back to the house. We found a pile of calla lilies on the front porch, leftovers from the funeral.

"That's nice," I said. "Reba dropped off some flowers."

"I'm surprised she had time between bonk sessions," Terry said.

"Now, now." I shook my finger at her. "It was a nice gesture."

She made a face. "I don't like having funeral flowers in the house. Seems like bad luck or something."

"But they're beautiful. It's a shame to waste them."

"Hey, let's give them to Jane. We haven't seen her in a long time."

Jane Doe was the wild deer who visited our backyard. Before the arrival of Muffy and Paquito, she had been kind of an unofficial pet. We sometimes left raw vegetables out for her, but flowers were her favorite treat. Giving her the lilies seemed like a good compromise. We wouldn't have fresh blooms in the house, but we might have a deer sighting. If she didn't show up tonight, the chances were good she'd drop by for breakfast.

After feeding the pups, we changed into jeans and went out back, placing the flowers at the edge of the wooded area where the canyon wall rose at a sixty-degree angle. There was enough light there to see Jane if she appeared, but not enough to frighten her off. We stationed ourselves on the back porch in the shadows, a spot that gave us a perfect line of sight, and sat on our haunches waiting and whispering.

"So, you think we should confront Reba and Eli?" Terry asked.

"Oh, what for?" I said, sighing. "Priss is right. They're grown-ups, they can do what they want."

"But why didn't they tell us? I feel so betrayed."

"Maybe they want to see if it's the real deal before they tell us. Or if it's just—" I swallowed hard, "a sexual thing."

"Eeeeyick."

"Oh, listen to us!" I said. "We're being really infantile about the whole thing. Seventy isn't dead—far from it these days. And when we're that age, do we want people looking at us and going, *Ewww, you actually use that old booty?*"

"Yeah. But maybe they don't see *us* as grown-ups who can appreciate mature love."

"It's possible," I said.

"Then maybe what we should do is say we saw them—"

"Say we saw them going at it like a couple of Viagra fiends?"

"What, then? Continue to live in denial?"

"Denial as a way of life is vastly underrated."

"Shhh, listen."

We heard the sound of twigs snapping. Was that Jane, making her way down the hill? She had the nimbleness of a mountain goat when negotiating the rocky ledge and a very sensitive radar for fresh edibles. But we had only just put out the flowers, so it might be a raccoon or a squirrel. We held our breath and waited for another sign that she was out there in the darkness.

Crunch. There it was, another delicate footfall. She was taking her time coming down the hill, cautious little woodland creature that she was. Ah, I thought, there's nothing like the natural world to put all of our human craziness in perspective.

We heard another step, another barely audible snapping of twigs under a dainty hoof.

Then there was a great rustling of leaves and crashing of branches like a heavy animal was sliding down the hill, hurtling through the underbrush and slamming into a tree, thudding against the trunk.

"Uggghh!" it exclaimed.

That was no deer. That was a person!

We jumped up to our feet.

"Who's there?" Terry yelled.

We heard someone thrashing in the leaves, twigs snapping like crazy. And involuntary noises of exertion as someone scrambled back up the hill.

"Ugh ugh ugh!"

"The flashlight!" Terry yelled.

We dashed through the back door into the kitchen. I grabbed the Mag-Lite flashlight, she ran into the living room and emerged with a baseball bat.

"Let's rumble!"

The pups barked and chased after us and we lost a few seconds trying to keep them in the house as we flew out the door. I shone the flashlight into the trees, waving the powerful beam back and forth like a searchlight.

No one was there.

We ran across the yard and I shone the light further up the hill. We could see where the earth and leaves had been displaced, a shallow tunnel dug by the sliding person. There was a narrow groove down the middle that was probably caused by the heel of a shoe.

I aimed the flashlight at the top of the rise and saw a figure in dark clothes running across the ridge to the south. He disappeared into the trees.

Terry and I clawed our way up to the top, pulling on saplings and grabbing tree trunks to hoist ourselves up the steep incline. I slipped once and fell hard on my knee. Terry beat me to the top, using the bat for leverage and to whack away at the densest foliage.

But when we reached the top, he was nowhere to be seen. He'd probably traversed the crest and gone back down through someone else's yard. I pointed the flashlight at the ground, illuminating some large footprints with a patterned rubber sole, like the sole of a running shoe.

"Well, hell," Terry said at last. "We've got a prowler."

"Or a murderer."

We went back inside and debated whether to call the police. Terry made the counterargument, of course.

"It's not like they're going to come out here and make a plaster cast of the footprints in the dirt, then compare them to a national database of backyard intruders."

"No, but if we tell them about Sergei, they'll take it seriously."

"Take it seriously? Get real. Are you forgetting the laughfest down at Parker Center? I'm not going to watch them spewing saliva while they hoot about *The Case of the Killer Raccoon!*"

"You know that wasn't a raccoon, Ter."

"I know it's a little scary, but we've spent enough time with the police lately. Let's not cry wolf until we *really* need them—"

"And when is that going to be? When Sergei actually makes it into the house and attempts to disembowel us or something?"

"Yeah, something like that."

"Oh great. Listen, why don't we just take our twelve thousand dollars and escape to Hawaii or somewhere until they catch him?"

"What? You didn't even want to take that money, any of it! And now you're proposing that we take it and flake off without even attempting to earn it?"

"Earn it? How do we do that, by getting killed? Let the police find their man!"

"That's chickenshit, Kerry."

"I never said I wasn't chicken! *Brawwwk! Brawwwk! Brawwwk!* See? I open my mouth and out it comes—my native tongue. Anyway, I never said I wanted to *die* for this stupid case."

"First of all, you're letting your imagination run away with you. *Someone* was in our backyard. It's a big leap from that to being stalked by a Russian murderer."

"We can get a kick-ass spring rate in Maui. Whaddaya say?"

"No."

I began to hula dance around the living room. "Come *on.* We'll get new bikinis. It'll be fun!"

She gave me a disgusted look and sat down on the couch, arms crossed.

I twirled my hands and gyrated my hips, singing in a Polynesian accent. "Oh we're going . . . to a hukilau—"

"Shut up!"

"The huki huki huki hukilau . . ." I mimed along with the song. "We throw our nets, into the sea . . . All the amaama come a swimming to me—"

"You're scaring the dogs! You're scaring *me*." Muffy and Paquito were sitting next to her, heads on their paws with their ears back.

"Oh, okay, spoilsport."

I'd made my point. I bent at the waist to take a bow.

And then came the explosion.

It sounded like a shotgun blast and a car crashing through the front of the house simultaneously. Shattered glass rained down around me. Plaster exploded from the wall above the couch.

I threw myself on the floor. Terry dived off the couch.

She grabbed Paquito and I grabbed Muffy and we scrambled away from the front door, the dogs yapping in terror.

I grabbed the phone and punched in 911.

"Nine-one-one Operator. What's your emergency?"

"Someone just shot into our house!"

It seemed like an eternity but it was only five minutes by my watch. We huddled on the floor in the alcove between the living room and the dining nook, clutching the dogs and trembling, eyes trained on the front door. Terry had the baseball bat next to her leg.

Finally a light shone in the blasted-out front window and we heard that blessed word.

"Police!"

We leaped to our feet and ran to the door, glass crunching underfoot. Terry unlocked the door and threw it open. Two officers stood on the porch, one blond, one African American. They looked capable and square-jawed, as tough as Marines, and they were instantly the best friends I'd ever had.

"Come in," Terry said to them.

They entered, looking around.

"You ladies made the call?" the blond one asked.

We nodded.

"Are you all right? Were you hurt?"

We shook our heads.

"Are you two twins?" the black cop asked.

"Yes sir, we are," Terry said, and I almost had a stroke. It was the first time in her life to give a straight answer to that question—scared polite, I guess.

The blond was the first to spot the hole in the wall above the couch. He went over to inspect it. "Heavy artillery," he said. "You ladies see or hear anything before the shot?"

"Well, not right before the shot," I said. "A few minutes earlier we had been in the backyard and we heard someone on the hill. We ran out with a flashlight and a baseball bat, but he got away."

The black officer crossed to the back door, looking out into the yard. He spoke into a microphone under his chin. "Witness reports sighting of a man in the backyard."

"We don't know for sure it was a man," Terry said.

"Oh, for once shut up with the feminist crap!" I said, exasperated.

The cops spun around at my outburst.

I almost told them about Sergei, but thought better of it. That was a conversation for when things calmed down. "It was a man, officers," I assured them. "A man in dark clothes. She thinks we have to allow for women in every aspect of society and I guess that includes shotgun killers."

"Possibly a woman," the blond officer said into his mic. Obviously he'd been through sensitivity training at the Academy.

"We've got other officers outside, checking out the perimeter," the black cop said. "Did this person say anything to you? Did you hear a voice?"

We shook our heads.

"He slipped on the hill and hit a tree," I told them. "We heard him say *Ugh*, but that's all."

"We had an earlier report of a prowler in the area," the blond cop said.

I glared at Terry. "When was this?"

"About a half hour before your incident," the black cop answered. "Were you in this room when the shot came through?"

I pointed to the couch. "My sister was sitting there, and I was over here." I moved to the spot where I had been.

"You were standing right there?"

"No, officer," Terry said. "She was not standing. She was dancing the hula."

He gave her a stern face. "I know you're upset, miss. But we don't need sarcasm right now."

"I'm telling the truth!" Terry protested. "She *was* hula dancing."

"Oh."

The officers exchanged a look, then the blond turned to me. "Can you show us what you were doing and where you were doing it?"

Oh fine.

Just *fine*.

Terry stifled a giggle, while the blond officer went out to the porch, closed the door, and looked through the blast hole. "Go ahead," he said.

I twirled my hands and wagged my hips, Terry humming an accompaniment. I gave it a few seconds, then stopped. I was already traumatized enough. Anyway, it was hard to imagine I was shot at just because I got a little carried away with a luau fantasy. Nobody's *that* tough a critic.

"It was something like that," I said.

"And were you dancing when the shot came through?" the black officer wanted to know.

I nodded.

"And singing," Terry said. "Sing for them, Kerry."

I glared at her, telegraphing an image of her hanging from a meat hook by the nostril.

"That's not necessary," he said, then smiled for the first time since he got there. "Unless you're inspired."

"Well, either he wasn't a very good shot or he didn't intend to hit you," the blond said, coming back inside. "You'd be hard to miss at that angle."

I suddenly remembered. "No, I took a bow. I bent over like this the second the gun went off." I demonstrated for them.

The black cop whistled. "Lucky lady."

The officers got a squawk on their radios. They'd caught someone outside and were bringing him to the house for possible identification.

Terry ran to the door, but I stayed glued to the spot. The black officer put a hand on my shoulder, sensing my fear. "It's okay," he said. "They've got it under control."

We looked outside and saw the patrol cars with their lights flashing, and an officer waving traffic through on Beverly Glen.

Two more cops in flak vests appeared dragging a huge man between them, his hands cuffed behind his back, wearing a black trench coat and dark glasses. He had a thick neck and a jarhead topped with brushy blond hair. Terry and I recognized him at once.

"Lance!" we yelled.

One of the officers said, "Do you know this man?"

"Yes!" I said. "Lance, did you shoot at us?"

"No, I swear!"

"He says he's your bodyguard."

Terry rolled her eyes. "He's an actor. He's going to *play* a bodyguard in the movies."

"Your aunt hired me," Lance whimpered. "She rehired me, I mean."

"When?"

"This morning. I told her I wouldn't work in the same house with the Irish she-devil, but you two were okay."

"Well, you're fired!" I yelled at him. "We just got shot at!"

Lance looked down at his feet. "I couldn't get a parking space, so I went to Starbuck's for a mocha frappuccino. When I came back, all hell had broken loose."

"Is this for real?" the black officer said to me, incredulous.

" 'Fraid so," Terry said. "It's something our aunt *would* do."

I suddenly made the connection.

"Do you have a gray sedan?" I asked Lance. He gave a rueful nod. "What about a yellow VW Bug?"

"They're rentals. I told your aunt that you had caught on to me in the sedan, so she had me rent the Bug. She didn't want you to know you were being guarded. Said you'd be too proud, or something."

"Well, we're bursting with pride right now," I said.

The officers spent another hour at the house. They recovered the shell casing from the front porch and a 9mm slug from the wall, bagging them for evidence. They also combed the neighborhood for the shooter, but without success.

At some point I cornered the blond officer and told him that we were private investigators and that we'd been running an investigation that may have brought us to the attention of Sergei Pavlov, an escaped Russian hijacker who was suspected of killing a junkie plastic surgeon and his office manager—his cohorts in a scheme to run illegal drugs through the Dauphine Hotel—all of them aided and abetted by a criminal mastermind in the person of a silver-haired Beverly Hills attorney named Hugh Binion. . . .

"Yeah, I like those Jackie Collins novels, too," he said, walking away.

Hmmmph.

The cops called Reba, who confirmed by phone that she had indeed hired Lance to watch us. It was clear he wasn't the same man dressed in black who'd been running through our yard, so the cops released him and Lance went sniveling back to Reba's house.

We had to clean up the glass first, so the dogs wouldn't step on it and lacerate their paws, and we didn't get around to speaking to Reba until forty-five minutes later. She was verging on hysterical when we called. "You're all right?" she said. "Tell me you're all right!"

"We're fine," Terry told her.

"Just a little shaken up," I said. Like a hamster in a blender.

"Well, you're not to spend another night in that house. Get over here as soon as you can."

"He won't be back tonight," Terry said. "Don't worry."

Easy for her to say—no metal-jacketed missile had gone whizzing past *her* pootie tang.

"Really," I said, trying to convince myself as much as Reba, "we're okay here."

"Just a moment." We heard Reba calling out, "Eli, they say they won't come over. They say he won't be back tonight."

A man's voice rumbled in the background, then Reba came back on the line. "He says you're to come over here, anyway."

"Uh, Reba?" Terry said, stifling a laugh. "What's Eli doing there at this time of night?"

"We're soul mates," Reba said as if that explained everything, then handed off the phone.

"Kerry? Terry? It's Eli. You all right? Who shot at you?"

"Sergei Pavlov," I said. "He's bumping people off left and right, and hiding in plain sight, thanks to your buddy Binion. And I can promise you Binion knows what his boy is up to. He's sitting up there in his fancy office and pulling Sergei's strings and—"

"Hey!"

"What?"

"I know you're scared, kid, but I gotta say, you're running away with this. Turning it into one of your vast, *90210* conspiracies. Look, if you don't know who shot at you, don't make something up. It serves no purpose. You girls come over here for the night and we'll deal with it tomor—"

"What the hell . . . ?" came a startled voice from the doorway.

I turned and saw Boatwright standing on the threshold, looking like a contestant from *The Bachelorette* after stumbling onto a triple homicide. He was dressed in a navy sports coat, jeans, and a light blue button-down shirt that set off his gorgeous eyes. His mouth was open in shock (my, what a nice tongue), and a bottle of red wine hung forgotten at his side.

He stepped over the threshold, gawking at the hole in the door.

"I thought you were going to call," I said to Boatwright.

"Who's that?" Eli asked.

"Kerry's date," Terry said.

"No one answered," Boatwright said, his eyes wide. "I thought I'd come over and surprise you—"

"Gotta go," I said quickly into the phone.

"Who the hell shot into your house?" Boatwright asked.

"I can hear him," Eli said, chuckling. "It's the Beverly Hills dick, isn't it?"

"None of your business!" I yelled.

"None of my business?" Boatwright said, thinking I was yelling at him. "I'm the police! It's sure as hell my business when people go shooting into houses!"

Eli chuckled again. "Hussy. Cop groupie—"

I hung up in his ear. Terry stayed on the line, whispering into the mouthpiece and laughing as she and Eli shared a joke at my expense.

Boatwright took me by the arms, studying my face. "You okay? What happened?"

I did my best to smile flirtatiously and took the bottle from his hand. "Merlot! Just what the doctor ordered after an evening of random violence."

"Random?" He knitted his thick brows. "What the hell's going on here?"

He followed me into the kitchen. I pulled out a corkscrew and went to work on the wine, while he stared at me with those piercing eyes, waiting for an explanation.

"I'm not getting any younger," he said.

I popped the cork. "Should we let it breathe?"

"Let it suffocate, I don't give a rat's ass! You gonna tell me what's going on here or do I have to play twenty questions?"

I pulled down a couple of Flintstones glasses and poured the wine. "You could play forty, I have no answers."

I gave him a Fred glass and I took Wilma. Unconscious role-playing, I guess—a little Flintstone foreplay. He chugged the wine and held his glass out for more. I refilled it and raised my glass in a salute.

"You must have *some* idea who it was," he prodded.

"Okay, I had an idea that it was Sergei Pavlov, but I probably made that up. Truth is, I'm clueless. At any rate, no one thinks he's coming back tonight."

"How do you figure that?"

"Look, you're not here as my personal response unit, it's supposed to be a date. Do you want to have a date or not?"

He looked at me, shaking his head. "If I knew you better, I'd spank you silly."

"If I knew you better I'd let you," I said coyly.

He smiled in spite of himself. "Then let's get to know each other quick."

He leaned against the counter with one of his slim, denim-clad hips and studied me closely, sipping his wine. Why did he have to be so damn gorgeous? He was making it *very* hard to maintain my cool. My eyes were involuntarily drawn to his pelvic area. I had a flash-fantasy of grabbing those narrow hips like handles, pulling him between my legs . . .

Uh-oh. Caught me looking.

I turned away before he could discern the awful truth—I was a hussy cop groupie.

Wouldn't do to play my hand too quickly, I reminded myself.

I leaned against the kitchen table, the same one where I'd eaten breakfast with my grandparents—cereal loaded with sugar. Grandma'd had this quaint notion that we should consume actual food at our meals, so she'd always put apple or banana slices on top of the fluorescent-colored glop that represented some toy tie-in or other.

I was a good girl. I'd indulge Grandma by eating prunes if it made her happy. But I wasn't that good anymore. Right now I wanted to skip the healthy stuff and go straight for the sugar. A hundred-and-eighty pounds of it.

"The police were here," I reassured him. "They took a report."

"Good move, calling the police." He grinned. "Exactly what I would have recommended myself."

The next thing I knew, he'd set down his wine, and his arms went around my body and pulled me to him. I was pressed against a wall of muscle, the smell of him making my head spin. Strong healthy man smell, accented with aftershave.

We kissed, hard.

Tongues going at it like we were trying to crawl into each other's mouths.

I felt his shoulder holster beneath my left breast—which was *very* erotic. I'd always been anti-gun, but that was on the streets, not in the bedroom. In the bedroom, I figured it was my God-given second amendment right to be aroused by a sidearm.

Somebody clamped her lips down on his neck and sucked. I guess it was me. I nibbled at his beautiful flesh, wanting all of him in my mouth.

I was lifted up. Strong hands grabbed my legs, which were immediately clamped like a wrestler's around his waist. He moved in a noisy shuffle across the kitchen floor, then smashed into the swinging door that led into the sitting room.

"Owww!" My head had taken the brunt of the crash.

"Sorry, sorry," he whispered in my ear, his breath hot.

Can ear canals have orgasms? I thought mine just had.

We pushed through the door, almost tumbling to the floor on the other side. My mouth was on his, my neck straining as I pushed into him, trying to meld completely with his teeth, his tongue, his luscious lips.

Then I was dropped like a load of cement.

I stumbled backward, the word *Shit!* strangling in my throat.

Boatwright caught me by the elbow to keep me from falling to the floor. I got my balance by waving my other arm in the air. Why had he dumped me?

"Excuse us," Boatwright said, straightening his jacket. "We got a little carried away."

Oops. We'd forgotten about Terry in our lust craze.

She gave us a knowing smirk. "Don't let *me* stop you."

I tugged down my shirt. "Um . . . John, why don't you grab Fred and Wilma and join me upstairs?"

"A foursome?" Terry said. "*Kinky.*"

Boatwright disappeared through the kitchen door and I ran to Terry's side.

"Please don't say anything or do anything or pull anything, okay?" I whispered desperately.

She was affronted. "Hey, I'm the one that told you to get laid."

"Good," I said. "Are you gonna—you know—be down here?"

"I *live* here," she said, thrusting out her chin. "That is, when I'm not under threat of death."

Boatwright came out of the kitchen, glasses and wine bottle in hand. He and Terry stared at each other for an awkward moment.

"So . . . upstairs?" he said to me, nodding toward the staircase.

"I'll have headphones on," Terry said. "Feel free to make the wooden platform creak all you want."

I turned and ran up the stairs, with Boatwright right behind me.

When I got to the loft I fell down on the bed. He set the glasses and bottle on the bedside table, then stared down at me as he peeled off his jacket.

He tossed it on the chair in the corner. Then he started stripping off his holster. He popped the fasteners and pulled the leather straps off one broad shoulder, and I almost came on the spot. Keep your lap dancers. I'll take a gun-stripping homicide detective any day.

The gun got more careful treatment than his jacket. He bent down and slipped it under the bed. Then he stood at the edge of the bed and unbuttoned his shirt.

His chest was hard and muscled and covered in silky dark hair. He untucked his shirttails and let the shirt fall open around the chiseled stomach, watching me intently the whole time.

"What?" I said when his gaze became unbearable.

"You look so—"

Beautiful? Ravishing? Fuckable? I supplied mentally.

"Uncomfortable."

Huh?

He put one knee on the bed and leaned over. He reached under my shirt, running his hand over my belly, and causing my skin to tingle with a sensation like tiny electric shocks. His hand found the wire of my bra and he slipped his fingers underneath it as I held my breath.

"All cinched in," he said, running his fingertips around my shivering rib cage to the back. He fumbled with the hook, then the bra went loose.

"*Much* better," I said, letting out my breath.

He smiled and moved his hand slowly around to my breast, gently grazing my nipple, which sprang up like a little pink soldier on parade. He closed his eyes, breathing through parted lips, and performed the same maneuver with the other nipple.

I couldn't stand it. I was going to explode or scream or undergo a complete meltdown from wanting him. I ran my fingertips up his nice hard stomach muscles, making a mental note to straddle them later.

"I'm even more cinched by these jeans," I said.

"That's what I was afraid of."

Pop went the offending button on my jeans, *down* went the zipper, and now the cool smooth hand was traveling down my lower abdomen toward its reward.

"Do it," I whispered, arching my hips.

"Do what?" he whispered back.

"Anything!"

Glass crashed downstairs.

Boatwright's hand jerked out of my pants. He dived off the bed, going for the gun. He sprang up with it in his hand and was down the stairs before I even knew what had happened.

I scrambled off the bed and followed him, pulling down my T-shirt and fumbling with my zipper.

He was crouched halfway down the stairs, arms out with the gun aimed at the front door.

Terry stood there giving him an apologetic look. She wore leather work gloves and was holding a hammer in one hand, a big shard of glass in the other.

"Sorry," she said. "I was trying to get this glass out of the window before it fell down. If it shattered and fell, the dogs could step on it."

Boatwright relaxed his arms, bringing down the gun.

Good thing he was between me and Terry. I would have had to get around him to pummel her senseless. And if I did that, he'd have to arrest me for assault.

"You didn't think that could wait till later?" I snapped at her.

She shrugged. "Thought it was too much of a hazard to wait."

Boatwright sighed and looked at me. "She's right about that. It *is* a hazard."

Terry might not technically be from Venus, but she sure knew how to bring out the Martian in a man.

"Hope I didn't interrupt anything," she said.

"Oh *no-o-o-o*," I said, bitterly.

Just the lay of the century, you passive-aggressive—

"I'll give you a hand," Boatwright said to her, heading down the stairs.

I watched them remove the rest of the broken panes from the window and sweep the area again, going over it with wet paper towels to make sure there were no glass splinters. Then Boatwright nailed a piece of plywood over the hole in the door.

It might have been a good idea, even necessary, but that wasn't why Terry had picked this moment to do it. She was trying to sabotage my relationship with Boatwright out of jealousy, I just knew it.

By the time they were finished, the moment had been lost.

"Want me to stay?" Boatwright said to me, stroking my cheek.

"No thanks. We'll be fine." I didn't want to force the intimacy issue now. I wanted him to stay because he wanted me, not because his guard dog instincts were aroused.

He looked around. "I'd feel better if you had a gun. Or even an alarm system."

"I think we'll stay with our great-aunt tonight. She'll have a cow if we don't."

He nodded. "Good idea."

We stood in awkward silence for a moment.

"So, I'll call you?" he said.

If you value your life.

"Sure," I said lightly. "Give me a call."

He smiled and reached for the doorknob. "Good night, Terry!"

" 'Bye!" she called back from the kitchen. "Thanks for the help!"

I gave Boatwright a kiss on the lips, inhaling his scent so I could remember it after he'd gone.

He stepped onto the porch, waving good-bye. I waved back, and when he was out of sight, I picked up the hammer and headed for Terry in the kitchen.

Justifiable homicide, if ever there was one, I thought. Manslaughter second-degree murder at the most. Five years' probation—

The phone rang, snapping me back to my senses.

It had to be Boatwright, calling on his cell phone to say he couldn't wait to see me again, it *had* to be tomorrow, he could still smell my perfume on his hands, it was driving him crazy, he'd never wanted anyone so much in his life—

I grabbed the receiver. "Hello?"

"Kerry? Terry?"

Damn, it was Eli.

"Hi, it's Kerry. Whassup?"

"What did I tell you about jumping to conclusions?"

"I got it. You don't have to beat me over the—"

"Binion bit it earlier tonight," he said.

My jaw dropped. "What?"

"He isn't your criminal mastermind, after all."

"When? *How?*"

"Channel four," he said, then hung up.

seventeen

I ran to the TV yelling for Terry. She rushed in from the kitchen with an apple in her mouth, blissfully unaware that it had almost been her last.

"We'll have more on the brutal slaying of one of Beverly Hills's most prominent attorneys right after this message," an announcer said.

"Binion?" Terry said, chewing the apple. Then she frowned at seeing the hammer in my hand.

"Um . . . had it for self-protection," I said, tossing the hammer on the couch. I could always kill her later, we had other concerns at the moment.

"Yeah, it was Binion," I told her. "Eli just called with the news."

"Who did it? Sergei?"

"Why would Sergei do it? Binion's his protector."

She shrugged. "Maybe it's what you said after Suzie was

killed. Dishonor among scumbags. They're all into something together, and one of them is bumping off the rest."

We waited through the commercials for feminine spray, and Scrubbing Bubbles toilet cleanser, and something called an "in-the-egg scrambler," which was a tiny drill poked through the top of an unfertilized egg for the purpose of whipping the yolk and the white together without the bothersome chore of cracking the shell.

I groaned at the commercial.

"Hey, don't knock American innovation," Terry said. "It took us to the moon."

When the news finally came back on, they broadcast a prerecorded segment showing Binion's high-rise apartment on Wilshire Boulevard, with the usual three-ring circus of cops, looky-lou's, crime-scene techs, and ambulances. An on-the-scene reporter recounted how the famous lawyer had been found in the Jacuzzi of the luxury condominium, nude. The reporter confirmed that Binion's throat had been slashed, and added a sumptuous detail for any viewers who might be trying to swallow their dinners: Binion had been in the pool for hours, and was found floating in water that had been dyed red by the blood.

"Police are anxious to speak to a young woman who was seen in Binion's company earlier in the evening by building staff. She is said to be in her twenties or thirties, with dark hair."

"That rules out Pavlov," Terry mused. "Unless it's *Mrs.* Pavlov."

I stared at the image on the TV. Something had caught my eye in the throng of the curious onlookers. I ran to the screen and pointed to a half-visible woman in the right foreground. She wore a police uniform and had her back to us, hands on her hips, head turned to the right as she spoke to someone off-screen, showing a one-quarter profile.

"Terry," I said. "Who is that? In the foreground. Get a good look."

Terry squinted at the screen, focusing on the dark outline of the woman. "Oh, it's Dinah, isn't it?"

"Yep. Miss Johnny-on-the-Spot."

"Well, what do you know."

I gave Terry a searching look. "*Why* is she on the spot whenever someone gets killed?"

"Oh God," Terry said, rolling her eyes heavenward. "Now what?"

"You do realize that Binion's death blows our whole theory of the crimes."

"How so?"

"He helped Sergei evade the authorities. He was an ally, someone who could help him in the future . . . I say it again, why would Sergei kill him?"

"Maybe he thought Binion was going to give him up."

"Binion'd go out of business in a second if he gave up his clients. And they'd have a hell of a time forcing him to, because of lawyer-client privilege."

"What are you trying to say?"

"That we may have been focusing on the wrong person. Maybe nobody's been able to locate Sergei because he's worm food. Someone else could be doing the killing, knowing he'd get credit for it. Maybe you were right and it *was* a woman who shot at us tonight."

She shook her head. "I don't think I like where this is going."

"You have to admit, there's something very strange about Dinah."

"She works a lot and she dresses like a cowboy, so? That doesn't make her a mass murderer. Anyway, you were completely convinced that Sergei was the bad guy not five minutes ago."

"Sometimes you don't see the obvious because you're convinced of something else." I chewed my nail, trying to banish the image of Boatwright's perfectly sculpted chest from my mind.

"But they said they wanted to question a woman with dark hair," Terry argued. "Dinah has blond hair."

"Hello! Ever heard of wigs? Seen one on your own aunt, lately?"

"Yeah, so maybe Reba did it."

"I'm serious about this."

"Seriously whacked."

"Humor me," I said.

"And how would I do that?"

"Let's invite Dinah out for another drink, feel her out."

Terry let out a melodramatic sigh. "Fine. If it will ease your paranoia, call her."

It felt like the middle of the night but it was only ten o'clock—still a decent hour to call up a friend for drinks. Dinah was listed in the Beverly Hills directory. She answered on the second ring, and I would have sworn she was surprised to hear from us.

"You guys okay? Heard you had some trouble tonight."

I mouthed to Terry—*Surprised we're alive?*

"Yeah, we're all right," Terry said, giving me a disgusted look.

"I told you this case might bite you in the butt," Dinah said.

"Listen," I said, "we'd like to talk to you about these developments. Are you free for a drink?"

"Oh, uh . . . I'd like to, but I promised Helga I'd stay home tonight. I've been out late a few nights in a row."

Who's Helga? Terry mouthed to me. *Lover?*

Dog, I mouthed back.

"I tell you what," Dinah said. "Why don't you girls come over here for a drink? You can bring your dogs if you want, and they can play with Helga."

Yeah, play *dead*. Dinah had said she had a German shepherd. I didn't think throwing a pug and a Pom puppy and a shepherd in the ring together would be much of a fair fight.

"Another time. We'll come by ourselves. Where do you live?" Terry said, snapping her fingers for the steno pad and a pen.

Yes, memsahib I mouthed to her, handing them over.

She wrote down Dinah's address, an apartment on Gregory Way, then hung up the phone.

"Let's rip," she said.

"Uh. We're going to her place?"

"That's where she is," Terry said slowly. "You wanted to talk to her, that's where we have to go."

"Maybe we should wait until tomorrow. It's late and we've been through a lot—"

"No! You insisted we call and we called. Now we're going." She grabbed her leather jacket and pushed me toward the door.

"I'd feel better if we had protection."

Terry howled with laughter. "Oh, *now* you want a weapon? It's like they always say, a conservative is just a liberal who's been shot at."

"Okay, I'm a big fat hypocrite," I admitted. "But I'm kind of shaky right now." Like a tub full of Jell-O.

She patted me on the shoulder. "All the more reason to go. You'll feel better once you get over this crazy suspicion of Dinah. She's just a good ol' gal bull dyke and a good cop. She's not the one we have to worry about. Bring your hammer if it makes you feel any better."

"Better not." It might come crashing down on your skull on the way there.

I walked out the door, trying to rationalize the situation. We were going to an apartment building with lots of other tenants. Even if she was the bad guy, Dinah wouldn't bump us off right there, would she?

We pulled up in front of a four-story brick apartment building in Beverly Hills' version of a ghetto—a string of housing units built in the forties and fifties at the southernmost edge of the city. The brick buildings were well-maintained and nicely landscaped. Nothing fancy, but the rents were reasonable and you had your own police force at your door within seconds of a prowler sighting.

"I'll bet the neighbors love having a cop in the building," Terry said.

I arched an eyebrow. "I guess that would depend on who the cop was."

She made a face and knocked on the door. We waited a few seconds then heard a bestial yowl like the hound of the Baskervilles, echoing thunderously down the block.

The door swung open and a huge hairy beast leaped out at me, fangs bared. Its massive paws landed on my shoulders, its maw gaped in my face. I felt its hot wet breath on my skin as I stumbled backward, and I knew with absolute certainty that I was going to die.

"Helga, no!" Dinah yelled. She yanked the gray and black slavering monster off of me. But Helga continued to bark, straining against her choke chain.

"I'm sorry, she just loves women," Dinah said, hauling Helga away from the door, the dog's claws scraping against the floor as she tried to lunge at my throat again. "Come on in."

Terry strolled right in without a second thought. "She doesn't bite?"

Dinah gave her a crooked smile. "Only if I tell her to."

Oh, great. Where's my Uzi?

I brushed off my shirt and followed Terry into the apartment, keeping her between me and the dog. It was then that I noticed that Dinah was still in uniform, shirt tucked in and everything. Sure didn't *look* like she had planned to spend the evening lounging about.

I glanced around the living room, which was decorated in early Roy Rogers: a wooden rocking chair on a Navajo rug, wagon-wheel coffee table, and a daybed covered in horse blankets with real horse hair stuck to them—a pinto by the looks of it. A white child-sized saddle with turquoise stitching sat on a stand in the corner, and a family portrait hung on the wall below a rusted spur. I walked over to the photograph to take a closer look.

It appeared to be mom, dad, Dinah, and baby brother. Dinah was only about eight years old, but her parents looked sixty. They were careworn and weather-beaten, like people who had lived their entire lives outdoors, with little money or amenities, or whatever lightens a person's load in this life.

"That's my family," Dinah said, noticing my interest in the photo. "My dad Billy, my mom Lou Ann, and my little brother Jonah."

"Dinah and Jonah," Terry said. "That's nice."

"They named him that 'cause my mom was so darn big when she was pregnant, my dad said she looked like a whale. And then she said they should name the baby Jonah if it was a boy," Dinah said with a dopey grin, as if this was the most wonderful family legend anyone had ever heard.

Terry and I smiled. "Ha ha, that's good," we said in tandem.

"Where's Jonah now?" I asked.

Dinah didn't answer right away. She stared at the baby for a long moment, then her smile disappeared.

"Dead," she said at last.

I swallowed. "That's too bad."

"It was his own damn fault!"

Dinah's outburst hung in the air like a nuclear cloud. We backed up a step, clearing our throats. "Um, how about your parents?" Terry said.

"Huh?" Dinah wrenched her eyes from the photograph.

"Are your parents alive?"

"Nope," Dinah said, her tone completely flat. "Everybody's dead."

We stood there tongue-tied for about fifteen seconds.

Suddenly Dinah clapped her hands. "So!" she said brightly. "How about that drink?"

"Sure!" Terry and I said, clapping our hands in response.

"Come on out to the kitchen. I'll feed Helga and get us some beer."

The overhead kitchen light cast long shadows beneath our noses. There was a big iron kettle and matching skillet on the stove, and a gingham dish towel hanging off the dish drainer, which contained a single bowl and a wooden spoon. I wondered what Dinah cooked in the iron pots. Probably baked beans with ham hocks in the big one, bacon and fried eggs in the skillet.

An ancient aluminum coffee percolator sat on a third burner. Well, she was only forty years behind the times. Had she never heard of Mr. Coffee? Never known the joy of a pre-set timer that brewed your first cup before you even rolled out of bed?

She was more peculiar than I'd imagined, even allowing for regional differences. I wondered if Jonah had died later in life, or if it was somehow "his fault" that he died as an infant. Maybe he'd cried too much and had to be shut up with a pillow over his face.

Dinah opened the fridge while Helga did a little dance in the middle of the kitchen, whimpering in anticipation.

"Hold on there, girl. It's comin'!" Dinah said. She hauled

out a raw rump roast, thumping it on a wooden board with a wet slapping sound. Blood pooled under the meat, reminding me of all the carnage we'd seen in the past few days.

I felt my stomach spasm.

I started to excuse myself to go to the bathroom, but Dinah picked up a meat cleaver, swung it into the air just inches from Terry's head, and then slammed the sharpened blade down into the wet hunk of meat.

I screamed.

Dinah wheeled around in shock, one hand holding the meat, the other gripping the bloody cleaver. "What the hell's the matter with you?" she yelled.

In a split second, Helga jumped into the air and snapped the meat out of Dinah's hand, biting her finger in the process. Helga then wrestled the meat to the floor, ripping into it like a hyena into carrion.

Dinah looked at the blood beading up on her finger and grabbed for the dish towel, scowling at the dog. "She's never bit me before."

I had a flash of Helga losing her fluffy plume of a tail to the angry meat cleaver, leaving her with only a bloody stump.

"It . . . it was my fault," I stammered. "I thought . . . I thought you were gonna chop off your hand. The cleaver looked like it was headed straight for your wrist."

Terry sighed noisily, her eyes rolling.

"Raw meat's tough," Dinah said slowly, as if to an idiot or a small child. "You have to really *whack* at it."

"Oh, is that right?" I said, nodding my head eagerly. I was willing to learn all about hacking raw meat, as long as I wasn't the raw meat in question.

"When she was little I used to give her raw chicken," Dinah said. "I'd chop apart the whole chicken and toss it to her piece by piece. I'd hate to see how you'd react if I hacked up an entire bird!" She ran cold water over her hand.

"You can give a dog chicken bones?" Terry said. "I always thought that choked them."

"That's only cooked chicken bones," Dinah explained. "Anyway, Helga's no dog. She's eighty percent timberland wolf, twenty percent shepherd. Wolf hybrids can eat raw bones with no trouble." She looked down at Helga with obvious pride.

"But don't tell anyone about that, okay?" Dinah said. "People don't like to know they're living next to a wild animal, and I hate to think what would happen to my little girl if the neighbors found out. They'd probably run her outta town or shoot her or something."

Yeah, probably. If they had a gun.

"Listen, I better put something on this, okay? You all help yourselves to some beer. I'll be right back." She exited the kitchen, clutching a paper towel to her finger.

When she was out of earshot I started across the kitchen to strongly suggest to Terry that we get our asses out of there. But I must have stepped into Helga's zone of discomfort. She looked up from the raw meat she was gnawing and growled from somewhere deep in her belly, her black lips curling up over the yellow fangs.

I backed up against the sink, breathing shallowly.

"Don't show fear," Terry whispered to me.

"Would that encompass wetting my pants?" I squeaked.

"Take it easy. She's not going to attack you with her mistress in the other room."

"No, but she may attack us when her mistress comes back in the room, on her say-so!"

"What are you all whispering about in there?" Dinah called from the bathroom. "You aren't talking about me, are you?"

I grimaced and put a finger to my lips, but Terry shouted back to her, "Yeah, we were just talking about what a great apartment this is! Do you live alone?"

The toilet flushed, followed by the sound of running water. Then Dinah came sauntering back into the kitchen with a bandaged hand.

"Did you get a beer?"

We shook our heads, but didn't volunteer that we were too scared to walk past Helga the Killer Wolf to get to the fridge. Helga was now licking her paws, looking perfectly sated and domesticated, and Dinah reached down to pet her.

"That's my little angel," she said. "She's such a good girl."

Helga jumped to her feet and whipped her tail around.

"No, that's enough meat for right now," Dinah admonished her. "Maybe you'll get more later if you're good," she said, winking at me.

And just what was that supposed to mean?

Were Terry and I about to become a treat for a rabid wolf owned by a psychopathic serial killer?

"So . . . pretty weird about Hugh Binion," Terry said to Dinah.

"Yeah, can you believe it?" Dinah said, as she pulled a long-neck bottle of Corona out of the refrigerator.

"What a horrible way to go," I said, trying to cover my terror with idle chitchat.

"Godammit!" Dinah shouted.

I jumped a foot in the air. *What? What'd I say?*

"The beer's not cold!" she huffed. "The landlord was supposed to fix the fridge. If you'll reach up and get the glasses down out of that cabinet there, I'll get some ice. Can't drink warm beer."

I reached into the cabinet as instructed and brought down three glasses with shaking hands. Terry grabbed one from me, popped the top off her beer, and poured it into the glass. I started to do the same, but then Dinah reached into the freezer and pulled out a hand tool.

It was an ice pick.

Suddenly I couldn't breathe. I made a desperate attempt to signal to Terry that it was time to go, but the idiot ignored me.

What was *wrong* with her? Where the hell was her famous intuition? Did Dinah have to have "Psycho-killer" stamped on her forehead before Terry would get clued in?

Dinah palmed the ice pick and jammed it into the old-fashioned freezer, chipping off hunks of ice as the razor-sharp pick snicked away.

" 'Course, I've noticed that most people who get killed that way have done something to bring it on themselves, you know what I mean?" she said, looking directly at me.

Snick.

Snick, snick.

"How so?" Terry asked curiously.

"That Binion, I'm pretty sure he was involved in criminal activities."

"How . . . how would you know that?" I said, a little quaver in my voice.

Dinah shrugged. "I know my beat."

"Well, nobody deserves to be brutally killed," I said.

She turned and looked me straight in the eyes, pointing the ice pick for emphasis. "No, but you could say that it's inevitable sometimes, when people get involved in things they shouldn't be involved with." She gave me a quick smile, then returned to chipping ice.

I was sure I would faint. Or puke. Or puke while fainting.

"Could I use the bathroom?" I said weakly.

"Sure," Dinah said. "Right back there." She pointed past my nose with the ice pick. I dodged it reflexively.

"Sorry, that was kinda close," Dinah said.

I tried to give a casual laugh, but sounded like I was coughing up a hairball instead. *Heccch.*

Terry gave me a bewildered look.

"Be right back!" I sang out.

I scurried down the hallway to the bathroom, attempting to slow my breath and my heartbeat. What had I just done? I'd left my sister alone in the kitchen with an ice-cleaver, meat-pick murderer! But I thought that if I could get away for a few minutes my fear would subside, my senses would return, and I'd be able to think of a way out of this mess before we got stabbed into Swiss cheese.

Once inside the bathroom, I shut the door and splashed water over my face. I looked at myself in the medicine cabinet mirror. My eyes stared back at me, wide and dazed.

On a sudden hunch, I opened the cabinet.

It was *packed* with drugs. Rows and rows of brown plastic vials marked "Sample."

Oh my God. Dinah had a heavy prescription drug habit. What else was she hiding? I wondered.

I turned off the water and slipped out into the hallway, creeping further away from the kitchen toward the bedroom. It was dark but I didn't dare turn on a light. I pushed open the door, which emitted a little creak. I stood stock-still for a moment, holding my breath.

No sound from the kitchen but Terry's and Dinah's voices, conversational and relaxed. Terry even laughed a bit.

Way to go, sis. Keep her calm and occupied.

I ducked into the bedroom. In the half-light I could see a large bed with a plaid coverlet. There was a dresser to my right with two cowboy boots on top, serving as bookends for volumes on criminology and forensics. I panned around the room, looking for anything incriminating.

Nothing to see here. I turned to leave and tripped on something, catching myself on the dresser. I looked down and saw a running shoe poking out from under the bed. I reached down to grab the shoe and its mate.

They were enormous.

Easily a man's size ten.

Just the right size for kicking me in the face in the doctor's office. Just the right size for leaving prints in our backyard.

I dropped them on the floor and flew down the hallway into the kitchen. Dinah and Terry leaned against the counter drinking their iced beers and chatting animatedly, the hell-hound dozing at their feet.

"I gotta—we gotta go!" I yelled. "Sorry, Dinah!"

Terry and Dinah frowned at me.

"I gotta—we gotta—do that thing, you know? That thing that—we were supposed to do?"

Dinah cut a suspicious eye to Terry.

"Huh?" Terry said.

Okay, maybe I wasn't the smoothest, but if Terry would just *get the goddamned message* we could run out the door and maybe make it out of there alive with only a little flesh missing from our butts when Dinah sicced her wolf on us.

Terry set her drink on the counter. "Oh yeah, I forgot," she said, turning to Dinah. "We've gotta do something."

"What?" Dinah asked. "What do you have to do?"

Gulp. Hadn't thought that far ahead.

"We have to get home and feed the dogs," Terry said, and I heaped a thousand blessings on her quick-thinking head.

Dinah gave us a slitty-eyed look, pointing to our business card on the refrigerator door. "The caller ID said you were calling from your house."

"Yeah, but we forgot to feed the dogs. Slipped our minds," I said, grabbing Terry's sleeve.

Helga jumped up, barking in my face. I jerked back in terror.

"She doesn't want you to leave," Dinah said. "You sure you have to go?" She gave me an ingratiating smile, and I could imagine blood dripping from her own prominent canines.

"Uh yeah, sorry," I said, pointing to Helga. "Could you hold on to her, please?"

"Oh, she won't hurt you."

"Would you just hold on to the goddamned wolf?"

Terry gave Dinah a sheepish grin. "She's been like this ever since we were kids. Too many nights with *Red Riding Hood* under the covers."

I grabbed Terry's hand and we scooted across the living room to the front door. "Thanks a lot, Dinah," Terry said, waving. "Sorry to drink and run. We'll talk to you later."

"Yeah, okay." Dinah followed us through the front room gripping Helga by the choke chain. "Thanks for comin' by!"

I whipped open the front door and felt the cool evening air hit my face. We were almost home free. At least I could scream my lungs out now and someone would probably come to our rescue.

"Ya'll watch yourselves!" Dinah said.

"We will!" I slammed the door in her face and we leaped over the porch and were at the bike in two shakes. Terry pulled on her helmet and revved the engine, screeching away from the curb only seconds after I'd hopped on behind her.

I looked back at the apartment as we tore away.

The curtain was drawn back from the bedroom window. Dinah was silhouetted there, watching us leave. Had she noticed that the room was disturbed? Had I left tracks on the carpet?

We sped down to Olympic Boulevard, then Terry pulled into a darkened parking lot and cut the engine. She took off her helmet and sighed, leaning on the handles.

"This had better be good," she said.

I jumped from the bike and yanked off my helmet in one move. "Good? How good is this? While you were chatting so pleasantly in the kitchen, I actually did some detecting . . ."

She gave me a sideways look, waiting.

"I went into the bathroom and guess what she had in there?"

"A dead body dangling from the shower massage?"

"The medicine cabinet was full of drugs in brown pill bottles, marked 'sample.'"

"So what?"

"So what?" I yelled. "This whole thing has been about prescription drug dealing! And what's a cop doing with a cabinet full of promotional drugs?"

"I don't know, but 'sample' sounds like something you get in a hospital, not something that falls off the back of a truck."

"All right, then. What about the meat cleaver and the ice pick?"

"She's from Oklahoma! Country people use those kinds of implements. They go out and slaughter animals for their Sunday dinner. They're not squeamish like us."

Squeamish like us?

"Oh, pardon me for being squeamish when we're in the kitchen of someone who killed her whole family and half the widows of Beverly Hills," I said.

Terry crossed her arms over her chest. "I told you to get laid, didn't I? This is what comes from not getting laid. A completely out-of-whack perspective."

"I was *trying* to get laid!" I said, almost choking on the words. "I was *just about* to get laid when you went into front-door demolition mode!"

"Well, excuse *me*. I was *trying* to protect the dogs."

I sighed in frustration. "You are completely missing the point!"

"Please," she said. "Tell me the point."

"Dinah's our butcher. A twisted mass murderer of biblical proportions."

"And what is her motive? Or don't you need motivation in the Bible?"

"I'll tell you her motive," I said, nodding madly. "She's anxious to get ahead, to make it to the Homicide squad—"

"And?"

"She knows her beat, like she said. She takes the bogus burglary report from Suzie Magnuson and smells a rat. She knows there's fraud going on, she makes the connection between Binion and Lenore and Suzie and Hattrick—all of them—and she thinks, 'Great. Here's a bunch of dirtbags I can use for my own purpose.' "

"Which is?"

"Homicides, lots of 'em. In a town not known for its murder rate. She does the killing, then gets a chance to shine in front of her superiors, always the first one on the scene and full of bright ideas. Anyone looking into the deaths would see a bunch of double-dealing lowlifes bumping each other off one by one!"

"Okay, so how does she manage to do all this killing while she's on duty?"

"I don't know, she's fiendishly clever!"

Terry laughed again, shaking her head.

"Oh, and I forgot the best part!" I said. "I found running shoes under her bed. They're big, about a man's size ten!"

"That's the best part?" Terry hooted. "She's got big feet! She *must* be a killer!"

"I looked at her feet, Terry. They're not that big."

"So you think she puts on men's running shoes so she can't be tracked by her footprints?"

"It's a damn good idea, you have to admit."

She made a skeptical face. "I don't know—"

"It all adds up."

"I'm not sure it adds up. We'd have to sit down and chart it. Who died when, who's connected to who—that kind of thing. We'd have to know when Dinah was on duty and when she wasn't . . ."

What was this, role reversal? Suddenly the ever impetuous Terry wanted to sit down and diagram things while I was making the call to action.

"We don't have time for that!" I said.

"Why not?"

"The noose is tightening around Dinah's neck. She knows it. That's why she shot into our house. She tried to warn us that night in Hattrick's office, but we didn't get the message. You heard her—'When you get involved with things you shouldn't, you bring it on yourself.' What was that, if not a statement of intent?"

Terry shook her head. "I can't buy into any of this."

"Well, I can!"

"Hey, we agreed a long time ago that I was the better judge of character."

"No, *you* decided that."

"I thought you trusted my instincts!"

"I do when you're not blinded by politics."

"What does *that* mean?"

"You don't want to believe Dinah's the bad guy because she's gay!"

She guffawed. "Come on, it's such a horrible cliché: *the twisted homosexual killer!*"

"Ter, we're not talking about the movies, we're talking about real life. And in real life there are people who kill for all kinds of reasons."

"Look, if what you say is true, if she's trying to win points with her superiors, she'd have to close some cases, right? Deliver a perpetrator. How's she gonna do that if she's the killer herself?"

"Maybe she's going to give them Sergei."

"How?"

"Maybe she's got him stashed somewhere. She makes sure all the evidence points to him, and when she's eliminated the rest of the players, she'll choose her moment to kill him, then lead them to his body."

"Oh, man," she said. "Do you realize how far-fetched this is?"

"Yeah, well truth is stranger than fiction, sometimes."

"I'm not at all sure you'd know the difference right now."

We sat there in silence for a minute, listening to the traffic roll by on Olympic Boulevard.

"Just promise me you won't rule her out as a suspect," I said.

"Okay, she's not ruled out. Can we go now?"

"Yeah, let's go home. I'm exhausted."

"I imagine paranoid schizophrenia *can* be taxing," Terry said, yanking on her helmet.

eighteen

Our plan was to pack our clothes, round up the dogs and their paraphernalia, and take a taxi over to Reba's. We didn't want her and Eli to stay up worrying all night, and personally, I didn't want to risk another potshot at my wagging behind.

When we arrived back at the house, the sound of excited yapping reached us on the porch.

"Nice to have someone to come home to after a hard day of tracking serial killers, isn't it?" I said, pushing open the door.

But no dogs came to welcome us when we walked into the darkened house.

"Where are our babies?" Terry said, flipping on the lights and locking the door behind us.

The dogs barked again, from the kitchen. I stared at the closed kitchen door in confusion. How had the pups gotten themselves locked up in there?

"Hey, who closed the—?" I started to say, then heard the faint rustling of nylon. My gut clenched as I realized we weren't alone. I grabbed for Terry's arm at the same instant someone stepped out of the shadows.

It took a second for me to register who it was:

Barbie. And she was pointing a twelve-inch butcher knife at us.

"I left your babies up in the kitchen," she said, advancing on us with her slinky walk. She flashed a deranged, Ultrabrite smile, her eyes glittering like icy marbles. "Play your cards right, and I'll let them live."

She wore black sweatpants and a bulky pea jacket, her feet encased in large, black running shoes, her blond hair stuffed under a knit watch cap.

"Welcome home," she said, striding up to me, as I moved back against the wall.

Her hand snaked out and I felt a sharp stinging pain as the knife grazed my ribs. I gasped and looked down in horror. The point of the blade had pierced my skin, but she hadn't thrust it home.

"Don't do it!" Terry screamed.

"Don't do it! Don't do it!" Barbie shrilled mockingly.

I realized then that the woman was nuts—stark raving mad. I whimpered as she pushed harder up against me, the cool metal of the knife against my stomach, contrasting with the warm sticky blood soaking my shirt.

"Barbie, take it easy, now," Terry said, hands up in surrender. "Whatever it is you want us to do, we'll do."

"I *know* you will." Barbie chuckled. "Hey, how did you like the funeral flowers I left on the porch? I thought they were a nice touch."

Terry looked over, trying to reassure me with her eyes.

"Yes, very clever," she said to Barbie. I knew she was trying to keep her talking in an attempt to defuse the situation. I was gasping for breath, fighting the surge of panic welling up inside me. "Just like the needles in Hattrick's eyes. You're a real artist."

"Thanks," Barbie said, an attractive blush spreading across her cheek implants.

"And the big shoes—also inspired," Terry said, taking a tiny step forward. "You knew it would make us suspect a man."

Barbie's smile evaporated and she looked down in disgust. "Damn feet," she said. "A dead giveaway. Feet, calf muscles, hands. But what can you do? Hasn't kept me from getting dates."

Suddenly it came to me in a blinding flash:

The impossibly tiny hips.

The muscled legs.

The gravity-defying butt.

"You're a *he!*" I said, gaping at Barbie, even as the burning in my side increased.

"I'm in transition," she said. "I think it's politically correct to refer to me as *she*."

"Ms. . . . Sergei Pavlov?"

Barbie nodded, the tip of her tongue poking through her teeth, and she gave me a sick little giggle.

Terry and I looked at each other, dumbfounded.

"But you have no accent," Terry said.

"Do I need one?" Barbie cooed in her dolly voice. Then she pitched it low with disdain. "I've been in this country since I was ten, stupid."

"But, Tatiana—"

"Is fresh off the boatsky . . . Backstabbing little *user*. She dumped me like a hot potato when I got arrested."

"I don't think you can talk about *using*, Barbie," I said in a low voice, risking her wrath in the hopes of throwing her off-balance psychologically. "*Nor* about stabbing. You used Hattrick to give you a new identity, then you killed him. You used Binion to keep you out of prison, and then you killed him, too."

"Oh, good guess," Barbie said. "Give the girl a cigar!"

"Jesus," Terry said. "What did Janice do to deserve her fate?"

"I used her to get to you, obviously. Poor thing didn't want to do it, but I had her by the short hairs. Too bad I didn't give you enough morphine to do the job—but as you probably know, I don't have any real medical training."

"You killed Mario, too?" I said, desperate to keep Barbie occupied until I could conceive of a method of escape.

She smiled at the memory, licking her frosted lips. "I called him, pretending to be Tatiana. I asked him to meet me at her apartment for a little *cerveza*. He was so hot for her, I knew he'd walk right into my trap."

"Men are so predictable, aren't they?" I said, forcing a sardonic laugh.

Barbie's smile faltered—had she just been insulted?

"Why did you kill Suzie Magnuson?" Terry asked her, before she could react to the insult.

Barbie blinked and shook her head. "Suzie Magnuson? Who the hell is that?"

"Didn't you steal the Bacon?" I said, amazed that I bothered to ask in light of the slightly more pressing issue of a knife in my gut.

"You're going to die and you're asking me about *bacon?*"

Terry and I looked at each other, baffled.

"Look, if we're going to die, you could at least tell us why," Terry said.

"As if you don't know!" Barbie said. "Just tell me where it is!"

"Where *what* is?"

"Don't play innocent!" She slammed me against the wall again and poked the blade in another millimeter. I cried out and sucked in my abs, flattening my internal organs against my spine. "Lenore had it and you worked for her," she said, scowling at me. "You've been snooping around ever since she died. Were you going to try to blackmail me with it next?"

"Please," I begged, "if we knew what you were looking for—"

"The skin!" Barbie screamed. "And don't talk to me about pigskin!"

"What? *Football?*" Terry said, now utterly confused.

Barbie rolled her eyes. "You idiots. *My* skin. The trimmings Janice took from my cosmetic surgery and gave to your little friend Lenore, who tried to blackmail me with them!"

"Ohhhhh." Terry slapped her forehead. "*That's* the mystery object?"

"They threatened to go to the FBI with it. The DNA is the only way anyone can identify me."

"Wrong, Barbie," I said evenly. "They can identify you with fingerprints."

She ran a smooth finger down the side of my cheek. "Don't have any. Hattrick burned them off." She dug the tip of her nail into my skin.

I saw Terry edging sideways out of the room.

Barbie saw it, too. "Don't get cute!" she yelled, and in a flash, she'd moved around and grabbed me from behind, pressing her rock-hard breasts into my back. Her left hand was across my chest, the blade of the knife against my right jugular vein. "One more step and I'll slice your sister's neck!"

"You're going to, anyway," Terry said with regret. "Might as well salvage something of the gene pool."

Barbie dug the blade in deeper. I felt warm blood trickle down my skin.

"Terry!" I yelled. "Quit messing around!"

She froze in place.

"*Where is the skin?* I promise I'll let you go," Barbie said seductively, "if you tell me where it is."

Terry stared at Barbie for a moment, then shook her head, moving toward us with her hands tensed, menace flaring in her eyes. "No you won't, Barbie. You can't afford to let us go. You've killed everyone who knows who you really are, and now we know, too." She gave Barbie a disgusted sneer. "And you'll like doing it, won't you? You love butchering people. You're a ruthless, psychotic, *killer bimbo!*"

"I am not a bimbo," Barbie snarled. "I'm a babe!"

"Gonna kill Tatiana, too?" I said, picking up on Terry's accusatory tone, trusting that she had a plan. "Going to destroy all that beauty just because she rejected you?"

A pitiful wail escaped Barbie's throat.

"She *left* me just when I needed her most. Faithless bitch!"

"Who's the bitch now, *Sergei?*" Terry said, advancing on us with her eyes locked on Barbie's. "Tatiana fell in love with a man. She married you as a man. And you *cut off your manhood* to escape prosecution!"

"I'm still a man!" Barbie shrieked. "Still a man in the only way that counts, the rest of it's reversible!"

It was suddenly clear to me what Terry had in mind.

"So you've still got your package!" Terry yelled.

I swung up my leg in a balletic lift to expose his groin, and in a seamlessly choreographed move, Terry whipped her boot up between Sergei's shapely legs and kicked his nuts all the way into his throat.

He howled in pain, the knife jerking away from my neck, his arm releasing my chest. I dived away from him and tried to run, but he was right behind me. He grabbed my jacket and yanked me back. I brought my heel scraping down on his shin and he cried out, falling backward to the floor, releasing me as he went.

Terry and I both raced to the front door. Terry fumbled

with the lock, then threw open the door and catapulted herself onto the porch. I tried to follow but Sergei grabbed my ankle. I tripped and slammed down hard on the concrete, breaking the fall with my hand. I heard my wrist snap and screamed as excruciating pain shot up my arm.

I tried to drag myself forward with my good hand. Terry grabbed my arm and pulled, while Sergei tried to stab at my leg with the knife, missing me by centimeters. Finally Terry sprang forward and clambered across my back, having no other way to get to Sergei, and before he could stand up, she hauled back with her boot, kicking him square in the face.

His head jerked back with a sickening cracking sound, and he let out a cry like a wounded animal.

Clutching my broken wrist to my bloodstained shirt, I managed to stumble off the porch. Terry raced to my side and I fell into her, dazed and unsure what to do next. Then I heard movement behind me and turned around to see Sergei, wild-eyed and grimacing in rage. He held the knife in the air as he lunged toward us through the door, screaming, *"Yahhhhhhhhh!"*

I froze. I'm not sure why. Maybe it's because I heard someone yelling, "Freeze!"

Little pleaser that I am, I tend to follow orders without thinking—especially those shouted by someone in uniform.

The someone in uniform was Dinah!

"Freeze, police!" she shouted again.

I looked up and saw the knife gripped in Sergei's hand, coming straight for my heart. I tried to unfreeze, to lurch away from the steel blade, but my legs were locked in terror.

There was a concussive blast next to my ear. A gunshot.

Blood spread like paintball splatter on Sergei's chest.

The world of motion slowed to a crawl as he hung suspended in air, knife held aloft for endless seconds . . . then time sped up again and he collapsed on the grass, his startled blue eyes staring up into mine.

"*Tattttiiiii—*" he moaned, expelling his final breath.

And Sergei Pavlov died from the bullet that had pierced his saline breast.

We remained in shock for several moments, our adrenaline-drenched brains trying to bring things into focus. Dinah was the first to speak.

"That was close!"

I was the second.

"Jesus Christ!"

I looked down at my blood-soaked shirt and started to snivel. Shaking, the tears coming, I grabbed at the front of it, trying to rip it from my body. I suddenly couldn't stand the sight of blood, even though it was my own. I tore it off, buttons flying, and threw it to the grass.

Dinah took off her down vest and put it over my shoulders. I tried to thank her but my teeth were chattering so hard I thought they would splinter. My wrist was swollen to three times its normal size. I couldn't stop shivering.

"You girls okay?" Dinah said, checking us over with practiced eyes.

"Yeah," Terry said, putting an arm around me.

"I think my wrist is broken," I managed to say.

"Help is on the way," Dinah said.

Then she ran into the house to call the cavalry.

The paramedics came and shot me up with something that made me feel warm and at peace. And happy, quite happy to be sitting inside the ambulance being attended to, while I experienced my own kaleidoscopic version of reality.

Time became flexible. It stretched out and contracted as the events of the past few days swirled in front of my eyes, merging with the current moment in a kind of impressionistic foreign movie.

One minute I was shrieking at Dinah's cleaver, then the EMTs were putting a temporary splint on my wrist. I zoomed in on an image of Hattrick with hypodermic needles poking from his eye sockets, then pulled back to a wide shot of Dinah draping a blanket over Terry's shoulders.

I looked at Sergei's corpse as they took it away and felt a surge of compassion for his ruined body, his wasted life. That had to be the drugs—how could I feel any human emotion for such a monster?

That's what makes you human, said a voice inside my head.

But I had believed Dinah was the monster and I was so, so wrong. Where was she, anyway? I heaved my butt off the back of the ambulance and stumbled around looking for her. I had to thank her for saving my life.

I saw her deep in conversation with a handsome black man in street clothes. Maybe a detective, or a plainclothes cop.

I weaved my way over to them.

"How are you feeling, Kerry?" Dinah said. She pointed to the man. "This is my boyfriend, Dale."

Her *boyfriend?* Now I knew I was hallucinating!

Terry appeared at my side. "Yeah," she said, "we didn't get to meet Dale earlier tonight because he was on duty at USC Medical."

I gaped at the smiling man. "You're a doctor?" I said, looking down at his size-ten running shoes.

"Pediatric nurse."

"Oh." I blinked a few hundred times. I think I may have drooled. Probably the drugs, but then again, it might just have been me.

"Dale and Dinah have been together since Tulsa," Terry explained.

"We met at Oral Roberts U.," Dinah said. "But we had to get away. They're not too open-minded about mixed marriages in Oklahoma."

My jaw started working seconds before any sound came out of my mouth. "You're . . . married?"

"No, but he finally popped the question about ten minutes ago. I guess there's nothing like a close call to bring out the commitment in a guy," Dinah said, smirking. "And I owe it all to you two. Want to be my best maids?"

"Sure," Terry said, speaking for both of us. "We'd be honored."

I turned and saw her giving me a wry grin.

It occurred to me then that most people don't ever really know what they look like. Oh sure, they see themselves from the same angle when they look in the bathroom mirror every morning, and sometimes they get a glimpse of themselves from the back in a dressing room mirror or at the beauty shop.

But only an identical twin knows for sure what she looks like from every possible angle, every moment of the day, in every state of dress or undress, with every conceivable facial expression.

Only an identical twin knows what it's like to see her own face mocking her with her own smile. Her own eyes telling her that she's been a complete horse's ass.

Well you thought she was gay, too! I beamed to Terry.

"Too bad your family won't be at the wedding," I said, turning to Dinah. "How did Jonah die, anyway? Did he die as a baby?"

She shook her head in disgust. "Nah, he wrapped his pickup around a telephone pole about three years back. Drunk driving incident. Fortunately, he didn't take anyone else with him."

"I thought it was probably something like that," I said.

But I didn't give Terry the satisfaction of meeting her eyes again.

I heard later that Boatwright showed up after we'd left. He'd been at the scene of another homicide, and by the time he got to our house I'd already been taken to the hospital. They transported me in the ambulance and I begged them to play the siren even though it wasn't an emergency. The driver finally relented and the *Wheeeeeeeee!* ricocheted insanely off the inside of my skull.

I waved out the back window to Terry. She was following in Dinah's off-duty Nissan with Dinah, Dale, and the dogs. They were using the ambulance to run interference as we gunned it through red lights and past the cars that were stopped respectfully by the side of the road.

My wrist was X-rayed and set, the wound in my abdomen cleaned and stitched. The nice ER doctor gave me some pain medication to tide me over until I filled his prescription, but when we got outside, I opened up the vial and tossed the pills into the gutter.

"Are you crazy?" Terry said. "That's gonna hurt like a mother later."

"I'll see what I can do with aspirin," I said.

"Yeah, you talk big *now*."

Dinah and Dale dropped us off at Reba's at three o'clock in the morning. Reba and Robert had waited up for us, greeting us like conquering heroes despite the late hour. Reba broke out the Cristal Rosé '95 and even poured a little for Robert, although he declined. He was still on his health kick, and he looked pretty good, considering.

He hadn't had a heart attack, as it turned out, but had fainted from overexertion on the back lawn. He had some bruising on his chest from Sven's resuscitation efforts, but was otherwise fine. The hospital had released him in the afternoon after giving him a few precautionary workups.

We told our story, and I think Robert was the most amused of all.

"Let me get this straight," he said. "You, Kerry, suspected the lovelorn lesbian cop, who was in fact engaged to a black male nurse with size-ten feet, and you, Terry, suspected the Russian prescription drug kingpin, who unbeknownst to you was now a trannie named Barbie, who lunged at Kerry with a knife and was shot to death by said lady cop, who'd followed you home because she thought *you* were behaving suspiciously."

"Right," Terry said.

"And the extortion, how did that come in?"

"Lenore, Rini, and Mario were co-conspirators, blackmailing people in Beverly Hills," I told him.

"But they weren't very good at it," Terry said. "They were still hard up for cash. Lenore was a patient and a customer of Dr. Hattrick's, and somehow she found out about his work on Sergei. So she leaned on Janice, who had assisted illegally during the operations, to take some of Sergei's cutaway flesh. The doctor wouldn't have noticed anything, he was way too stoned."

"Had Sergei, you know . . . ?" Reba scissored two fingers through the air. "Snip, snip?"

"No. A lot of them never do," Terry said knowledgeably. "They say they're women trapped in men's bodies, but when it comes right down to it—after they've gone through the breast augmentation, the electrolysis, the cheek implants, the shaving of the Adam's apple and all of that—they don't go for the cruelest cut. Can't imagine life without their pal, One-eyed Jack."

"So that was the 'it' Sergei was after?" Robert asked, wide-eyed. "His own tissue?"

I nodded and picked up the narrative. "Lenore and Mario had decided to go after this big fish, one big job that would send them to France in style. They put the screws to Sergei, threatening to expose his true identity to the FBI. He killed Mario right away and he probably would have killed Lenore, if she hadn't saved him the trouble by having an aneurysm."

"And why was Hugh Binion killed?" Reba asked.

Terry shrugged. "Probably because he knew Sergei's true identity. Binion had sent him to Hattrick to get his face and gender changed in order to evade the authorities."

"And how did Binion know Dr. Hattrick?" she wanted to know.

"Binion had represented Hattrick in an investigation by the medical board. He was probably in on the drug business, too. I guess it will all come out sooner or later."

"My, what busy little bees!" Robert said. "Drugging and dealing and hacking and blackmailing!"

We all laughed.

"So who broke into Lenore's?" Reba said.

"The selfsame drug lord, no doubt," Robert said, "looking for his moltings."

"Well," Reba said, "I'm glad it's all over. Though it's been a most invigorating piece of business." She winked at Eli who grinned back at her, completely besotted.

He lifted his champagne flute. "To Kerry—the best investigator I ever trained—and her baby sister!"

We all clinked and started to sip, but Robert held up a hand. "I hate to be a party pooper, but isn't there a teensy hole in all this?"

Terry glared at him. "Yes?"

"Where is it? The flesh, I mean."

Terry took a second to answer. "We don't know," she admitted.

"Well, then. Mightn't it be in the possession of someone else? Someone you haven't considered? Mightn't there be another blackmailer out there still?"

Terry and I frowned at each other.

Reba pursed her lips.

Eli scratched his nether regions.

"And come to think of it," Reba said, "who the devil has the Bacon?"

"And," Terry put in, "we still don't know who killed Suzie Magnuson or how she was connected to all this. Sergei said he didn't kill her, and he had no reason to lie. He was about to stab us to death."

"Well, okay. These are good questions," I said, pulling out my steno pad.

Terry kicked the pad and it went flying across the room, pages fluttering. Fortunately for her, she'd kicked my good hand.

"Why don't you go to bed?" she said.

"I believe I will."

I realized for the first time how wrecked I was after this week. I'd been drugged and arrested, I'd come within inches of being stabbed to death, my hearing had been blown out by a gunshot next to my ear, my wrist had been shattered, and all I wanted in the world was to snuggle up with one of the dogs and go to sleep.

I left them all in the living room arguing the fine points of the case, snatched Paquito from the kitchen, and made my way up the marble staircase to one of the guest bedrooms. On the way, I stopped and borrowed one of Robert's silk pajama tops.

" 'Night, everybody," I called down from the landing.

"Sweet dreams," Reba called up to me.

"Yeah, right," I muttered.

I crawled into bed, situating Paquito on the pillow next to my head. Then I pulled the covers up under my chin and drifted off into oblivion.

Blades. Sharp and deadly. Slashing at me, stabbing at my chest, my hands, my face. I tried to turn, to roll away, but I was stuck in something wet and slimy. Sinking, the more I struggled.

Quicksand.

My arms strained for the rope that appeared just beyond my reach. My hand closed around the knot at the end of the rope. I got it!

Paquito was on solid ground with the other end of the rope in his mouth, trying to pull me to safety. But he was too tiny. I was too heavy. It was hopeless.

His paws slid toward the quicksand, toenails digging little ditches in the dirt. He was getting closer, closer . . .

I released the rope. I wouldn't drag him into the killer sand with me. Couldn't stand the thought of that trusting little soul being smothered as I myself would be within seconds.

The quicksand reached my mouth. I tried to spit it out, but hundreds of pounds of pressure forced the granular muck between my lips.

Glub.

Glub glub.

I gave myself up to my fate.

Then I hit the floor.

I woke instantly, a stabbing pain in my wrist. It took me a minute to remember that I was in Reba's guest room. The bedcovers were entwined in my legs, snagged under my armpits, and wrapped around my neck, strangling me.

Paquito! I thought desperately. I've killed him!

Then I heard little claws hitting the floor next to my head and a wet tongue snaked out and kissed me on the eyelid. "Baby! You're alive!" He gave me another kiss, this one on the underside of my nose.

"Sor-r-r-y," I moaned, reaching out and pulling him to my chest with my plastered hand. "Go to sleep, honey." I loosened the sheet around my neck with my good hand, and curled up on the floor.

I had no intention of getting back on the bed. I was too tired, and I thought if we slept here on the floor, Paquito had a better chance of surviving the night. He could run for his life if it looked like I was going to squash him with my huge, thrashing body.

That was my last coherent thought before I heard a *slerghhh* sound coming from my own mouth. Then I slipped behind the curtain of unconsciousness, wedged between the bed and the wall.

When I awoke Paquito was gone. I didn't know the time. There was a cast where my watch should have been.

My forearm was throbbing. I unwrapped the sheets and blankets and pulled myself up by means of the bed. I peered over the side to look for Paquito. The door was open, so he'd probably gone downstairs for kibble.

I myself had no thought of kibble, although coffee might be nice. But first I had to find aspirin.

I stumbled down the hallway, looking in the empty rooms. Had I slept right through breakfast? No one was in Robert's room. Reba and Eli weren't asleep in her canopied bed. There was no sign of Terry anywhere.

I looked out the window. Still dark, couldn't be past six o'clock. Where was everybody? Why were they up so early?

Aspirin. I had to have aspirin before I could think.

I went into the guest bathroom and opened the cabinet. Toothpaste, hand cream, a perfumed soap from the Dauphine Hotel, but no Bayer, no Excedrin, nothing.

Terry was right. I hurt like a mother. I'd been rash to throw away those drugs, but after all the death and indignity heaped on those who'd been addicted to them, I hadn't wanted any part of the painkillers. Seemed to me they should be called *peoplekillers*.

I went across the landing to Robert's studio at the top of the stairs. I peeked in, thinking he might be at work. He wasn't there, but the portrait of Lenore smiled out at me from its cracked golden frame like the Wicked Queen peering out from her dastardly mirror.

Reba had given Robert the portrait to use as a canvas for one of his abstract artworks. He hadn't even bothered to remove it from the frame, but had already begun to obliterate Lenore's satin gown with bold strokes of yellow paint.

It made me think of that other painting.

Where oh where was the Bacon?

Which reminded me of breakfast. Which reminded me of coffee, which I didn't smell wafting up to my nose at the top of the stairs.

I looked down the staircase expecting someone, Grizzie most likely, to scurry by. I was just about to call out when something caught my eye.

The front door was open a crack, and there was a cable running the length of the foyer into the dining room, plugged into a socket by the front door. It was thick, like those used for lighting equipment on a movie set.

Huh.

I tried to make sense out of this but the pain was clouding my mind.

I padded down the stairs in my bare feet. Was there a repairman in the dining room with a drill or an electric sander, waiting for a decent hour to start his work? Reba hadn't mentioned any pending repairs.

I shuffled to the dining room door, and there everybody was, seated around the dining room table: Reba, Robert, Eli, Terry, Grizzie. I opened my mouth to say hello when I realized they were all staring at me, their eyes like saucers . . .

. . . their bodies tied to the chairs and their mouths gagged!

Terry made little hitching motions with her head toward the living room. Someone was in there. Someone who had kidnapped the whole household and tied them up while I slept. Someone on the other end of that cable—

BZZZZZZZZ!

Omigod! He was revving a chain saw!

BZZZZZZZZZZZZZ!

I ducked back into the foyer and crouched behind a planter with a blooming hibiscus. My heart jumped into my throat and pounded on my thyroid gland. Cortisol surged through my bloodstream causing my teeth to clack like castanets. I had to get to a phone but I didn't think I could move.

Oh sure. Get to a phone and call the police. They'll be here in three to four minutes. In that time your aunt could be missing a finger, your sister could be minus a leg, the dogs could be tailless.

Where were the dogs?

I looked at the cable. I could unplug it first, then rush upstairs and call 911. Or I could go out the front door and run down the street screaming my head off.

I'd never even make it to the gate.

I had to unplug the cable. But if I did, he would simply come out and replug it, then proceed with the dismembering. But if he came out here into the foyer, I'd have a chance to brain him with—

What?

I tugged on the lip of the planter. It weighed two hundred pounds at least. I looked around frantically for another weapon and saw nothing but the Ming vase sitting pricelessly on its pedestal. I could break it over somebody's skull but would that really knock him out?

It always worked in the *Three Stooges* episodes.

Jesus Christ, Kerry! This isn't the *Three Stooges*, this is serious!

BZZZZZZZZ!

A man's voice: "Tell me where she is, or I'll take a pinky from the fat guy over there!"

Which fat guy? I wondered irrationally.

Then I recognized the voice with a start. Sidney Lefler of Whitechapel Mutual. What was he doing here, holding everyone hostage?

No time to wonder.

I dashed out from behind the planter and grabbed the cable, yanking it out of the wall socket.

BZZZZzzz-phut-phut.

The cable was still in my hand when I leaped up the stairs, slipping on the slick marble, scrabbling at the banister. I pounded up to the landing where the cable ran out. I dropped the plug and dived into Robert's studio.

I snatched up the phone. The line was dead. He must have cut it and disabled the alarm before he broke into the house.

"Hey, Kerry!" a voice yelled downstairs. "That you . . . ?"

I heard him coming up the stairs, and looked around desperately for a place to hide, then slipped behind Lenore's portrait. I held the sides of the frame with the tips of my fingers, turning my face sideways so the portrait wouldn't protrude, giving me away.

His footsteps came to the door.

A gun was cocked. I waited breathlessly for the shot.

No shot.

After a few seconds, the footsteps receded down the hall. I sweated it out, trying desperately to think without the aid of caffeine, my nerve endings screaming in pain.

No phone, no phone, no phone.

But there *is* a computer.

The computer had a DSL Internet connection. Could you dial 911 online? I thought you could, I'd seen it in a movie.

I didn't dare come out from behind the portrait.

I lifted it with my fingertips. Pain streaked through my arm but I ignored it, shifting the portrait a foot to the left. I peered out from the side of the canvas. The computer was a few feet away. Only a few feet.

I inhaled and picked up the portrait again, moving it toward the computer. I gained another foot, then—

"Well, what do you know?" Sidney's voice came from the doorway. "The portrait's moving."

I swallowed hard.

"That's not you back there, is it, Kerry?"

He grabbed the top of the frame and something took over in me. Pure adrenaline-driven instinct. I picked up the sides of the portrait with superhuman strength, impervious to the pain in my wrist. I charged him with it, holding it in front of me like a giant shield.

I heard an *Oouf!* and a *Shit!* on the other side of the painting but I hadn't succeeded in knocking him to the ground, I knew, because I could hear him shuffling and stumbling in front of me.

I pushed with all the strength I had, blindly plowing ahead. I passed through the studio door—thank God for the tall doorways in the house—and if I was through the door that meant the staircase was directly in front of me and that meant—

"*Aieeeyeeeee-eee-eee*!" Sidney screamed.

I heard tumbling noises and snapping sounds, which I

hoped were bones, and feet hitting walls, and a head bonking on marble steps, and then I lost my balance.

I toppled onto the stairs, the portrait beneath me, and sledded down the staircase at eighty miles an hour, bouncing right over Sidney like he was a minor mogul. I slid straight to the bottom, then zipped across the marble foyer and into the kitchen, where I sailed right past the service island and slammed into the refrigerator headfirst. Birds twittered and bells rang, and I was sucked up into a vortex of colored lights, traveling through space toward a distant pinpoint of white light. I succumbed to an indescribable sense of peace and well-being as the light drew nearer. Endorphin City. When at last I reached the source of the light, a group of angelic beings approached me.

A beautiful woman told me without speaking that I was in the place whence all life originated. She held out a scroll of luminescent parchment, the words *Secrets of the Universe* inscribed on it in gold.

I took the document, trembling with awe. I was holding the *Secrets of the Universe* in my unworthy hands! But I had one tiny question before proceeding.

"What about my sister?" I asked the beings of light. "Is she coming?"

They sent the answer back, their voices like celestial music playing in my head.

"No, not for another fifty years. She has many karmic issues to work out on the Earth plane. And personality problems such as anger, self-loathing, and a propensity toward violence. It will take her a long time to work through them."

"But, shouldn't I . . . shouldn't I be there to help her work through these issues?"

"As you wish."

Before I knew what was happening, I was sucked back into

the vortex at a violent speed, colors racing past me like streaks of neon.

"Wait!" I yelled back at the angels. "Don't I get a second to *think* about it?"

Then I was shot back out through the end of the tunnel with a rude expulsion of cosmic air. And my head hurt like a sonofabitch.

I opened my eyes on the world. Or the kitchen, as it were. And I remembered what had brought me to the kitchen, plowing me into the fridge in the first place. I got up and stumbled into the foyer.

Sidney lay motionless on the marble floor. Eyes staring sightlessly, chest still. I wondered if it was his fall or my sledding over him that had caused his death.

It didn't matter. Dead, he was. Probably holding my *Secrets of the Universe* at that very moment.

Read 'em and weep, Sidney.

I limped into the dining room to untie the victims. "It's okay, everybody," I said, feeling rather macho. "He's dead."

"*MMMMmmmmPhhhhhhggggg!*" they said in chorus, which I took to mean *Way to go, Kerry! Way to save us!*

But I was wrong.

What they were trying to say was, *Look out! He's right behind you!*

I figured it out when I felt the hard gun barrel jammed into my back.

"Hold it!" Sidney snarled. "Don't make a move!"

"Who are you, the Terminator?" I cried. "What do you *want?*"

"I just want a life! I'm tired of sitting in my car getting hemorrhoids while other people live in fabulous mansions, lining their pockets with stolen money!"

"How can I help you?"

Ouch. The barrel nicked my spine.

"You can help me by dying. Then I'm going to walk out of here with the Bacon."

"We don't *have* it," I said through clenched teeth.

"Oh, yes you do," he said, jabbing my kidney.

"I get the point, you have a gun! But we don't have the Bacon!"

"Freeze!" a male voice boomed from the foyer.

I spun around at the same instant as Sidney and saw Lance crouched in a firing position, his arms out in front of him aiming his—

Empty hands?

"You don't have a gun, asshole!" Sidney yelled.

Lance looked down at his hands, then back up at Sidney.

"Right," he said.

Sidney fired off a shot and I watched in horror as Lance flew backward, his enormous bulk smashing against the wall, spraying it with red.

"You bastard!" I yelled, jumping on Sidney's back. "He's an innocent actor!"

I grabbed Sidney around the neck and squeezed as hard as I could, strangling him as I sank my teeth into the top of his head.

Sidney lurched around, howling—trying to dislodge the rabid orangutan from his back—and somehow while he was trying to shake me off, the gun in his hand discharged with a deafening report.

The bullet pinged off a marble step and ricocheted, lodging in Sidney's shinbone. He screamed and fell, taking me with him as he hit the floor face-first, his forehead cracking on marble. My upper lip split on my own tooth as my face slammed into the back of his skull.

I lay on top of him, breathing heavily. Waiting for his next move.

But this time Sidney was truly down for the count.

I stood up and kicked him, just to be sure.

"Okay, who else?" I screamed. "Bring it on! Anybody else want a piece of me?"

Lance looked up from the floor. "Um, no. But would you mind calling 911? I've been shot."

"Sure," I said, running into the living room to find a cell phone. "Sorry, Lance. I got a little carried away."

nineteen

$\mathcal{W}$ell, who'd have thought *I'd* be the girl of the hour? The one who wiped out a bad guy single-handedly, saving my whole family and three others in the bargain?

I could hardly believe it myself. I hadn't really been courageous—just impulsive. But at least now I knew that blind instinct would serve me in a crisis, even if I *was* scared stupid. And that would be enough to give me confidence if Terry and I continued to work as investigators.

And why wouldn't we? Now that we were flush, we could pick and choose our cases for a while. We still had the twelve thousand dollars, plus a generous reward from Whitechapel Mutual for returning the painting. (The Francis Bacon would go to Suzie's estate, and ultimately be sold in order to liquidate some of her debts.)

Terry and I planned to pick up where we left off as soon as we got back from our trip to Hawaii. She had it all planned out. We would go shell collecting and parasailing and deep-sea diving and speeding around in those little rafts and hiking through the jungle . . .

I let her think we would, anyway. But actually I had a secret agenda.

I figured once I got there, I'd put on my new Pucci-print bikini, dig myself a hole in the sand, and have daiquiris brought to me by the hundreds, never moving a muscle except for those in my drinking hand, lips, and esophagus for the whole week.

Well, I might make one exception. I might get up and dance the hukilau, for luck.

But wait. I'm getting way ahead of myself.

After I called 911, I gave Lance a stack of towels and told him to apply pressure to his head. Fortunately the bullet hadn't pierced his skull, but scalp wounds tend to bleed profusely and I worried that Lance might panic from the sight of all that blood. Instead, he held up like a champ.

It turned out that Reba had retained Lance as her bodyguard after we'd fired him, having promised to keep Grizzie at a distance, and he'd reported to work at 7:00 a.m. as requested. And you know what happened after that.

While we were waiting for the paramedics, Lance called his agent to tell her about the incident. She got quite excited, saying that with all the publicity and the scar, his career was going to really take off. He could transition from playing silent good guys keeping watch in the background to playing bad guys with big gnarly scars. And she assured him that there was much more of a market for bad guys than good guys in the movies.

I hurriedly untied the rest of the gang and then located the dogs, who'd been cooped up in the laundry room. I had feared the worst, but there they were, unharmed. They leaped at my shins happily, barking and snorting and wagging their tails. After that, Reba gave me the longest, boniest bird hug I'd ever had from her and Robert grabbed me in a well-cushioned bear grip. Eli wiped tears from his eyes, and Grizzie kept saying, "Well, I'll be a baboon's spittoon! What a brave lass ye turned out ta be!"

And Terry? Terry only smiled, but I could read her mind. She was thinking—*Fucking A, Ker!*

We tied Sidney up with his own extension cord, and when he came to, he helped to put the final pieces of the puzzle into place.

The insurance company had been suspicious of Suzie Magnuson's theft report from the beginning, so they put Sidney on the case. But as he surveilled Suzie's house, he developed his own evil agenda. He suspected that she had the Bacon stashed somewhere in her home, and he determined to break in and steal it. He saw his opportunity on the morning the servants moved out. Suzie would be alone, he figured, an old lady easily overtaken. He'd introduce himself as the representative of the insurance company, then force his way in, tie her up, and torture her if necessary to learn the whereabouts of the painting, killing her afterward.

That night, he had set up his video camera on a tripod and taped himself going into the house, secure in the knowledge that he would be unidentifiable at that distance. In this way he'd given himself the perfect alibi.

To his surprise, he found the front door open, and Suzie lying unconscious in her bedroom, the apparent victim of an overdose. Though she was obviously at death's door, he stabbed her anyway, believing a murder would deflect police attention from his proposed theft.

But the painting was nowhere to be found.

He soon figured out Lenore had it—she had provided the canasta alibi for Suzie when the painting was allegedly stolen. He was waiting for his moment to break into Lenore's, when Sergei provided him with the perfect opportunity by breaking in first to look for his cuttings.

As Lenore's lawyer, Binion knew there was nothing left of Lenore's estate other than what was in the house, so he conspired with Sidney to grab anything of value after she died. Sidney hired a truck to deliver the rugs to Binion, but kept the information about the Bacon to himself. Only he was afraid to leave the premises with it, so he took the portrait of Lenore from the garage, pulled it off the studs and stretched the Bacon underneath it, replacing the staples afterward. He had assumed that no one would want the ghastly portrait and that it would be his for the taking when the unclaimed items were disposed of.

What Sidney hadn't counted on was Reba taking the portrait for the funeral, much less giving it to Robert to use for a canvas, all of which forced him into this desperate kidnap and murder attempt. After hearing his confession, we took Lenore's portrait out of its frame, tore the staples out of the canvas, and there he was—Bacon's *Man With a Watch*, blithely contemplating his mortality.

The police took Sidney away and Lance was off to the emergency room courtesy of the EMTs, who joked that Reba's house was becoming a regular stop on their route.

So everything was fairly well wrapped up, except that it appeared we'd never know where Sergei's purloined flesh had got to.

It wasn't until the following week that we received the letter and documentation from Gentex Labs. Reba had threatened Hartford, Huntington et al with litigation unless they gave us unfettered access to all of Lenore's papers, files, and incoming mail. She was the rightful heir, after all.

"Gentex Labs," Terry mused, ripping into the envelope. "I wonder what this could be? Do you suppose she had some kind of terminal disease, and that's why she got involved with all the criminal stuff? Maybe she couldn't pay the medical bills, or she just figured on going out in style."

"Interesting theory," I said. "Does it say what she had?"

Terry read the letter frowning, her eyes going wide. Then she whooped and threw the paper into the air and collapsed on the floor, howling with laughter.

"What?" I said, chasing after the paper. "What did she have?"

But Terry just squealed and guffawed, her black baby tee riding up to show her silver belly button ring, her feet pounding the floor.

People sometimes had hysterical reactions to terrible things, I knew. Still, I didn't think I was going to be half so amused to learn that Lenore was suffering from some horrible illness or other.

But it wasn't that kind of lab report. It was a bill and a disclaimer.

Gentex specialized in the analysis of DNA. Lenore had given them a biological sample, asking them to isolate any human DNA it contained for genotype testing. They were unable to find any human DNA, they said, and were returning the residual testing matter under separate cover.

On the report attached to the letter and invoice there was a section labeled "Source Material." And in the little square underneath it someone had inked in a cramped scientist's hand: *Feces, canine.*

I guess Lenore had learned all about bluffing in her years of canasta playing, but she'd bluffed her last with Sergei Pavlov. She didn't even have his flesh at the time she tried to blackmail him. She'd obtained it from Janice at Hattrick's office and secreted it in the Judith Leiber bag, intending to hold it at her house until Sergei came through with the money. But Paquito had apparently smelled the fresh meat and chewed through the leather purse to get at it, gobbling it all up.

Lenore had preserved Paquito's poop and had sent it to Gentex for analysis in the hopes that Sergei's DNA would show up in his stool. How she thought she'd get away with giving Sergei the dog doo in exchange for the big bucks she was hoping to nail him for, we'll never know.

She can't tell us. She's gone forever.

Just days after finally discovering the purpose behind that mysterious Tupperware in Lenore's fridge, her ashes were scattered to the wind from the rooftop parking lot of Neiman Marcus, by her dear friend Reba Price-Slatherton.

You're probably expecting to hear about my follow-up date with Detective Boatwright. I can't tell you about it because it didn't happen.

Oh he called, all right. And came over to the house with a nice bouquet of flowers and another bottle of red wine.

When the door was opened, he yelled, "You don't know how worried I was about you! You almost got yourself killed!" Then he grabbed me in his arms and planted a big wet kiss on my mouth, which lasted just about *forever*.

Could you tell us about the kiss perhaps? Could ya rhapsodize about the warmth going through your body and the tingles running down your spine? Could we at least hear about his manly smell again?

No, because I didn't actually receive the kiss.

Terry did.

She claims she tried to tell him that she was the wrong sister, says she tried desperately to push him away, but he was too forceful and he simply overwhelmed her. It was only when he came up for air that she was able to tell him which twin she was.

He stared at her and said, "Oh really?"

Then he looked into the living room and saw me standing there with my black eyes and my swollen lip, feebly waving my plastered wrist.

"Oh hey," he said. "Sorry about that."

And I guess I kind of overreacted. I called him a bastard and then I stormed upstairs, slamming my closet door for effect because there's no actual door to my loft.

Terry grabbed the flowers and hit Boatwright over the head with them, then she smashed the wine overhanded on the porch.

Boatwright left pretty soon after that.

Why punish him for an honest mistake, you ask?

Well, when I reflected on all the insanity that seemed to follow me around like, say, an evil doppelgänger, I figured I was actually doing Boatwright a favor. Going out with me would be pure misadventure. Plus, I didn't think I'd ever get that image of him and Terry out of my mind. There were plenty of other fish in the sea who had not actually French kissed my sister.

Besides, I had someone else in mind to punish. Someone whose mistake was less than honest. Someone who knew damn well that Boatwright thought she was me, and went right ahead and let him kiss her.

And I figured, what the hell? I have the rest of my life to punish *her*.

THE END

Kerry is a paranoid nutball.

THE END

P.S. There *is* no Beverly. The city of Beverly Hills was developed by oilman Burton E. Green, who named it after Beverly Farms, Massachusetts. Who knew?

Read on for a sneak peek at

The Mangler of Malibu Canyon,

the next installment in the series featuring

the McAfee twins, by Jennifer Colt, available from

Broadway Books in January 2006.

"Excuse me?" I said, blinking.

But Grizzie had already stomped off in the direction of the kitchen, muttering under her breath. Terry and I looked at each other, wondering if we'd heard her correctly.

"Darlings!"

Aunt Reba breezed in wearing her beach attire—an African-themed caftan in bold yellows and reds, with a thick elastic band holding back the hennaed hair from her high-boned, patrician face. Gloria Swanson does Nairobi. "I'm so glad you're here! I've been at my wits' end."

"Hi Reba," we said in tandem, receiving our air kisses. "What's up?"

"Well, it's been hell around here. Robert missing and Eli leaving me because he's too bored at the beach and—"

"And a dead body somewhere?" I inquired, just to test my hearing.

She made a little moue of distaste. "Let's have coffee first, before we jump right into the unpleasantness."

Unpleasantness? *Okay* . . .

Terry looked at me goggle-eyed. I shrugged back at her, then followed Reba as she scuffed on her red leather sling-backs into the breakfast room, which was paneled with light wood and had a spectacular view of the ocean through a spotless plate-glass window. Grizzie plunked down a tray with ceramic cups, a milk jug, a thermos pitcher, and a bowl containing large brown lumps of natural sugar.

"Where's the silver service?" I asked. Reba'd been using the same silver coffee service for as long as I could remember, buffed to a mirror sheen by Grizzie's chapped, red hands. Its absence seemed somehow sinister.

"Hmmph!" Grizzie said, before stomping back into the kitchen to prepare the muffins and mangoes that always accompanied the coffee.

"It's too 'heirloom' for the beach," Reba said. "We're much more relaxed out here."

Terry kicked me under the table. "I know I'm relaxed, aren't *you*?" she said.

I shrugged and waited impatiently for Reba to come to the point. We were used to her going miles around "unpleasant" issues, but if there was a dead body somewhere in the vicinity, I really wanted to know what the story was.

"As I was saying," Reba started, pouring the coffee with upraised pinkies, "Eli got bored. I should have known that such a vital, virile man would have difficulty adjusting to a life of leisure. I just didn't think about it. I was too blinded by love."

Eli was smart and funny, a peerless criminal attorney who had taken up with Reba during our last case. He was also my former boss. He had a stogie surgically attached to his bottom lip, suits that were a testament to the indestructibility of polyester, since they dated from the mid-seventies, and he looked like a giant, pockmarked Teletubby, minus the head antennae. I loved Eli, too. But you'd almost *have* to be blind to be romantically attracted to him.

"Not enough challenge without his legal practice?" Terry asked.

"Precisely."

"Well, perhaps if you told him you'd found a *dead body* . . ." I suggested.

"Well, that's just the thing, dears," Reba said, waving a diamond-encrusted hand in the air. "I drag him to the beach, he gives up his practice, then I present him with a missing son and a dead body in my rug? I don't know how much strain a new relationship can be expected to endure—"

"WHAT BODY?" Terry yelled.

Reba's jaw flapped open at this rudeness. "Well, I was getting to that, Missy, if you'll just hold your horses."

Terry fell forward, sinking her head in her hands. I leaned back in my chair and took a sip of coffee. We'd have to play it Reba's way, however insane. She took a deep breath, smoothed out her caftan, and finally dove into the story with morbid zest.

"I went into the guest bedroom earlier, where I'd stored the rugs that Lenore left me in her will. . . ."

We nodded.

"I wanted to see if any of them were suited to the new house, and I thought perhaps you girls would like one for your little cabin. You know, to dress it up a bit—"

Terry waved impatiently. "Stick to the body. Where was it?"

"I was *getting* to that," Reba huffed. "I noticed that one of the rugs—a Turkish dinner rug, actually—well, it was rather lumpy. So I took it by the corner and unrolled it and what do you know? Out she came!"

"She?" we asked. "A girl?"

"A young woman. Somewhere in her twenties, with blond hair, bleached to within an inch of its life." She clapped a hand over her mouth. "Oh dear, that was insensitive, wasn't it?"

I rolled my eyes. "Reba, I don't think this woman's in a position to mind a catty remark. What else? Do you know what killed her?"

Reba frowned. "Well, how would I know that?"

"Was there any obvious cause of death, like a bullet hole, stab wounds . . . ?"

"Oh my, yes."

"What was it?" Terry asked.

"Well, the decapitation, I should think."

"DECAPITATION!" I shouted, and watched in alarm as Terry's face practically turned purple. "Why didn't you say anything about this when you called?"

"Well, you never know who could be listening in on a phone call, do you? I thought it more prudent to discuss it in person."

"All right, please continue," I said. "So the head was forcibly separated from the body?"

"Well, that's a reasonable assumption, isn't it? There aren't too many people walking around headless, that I know of."

"So what you actually found was the head," Terry said.

"No."

"I thought you said she was a bottle blond."

Reba pursed her lips in distaste. "Yes, but I wasn't referring to her *head* hair."

Dear God in heaven. Why did we ever come home?

How did the dead girl get there, who could she possibly be, had there been any strange persons lurking about the house . . . ? Reba had no answers, no ideas.

"And how long have the rugs been here?" Terry asked.

"Oh, a couple of weeks," Reba said.

"And you just now noticed this 'lump'?"

"It wasn't there before, I assure you."

"No, it wouldn't have been," I said. "The body can't have been delivered in a rug two weeks ago. You'd have noticed the smell, no way around that." I finally thought to ask her, "You have called the police, haven't you?"

Reba leaned in and whispered, "I thought it best to keep this en famille for the moment."

"But . . . when did you find it?" Terry asked, her mouth agape.

"This morning."

Terry slapped her forehead. "You found the body this morning, and you waited for us to get back from Hawaii? Reba, do you know how this looks?"

"How?" she asked, her eyes big and innocent.

"Bad," I said.

"Well, I don't see why the big rush. She's not going any-where . . . anyway, it was closer to noon, now that I think about it."

Something was very wrong here. And I wasn't thinking only of the brutally murdered woman. It was Reba's reaction to it that was bothering me. Even for someone with her boundless capacity for denial, this was much too casual a response to such an outrageous occurrence.

Then it hit me. She'd been *afraid* to call the police. But why? Did she think someone in the household had had something to do with the heinous deed?

No. The idea was ridiculous.

We convinced Reba that the police had to be called. And even though the last time I'd seen him, I hadn't been too friendly to Detective John Boatwright of the Beverly Hills PD homicide division, I decided to call him on the grounds that it would be best to report this to someone who knew us.

Okay, maybe "not too friendly" isn't the right way to describe what happened. He'd come over to take me out on a date, and there'd been a little case of mistaken identity, wherein he stuck his tongue down Terry's throat. I called him a bastard, and Terry bashed him over the head with the flowers he'd brought for me.

So what first date is perfect?

Still, I was pretty sure he'd give us the benefit of the doubt when it came to a dead body in our aunt's house. Whatever the idiosyncrasies of our family, I didn't think he'd suspect us all of some big plot to murder an anonymous blond. Or whatever color her hair was.

I called Boatwright's office and he wasn't there, so I tried his cell phone. He seemed genuinely happy to hear from me—he probably thought I was calling to apologize for the kiss snafu—but I got down to the new business right away.

"I was hoping you could help us with something," I ventured.

"I can't fix traffic tickets."

"Ha. I wish it was that simple."

"Okay, what is it?"

"Well, my aunt Reba left Beverly Hills and moved out to Malibu. She, uh, bought a house on the beach, and she's found . . . well, she's found a corpse in it."

There was a long silence on the line. "You're kidding, right?"

"Um, no."

"By corpse, do you mean a human body? I mean, we're not talking about a dead seagull or something like that."

"No, it's a human body. One that, unfortunately, is missing its head. So I guess it's more of a torso, strictly speaking."

"Arms and legs intact?"

"I'm assuming. I didn't look. Didn't want to mix my DNA up with the scene, you know what I mean?"

"Then we'll call it a body for now. Male or female?"

"Female, twenties."

"And where did your aunt find this body?"

In her spare bedroom. One of her spare bedrooms, I should say."

He cleared his throat. "Where was it exactly?"

"Well, she'd had a bunch of Oriental rugs shipped to her by a Beverly Hills law firm—you remember that business with Lenore Richling?"

"Uh-huh."

"Anyway, the rugs had been housed in a storage facility, then shipped to Reba after the will was probated. And she started to roll them out to, you know, see if any of them were suited to her new beach lifestyle, because they might be too heirloom—"

"Too formal," Reba corrected me in the background. "Silver can be heirloom, not rugs."

"Sorry, uh, too *formal* for the beach. So she rolled out a Turkish dinner rug, and what do you know? Out tumbled a headless body!"

He sighed like Sisyphus, looking up a big friggin' hill. "Look. If you're in Malibu, you need the sheriff's department. But if you want, I can make the call for you."

Uh-oh. The word *sheriff* conjured up someone with a pair of six-shooters and a ten-gallon Stetson who referred to women

about the author

JENNIFER COLT is a screenwriter in Santa Monica, California. She has written for Dimension Films and Playboy Enterprises and has worked in the nontheatrical division of MGM/United Artists in LA.

WITHDRAWN

as "little lady." I wouldn't mind too much, but if someone called Terry "little lady," she'd probably end up back in the slammer for assaulting an officer.

"Can't you come, too?" I asked a little more timorously than I'd planned. "I mean, I know it's not your beat, but—"

"I wish I could," Boatwright said, "but I'm tied up at a triple homicide."

"Well, okay. If you think that's more *important* . . . " I heard another sigh, so I went into placating mode: "But it does make me feel better to know you're going to speak to them on our behalf. You'll tell them we're not murderers, right?"

"I'll vouch for you not being a murderer, but I don't know about your sister. Listen, I don't have to tell you not to touch anything, do I?"

"No, uh-uh," I said. Dead-torso touching was not high on my list of fun activities. I gave him Reba's new address.

"Okay, 'bye," he said, like we'd just had a normal conversation, then hung up.

I let out my breath. "He's calling the sheriff for us," I announced to Reba and Terry.

"Well, I feel better already," Reba said. "That's a tremendous weight off my shoulders." Then she clapped a hand to her mouth again. "Oh my, that was insensitive, wasn't it?"